The Pleasure Project

Also by JAX

The Bid

Also by Jenna McCormick

No Limits
No Mercy

Also by Cassie Ryan

Ceremony of Seduction
Vision of Seduction
Trio of Seduction

The Pleasure Project

JAX

JENNA McCORMICK

CASSIE RYAN

APHRODISIA

KENSINGTON PUBLISHING CORP.

www.kensingtonbooks.com

APHRODISIA BOOKS are published by

Kensington Publishing Corp.
119 West 40th Street
New York, NY 10018

All Kensington titles, imprints, and distributed lines are available at special quantity discounts for bulk purchases for sales promotion, premiums, fund-raising, and educational or institutional use.

Special book excerpts or customized printings can also be created to fit specific needs. For details, write or phone the office of the Kensington Special Sales Manager: Kensington Publishing Corp., 119 West 40th Street, New York, NY 10018. Attn. Special Sales Department. Phone: 1-800-221-2647.

ISBN-13: 978-0-7582-4179-5
ISBN-10: 0-7582-4179-8

First Kensington Trade Paperback Printing: April 2013

10 9 8 7 6 5 4 3 2 1

Printed in the United States of America

CONTENTS

The Science of Pleasure

JAX

For Renee.
Best friends for life.
No matter how many miles
or how many years,
I know you are with me.

1

Dr. Jenesis DeBruehl looked down the rows of tidy little cages with rats of all sorts of colors within them, one rat per cage, nearly one hundred of them on her right side. Steel lab tables gleamed with cold perfection and brand-new equipment, including the latest in centrifuges, note centers, and high-powered microscopes. Mirrors lined the ceilings along with bright fluorescent lighting, to help others watch the work of the researchers without overcrowding them.

Jenesis's heart was pounding with excitement. This gift affected her like diamonds or new shoes might affect some other woman. Her palms were moist and she surreptitiously wiped them down over her hips, her new lab coat crinkling with starch.

"So . . . where is my desk?" She looked at the young lab technician, wanting to remember his name but too overwhelmed by the rushing sound of her own blood in her ears.

Hers. This whole lab was all hers. Fully funded. Fully staffed. Fully stocked. And, apparently, brand spanking new. Who the hell ever got brand-new anything in a lab? In her last research project, even her lab coat had had someone else's name on it at first until she'd had it patched over. Granted, that had been her very first solo lab since . . .

Since she'd been over-recognized, made notorious, and seriously disrespected after the painful separation of her life from that of one maniacal Dr. Eric Paulson. After that, the responsibility of an entire lab had been hard to come by.

As usual, the thought of Paulson sent a horrid shiver down her spine. She had barely managed to escape jail time because of that lunatic. But what the outside world had not understood about the Phoenix Project was that below a certain level, the people working in Paulson's labs had had no idea he'd been experimenting on captive humans with the untried methods they were in charge of creating. It was supposed to have been a simple study on interrupting the natural decomposing cycles of the human cell, also known as an antiaging process. But regardless of too-obvious applications in the world's beauty markets, there had been whole sections of the labs that had had a much loftier goal.

Imagine, she thought, as she had thought when she had first signed on to the Phoenix Project, the possibilities for human beings riddled with cancer or leukemia if the precious and fragile healthy cells they had left could be preserved from the natural shedding process just long enough to help them through the chemotherapy or radiation processes. Jenesis herself had been designing the tag meant to differentiate a healthy cell from an unhealthy cell, so when the delivery took place, only the healthy cells received the strengthening alterations.

But then it had all gone to hell. That monster Paulson had been using her work—*her* work—to torture, murder, and mutate innocent human beings. He had bastardized her precious cellular tag to deliver specified cellular mutation commands.

He had used her and some of the best minds in the medical research world to create the Morphates, a new species of superhuman, in his quest to play God with others and find immortality for himself.

And she had been none the wiser until the day the Federated police had raided the labs and arrested her. Her life had been ruined, her reputation trashed. Now here she was, seven years later . . .

Seven years later and she finally had her own lab again. Someone had finally decided she was once again worthy of the honor that a woman who had earned her doctorate by the age of twenty-five deserved.

Someone . . .

Someone who hated her.

"I'll show you," the lab tech said.

Was it her imagination or was he looking at her with disdain? As she followed him through one perfect lab room after another, one beautiful display of expensive equipment after another, she realized everyone was watching her. They didn't even bother to pretend they weren't doing so. They flat out gawked at her. She could hear the accusations in their looks.

Monster . . . Dr. Frankenstein . . . mad scientist . . .

She had heard the accusations hurled at her for years. No one cared about the details. No one cared that she had been used and destroyed almost as badly those innocent humans whom they now called Morphates. And perhaps they weren't that wrong. She was supposed to have been this incredible genius of the research world. How could she have been so stupid? So wrong? So dense?

Oh, she knew exactly how.

But she refused to let her new subordinates see how insecure she was, or how desperate she was to make this work. She didn't want to feel that desperation, but it was better than the clinical drive and the associated tunnel vision that had allowed her to be so ignorant of what Paulson had been using her for.

As she was led around the network of the lab, she began to

realize the enormity of this project—that and the sheer wealth of its benefactor. If it hadn't been so perfect, she might have found it obscene.

The tech led her to her office, which, it turned out, was at the center of the lab, like the hub of a wheel with 360-degree windows or doors exposing each spoke of the lab as it stretched out and away from her. She would be able to see almost everyone as they worked, and would be within visual beckoning if anyone needed her. The glass was, however, threaded with steel fibers so it couldn't be easily broken or breached, and if she wasn't mistaken, it was also smart glass. All the doors were secure locked, requiring not only a key card but a thumbprint to cross from one section to another. They even had an entirely "clean" environment in one section, requiring very stringent protocols before workers entered or left the environment to keep it as uncontaminated as possible.

Everyone seemed busy as she stood in her office looking around, but she knew it was all just equipment testing and that everyone was getting their bearings just like she was. The lab had not been used until that day. There were seals on all the refrigeration units, blue protective plastic on all the displays, and hardly a single fingerprint on the metallic surfaces.

It was all waiting for her. Regardless of how they felt about her personally or even professionally, her staff was all waiting for her. And it was high time she started.

"Are you my go to?" she asked the technician as she lightly touched the state-of-the-art laptop sitting next to the desktop computer. Portable data next to fixed data. All of it, no doubt, linked to a central database. An empty database, perhaps? Most likely. She had lost everything she had been working on in the Phoenix Project when the labs had been destroyed by the government. Although long before the agents' arrival the data had apparently been decimated by Paulson himself before he'd escaped into the unknown. She didn't know which disturbed her more: losing all the magnificent advances she had made, or the idea that Paulson was still out there.

"No, Doctor, I'm not your lackey," the tech bit out, sounding mightily offended by the idea.

"I hardly consider my go to as my lackey. I consider him or her my lifeline to what is going on in the entire lab, the one person besides myself who will have his finger on the pulse of the bigger picture here. I consider my go to to be a crucial sounding board, a secondary voice to the one in my own brain. A fresh font of ideas, perhaps. Or even the voice of my conscience. You see, Paulson had no go to. He never thought he needed one. He was quite brilliant, you know, but also quite without conscience. I do not aspire to his type of brilliance."

"I'll be your go to, Dr. DeBruehl," a sophisticated, feminine voice spoke up. Jenesis turned to look over her shoulder to see a beautiful brunette woman in the doorway. She had fair-colored eyes, hair of indeterminate length twisted neatly at the back of her head, and she wore a smart vintage Chanel skirt and Possessiere blouse beneath a neatly tailored lab coat that hung open. Her name had been tightly stitched over her left breast in bright red thread: *Dr. D. Chandler.*

"Thank you, Dr. Chandler. I wasn't allowed to bring any of my own staff. It will be awkward until I learn everyone's capabilities." And beggars couldn't be choosers, Jenesis thought wryly. She had been in no position to make any demands for staff or anything else, to be honest. As it was, she had no idea why she'd been given this spectacular lab in the first place. With her besmirched history, she was still considered toxic goods. And considering this lab was owned and run by the Dark Philadelphia Morphate clan . . . Jenesis had her theories on why they had chosen her to head up the lab, but she would have thought that would be all the more reason for them not to want anything to do with her.

"Devona Chandler," the doctor introduced herself, holding

out her hand to Jenesis. "I'm in charge of your zoologicals. I'll be keeping the test animals happy and healthy. As happy as they can be, in any event."

Jenesis slowly reached out for the doctor's hand, her own hand shaking as they made contact. "Dr. Chandler. Your reputation . . . well, it's as colored as my own," she said with a self-mocking grimace.

A Morphate. Chandler was a Morphate. The first she had ever met, never mind touched. Jenesis felt a little sickly as they shook hands. It was because of her that this woman was now a cross between a savage beast and a human, and was also immortal in every sense of the word.

Morphates could not be killed. The tag that had led Paulson's genetic modifiers into her cells had made those cells indestructible, unaging, and had given them the most incredible regenerative ability known on Earth. A Morphate could be shot right through the head and could still heal and eventually fully recover with perfect integrity. It was also a surprisingly fast process. So as she shook Dr. Chandler's hand, she was overwhelmed with a combination of utter guilt and absolute fascination. Oh, she knew she had had nothing to do with the creation of the actual genetic modifiers that had caused this woman to mutate, she had only created the delivery system, but still . . . it would be as ignorant to say she hadn't created the bomb, she'd only discovered how to split the atom.

"I . . ." What could she say? That she was sorry? That she hadn't meant any harm? Hadn't meant to be a part of making her inhuman? If she said the wrong thing, the woman was now strong enough to rip her head off in a single punch. And she'd have every right to do so.

"Eric Paulson asked me to be a part of his work," Devona Chandler said in her soft, refined accent. "I was honored and thrilled. I accepted before he even offered me my salary. After all, it was Eric Paulson. He was a genius and the most powerful researcher I knew of. It wasn't until I realized his zoologicals were actually humans that I comprehended what I had signed on for. I quit on the spot. Tried to walk away. But he was having none of that. He gave me a choice: work with him or for him. What he meant was he knew I would speak against him if he let me go. I would either take care of his test group as I'd been hired to do . . . or I would become one of them. I chose the latter. I like to think that had you been aware of the nature of what your work was being applied to, you would have made the same choice."

Jenesis nodded mutely, but she could not affirm that with any honesty, so she didn't try. It was easy to say she would have made the right choice in a crucible of morality, but the fact was, no one could honestly answer a problem like that unless they were actually in the situation.

"I would like to think that as well," Jenesis agreed grimly. "But only you have the real answer."

Dr. Chandler gave her a slow nod and a half smile.

"Come. Let me give you a more in-depth tour of the lab," she said, pulling Jenesis into position at her side.

Kincaid Gregory stood with his feet braced hard apart and his arms folded tightly over the expanse of his chest as he stared fixedly at the monitors on the wall. Behind each mirrored run along the lab ceilings was a multitude of cameras, one for each workstation at minimum and dozens of others besides that were less hidden. The security cameras in the corners of the labs were par for the course and to be expected, but these others were for his purposes, although it benefitted everyone that there was always a second witness to the techniques, actions, and culpability of all events in the laboratory.

He had gone from being one of those anonymous little rats in Paulson's cages to being Paulson himself.

The parallel was not lost on him, and it didn't fail to make him just a little bit sick to his stomach. But unlike the demented Eric Paulson, Kin Gregory was not trying to recklessly mutate innocent humans, although it had become quite apparent early on that the mighty Dr. Paulson had never intended for his creations to become indestructible. Quite the contrary. That outcome had not suited his methods of illegal and inhumane research at all. After all, how could he possibly get away with what he was doing if he couldn't destroy the evidence?

Kincaid narrowed his focus onto the smooth little blond doctor he'd hired to run his lab. She had been one of Paulson's weapons in a vast arsenal of scientists. A key weapon, as it turned out. Without her, without that damnable tag of hers that had ferreted out the perfect cells necessary for transforming Paulson's human rats into the inhuman Morphates, he might never have succeeded.

Without her, Kincaid might still have the human life of a Federated police agent he had once been so proud of. His brother, Nick, would also be the human cop he deserved to be. Now, instead, they were . . .

Alphas. Beastly leaders of a beastly species, condemned to live this parody of freedom as the leaders of two out of the six Dark Cities. Seven years ago, no one in their right mind would want to purposely set foot in one of the Dark Cities. They had been overrun with the scum of the earth. Gangs. Rapists. Pedophiles. Thieves. They had claimed Dark New York, Dark Philadelphia, and four other cities for their own, making certain no decent person would want to go anywhere near them. Law-abiding citizens had then walled those cities off, isolating the bad things where they could keep an eye on them. Then they had stuck their heads in the sand, pretending that the scum of the earth would be quite content with their lot and never want to expand their territory.

The walls had kept people out of the Dark Cities, but not in. The pestilence of poverty and violence had been creeping over the walls slowly, bleeding into the New Cities as well as the workhouses, industrial parks, and the low-income housing along the Dark City walls that no one else wanted to be near.

And then the Morphates had come.

Much in the way Native Americans had been given reservations, the Federated government had given the Morphates the dubious benefit, at Nick Gregory's suggestion, of taking over the Dark Cities. Normal people had been given the illusory comfort of putting the scary Morphates they hardly understood behind high walls with all the other things they didn't understand or were afraid of, and the Morphates found themselves in charge of huge amounts of real estate that, up until then, had been controlled by the baddest asses of the moment. Well, there was nothing more badass than a Morphate. It hadn't taken long for the criminal element behind the Dark City walls to realize there was a new sheriff in town, and that sheriff couldn't be dealt with the way they had dealt with previous mortal competitors.

Each Alpha in each City ran things his own way, and those Alphas took part in the Alpha Council, which was loosely responsible for keeping each group of Morphates under a modicum of control and helping the Morphates maintain representation in the government. After all, what the government had given, the government could just as easily decide to try and take away.

If they were stupid, that is. But no one had ever accused the government of being overtly smart. Over the past seven years, Dark New York and Dark Philadelphia, the cities run by the Gregory brothers, had undergone massive restructuring. The cleanup was moving along in both cities and, for the most part, the criminal element had been cleaned up along with it.

Kincaid smiled, a feral showing of his teeth.

Not that they'd had many other options, he thought.

Kin watched the monitor as Devona made nice with the new doctor, his eyes narrowing on the delicateness of Jenesis

DeBreuhl's wrist. The monitors were sharp, the cameras high-definition color, to the point that he could see the beat of her pulse through the tiny veins there. The sight of it was a little like dangling chocolate in front of a PMSing woman. There was an instant reaction of craving inside his body as a whole, quickly followed by the push/pull effect of wanting something on a visceral reactive level and yet knowing it wasn't good for him in any way except to provide a brief moment of pleasure, but with no real long-lasting satisfaction.

Kin frowned. He didn't usually drop and get hard at the idea of the warm blood in a woman's body, even though there was always a craving for it. But ever since his transformation, he had directed his craving solely at Morphate women. The only women, in his opinion, who were capable of holding up under the savage need a Morphate male felt when sexually aroused. In fact, it was something of an unwritten law among Morphates that they should only breed and feed amongst themselves. Both feeding and breeding could get so out of control sometimes that fragile mortal lives could easily be lost. They had learned that in Paulson's Phoenix Project, when he had "fed" unchanged humans to the Morphates. Just for shits and giggles. Just to see what would happen.

The results had not been pretty. True, the Morphates had just been turned and had had very little idea of what they were and even less control over what they had become, but quite a few of them had been scarred by their own savagery and behavior.

Kincaid shrugged a shoulder harshly, pushing the heat-inspiring reaction to the doctor away. He put it down to a lifetime weakness for blondes, especially the pale pretty ones. And this blonde in particular looked like she hadn't been touched by sunlight once in her life. It wasn't an unattractive paleness. It was a cool, fragile one. If he looked at her pulse points, like along her long neck or her cleavage, which was presently being displayed in the simple white blouse she was wearing, he could see the spidery blue ghosts of her veins painted delicately beneath her skin. That had once been a mild turn-on for him in a strange secondary way, but now there was nothing mild about it. It was hard and brisk. Right in his face.

Strange. While she was measurably pretty, she wasn't as drop-dead hot and viscerally sexual as the Morphate women who had been gracing his bed since . . . Still, he found her physically compelling. But only enough to acknowledge it and push past it. He had uses for Jenesis DeBruehl, and they absolutely did not include bedding or blooding her.

2

The next morning, Jenesis arrived at the lab very early, needing to get there before anyone else. She couldn't explain why, but she felt she needed a few minutes of silence and exploration on her own to connect to the nuances of what she was going to have available to her. This way, shallow, surface things like judgmental looks and outright hostilities wouldn't distract her. She needed to find her stride, dig in her own roots. The rest, including the opinions of her staff, would fall into place slowly over time. She recognized that they felt she deserved censure. Besides, who knew how many of them were actual Morphates? It was very likely a large majority, considering the lab was in the heart of Dark Philly. After all, there were very strict rules about regular mortal humans entering and exiting the Dark cities. Not many volunteered for that sort of thing. Only people who were desperate to make money or make a new start would put their necks on the line and do such a thing. The Morphates paid huge salaries in order to coax fresh manpower into the jobs they had available.

But though the pay was impressive, she hadn't come here for money.

"Right, boys?" she said to the rows of rats housed in the room. She leaned forward to peer through the cage bars at a strangely spotted rat, his pink nose wobbling fiercely as he munched on something he'd captured between his front paws. He was up on his haunches and his glassy black eyes were fixed on her carefully as he ate. "I see you don't trust me either," she observed.

"Should he?"

Jenesis made a small exclamation of sound, whirling around to face the man who had spoken up behind her. She hadn't even heard him approach her. There'd been no telltale click of a door opening or closing, no squeak or tap of a shoe on the brisk floor tiles. Not even so much as a rustling sound from the crisp oxford shirt he wore or the worn denim jeans that fit him like the proverbial glove. Then again, denim wouldn't really make a sound if it fit that well, now would it?

"I-I didn't know anyone else was here," she said a bit lamely as she let her instinctively analytical mind work in the background to figure out who he was. A lab worker? Where was his coat? Where was the I.D. she had been told everyone must wear clipped to their lapel or on a lanyard where it could be immediately seen by security at all times? Even the janitorial staff had to have their I.D. on them. It had been made very clear to her that security was of paramount concern in the lab. "I'm sorry, you are?"

"You're here very early," he noted, ignoring her hunt for identification.

"So are you," she returned with a frown. She eyed him carefully, and not a little bit nervously. She might be 5'9"—relatively tall for a woman—but there was no way she could go head-to-head with a man as big and, if she were going to be blunt, buff as he was. That pale blue oxford shirt was stretched out tight over a pair of thick shoulders and impressive biceps. There was nothing easy about his build. It was clearly something that was worked at and religiously maintained. Nothing ridiculously bulging, but he was a strong and imposing man, no two ways about it. Imposing enough to make her nervous, being in a vast lab seemingly all alone with him. She glanced at the glass walls and deeper into other parts of the lab, looking for what she already knew was not going to be there. Her gaze shifted to the cameras in the corners of the room, and he took notice of the obvious action.

He smiled in what she could only describe as a feral fashion. The anger of the insult he felt was in his dark blue eyes, and she imagined she could see the hackles of his short, military-grade haircut prickling up along the back of his neck. He was just shy of being a blond, and probably would be more apparently so if he let his hair grow out. Just the same, he would be a very different sort of blond from her own waves of obvious gold, which were tucked up and around in a relaxed, pretzel-like knot at the base of her skull.

"What's the matter, Doctor? Afraid to be alone with one of your own creations?"

He leaned in closer, purposely taking away all of her personal space, coming so close her nose touched his sternum for an instant before she backed up a step. But her backside almost immediately came up against the steel lab table behind her.

She was stuck there with the rats at her back and what she now realized was a Morphate male at her front. Her stomach bottomed out, her fear blossoming to such a degree that she thought she could taste it on her own tongue, and it wasn't a pleasant thing to experience at all. Her heart began to race and she tried not to let all of her instinctual reactions be obvious, but he was a Morphate, for God's sake. She had heard the stories, watched the news, and read every tell-all book anyone who had been in the Phoenix Project had thought to write. Where most of the Morphates had chosen to be more circumspect about the details, not wishing for the normal human race to be any more afraid of them than they already were upon learning they drank blood during some of the most savage sex known to man, as well as for sustenance, other Morphate individuals had made their stories public. And while for everyone else it might be a morbid fascination like craning your neck to see what is happening when you're passing a car wreck on the highway, for her reading them had been an exercise in self-recrimination.

It was a wonder she'd ever set foot in a lab again.

"What do you want?" she asked, her words bursting out in a combination of bravado and resignation. After all, she'd always felt it was only a matter of time before the Morphates cornered her, pinned her down, and made her pay for what she had done to them. "Whatever it is you feel you need to do, just do it and get it over with. Or go slowly if that's your preference. Make me suffer. There's nothing I can do to make you happy. None of it will make you what you used to be."

His face was handsome and somehow familiar to her, though she couldn't figure out why. When he lifted a brow it made him look curiously amused, even though nothing else about him looked at all entertained. He was a crowding wall of genetically hyped-up masculinity obviously looking down his nose at her—literally as well as physically.

"Are you really so naïve that you've stepped into yet another lab, Doctor, without realizing what that lab's purpose is? What your work is going to be used for? Haven't you learned from your mistakes yet?"

Jenesis swallowed and forced herself to meet his eyes. She was frightened and she was guilty as charged, but she was no coward.

"No, I'm not that stupid," she bit back. "The party line is

that you're looking to understand what you are, what you've become, and searching for ways to better your lives as Morphates. But I knew the minute you came looking for me that what you were really looking for was a way to change yourselves back to human."

He took a slow breath in; she could see his nostrils flaring and she knew it had very little to do with the need to breathe. He was taking in her scent. His lip lifted momentarily, a brief flash of teeth that made her heart seize in her chest with wild shock.

"Really?" he said. "So you think we hate ourselves so much that we need you to fix us? That we are so reprehensible?"

"I don't think you are anything of the kind. I think you are wondrous and unfortunate. I think you are miraculous and tragic. I think you might end up being the ones to inherit this earth because you are invincible in the face of the things that may one day destroy the rest of us." She swallowed as she saw him tighten his hands into fists, the clenching of the muscles of his arms rippling up his forearms and biceps, and turning his shoulders visibly hard as rocks.

"So you think we want you to change us back. To make us weak and civilized like you. To make us better, hmm?" He made a sound of utter disgust as he reached up to nab her by the chin, making certain she was there when he looked into her eyes. His irises were a strange marbleized blue and gold, the blue as cool as the feathers of a jay with veins of gold swirling throughout like stardust in a picture of the cosmos. "So in your estimation, I despise myself?"

"I don't know you." Jenesis breathed softly. "And I would be the last person to presume to make any kinds of judgments about you. It's not my place. It's no one's place. You never asked to be what you are any more than I asked to be what I am. But the only reason you could possibly want me, the dregs of the Phoenix Project and the inventor of the tag that was so instrumental in changing you, would be to create more change . . . or reverse the process."

"Perhaps." He tilted her face left and then right, examining the shape of her brows, the way the widow's peak of her hairline made a classic sweetheart shape of her face. She was an understated sort of pretty, but he found the more he looked at her, the more appealing she became. And this time Kincaid couldn't blame it on the attractive beat of her pulse under her skin, although he could clearly see that at the line of her neck where the thick carotid artery was working overtime to compensate for her stress and fear. "But the best-selling books and news exposés about us are not all that in-depth, Dr. DeBruehl. There are things we don't care for the public to know about us. And you are going to help us with one or two of those things."

"I'll help you. There's no need for you to bully me or try to intimidate me. I'll help the Morphates in any way I can."

It was the least she could do.

She didn't say it out loud or even think it to herself in that moment, but it was the unspoken understanding between them—she thought it out of guilt, he as accusation—and each of them understood the other's position quite clearly. What Kincaid didn't understand was why she would ever agree to set foot behind Dark City walls. Was it really all about some skewed need for redemption? Or was it more that she wished to be punished for her crimes? The courts had not found her guilty, and with quite a bit of ease considering other members of Paulson's teams had been legally eviscerated. The Federated government didn't want to admit that it had fallen down on the job, that it had allowed such atrocities to go on for so long and with such a horrific end result, and that in the end they had let Paulson get away from them. Someone had to pay, and Paulson's staff members, those who had survived at any rate, had taken the brunt of it. And for the most part, "I was just following orders" had been found to be an incredibly lame defense.

But Dr. DeBruehl had never claimed that kind of defense. She and her staff had been guilty of nothing more than total ignorance, and their handwritten data had proved that.

Lucky for them. Paulson had destroyed all remnants of electronic data. If not for their fastidious note taking, they would have been lumped in with the rest of those to blame. Kincaid wasn't certain they still shouldn't be. And he could tell after just a few moments of talking to her that she felt exactly the same way.

"Fine. Let's start with me."

Kincaid grabbed her by the hand and, turning on his heel, yanked her along in his wake. He pulled her into one of the phlebotomy sections of the lab, threw himself into the chair, and presented her with his arm as he rolled up his sleeve in quick, distinct jerks. Everything about him screamed that his anger was barely repressed, and she very nervously approached him. She looked around at all the sample tubes, the typical chairs for drawing blood, the boxes of gloves and packages of sterile needles and catheters. She plucked out a pair of medium-sized gloves and put them on, frowning as she habitually looked at the integrity of his arm for the proper vein she required.

"It's not so easy," she muttered as she popped open packages and chose the tube types she wanted. Even as she was resisting him verbally, her curious scientist's brain was getting excited by the idea of looking at his blood composition on all levels. From the basics to the nuclear, she had been wanting to see a Morphate blood panel for quite some time now. Sure, the overall animalism in their natures fascinated her, particularly their need for blood both nutritionally and sexually, but what it really came down to was the indestructibility of their cells. That had been the ultimate side effect of her work. Her tag had sought out the healthiest cells, the goal had been to keep those cells healthy for longer than their natural life span, but who would have ever thought they would so thoroughly overshoot the mark? And where, in any of it, had they stimulated the cells to regenerate in such a rapid fashion? They had planned to get to that eventually, but as far as her lab had been concerned, they had not yet reached that stage of the experiment.

But then again, as far as her lab had been concerned, they had not yet reached the stage for human testing. As far as her lab had been concerned, the rats they had been testing on were only at a seventy-three percent success rate. Not enough of a success, in her mind, to warrant moving up to primate testing. And nowhere in her testing had they noted the primal behaviors the Morphates ended up exhibiting.

"What's not so easy?" he asked her. "You have a guinea pig. Start testing it. I know you're dying of curiosity. It's your nature, I think, to be curious to the point of recklessness."

"Shows what you know about me," she bit out as she ran her finger over one of the many ropey veins wending its way down the length of his arm. The plastic of the glove snagged infinitesimally on the dark gold hairs that peppered his skin. "I am curious, I won't deny that, but never to the point of recklessness. I never knowingly hurt anyone. Or anything, for that matter. Except for maybe a few hundred innocent rats. Perhaps I'll have to answer for that when I meet my maker."

"I'd say you have a lot more to answer for than the deaths of a few hundred rats."

Jenesis pressed her lips together and sent the needle into his arm. She popped the first tube into the hub and it immediately began to fill.

"I need a name for these samples," she said.

"Kincaid Gregory."

That made her stop in the midst of switching to a fresh tube. She looked up into those marbleized blue eyes and her breath caught. This was the man who had hired her. He was the reason she was here. He was the leader of the Dark Philadelphia clan.

The clan's Alpha. He had proved to all of the other badass Morphates that he was the baddest ass of them all.

"I thought I recognized you, but I couldn't recall a name to fit the face," she said simply. What else was there to say?

"Well, when you've seen one Morphate . . ." he said with a leading shrug.

Jenesis smacked the tube down on the steel table a little recklessly in her temper. "You know, not everyone thinks like that. Not everyone hates you. It's even quite possible that there are a lot of people out there who don't even think about you at all. After all, you look just like any other human being."

"Most of us. Until we get pissed off at any rate. Or turned on." Kincaid reached out to brush a finger down her chest, ending just shy of her cleavage. It was an overt act of sexual harassment, he knew, but he did it anyway. He liked the startled way she caught her breath and the way she suddenly turned pink around her ears and neck. He liked the way he could smell her warmth increasing, and the way her scent reminded him of clean linen.

She had a tight, intriguing figure, he found himself realizing. She wore very professional designer clothes along with that lab coat she had donned like a suit of protective armor. Even though she had thought no one else was around, she had still girded herself with her crisp, clean lab coat.

"Don't touch me like that," she said, her words rushed and breathy because she was breathing so hard. "You have no right."

"How does that feel, Doctor?" he asked as he took hold of her by her hip and pulled her closer. "Being touched by the freak you created?"

"I didn't create you!" she burst out, yanking the needle out of his arm prematurely so she wouldn't have to stand so close to him any longer. Blood quickly welled up out of the puncture site and she fumbled to reach for some gauze while he drew her so close her breasts were practically in his face. "Paulson bastardized my work and *he* created the mutations you suffer from!"

"If that's true, Doctor, then why do you think you deserve penance? Why are you here so wracked with guilt?"

Kincaid found himself trapped in a web of his own making. By drawing her close, he was stimulating himself on a very base level. There was something about her, the smell of her. Intellectually, she hit just about every negative note he could think of, but physically, the Morphate animal inside of him was responding to the attractive curves of her body and the deliciousness of her smell. Her warmth radiated against him to such an incredible degree that he couldn't help but think of the blood in her body that made her that warm. It was disturbing to him because he never craved blood on that kind of conscious level. It was somehow always just a sudden need easily fulfilled by the nearest Morphate female.

But this was twice now the idea of her blood had compelled such a powerful response in his body. Twice. And as wild as his first hours as a Morphate male had been, as savage and uncontrolled as all those initial learning sensations had been, he couldn't remember it being like this.

He surged up out of the phlebotomy chair, crowding his body into hers even though his logical mind was demanding he shove her away, demanding he put a good distance between them. He tried to tell himself he was not the beast they had made him become. That he was above knee-jerk cravings and uncontrolled desires. He was a civilized being as controlled and thoughtful as any other human being on the planet.

Jenesis wanted to escape him, but he was everywhere at once. He was probably one of the biggest men she'd ever come up against. Certainly one of the most intimidating. He was also Kincaid Gregory, the man in charge of Dark Philadelphia and her entire future. He owned this lab. He owned *her*.

So when he ran a sudden and fierce hand from her waist to her backside, gripping hold of her ass and hauling her into the bend of his body as tightly as if he'd glued her to himself, she was paralyzed into inaction. He growled fiercely, the sound chilling and savage, like nothing she'd ever heard from anyone before. Her heart seized, every latent instinct in her body coming suddenly to life in a classic flight-or-fight reaction.

"My guilt does not permit you to use me like this!"

She hauled off and belted him hard across the face as her whole body lurched backward from his hold on her. But there was no escape for her. He was far too strong and much more determined than she would ever have thought. And while slapping another man that hard across the face might have sent a significant message to his conscience, this man recoiled from the strike with a savage sound and a flash of ivory fangs that had not been present an instant earlier.

And as terrified as she was to find herself in this situation, a back part of Jenesis's brain was utterly fascinated by the mechanics of the clearly retractable fangs he was sporting. That was how she found herself torn by the possible option of kneeing him between the legs to reinforce her message that she wasn't going to let him maul her like some piece of meat . . . or reaching up to touch those magnificent fangs.

For some reason, she gave in to the latter impulse, her fingers shaking as she touched the tip of the lower bicuspid.

"Do they retract fully into the jaw? Does it hurt when they do so?"

Her curiosity had the power to do what her slap had failed to do. It took him aback, made him hesitate, even though his body was hard with need and hungers. He felt his own pulse as it shot through the seat of his testicles and down the length of his rigid cock. The sound of it was raging in his ears, making him realize he was listening far too keenly to voices that were far too formidable within him. Kincaid recognized that he'd allowed the beastly Morphate to command him and the situation.

"Fuck!"

He spat the invective an instant before shoving her away from him. He snarled at her viciously, a gnashing of those fangs that so fascinated her. The curse sounded funny, a little lisped because it was no easy trick to make the "f" sound around a mouthful of fangs.

"Do you see? Are you fascinated?" he demanded of her as he reached for a rack of specimen tubes and threw them violently against the far wall. "Does it pique your scientific curiosity to know that this man who used to live and breathe the law as a Federated officer could lower himself to molestation and possibly even rape thanks to your brilliance?"

"Do you think this pleases me on any level?" she railed back at him. "But I can't sit here and wallow or beg your forgiveness for things I can't change, and you are clearly in no frame of mind to forgive! And before you say anything, I have never even asked for your forgiveness or your understanding! I have never even suggested that I deserve it! But you brought me here for a reason, and whatever those motives are, I have to start by fully understanding what it is that Paulson did to you. Blood chemistry is the smallest portion of this, albeit the keycode to what was done. But unlocking that code will be nearly impossible if I don't have a hypothesis about where to start looking."

Kincaid was breathing hard, like an enraged bull she had swatted in the face a few times. And to be technical, she had swatted him in the face at least once. But he was clearly and visibly drawing himself back together, gathering his civil self back up again instead of letting the bestial half hold reign over him. From the look of him, from what she had seen and felt so far, it was something of a monumental effort.

"I don't know anything about you that I haven't seen in the

news or read in someone else's editorial about you," she said quietly. "But your record of valor and achievements as a cop say a great deal about the man you once were and, somewhere, still are."

"Now who thinks they know everything," he accused bitterly.

"Hardly that," she assured him. "And I don't presume for even a second to know how difficult this struggle you are fighting with yourself must be. But I do know it is in my power to help . . . if you'll only tell me what it is you want from me."

He took a deep breath, his stone-cold blue eyes pinning her in place once again, no hands necessary.

"I want two things, Dr. DeBruehl. I want to figure out how to control this thing inside of me. In seven years I've learned that there are no longer any guarantees that the man of law and morals I once was and, at my core, still am is strong enough to stop me from hurting someone while I am caught up in the urges of the beast I now harbor."

"I can understand that. You might not like some of the solutions that immediately come to my mind. And what is the second thing?"

"I need to learn how to kill a Morphate."

3

"Morphates under my control and my brother's control respect the will of their Alphas for the most part," Kincaid said with a frown. Jenesis was realizing that frown was almost ever-present, marring what were otherwise good looks. "But Alphas don't necessarily have to mind the rules we've drawn up for ourselves, or the rules of human society for that matter. After all, what can you do to them if they don't behave?"

He glanced at her from under his thick, dark lashes, making her realize he was judging her responses, perhaps even baiting her. "I see the writing on the wall, Doctor. I see there are other Alphas on the Alpha Council who are chafing at the limitations of polite society and the scraps of life you have reluctantly thrown us. I was a cop for a lot of years. I know a bad sort when I see one, and Paulson culled his lab rats from all kinds of society . . . including some who were criminally insane. Can you imagine it? Criminally insane Morphates?" he offered, the idea making him tense throughout his body. "A monster with no equal to hold him in check."

"Except Morphates like you," Jenesis said carefully. "You

are still the cop you once were. At heart, it seems, if not in practice. And I have no doubt it's in practice as well. The role has merely changed you from being a deputy to having become the sheriff," she pointed out insistently when he gave her a dark look. "And if you didn't still have the heart for it, Mr. Gregory, you wouldn't be here asking me to help you control yourself, as well as others around you. You aren't doing it for ultimate power and domination. I can feel that. You want me to think your desire to control the animalistic side of you is a purely selfish desire, but I am willing to bet you would share it in a heartbeat."

Kincaid made a dismissive sound, turning away from the divining strength of her eyes. How was it that she could figure these things out about him so quickly, and yet she'd never known what Paulson was? What he was doing? It made him even more suspicious of her than ever. He couldn't figure out if she was the consummate actress or the dupe she professed to be. As a person, he knew he couldn't trust her at all, but there was no denying the power of her skill as a scientist. If he'd had another choice, he might have taken it, but the truth was she'd already walked in the footprints of the science used to create the Morphates. She wouldn't be starting cold the way anyone else would.

Anyone walking around free, that is. The idea of recruiting anyone from the original Phoenix Project had gone against everything inside of him, but he had considered making a deal with the government to bring in one of the scientists they'd imprisoned in the wake of the project's demise. Until he'd come across the stories about Dr. DeBruehl. Until Devona Chandler, an incredible doctoral mind in her own right, had made him understand that Jenesis DeBruehl was probably his best chance to bring about the change and the control he knew the Morphates needed. Devona had made him understand the science as much as he needed to. He didn't have the kind of intelligence it took to fully comprehend the vast details of genetic tags and cellular alteration, all he knew was the results of the practical application of it. He lived with them every second of every day.

He had just given the doctor a close-up encounter with the hell of being a Morphate.

Well, good. *She fucking deserved it,* he thought bitterly. She deserved anything she got as far as he was concerned. Fit punishment for an obscene crime. She deserved to meet the vicious monsters she had unleashed in them all.

And the moment he had the thought, Kincaid felt sick to his stomach for it. He'd never been an easy man, but he liked to think he'd always been a decent one. Even she was assuming he had once been a decent human being. But he'd always wanted punishment for a crime committed.

Did her crimes mean she deserved the beast of his Morphate turned loose on her?

Kincaid was still very close to her. Close enough to continue to smell her, a scent that he was finding far too compelling.

He made a sound low in his throat, his head dipping until his nose lightly brushed beneath her ear. His breath blew out through her hair, coasting over her ear until she felt her heart skipping a beat as it tripped over itself to speed up. She wanted to tell herself it was fear alone that caused the reaction, but the chills rippling down her chest and breasts forced her to be a bit more honest with herself. As intimidating as Kincaid Gregory was, there was something dangerously exciting about him. It was, she realized, that male beast that a female mate responded to on primitive levels. She did not need to be a Morphate female to recognize there were base things inside of her that would find the baser things he represented exciting, perhaps even appealing.

And it didn't hurt that he was incredibly easy on the eyes and quite beautifully built. His body and physicality were the equivalent of bright plumage on a male bird. They were meant to attract a female. The brighter the plumage and the more attention getting the strut, the more she was instinctively going to find it attractive.

At least that's how her scientist's brain tried to quickly explain away the reaction. It was all about nature. All about those latent needs and desires that years of evolution and civilization still had not bred out of them.

"I know I'm no better than a low beast," he growled against her ear. "I know it because all I can think about when I smell you is getting myself under your clothes, touching your skin, sucking on anything I can get my mouth on, and then fucking you until I can't make myself come anymore. This is what I've been reduced to."

His words were like having molten gold poured down the center of her body. The heat and weight of it scorched her in a wild splatter pattern of internal burns. The result was a sudden wetness between her legs. It had been such a long time since she had felt anything like it that the unexpected alienness of the response made her feel awkward and gauche. She should be put off by him. The way he had spoken said he expected her to be offended by his behavior. But she wasn't. And as much as she could analyze the whys and wherefores and the science behind basic things like attraction and sexual need, there was nothing in her coping repertoire that had ever experienced something so enlivening and so obviously forbidden.

"I thought Morphates couldn't have sex with regular humans," she said, her voice a raspy, catching whisper. He was still nuzzling her cheek, his thigh now pressed against the side of hers and shifting restlessly.

"Hmm. Not can't. Shouldn't. We're too . . . savage. We bite our mates. We drink our mates." Jenesis felt something sharp running down the back of her neck. "We claw our mates in the heat of our coupling. What fragile, normal human would want to experience such a thing?"

Jenesis reached a shaking hand up to the back of her neck, her fingers gripping hold of his and bringing his hand around to where she could see it. He'd had normal nails moments ago. Now, thick, ivory-colored claws curved out from the nail beds. They were a good inch extended past the tip of his blunt fingertips.

Kincaid knew immediately that she had shifted back to being the curious scientist as she touched one of his claws, tracing it for its strength and permanency. He wished he could switch gears that easily. Perhaps once upon a time he had been able to. After seven years of wrestling with this dominant demon inside of him, he couldn't even remember anymore.

"There are quite a few humans who would be attracted to the idea of all those things," she said, drawing her eyes from his hand and meeting his hard gaze. "We shouldn't be lumped into absolutes any more than you should be."

"True. I've heard stories of humans knocking at Morphate doors in search of a new kind of kink. And the government hasn't made it illegal. However, since all pedestrian measures of birth control, other than condoms, fail to be effective for us and we have no desire to start creating half-breeds when we barely understand ourselves as a breed . . ."

"I remember reading about that. That birth control doesn't work for you. Perhaps we can work on something."

"I think that would be most welcome. The heat of a female is very hard to resist. And if she's in heat, she is ripe for impregnation. We have nearly doubled our numbers because our instincts overwhelm precaution. And we barely know how to raise these Morphate children. I will show you what I mean. A Morphate child is nothing like any child you've ever seen."

Jenesis had heard very little about Morphate children. No one had. The Dark City enclaves and the clans within them were very tightly guarded and very well protected. The only pictures out there of Morphate children had been taken with powerful telescopic lenses, and yet were still blurry and unrevealing. There had been a few stories about photographers who had potentially caught a good picture of a Morphate child, only to suddenly and inexpicably disappear before it could be published.

Of course, that was just a silly urban legend.

She hoped.

Jenesis cleared her throat and tried to take a step back from him. She couldn't focus clearly when he was leaning up against her, oozing all that masculinity all over her. She needed to gather her professionalism back up. She needed to remember to approach him in a completely clinical manner. "If you want me to do my job effectively, I have to maintain a clinical distance."

"Fuck your clinical distance," he told her in no uncertain terms. "Your clinical distances have done you no favors, Jenny. Hasn't that been proved?"

"Don't call me J-Jenny," she stammered.

"What? I'm not good enough to know you that well?" he demanded of her, his hands closing tightly around her arms. The only thing he didn't do was to give her a good shake. But somehow she felt it was only through a tremendous act of self-control that he did not.

Jenesis pushed a hand hard against his chest, an act of resistance in gesture only because they both knew she didn't have the strength to fight him off for real. They had already had one tussle that had proved that. But this act, just like the earlier slap, grabbed the attention of the civilized man inside of him.

"I don't like anyone to call me Jenny," she bit out between tightly clenched teeth. "Do you want me to tell you the story about the uncle who called me Jenny and liked to touch me a little too lovingly when I was a kid, or will you give me the common courtesy of respecting my wishes?"

The remark, so full of acid and so cutting, made Kincaid go

quite still. He didn't let her go, didn't allow her distance; he couldn't control himself to that degree in that moment, it seemed. But she had his full attention.

"So not Jenny," he said. "Are you opposed to Jen? Or am I supposed to call you Doctor, like a well-behaved lab rat should?"

Jenesis imagined this had been part of Paulson's protocols during the Phoenix Project. It wouldn't have surprised her if the maniac had reduced his human specimens to numbers. She glanced through the glass to the rows of rats in the next room. Each was numbered quite carefully. But invariably someone working with them would get attached enough to one or two of them and give them nicknames. It always happened that way. Personalizing the animals was just part of human nature, even though they knew the rodents were not likely to have very long lives. Kincaid Gregory's need to call her by a more personal name, however, seemed to be more seated in the need to strip her of her power and title of "doctor." Honestly, who could blame him? The last doctors he had come across, no doubt, had been . . .

"Jenesis or Jena. Not Gina . . . Jen-ah."

There was something to that well-practiced distinction. But just the same, Kincaid saw it as a form of progress. Maybe even a form of advantage. But he didn't know to whom the advantage was. He didn't want to examine his own motivations too closely.

"I should make you continue to call me Mr. Gregory," he said, his smirk at her dirty look the closest thing she figured she would ever get to having Kincaid Gregory lighten up. She decided she would take what she could get. "But Kincaid or Kin works. Just don't call me Rat Number One."

"I wouldn't do that," she told him, this time succeeding when she tried to step away from him. Perhaps he didn't realize it consciously, but personalizing her with a mutually agreed upon nickname gave her an altered status in his subconscious. It was enough to give her the right to a little bit of distance.

But she made no mistake about it. Kincaid Gregory had claimed dominance over her, and he would find a way to prove it if he could. She was starting to see the base characteristics of what he was up close, rather than reading about those traits from a distance. She might have wondered if this whole project was a matter of biting off more than she could chew, but she felt it was more than fair that she be made to face the ramifications of her work up close and uncomfortably. Besides, what better way of understanding what had happened than by putting it all under scrutiny? She couldn't truly understand a creature if all she was going to do was study it behind the safety fences and glass of the zoo designed to keep her safe from it. She needed to work with the Morphates. To watch them eat, sleep, breed, and interact in all manners natural to them.

And most importantly, she needed to see how their humanity had survived in them. Nick and Amara Gregory, the Alphas of Dark Manhattan, seemed as normal and civilized as a human could be. They were intellectual and practical and well-spoken whenever they made public appearances or spoke for the needs of their breed.

But here was Nick Gregory's very own brother, and while he was also intelligent, he was clearly not so able to manage his baser side. He certainly made very few public appearances. That was why she had not been able to place his face when she'd first seen him.

"I was wondering . . ." she began awkwardly, not knowing what would set him off next.

"Morning, folks."

The lab tech sauntered into the room, hitting the lights as he went, for the first time making Jenesis realize she had been maneuvering with only sunlight from the outer windows to light her way. Considering the vastness of the lab, that was highly insufficient. But Kincaid Gregory had had her so flustered from the start that she hadn't even thought about it.

"There's bloodwork to be analyzed," she said, gesturing to the tubes and their colored stoppers that spoke for themselves as to which tests would be wanted.

"Sure, Dr. DeBruehl." He clapped his hands together, rubbing them eagerly. "Let's get this show under way, eh?"

His eagerness made her smile. His name tag said, TAD UNDERWOOD, SENIOR PHLEBOTOMIST. That meant he was going to be in charge of her phlebotomy lab.

"Thank you, Mr. Underwood," she said with a smile.

But her smile faded instantly when an aggressive sound rolled out of the Morphate who was suddenly standing up against her once more. Her entire back half was plastered with muscle and heat and the implied aggression that came with it. Jena's heart leaped up into her throat, her whole body going hot and cold all at once. The sensation was too overwhelming to sort out and the moment too dangerous to waste time thinking too deeply about anything.

Tad went instantly stiff at the aggressive sound, but a moment later he lowered his head and eyes, bending his neck and completely submitting to the other male in the room much the way a wolf in a pack would show submission to its leader. The action fascinated her, as did the way Kincaid significantly relaxed behind her, although he was still preening with dominance.

In a heartbeat she had learned that Tad was Morphate and she had just learned something about Morphate social structure. If it truly was akin to the ways wolves behaved, then that meant Tad knew who his leader was. But the interaction had gone a step beyond that. Of course Tad would know who his leader was. They all would. The only reason for Kincaid to feel he needed to set Tad down with a sharp reminder would be if he was marking new territory.

Or more specifically, warning a male away from a female he had claimed for himself.

Jenesis's face burned with embarrassment and anger. She reached behind herself and grabbed hold of Kincaid's shirt along the button line, using all of her strength to jerk him forward in her wake. He was so surprised to be manhandled in such a way that he stumbled along obediently. She had no doubt that he was surprised. For the past seven years he'd probably had people, Morphates, bowing and scraping at his significant dominance. He'd probably gotten used to no one countermanding him in any way.

She yanked him into her office at the center of the labs, slamming the door shut so hard that she might have shattered the glass in it if not for the metal reinforcement running through it.

Then she turned on him.

"You listen to me, Kincaid Gregory," she railed. "I'm going to have a hard enough time earning the respect of the people in this lab on my own merits. I don't need your Morphate posturing and whatever the hell that was supposed to be undermining my authority here!"

"This is a ninety percent Morphate-populated lab, Dr. DeBruehl," he said with an almost wickedly mischievous smile. "They know who you are, what you've done to help them become what they never asked to be. There's only one way they'll ever respect you, and that's if a stronger Morphate than they are tells them to."

"I don't believe that," she argued hotly. "By your theory, you're all no better than animals following instinctual demands. But in just a half hour in your company I can tell you that you are better than that! Like all humans, you have tendencies to be savage and the ability to be civilized. You are the one in charge of which you choose to indulge in from one moment to the next!"

"How interesting that you're so sure of that after less than a few hours in Morphate company," he said dangerously.

Next thing she knew he had hold of her beneath an arm and was hauling her up against the door. He slapped a button near the lock as he did this and all of the glass windows around them clouded over, going completely opaque with smart glass technology and blocking the arriving technicians from seeing into the room. They were instantly closed away. Jenesis was neatly cut off from everyone. As thick as the glass was, she doubted anyone would even hear her scream. Not that it mattered. With the pecking order being what it was, she doubted anyone would dare to challenge this Morphate male.

She doubted any of them gave a damn what happened to her.

His blue eyes, so remarkably pretty and yet so bitingly cold, fixed on to hers and he gnashed his as yet fangless teeth at her, growling menacingly in her face.

"Fuck you too!" she blurted out, unable to hold her tongue or her temper any longer. She wasn't going to get a damn thing done in an environment where she was going to be everybody's scapegoat and whipping boy. She might feel guilty and have regrets, but she was going to make amends *her* way, not his.

Her surprising show of backbone brought him up short. No, more than that. It turned him on. As much as it impressed him, it excited him. A lot of things about her, he realized, excited him.

He wanted the realization to revolt him. He wanted the logical human she kept insisting still existed inside of him to find her offensive and insulting. Instead, she kept sinking into him with these claws of inexplicable attraction.

Purely physical, he told himself hastily. She was attractive, smelled good, and appealed to the beast inside of him with her smooth skin and gorgeous blond hair. He wanted to fuck her, he acknowledged. But he wanted to fuck a lot of women. It came with the Morphate genes.

"Hmm," he rumbled in her face. "I can take that as an invitation."

That speculation made Jenesis catch her breath. He'd made no further overt moves on her, but her brain immediately started to recall his earlier blatant actions. And those recollections came with uncontrollable responses.

But despite all his threats and all the privacy and opportunity he had given himself, Kincaid suddenly pushed away from her, pulled her out of the way of the door, and yanked it open. The minute he did so, the smart glass went clear because it needed a continuous connection to maintain the current that excited the particles within it and made it go opaque.

He strode out of the door like a dark storm menacing the sky. The lab was still only lightly populated, but as she watched him leave she saw each person he passed react. She immediately could tell who was Morphate and who was human. The distinction fascinated her, even as she dropped into her desk chair and tried to figure out how to catch her breath.

And how she was going to spend the next several years in head-to-head combat with Kincaid Gregory.

4

Jenesis was exhausted.

She'd spent every minute of every day, weekend, and night in the lab. She wasn't trying to prove anything to her staff by her behavior. She wanted her work to speak for itself. But the work had drawn her in in a way she had never expected. Sure, she'd always gotten a little obsessed with her work through the years. What scientist didn't? Especially when they felt a breakthrough was imminent. But she was nowhere near any such breakthrough. However, the work she was doing was groundbreaking in many ways just in its infantile stages. Outside of the initial government testing the Morphates had endured during the exposure of the Phoenix Project, no other testing or work had been done on them. And certainly none of the information that the government had gleaned had ever become public information.

This she knew for a fact because she had searched exhaustively for it. And in ways normal people might not do. She knew how the government worked, and she was very certain that Kincaid Gregory wasn't the only one wanting to know how to kill a Morphate. It was simply the darker side of human nature to fear what it didn't fully understand, and in that fear want to know how to destroy it. Perhaps it was a self-preservation instinct . . . but she was more inclined to think of it as human ignorance.

Over the past two weeks she had seen very little of Kin Gregory, but she knew he was there. Knew he was watching her. She could almost feel his disdain following her around like a dogged, nasty pit bull that simply would not unclamp its jaws now that it had hold of her. The few times she had been in the same room as he, she'd made certain to walk a wide circle around him. It was just better that way.

The labs were in the same building as the condos the human lab members had been given, so she never had far to go to get home. The lab building had been designed that way to keep humans from wandering too freely in the Dark City. The entire building was like a mini human city in the heart of Dark Philly. The shopping was all inside the building, from clothes to food, including even boutiques, all Morphate-run and all heavily guarded by security. It was clear that the security wasn't to protect the shop owners. It was there to regulate the interactions between the Morphates and the humans. At the end of the day, the Morphates left the building and the simple humans remained inside.

That wasn't to say they couldn't wander the City, but it had only been seven years ago that the Dark Cities had been hellholes devastated by criminals, addicts, and worse. The human and Morphate populations of Dark Philly were still a bit unnerving. Jenesis could easily see where some of her lab workers had come from. The scarring and the tattoos, the rough attitudes they had to work hard at keeping under control, made it clear that they had been reclaimed from the dregs of society.

In her opinion, that made the Morphates miracle workers.

They had been able to give second chances to people who had otherwise been given up on. They had saved countless human lives.

But that didn't mean Dark Philly was a garden city to be safely strolled around. However, the Morphate cops, known as the Watch, were very diligent. Especially, no doubt, as the Dark City allowed more and more humans in to fulfill specialty jobs like hers.

All of this raced through her head in a dizzying swirl as she dragged her feet into the elevator.

She didn't even register the man who entered the elevator with her. Not until he hit the Stop button between floors and abruptly cornered her at the back of the elevator. She heard the bell going off distantly, warning of the stopped elevator, but what she was focused on was the dark eyes of her assailant.

"Dr. DeBruehl, I have a message for you," he said quickly, his hand coming out to clamp on to her shoulder. The grip was painful, in contradiction to his next statement. "I am not here to hurt you. Only to tell you that there are interested parties who would be willing to reward you in impressive ways if you were to give them the results of your research instead of giving them to the Morphate."

Not Morphates. Morphate singular. It struck her that there was contempt in that acknowledgment of Kincaid Gregory.

"What people?" she demanded.

He smiled, but there was nothing comforting or amusing about the expression.

"No one you haven't already been willing to work with," he said. "Suffice it to say, there's a great deal of advantage for you in this proposition." His grip tightened so hard then that she cried out and her knees buckled. "And it would not be in your best interest to ignore this opportunity."

As he spoke, he hit the Continue button on the elevator

panel and pressed the button for the next floor as well. He didn't let go of her until the doors opened. Then he released her and hurried out into the hallway.

She slid down to the floor of the elevator, sitting there numb and scared as the doors shut and the lift continued on its way to her top-level apartment. As her floor approached, she picked herself up, cradling her left shoulder in her right hand. When the doors opened she made a cautious movement outside, looking into the hallway, cautiously inspecting both directions. She was in a bit of shock as she plodded onward to her apartment, nervously looking over both shoulders all the way to her door, where she pushed into what she hoped was the safety of her apartment.

The building was, for all intents and purposes, heavily secured. Where had her assailant come from? How had he gotten into the building past the notoriously thorough Watch? As dangerous a job placement as this was, she had felt ridiculously safe because of all the security measures, both Morphate and technological, that had been put in place. She should have known not to let her guard down, she thought bitterly. And what had he meant by—?

Jenesis dropped back hard against the door of her apartment, frightened fingers fumbling with the deadbolt lock, as if it would stand up to anyone really determined to get in. The ridiculousness of her action made her laugh until tears blurred her vision. She sank down onto her heels, her hand nursing the shoulder that still hurt. She suspected it wouldn't hurt so badly if she hadn't been so terrified.

The only person she could think of whom she had worked with in the past who would play such a ruthless game was Dr. Eric Paulson.

The rumor was he had turned himself into a Morphate. That he was as indestructible as they were. That there would never be any way of making him pay for his atrocious crimes. The understanding that he was out there was bad enough, but the prospect that he was out there doing the same kinds of experiments as he had been before was mind-numbing and fearfully paralyzing. And if he was looking for a way to kill other Morphates, then Kincaid Gregory and his people were in a great deal of danger. Especially considering that Paulson was powerfully persuasive enough to convince one of his agents to breach Morphate security in order to get to her.

Jenesis wouldn't be half so afraid, she supposed, if she wasn't already anticipating the fact that she would rather cut her own heart out than give that maniac one iota of her research ever again. That meant that somewhere in her future all she had waiting for her was the other side of Paulson's ultimatum.

Join or die.

She took a deep breath, gathering herself together as she picked herself up off her heels. She shook the tears out of her eyes, lifting her chin. So be it. She would deal with that when the time came. If the time ever came. So far no conventional method short of the intense equivalent radiation dump of a radical bomb had proved capable of killing Morphate cells. As it was, they had been forced to develop a special chamber in the lab to dispose of blood specimens. On the positive side, they didn't have to refrigerate Morphate blood. It never separated into serum and cells under normal conditions. It took a centrifuge, whereas human cells immediately began to break apart when taken out of the body. It had changed the protocol for preserving blood specimens completely.

Meaning there was no need for protocol. No need for preservatives. No need for any of it.

Moving to her kitchen, she pulled open the fridge door and looked for something to calm her nerves. The sight of almost completely empty shelves reminded her just where her priorities had been for these past few weeks.

She looked at the clock. It was nearly 3 A.M. Everything was closed. There would be no delivery services, no stores would be open, and she sure as hell was not setting foot outside of her door until daylight.

She tried not to give in to the urge to cry as she closed the refrigerator and looked around the room for something . . . anything . . . to help steady her nerves.

And there, written across the whiteboard she'd pinned above the countertop, was Kincaid Gregory's phone number. She'd written it there after she'd grown tired of looking for it every time she'd needed to call him to report the progress of the day. For some reason, she had always felt better making the call from her apartment instead of the lab. Frankly, whenever she heard his voice while she was in the lab, her skin went damp with a sensory memory of what his rough, dominant hands had felt like on her skin and his heated proposals had felt like against her ear. He had infected her like some kind of virus that day.

So maybe that was why she stumbled over to the phone and dialed his number.

He picked up instantly. He didn't even sound as if he were sleeping.

"Gregory."

"Kin? I . . . it's Jena."

Silence. Then . . .

"What happened?"

Somehow, he knew. The understanding made her whole body go weak with relief, and she had to drag herself onto the bar stool next to the counter to keep from ending up on the floor again.

"I was . . . I just needed someone to talk to," she hedged. Now that she was on the phone with him she was suddenly unsure of her actions. Kincaid Gregory was no friend of hers. He wasn't any kind of source of solace. Why was she turning to him?

Because he was Alpha. He was the leader and the strength of the strongest of people. If anyone could keep her safe, it would be he.

"Someone threatened me," she whispered into the phone. "I'll be right there."

Kin didn't bother with the elevator. He powered up the stairs at a feverish, thunderous pace. It didn't matter that she lived on the thirtieth floor and he had been on the fifth. He took twenty-five flights without a thought, his mind flooded with an interior growl, a rage of demands and instinctual responses he couldn't even try to soothe or sort out. He understood nothing but the realization that she had been so frightened by whatever threat she'd faced that she had turned to *him,* a creature she so clearly went out of her way to avoid. He knew that was his own fault, that he had given her cause to fear and avoid him.

By the time he reached her door he was covered in a sheen of sweat and was drawing hard for breath. He was Morphate, incredibly strong and fast by nature of his breed, but he was still affected by aerobics as anyone else would be under extreme duress.

When he knocked on the door, he knew she was right there, waiting. And still she stopped to look through the peephole, the sound of her breath reaching his keen ears. Had he not been hearing his own heart so loudly, he might have been able to hear hers, quick and flighty and fearful. When she opened the door it was only a crack, a moment to double-check it was him. Foolishness, really. Her weight against the door could not stop him from powering through it once she opened it. But this wasn't about judging her safety tactics. Not at the moment. He laid his hand on the door and looked into the single wary cocoa-colored eye peeking through that crack in the door.

"Let me in, Jen," he said as quietly and gently as he could manage.

She did. She let the door fall open as she took several quick steps backward toward the living room.

Scylla and Charybdis. She looked like Ulysses must have looked when he had to decide between those two horrible monsters, trying to figure out which would be the lesser evil.

He was her lesser evil in this particular situation apparently. So what could possibly be worse than him, he wondered.

He shut the door behind him, looking carefully at her as he stepped a little closer to her. His eyes had already tracked over the entire apartment and assessed it for threats. There was nothing there but the two of them.

And a chasm full of emotional flotsam.

And the smell of blood.

Blood.

It drifted into his senses like the teasing aroma of fresh-baked waffles coaxing him awake on a Sunday morning. It was her blood, he knew, because its makeup was so original and distinct to her. It bore the essence of what he knew her to be.

"You're injured?"

Her hand reflexively went to her shoulder. So, he thought, she'd suffered more than just a verbal threat.

"How did you . . . ?"

"You're bleeding."

She seemed startled by the information. Jena looked at her shoulder, struggled to see over it. He took the opportunity to close the distance she had put between them. He took her between his hands, not taking her startlement as a personal insult. He turned her so her back was to him and saw the white of her lab coat stained red on her shoulder. There, in a semicircular pattern, were four tears with the taint of an odor to them. The mark of another male. A Morphate male.

He reached for the lapels of the coat and drew it back over

her shoulders. She quietly allowed him to do so. He exposed the deep punctures in her shoulder. Without the weight of her coat on her, they began to bleed heavily into the fabric of her sleeveless silk blouse.

"He wounded you with his claws," he told her, his fingers pulling at the edge of her blouse to expose her damaged skin. It was strange how the sight of it made him feel. It was more than the idea that someone under his protection had been hurt, and by a subordinate Morphate no less. His reaction was something he couldn't acknowledge consciously just then.

"He said . . ." She swallowed loudly. "I didn't even realize he was a Morphate. My God," she rasped. "That makes what he was even worse." She turned around to look at him, her fragile state of mind evident in her eyes. "I think he was sent to me by Eric Paulson."

That name . . . *that goddamn name*. There was no describing the hatred it inspired in him. But he took a breath and tried to move past that instinctive reaction. There was time for that later.

"Let me take care of these," he said steadily, taking her arm to lead her into the bathroom, hoping she had some kind of first-aid kit. Maybe he could find some cotton to shove up his nose and block off that amazing, wondrous smell. . . .

"He wants to learn how to kill you," she pressed, feeling that he didn't understand the urgency of the situation because he wasn't reacting the way she was expecting him to react.

"I figured he would, Jen," he said as he turned on the lights in the bathroom. "And not just him. Everyone wants to know how to kill us."

"Then why press to discover it yourself? Isn't it best to leave it alone? That lab is full of hundreds of people, hundreds of witnesses you can't control forever, Kincaid. They will all take what they learn here with them. Information will be leaked everywhere."

"Perhaps." He found the first-aid kit and used the meager supplies to dress the wicked puncture marks. It was hard not to give in to the urge to bend his head and lick his tongue over those painful marks. Instinct was demanding he do so on two levels. First, he wanted to wash away the taint of the other male on her. Second, he craved the taste of her on his tongue in a way that almost blinded him.

Instead, he used gauze and conventional methods. He didn't know how he managed it, but he did. Even so, as he taped up each puncture, his anger began to boil higher. Paulson had made this threat for several reasons. Trying to manipulate Jenesis was only one of them. The more important message was being sent to Kincaid. It was Paulson's way of telling him that all of his precautions, all of his power, and all of his security meant nothing. It was his way of telling Kincaid that he was still nothing but a lab rat within his reach, and that Kin was never going to be free. He would live and die at Paulson's whim.

Seven years later, he still remembered the feeling of being under that man's utter control, of knowing there was nothing he could do to get away. He remembered the devices in his body that had kept him in line; the measures that had been used to keep him tame. The white walls. The gray sweats. The tests, the drugs, and the constant measuring of his every body function . . . the monitoring of his every physical or emotional reaction to something. That had been his life for weeks before Paulson had changed his strongest and healthiest specimens into Morphates in a mass genetic experiment.

Kincaid hadn't realized Jenesis had turned around to look at him. He didn't realize the expression on his face was radiating his every thought, his every fear. She saw his emotions in the widening pupillary reaction that made the crisp blue of his eyes little more than an accentuating rim.

"What is it?" she asked him in a whisper, her hand reaching to touch his bare chest. Her belief that he'd been wide awake when she had called him had been wrong. Clearly he had been asleep. He hadn't even stopped to dress himself properly before running to her side. He'd thrown on jeans and nothing else, leaving his feet as bare as his torso, his short, spiky hair sticking out in haphazard directions.

"Nothing," he said with a shake of his head.

They both knew he was lying. But he wasn't going to tell anyone about the things that haunted him. All of the things that haunted him.

Including the way she smelled.

She was wearing her golden hair in a ponytail, the end of which was stained red where it had touched her bleeding wound. He reached out for the tail, pulling it forward over her shoulder, drawing it up to his nose where he could smell the floral richness of her shampoo, the hairspray she had used to tame it, the perfume on her own hands that had been transferred to it as she had absently stroked her hands over her hair throughout the day.

And, yes . . . blood.

His eyes closed as it invaded him, called to him, begged for a deep, instinctual reaction from him. Kincaid took a deep breath, gritting his teeth as he looked down at her.

"If I were human," he said, "I would be more considerate of how you are feeling right now. I would consider your injured state. I would take a great deal of care with you."

"But you're not human," she said breathlessly. "So what does a Morphate do in this situation?"

"He protects you. Fiercely. Savagely, if need be." He pulled on her ponytail, drawing her closer, breathing a strangely relieved breath when she rested against his body. "And he reacts to his needs. Selfishly, it seems. Because I haven't been able to rid my mind and senses of you since the first day I met you. You irritate everything inside of me. I shouldn't even care that you're hurt by the man you once colluded with to hurt me."

She didn't argue the point. She was tired of defending herself. He could see that, even as he knew the wording was unfair and perhaps designed to piss her off. He needed her to get pissed off . . . he needed something to get in his way. Anything. Because as it stood, he was plowing a path that was incredibly dangerous. Especially for her.

"A Morphate male smells the blood on you and lets it call to him. Lets himself seek it out," he continued as he bent his head until his lips were touching the outer shell of her ear and the strands of her hair were filtering through his fingers. "Send me away, Jenesis, before I drink you to exhaustion. But not before I fuck you to within an inch of your life."

He watched her oh so carefully, wanting her to look horrified and offended, wanting her to throw herself away from him and accuse him of being the bastard that he was. Why wouldn't she? How could she possibly understand the Morphate drive that was motivating him? Surely she would envision the damage he could do to her fragile human self if he were to be given his head.

But she did none of that. Instead, she leaned into him just a little farther, touched her nose to the back of his jaw, and took in a deep breath. Took in the smell of him.

That was all he needed.

Kincaid grabbed her by both arms and propelled them both out of the too-small bathroom that he could barely move in. He burst into the living room with a mere pair of strides and found the nearest wall to slam her up against. He was too rough; he could tell by the breath that kicked out of her. But he ignored the sound as he buried his face deep against her neck and simply smelled of her. Her and the blood inside of her that he wanted so damn badly. But that was just the beginning of it all. Not the be all and end all of it. There were so many delicious things about her that he had wanted since he'd first laid eyes on her, always in antithesis to what his brain tried to lecture.

"Is this another experiment for you?" he wanted to know on a deep, dangerous growl. "Another curiosity you must satisfy no matter how perilous it might be for you?"

Jen was breathing hard, a world of excitement shuddering through her from blood to bones. She had never felt anything like this primal mixture of fear and excitement.

"Is there a measure of curiosity involved? I'd be a liar if I said no. There is always curiosity between new lovers. Isn't satisfying those curiosities so much of what motivates us all?"

"I am not motivated by curiosity," he reminded her, yanking her up tight against his mouth as he opened it on the fragile skin of her shoulder. "I want to eat you. In every way possible." He let his tongue splash across her in a long swipe, first in one direction and then the next.

An X to mark the spot.

"Oh, my God, you just made me wet," she gasped as she dropped her head back against the wall.

He had, indeed. Suddenly the aroma of her excitement was drifting into his senses. And just as suddenly he wanted to drink her in a completely different way. The stimulus of the thought had his claws and fangs lengthening into readiness. The whole of his mouth ached with the craving. Before he knew it, his hands were dragging at her skirt, pulling it up around her hips, exposing her as he moved back just enough to see her.

"Oh, Christ on a goddamn cross," he swore heavily. She wore garters. Straight and professional, neat and beautiful on the outside, but hiding something blessedly naughty underneath it all. Pristine white garters to match the sweet white panties she wore. A goddamn virgin sacrifice the way a man would want to have one. "Bad, bad girl, Dr. DeBruehl."

"T-they're practical f-for a tall woman. Pantyhose never fit right."

"Bullshit. Own it, Jen. You like the way it feels. Every so often in the middle of all that science in your day you stop and remember you're wearing these sexy little things. You remind yourself that you're a woman underneath it all."

"A practical woman," she allowed with a mischievous smile.

That gorgeous little smile of trouble made him suddenly weak in the knees. He let them bend and collapse, kneeling at her feet, his knees braced on the outsides of her ankles as his hands coasted down her hips and onto her thighs. How had he missed the fact that she had the most amazing legs? Pretty pale skin was everywhere, as well as the smell of her, which had intensified with the relocation of his nose. He leaned forward, burying his face directly against the silky white fabric covering her mound. He exhaled hard through the fabric, sending his hot breath against her. He felt the quiver of response that shuddered through her thighs. Her hands came to his head, her nails blindly plowing through the short edges of his hair. The sensation sent nerve impulses down through his body, making his cock ache as it shuddered through the thickness of his erection.

Jenesis felt his fingers hook through the wet crotch of her panties and he pulled them down her legs as far as the garters would allow him to. His fingers were shockingly burying themselves in her pubic hair and the folds of her labia the very next instant. He pulled her forward onto the open mouth and tongue he had waiting for her. She cried out as her long-dormant sex drive was called to attention by the swipe of his tongue over her clit. There was no seeking. No hunting. He knew exactly where to find it and wasted no time making use of it.

And all the while she knew he was thrusting that tongue against her through long, beautiful fangs. It hardly took anything at all for her to launch into a fast, fierce little orgasm. She came into his mouth with a startled cry, the sensation ripping through her almost painfully dazzling. Tears sprang up into her eyes and she quickly tried to blink them away. He wouldn't understand. He wasn't there to be understanding. Nor would he care that she hadn't been touched since her boyfriend had walked out on her in the wake of her fall from grace seven years ago.

He was there for one thing only. And that was fine with her. Oh so fine with her.

She couldn't know what the creaminess of her response on his tongue was doing to him. He couldn't have even explained it. The Morphate inside of him wasn't interested in anything but reflexive need.

He surged up to his full height, towering over her as she drew rapidly for breath. His fingers were still toying with her sex, making her squirm up onto the tips of her toes as she became overstimulated in the wake of that unexpected orgasm. He was breathing in deep, growling gusts against her face, forcing her to smell herself all over him even as he stared down into her eyes.

He said nothing, making the point on his mind by suddenly thrusting two large fingers deep inside of her, his lips remaining at a distance from hers. He would show her no affection, she thought even as she struggled up onto the tips of her toes in reaction to the stimulation. He felt no affection for her. She was pretty sure he didn't even like her. He was responding to a mating instinct, pure and simple. Regardless of what his mind might think of her, his biological imperatives were telling him she was an ideal mate.

It was sort of a compliment, she supposed. It told her that she was somehow superior in genetic material. Physically, intellectually . . .

Jena gasped as he thrust inside her again, wriggling his fingers in such a strange, thrilling undulation that she felt her whole body go weak and wet once again. That made his lips quirk up on one side. Perhaps a smile, perhaps an expression of superiority.

His free hand came up to streak across her body suddenly, half-extended claws ripping through the silk of her blouse, shredding it until he could pull it down her arms enough to expose the front of her torso and effectively pinning her arms to her sides as he twisted the torn fabric together and held on to it. At that same instant she felt what those half-grown claws felt like inside of her body, scraping against her cervix in a way that made her whole body jolt with the amazing ratcheting sensation of another orgasm building rapidly up inside of her. She was gasping in uncontrollable bursts of breath as he lowered his lips to her ear.

"With a Morphate female, we can smell her ripeness. She is aware of when she is prime for the making of a child. And the exchange of blood between mates during sex readies her reproductive cycle."

Jena would probably be the only woman on the planet who would find such information an absolute turn-on. It didn't hurt that he was leaning his big, heavy body against her, rubbing himself against her like a cat might rub its owner.

Then very abruptly he was away from her, flipping her front to back and stripping down the tattered remnants of her blouse. His hands raked over both of her hips, snapping the fragile garters easily and doing the same to her panties. He was able to spread her feet apart then, able to pull her hips out from the wall and into the cradle of his pelvis. Heated denim rubbed coarsely against her, as if he wanted to fuck her in spite of the impediment. Jena braced her palms against the wall, but a warning hand on her back prevented her from pushing away. Not that she was of a mind to. She was too overwhelmed by sensation, her head spinning as an unbelievable craving overcame her.

He leaned his head forward, sniffing at the wound he had dressed, deep, intimidating growls punching out of him. He stripped away the bandage and this time gave in to the desire to lick her wounds. He couldn't fuck her with the smell of another male seeping into her in even the smallest way. It made him angry that she had been hurt. It made him angrier that another male had dared to mark her first. He would remember that scent, though. As he washed it away with his tongue, it sank deep into his memory so he would know it the instant he came across it once more.

Then he would rip the fucker to shreds.

Oh, the dismemberment couldn't kill him . . . but it would hurt. A lot. Death was an agonizing experience . . . even more so when you couldn't actually die.

But all of that was pushed aside as a deeper need overcame the Morphate male. The need to take her. His way. And immediately. He was beyond the point of recognizing the dangers of that prospect. The animal inside of him had chosen its mate and nothing was going to gainsay him. Besides, looking at her, all unkempt and naked, all curves and femininity and nothing there reminding him she was the buttoned up brilliance that had made him what he was, he just wanted to ease the pounding need inside himself.

Kin ripped open his jeans, freeing his enormous cock, letting it fall against her curvy little ass, barely registering how massive it seemed to be in comparison to her petite backside. One hand reached for her hair, stripping it out of that neat ponytail and giving himself a mess of gold to grip on to. He fisted his hand into it and fit the crown of his penis to the entrance of her body. Driven purely by mating need, an overwhelming mating need, he began to thrust himself into her.

Jena cried out almost immediately. It didn't register on him that it wasn't a good sort of sound. He continued to try to force himself in, the clawing urge to come inside of her blinding him to everything else. There was no describing or controlling the imperative that overcame him. Even he was shocked and overwhelmed by it. He had felt Morphate need before, but nothing like this. And the tightness of her closing around him seemed to make it more and more intense by the second. In the back of his brain the man that he was whispered fiercely of the things he understood about women and their needs, but for some reason he could not make any of it come into play. This was a fuck. The Morphate wanted a fuck. It demanded it single-mindedly.

Jena was in pain. She couldn't see the size of the erection being pushed inside of her, but she didn't need to in order to understand that it was insanely out of proportion to her own body. It was a hell of a time for her to recall that there was a reason why Morphate males had required a specialized line of condoms in order to fit their exaggerated parts. It was a hell of a time for her to realize that he wasn't even using one of those condoms.

She didn't realize that the Morphate inside of her had never, ever forgotten a condom.

Instead, Kin couldn't distract himself from the idea of spilling himself inside her. He couldn't make himself fit inside her entirely, hard as he tried, so he had to be satisfied with a little over halfway and began to thrust in rapid succession into her.

Jen stretched to suit him, albeit painfully. But after a while that discomfort became something distant and unimportant, even though it never actually went away. The surge of all that masculinity up against the back of her body, the repetitive jolting she took against the wall, somehow overcame his lack of attention to her body in other ways. The primal starkness of it made her breasts and chest go heavy and hot; she creamed over him and it eased him along. He hit her harder then, a fierce snarl of need and coming climax barking out of him. And suddenly he jerked her back by her shoulders, throwing her head against his collarbone, and ferociously bit down into her in the very spot he had marked on her earlier with his tongue.

The agony was shocking and she screamed, but even as the fire of it burned through her she felt him starting to come in hard, savage bursts. The wildness of it touched on something that years of evolution couldn't breed out of her, though she had never known it was there. She exploded into the rawest and most shocking orgasm of her life. She would have thought there could be no pleasure in any of this, but there it was, spiraling through her and all around her. And every single sound he made, every growl big or small, sent a sense of wicked satisfaction down into the deepest core of her body. She took him and let him take her, in every way her limited humanity allowed her to do.

Kin could hardly decide which felt more glorious, the raging release inside of her or the heated delight of her blood sliding down his throat. Blood to him did not taste like blood had tasted when he had been human. Though there was that tang of salt and iron, there was a sweet, savory dimension to it that his human senses had been incapable of appreciating. And that was just the general bouquet of it. The special nuances that were Jenesis and Jenesis alone, nuances that no other woman would ever be able to duplicate, were unbelievable. It went through him like a potent liqueur, spreading warmth and languor in his chest, belly, and limbs.

His mouth came away from her ravaged shoulder, his forehead falling forward against the wall as he tried to catch his breath. His cock was still hard, still inside her, wrung out from his orgasm but clearly he was already contemplating using her for another. He felt the wetness of his come oozing all around himself as it sought ways to overflow her tightly occupied body. She was slick with sweat from head to toe, only her skirt bunched up around her hips providing evidence that she had been fully clothed just minutes ago. He was supporting a great deal of her weight, he realized. He turned his head a bit so he could see her face. Long, pretty blond lashes were resting against her cheeks, her eyes closed as she drew hard for breath. Her hands were against the wall, curled into fists.

The sight of her, just the aspects of her face, the paleness of her skin, and the smell of her in a postcoital state made him want to do it again. And again. The desperation of the thought took him aback, even as he felt wet warmth against his chest and realized he had unthinkingly left the wound on her shoulder open and bleeding. Bleeding quite freely down her back and chest at that. Her blood was seeping into the matte white paint of the wall where her breast touched it.

She went suddenly lax against him, and every protective instinct in his being raged violently to the surface.

No! No, I won't hurt you! Caring for you is my everything. It will be my everything!

He could no more control the thought than he could the impulses that came next to cradle her back against his body, pulling himself free of her while he brought her shoulder up to his lips and the intense brush of his tongue over her weeping wounds. There was something inside of him that would not only clean the area free of immediate bacteria, but would seal it and protect it from further infection. It was a secondary system, really, meant to support the powerful healing capabilities of a Morphate mate. Had she been Morphate, the wound would already be well into the healing process.

But she was not Morphate.

The understanding rang through him like a shrill note. Because she was not Morphate, he would need to protect her even more carefully. She would need all the protection and attention he could muster. Nothing must happen to her.

Nothing could happen to his mate.

"Jenesis?" He breathed it softly against her cheek.

"I'm fine," she said so quietly he would have thought he'd

imagined it had he not seen her lips move. But those lips were lacking their usual soft coral color, telling him she had lost a little too much blood for her system to handle. He had not taken much . . .

. . . for a Morphate mating.

"But you're no Morphate woman," he said under his breath as he scooped her up off her feet and carried her in to her bedroom.

"I'm woman enough," she pointed out with a mysterious little smile rippling over her pale lips.

5

Kincaid was at a loss. He didn't know how to react to all of the things he should be acknowledging and reacting to. He was acting on autopilot, his Morphate self seeming to have a better idea of what was to be done in the situation at hand. He laid her down on the bed and immediately took his place beside her. His hands shaped their way over every inch of her, inspecting her for further damage. He tried to recall reactions to his bestial handling of her that he'd had no interest in earlier. Suddenly what had started out as a passing mating impulse had taken on a far deeper aspect to that stubborn creature living inside of his skin.

Over the past seven years Kincaid had struggled with his animalistic self, trying to come to grips with it, trying to come to some sort of understanding. Just when he thought they had come to an agreement, that he would relish the beast's power, strength, and immortality, and the beast would have to be content to work within his moral compass and self-control, the Morphate inside of him would go and do something like this.

"See what your curiosity has gotten you?" he said starkly, even as he let careful hands run down the length of her milky white legs. Here was a woman who so rarely saw the light of day, who had no interest in tanning beds and other such vanities. She didn't care if she was perfectly kempt or coifed. She was tasteful, wore pretty, delicate clothes, keeping in touch with the need to present herself professionally and elegantly. Just enough, but not beyond. Her legs were shaved, her pussy was not. She was not a woman behaving in expectation of a lover.

Not that he had any right to call himself a lover.

"This was hardly a lark to satisfy doctoral inquisitiveness," she said with a sigh. "No scientist with proper ethics would use herself as part of an experiment. Nor would she make a sentient being like yourself feel like he was little more than a lab rat." She reached out to touch her fingers against his hair. "I am not Eric Paulson."

Well, shit. That made Kin feel even worse.

"How do you feel? Light-headed?" He wanted to bark at her, growl at her for her utter foolishness in giving him permission to treat her in such a disconnected and selfish manner. But it wasn't Jena he was truly angry with. His reaction left him feeling quite confused, really. How had everything devolved into this situation so quickly? How had he woken from his bed and ended up in hers in what had to have been under an hour?

That fucking animal inside him had wanted its way, no matter what, and he hadn't been able to gainsay it. Now he was left to pick up the pieces and figure out what the hell to do with her. And on top of it, he was overwhelmed with a compulsive urge to treat her caringly, gently, and protectively. The beast whispered things in the back of his mind that made no sense to him, that he did not want to listen to.

Goddamn it, *he* was in control here! *He* was the one who

was going to manage his life. He had a specific goal as far as Dr. Jenesis DeBruehl was concerned, and nothing was going to change that!

"Are you hurt . . . anywhere else?" he asked her in a rough bark of demand.

"There's no need to be polite, you know," she said wearily. "I'm a big girl. I can make big girl choices. I can take their consequences." She moved out of the shadow of his protective body and went to sit up, but he grabbed her by the arms and forced her back against the pillows.

"And you are going to faint like a big girl, too, if you get up right now, Jena. You've lost a lot of blood. I can see it all over you. And I know you can feel it. Christ, you're stubborn!"

"Back at you," she muttered. "I'm almost positive the gene strands you have are shared with wild primates and canids, which accounts for the tendency to express an Alpha hierarchy in your groups. But the way you act sometimes, I'd swear they shoved you full of bull and mule."

"What's your excuse?" he shot back at her. "You are like a dog with a bone in that lab, day after day immersing yourself in every test and discovery you can wrangle. You're trying to make up for what you let get by you in the past. You can't do it, Jen. You can't fix it. No matter how many Band-Aids you come up with."

"Screw you," she spat irritably, her head spinning and her stomach lurching with queasiness. "I'm a fucking brilliant geneticist, Kincaid Gregory. If I spend enough time, I'll figure out exactly what that prick did to you, and I'll figure out how to fix the damage too!"

Kin raised a brow at that.

"So that's what you're aiming for? You want to change us back?" He sighed. "Jen, the Morphates of Dark Philly are only one of six different protocols Paulson created. Each building in the Phoenix Project had a different experiment going on, a different twist on the theme. He dumped his poison into us, no doubt looking for the best result out of the six. My brother is very different than I am. He is much more clearheaded, has far more control over his beast. Some of the others on the council . . . in Phoenix it's more like a pride than a pack. They are more cat than dog. In L.A. they're more like . . . I don't know . . . insects. It's more like they have a queen, rather than an Alpha. With all that variety, do you think you're smart enough to figure it all out? To fix it all?"

Jenesis turned her head to the side, tears threatening in her eyes as frustration burned through her soul. She had not realized the Morphates were so different from one another. How could she have? There was just so little known about them.

"Then . . . even if I do figure out how to kill a Morphate, Kin, there's no guarantee the process will work on all of them. That changes everything." She ran her hands back through her hair in frustration. "It means I have to find the thing that made you all immortal and find a way to interrupt the process. Without Paulson's science and notes, that will be almost impossible."

"Then maybe we ought to be looking for Paulson," he said darkly, giving her a deep, inspecting look. "But all of the cities and the Federated government have been doggedly trying to do that for seven years. We haven't found so much as a single reliable clue to his whereabouts."

Jenesis looked at him suddenly, a bright light abruptly entering her eyes. It was very contradictory, to see her so pale and weak and yet suddenly so full of inner strength and determination.

"That's not true," she said in firm words.

It took a moment for Kincaid to catch up with her thoughts. But barely a moment. He'd been a cop for too long, had come up with the solutions to too many problems not to suddenly see what she was thinking.

Yes, of course! Paulson had just about walked into this very building and handed him the key to finding him. He could use Jena as bait somehow.

"He wants to know what you know just about as badly as we want to know what he knows. Paulson believes that you are going to be the key to figuring out how to kill Morphates."

"Why wouldn't he? You certainly did."

"Yes," Kin said with a frown. "I did. But it took me a long time to get you here. I needed money. To build a proper facility. If he wanted you, why not take you before this?"

"He doesn't want *me*. He wants the solution. And he's clever enough to let you spend the money and manage the financial headache of supporting me while I am trying to discover it."

Kin's laugh was short and wry, and obviously bitter.

"I swear, I'm never going to get away from that motherfucker. He's going to haunt my every step from now until the day I figure out how to die."

"Only if you let him," Jen said softly, placing a hand of comfort on his biceps. "And you don't strike me as a man in a hurry to die."

"No, not particularly. But I'm not so certain I want to live forever either."

Jena sighed. "He may be insane, but I have to admit, Paulson is a goddamn genius. In the lab all I was ever able to do was suspend cellular life for three weeks maximum. How he managed to do it infinitely I'm not sure I'll ever know. I'm not certain even he knows. And I doubt I'll be able to figure that out in the course of my regular lifetime. But what I can do is help you figure out a way to get Paulson. I think we both know how to coax him out of hiding. We use me as bait."

Kin was nodding, ready to agree, but something inside of him began to balk at the idea with about as much power as he felt when he went into a rage or flung himself into his beastly passions.

No! We will not put our mate in danger!

We. Our. Christ, he had truly gone crazy if he was referring to himself in plurals. It seemed the further into this he went, the more distinctive the two halves of himself became. And from one minute to the next his other half was constantly shifting focus and desire. Not fifteen minutes ago he'd been using her without regard for her fragility or her humanity. Now, suddenly, he was protective of her? It didn't make sense. It never seemed to make any sense.

"That's not the smartest idea you've ever had, Doctor," he said grimly. "You forget what you are dealing with here. Creatures that are more animal than human. And they aren't afraid of dying, because, unlike you, they *can't* die."

"You're assuming Paulson has changed himself into a Morphate."

"His goal might have just been an extension of natural life, but once he saw he'd made us indestructible . . . hell yeah. Paulson already thought he was a god. He would only assume immortality was his due."

Jena watched him as he frowned and wondered if he realized he was petting soft, circular patterns onto her bare midriff. It was the first act of true affection she'd ever seen from him. Strange that he should be doing it right then. Stranger that he should be showing her any affection at all. She tried not to read anything into it, but it was difficult because it felt so outlandishly good. His fingertips were wide and warm, smooth and hard. His nails were longer than what she might find on the average man. Probably because of the way his claws retracted and extended. But honestly, right now she couldn't tell a damn bit of difference between him and a human male. Not at first blush, anyway. She imagined he was very much like he had been before he had been changed. Perhaps a bit more muscular or defined. She didn't have the original to compare him to, so she couldn't speak with any assuredness.

"I doubt it's as much a matter of arrogance with Paulson as it is the traits of a psychopath or a sociopath. He knows his own brilliance, and he considers himself far and away above the rules of society. You might see that as godlike. He is more likely to see his brilliance as a means to the end. The end game has more value, in his mind, than the methods he has to take to get there."

"Like war," Kin said grimly. "As long as we win, what's a few lives in the process?"

"Exactly." Jen smiled at him, her head tilting as her eyes brightened a little. "Kincaid Gregory, you are far better at higher reasoning than you would have others believe."

"Don't let my good moments fool you," he said wryly. "In some ways, I'm not so different from Paulson. Why else would I even be considering putting your life on the line?"

"Well . . ." Jen touched the tips of her fingers to the backs of his, stopping their play against her skin for a moment. "Whereas Paulson is into this for the single-minded achievement of his own science, you are looking at a different picture. You are trying to find a way to do damage control. The way any cop would. The perp is out in the world and wreaking havoc and must be stopped. Sometimes that means putting a confidential informant at risk. It's done all the time."

"Except a CI is usually a criminal themselves looking to cut a deal. It's a matter of using a smaller fish in hopes of catching a bigger, more important one."

Kin watched her look off to the side and a harsh protest kicked through his brain.

"You are not a criminal, Jenesis," he bit out.

"Since when do you actually believe that?" she countered

sharply. "You've held me responsible from the first moment I walked in your doors. No doubt for much longer than that."

He opened his mouth to argue but couldn't figure out what to say. If he contradicted her he would be admitting that he'd known she was innocent the entire time he'd been treating her like utter shit. What did that make him, exactly? Did it make him even worse that he wasn't willing to own up to his own mistakes and flaws?

Was he able to blame that on being forced into becoming a Morphate? Or had he always been that way? Maybe his brother had better control over his Morphate self because Nick had always been a better man overall.

Not at all prepared for such soul searching, Kin backed away from her and flung himself off the bed and onto his feet. He straightened his jeans, zipping himself up and running an agitated hand back through his bristling hair.

Christ, Kincaid, when did you become such a douchebag?

He had to ask himself that because he could see by her increasingly resolute expression that she was taking the weight for things that were honestly not her responsibility. He hadn't been sure when he'd first hired her, but after hours and hours spent watching her work through those damn security cameras and nightly reports of her progress when she'd sounded too tired to even be on her feet, he'd come to understand she was guilty of nothing more than being too dedicated to her science. What she was doing she did in a methodical manner and with ethics firmly in mind. At least she did now. If she had been in need of a readjustment in values, she'd certainly found it over the past seven years.

"Let me think about this," he said a little numbly. Somehow thinking didn't come so clearly anymore. For the past seven years he'd had her perfectly pegged, had thought of nothing else but the moment when he would have her under his control, doing his bidding . . . paying his price. Now everything was so damn complicated. "I'm going to get you something to eat. You need more nutrition than a half-eaten box of Twinkies is going to provide."

She was hungry and weak, so she didn't argue the point. Neither did she fight with him about his avoidance of the topic at hand. She wasn't exactly capable of heading out into the Dark City looking for all-night takeout. She wasn't even sure if she could get past the Watch at this hour. And frankly, it was too much of a challenge for her exhausted brain and body to cope with.

She heard the door to her apartment shut, and for a long minute she rested with her eyes closed.

They suddenly snapped open and her heart began to race. Fighting nausea and weakness, she struggled out of bed and onto her feet. She lurched into the bedroom doorway and then from one wall to another until she had staggered weakly into the kitchen. She started jerking open cabinet doors, the empty shelves glaring back at her until she pulled open the pathetically empty pantry.

Empty except for a half-full box of Twinkies.

"Son of a bitch," she said.

She turned around, ignoring the sway and list of the counter-tops, her keen eyes picking apart the bare, undecorated walls. Except for the delicate scrollwork clock that hung at the center of the trim running atop her cabinets.

"No, that's too awkward an angle," she muttered as she turned and began to map the kitchen out in her head in a series of ideal angles. After a moment she picked the angle most likely to give her a clear shot into the pantry, the angle she knew had been seen. With just a turn of her head she found herself staring straight into the microwave clock, the two dots separating hours from minutes blinking in half-second increments. She moved closer and looked past that distraction. Her movement made the lens behind the numbers autofocus.

"Son of a bitch!"

Every night. Every night that she'd been standing here in her kitchen calling him with her updates, doodling absently on her whiteboard, he'd been watching her! Making a bagel naked . . . singing the latest Aubrey song in her fucking panties!

And since she knew Kincaid Gregory wasn't the type to do things halfway, she knew there would be cameras in all of the rooms of her home.

Lurching over to the butcher block, she grabbed for the biggest knife it held. Then she slid down to the floor and rested there, conserving her unreliable strength, and waited for Kin to return.

6

Kincaid reentered Jen's condo about fifteen minutes later, having gathered a few groceries from his own home on the fifth floor, the bag full of them dangling from unconcerned fingertips as he glanced up and down the hall before shutting the door.

There was no explaining the sensation that crept across the back of his skull, warning him that danger was approaching him. He turned just fast enough to open his chest to what would have otherwise been a back stab.

She wasn't very strong at that moment, and his muscles, ribs, and sternum had been pretty impressive even before his transformation into a Morphate. That was why the knife never made it past the first two inches. It certainly wasn't for lack of fury or determination on her part. Instinct had him dropping the groceries and grabbing her by the throat, kicking her feet out from under her and following her all the way down to the floor as her back hit the tile. It also made him snarl viciously into her face as he reached to pull the knife out of his chest. Blood struck her face, splattering over her cheek, nose, and forehead. She cried out, the sound a combination of frustration, fury, and pain.

"Fuck you, you son of a bitch!"

She kicked at him, tried to rake his face with her nails, anything she could possibly manage as he threw the knife away hard, sending it four inches deep into the drywall across the room.

His reaction had no human component to it. He flipped her over, pushing her facedown into the floor, a deadly snap of fangs at her ear as he covered her body with his own. There was nothing human to the instant erection he felt shudder through his body, the incredible wave of arousal that was so powerful it made him weak in the knees. That was the reaction of an Alpha Morphate male getting bitch-slapped by his mate, just as a Morphate female would do to get his attention and force him to recognize he was supposed to be taking better care of her.

What was human was the part of him that kept him from fucking her to within an inch of her mortality, as an Alpha male might normally do to his female. But she was not Morphate, he forced himself to remember. She was fragile by any definition in his world, and even more so right now because of what he had put her through earlier. As he used a bloodied hand to pull her head back by her hair, he felt how limp she was. How quickly her strength was fading.

"What the fuck is wrong with you?" he shouted into her face, trying to blow off the kinetic fury of energy and craving clawing through him. "Are you trying to get me to kill you?" Because he knew she wasn't trying to kill him. He knew she was well aware of how impossible that was. But perhaps that was the point. Perhaps she really was trying to get his attention, to smack him around and force him to pay closer attention.

"You're a pig," she said through her teeth. "A lying, spying, untrustworthy, voyeuristic swine!"

Ah, hell. She really was too smart for her own good. He

now knew exactly what had changed between the moment he had left and the moment he had returned.

He rolled her over onto her back between the brace of his thighs, sitting back on his heels as they both panted hard. She glared at him angrily as she swiped at the blood on her face. He had already stopped bleeding, but there was still a long ribbon of red down his chest and belly. The stab wound was just to the left of his right nipple. But that wasn't his main concern at the moment. He knew that it would heal rapidly and was of no consequence.

"It's not just you," he tried to explain to her. "All of the apartments . . . hell, every inch of this building is covered by cameras."

"Well, clearly not for protection or I wouldn't have claw marks down my back!"

He winced at that. He didn't like the reaction. He didn't like the feeling that he had failed her.

"I had to protect my project! I had to keep an eye out. Watch for suspicious activity. I need to keep this project from turning into another Phoenix Project!"

"It became another Phoenix Project the minute you chose to rob people of their basic human rights like *privacy!*"

"Not people, scientists," he sneered at her. "Untrustworthy, scum-of-the-earth scientists whom I am forced to work with in order to understand myself!"

Her eyes went wide with disbelief as he flung the vicious insult right into her face. He realized his blunder a second after she reacted to it.

"Wait . . ."

"Get off of me and get out of my house! Get off!" She shoved at him with hard hands, proving herself to be much stronger than he had imagined her to be.

"You can't take care of yourself," he argued even as he did

so, letting her struggle up into an upright position. "Look at you! You can barely move."

"I'd rather drop dead naked in the middle of this floor than take one ounce of help from someone like you! I spent seven years putting distance between myself and Eric Paulson only to end up right back where I started! You have all your human subjects under watch, noting their every behavioral shift. What's next? Are you going to start putting drugs in our food supply?"

"I'm not Eric Paulson!" he shouted at her with ferocity.

"No, you're worse. *You* know what it's like to be one of those dehumanized subjects, and yet here you are, willing to do it to someone else. You disgust me. Get out."

"Don't you get it?" he said hoarsely. "I don't know who to trust! I trusted my brother to lead me out of that lab and into this City, but since then . . . I have nothing. Nowhere to put my faith. Nick has his own life. His own family. His own City. I can't let him worry about me. I'm the older brother and he doesn't need to be worrying about me.

"Everyone else in this place is subordinate to me because of some biological imperative, but that same biological imperative will tell them to take me out if I show an ounce of weakness, Jenesis. I feel like they are plotting it every damn second. I'm seething with paranoia because every time I think things are settling down, someone else wants to challenge me for Alpha. So what am I supposed to do? I don't know where to turn, who to trust. . . . All I want is two seconds of goddamn stability, and I can't even get that!"

Jenesis looked at him and for the first time saw the terrible vulnerability that was just beneath the surface of all his bravado. It went beyond his struggle with himself and his anger over the hand he had been dealt. He was truly alone.

Worse. He was lonely. There was a difference.

"Who is your Beta?" she asked softly. "In a social group there's an Alpha, a Beta, a Delta, and an Omega. The Omega is the group's weakest member, but the Beta should be your second hand. Your lieutenant. Devona . . . ?"

"She's Nick's Beta. Actually, I guess you'd call her Amara's Beta. Amara and Nick just lent her out to me for the project because she has one of those egghead degrees that I need. I . . . I don't have a Beta."

"You mean you don't trust anyone enough to choose one, because the Beta tends to be the second strongest in the group and the most likely to succeed the Alpha. You're afraid choosing a Beta will give that Beta delusions of grandeur. There is that chance, yes, Kin, but if you choose right, your Beta will be a source of relief for you. The protection and trust you are looking for."

Kincaid didn't know how to respond. He didn't know how to explain what it felt like to be in his position. The responsibility for an entire City's well-being, the dependents looking to him for food, shelter, and the medical evolutions they needed to stabilize their futures. On top of all of that, he had to cope with humans who didn't trust Morphates at all and a maniacal scientist who apparently wanted to regain control over his former test groups. Paulson's threats to Jenesis earlier told him that. He could easily imagine where Paulson's endgame was headed.

Jenesis could see the expressions warring over Kin's face, anger, doubt, and mistrust. It reminded her just how difficult his life had been these past seven years. As hard as it had been for her, at least she hadn't had to struggle with a volatile stranger inside of her the whole time. At least she hadn't been forced to adapt to rules of a new social order that she didn't understand. Or at least he didn't think he understood them.

With a sigh, she sat to face him, crossing her legs and relaxing.

"It's like when you were a cop. You need others you depend

on to have your back, Kincaid. Do they want your job? Sure they do. There's nothing wrong with ambition. But you have to find the ones who you know won't try to go through you to get that job. They'll wait until you retire out of it naturally or until you stop being effective in the role. Is that added pressure? I don't think so. No more than there will always be. No more than there was when you were just a cop in charge."

"Except this time if I screw up, a whole City suffers."

"And cities didn't suffer if you screwed up before? Of course, they did. Don't make this harder on yourself than it needs to be."

And it was at that moment that Kincaid finally realized why his Morphate self had chosen her as the perfect mate.

Because she was.

7

Kincaid was hovering around the lab again. Jenesis realized it might have been better if he'd gone back to watching her through those cameras of his. At least he wouldn't be staring at her in that unnerving way he had, and glaring and growling at anyone who so much as bumped into her the wrong way. She tried to remind herself that he was unable to help himself and that he was trying to be protective. She supposed being protective was better than being hateful and obnoxious. Although it was a little obnoxious in its own right.

"All right, this isn't working for me," Jenesis snapped, shutting down the centrifuge she was using and turning to face him when he tried to take a heavy microscope out of her hands.

"You're still weak," he said on a low breath, his blue eyes tracking the ridge of her shoulder, reminding her of the sore wound. The bite had been much deeper than she had initially realized. It was fascinating, really. If it had been just about finding a blood source, there were places where a much shallower bite would have served the purpose. But it hadn't been just about that. It was more like the way a chimpanzee or canine might bite to mark a member of its group, mark dominance or mark a mate. Those bites were nice and deep so they stuck around for a while.

Jen didn't know how she felt about that overall, but at the moment she was tired of being the fire hydrant he kept pissing on in order to tell everyone she was his. Especially when he really didn't feel that strongly about her.

"You need to stop breathing down my neck like a stalker, Kincaid. I can't work this way, and I honestly don't know how much more of it I can take before I punch you in the damn nose!"

Jenesis pulled her samples from the centrifuge with an irritated jerk, pulled an injection gun, and loaded the freshly made product into the injection chamber.

"I'm just trying—" he started.

"You're trying to irritate the crap out of me!" she bit out. Then she stormed past him, injection gun in hand, heading for the privacy of her office.

Jenesis closed the door to the office with a little too hard a slam, smacked the injector down on the table, and shrugged out of her jacket with heated temper even as she hit the button to activate the smart glass with her elbow. She was in the process of rolling up her sleeve as the door opened and shut to let in the storm that was Kincaid, the smart glass flashing clear and then clouding again as the connection was broken and then reengaged.

He opened his mouth to lambaste her, no doubt about it, but his words froze on his lips as the fact that she was giving herself an injection sank into his awareness. He watched the needle break her skin, watched her compress the injector.

"What is that?" he wanted to know.

"B12," she said dryly.

"You don't take B12 intravenously," he snapped.

She shrugged as she dropped the injector in the waste collector.

"Fine, since there's no way for you to argue with me about it. It's a tracer." She went to her laptop and turned the screen toward him; with a few taps she activated the tracing program, making sure to show him slowly how to do it. The shape of a body appeared, a warm red area slowly showing up around its inner right elbow. "In a few hours the red areas will have grown and spread throughout my body and the program. I used the same cellular tag Paulson did to attach nanobyte technology to my cells. The nanobytes are dormant, passive, and harmless. They have one purpose: They give off a GPS signal. That way if, for whatever reason, I should suddenly disappear, you are going to be able to use this laptop to track me down. This is the only tracking program I know of that is capable of doing this," she lied briefly, "so whatever you do, don't drop the damn laptop."

Kincaid was genuinely gape-mouthed as he stared at her and the tracing program alternately.

"You . . ." He couldn't seem to put together cohesive sentences. The implications of her actions were enormous. She had dedicated herself to the Morphate cause with that one injection. She had just acknowledged that she knew she was the bait Paulson wanted, and that she was willing to put herself on the line in order to help the Morphates finally track down their maker and . . . and do with them what they would. Exact revenge, extract information . . . whatever it was they wanted. "Jenesis, you are mortal," he found himself saying softly, for some reason that sentence being the only one he could manage. But when he thought about it, it really was the only one that mattered. "If you put yourself out there for him, he could kill you before we even have a chance to find you with this."

But Jena saw the way his big fingers were brushing over the pads of the laptop's unibody; the reverence and delicacy of the touch and the slight tremble in his big hands telling her just how badly he wanted this advantage, and just how much it meant to him. But she had known that already. It was why she had done it in the first place. It was only one of many ways she would use her brain and her science to help these people.

"Paulson doesn't want me dead. He wants my solutions. And once the nanobytes replicate far enough, they will remain in my body and working even if I am cut. I will bleed a trail of nanobytes with that tracer on them. Even if they do kill me, the trace won't die with me. You'll find me, and very likely you'll find him."

He smiled grimly. Not really a smile at all when she took in the sudden fury broiling in his eyes.

"And you think that's a fair solution? To give your life in exchange for tracking down Paulson?"

"I think that's as fair as it's going to get in this world," she said fatalistically.

He moved around the desk and grabbed hold of her in the span of a brief breath, her arms enclosed within his hands.

"I don't like it. It's unacceptable," he growled as his face burrowed into her hair, his breath coasting swift and hot against her ear. "It is beyond unacceptable to *me.*"

Jena couldn't resist the smile breaking over her lips. She knew this was the closest she would ever get to hearing him express concern for her. It felt ridiculously good for some reason.

"Nevertheless, it's done. Now all that's left is for us to put on a very convincing performance in the lab that will snag the attention of any of Paulson's spies and make him believe we have the solution he is looking for."

"And you think it could work that simply? That quickly?" he wanted to know.

"Paulson will want to snag the solution fast, in its earliest stages, before we have a chance to refine it and turn it into some kind of handheld defense weapon." She sighed. "It's what any brilliant psychopath would do. Steal it before you can use it against him."

Kincaid knew she was right. As he stood there with his face pressed against her ear, his senses absorbing the feel and aroma of her and how thoroughly she stimulated his entire being just by being that close to him, he felt torn violently in two directions. As usual. But in this case, it was the logical brain that agreed with her suggestion of taking the darker road while the beast within him wanted nothing to do with any of this plan and wanted only to protect her and keep her safe. He wanted to grab the laptop and smash it to bits, ending this insane plan right then and there.

"I don't want this," he gritted out from between tight teeth.

"You want nothing more than this," she countered softly.

He drew in a deep, quick breath, presumably to argue with her. But then it held. Ticktock. Ticktock. Just a few crucial beats of time. And to his credit, she could feel the energy of his internal struggle like a storm swirling against her body in powerful, turbulent waves.

"What do you suggest?" he asked finally on a rough exhale of breath, as if it took everything inside of him to make himself say the words. Again, it was the closest she imagined she would ever get to having him admit he cared about her. But in the end, she knew his passion for getting hold of Paulson meant far more. She didn't blame him. It was a top priority on her list as well. She would never be safe from the good doctor without the strength of Kincaid and the Morphates to protect her from him. They both had their reasons for using each other.

And they would always be using each other. As long as she was the scientist he needed and he was the Morphate she'd had a hand in creating, they could only ever use each other.

"I'll need a volunteer to die. The rest will be left to the imagination."

He lifted his head then, finally meeting her eyes, the blue of his gaze a turbulent storm of emotion and curiosity.

"A volunteer to die?"

"For all intents and purposes," she said. "It will be up to us to make it look real and to the volunteer to carry through the pretense. It has to be someone you trust, Kincaid. Who do you trust to disappear until Paulson takes the bait? It could be for a day . . . or it could be months."

"I don't know of anyone. Devona is the only one I trust . . ."

"But she's too important to your lab. And too close to you to make Paulson believe we'd choose to kill her. We'd pick someone lower in rank."

"Who would you pick, Jen? In the end, it would be . . . If it were for real, Jenesis, who would you pick as a sacrifice to prove you had a method to kill a Morphate?"

"No, Kincaid, in the end it would be *you*," she said as she looked hard into those marble blue eyes with those haunting veins of gold that laced them like a treasure she could never tap into. "As Alpha, as leader of these people, who would you pick? Who would you demand the sacrifice of? Where would you find a volunteer?" She reached to rake hard fingers through his haphazardly spiky hair. "What if I really needed someone to test my theory on? What if I really believed I had found a way to kill a Morphate? We'd need someone to test it on, wouldn't we? Who would we pick?"

"No one," he breathed against her mouth. "You would never kill someone. You'd never demand a Morphate lay his life down for your science. You are not that kind of person. You never have been. I know that."

He lurched forward, capturing her mouth with his and, for the very first time, kissing her. Truly kissing her with feeling and emotion behind it, putting himself into the expression of affection and accepting her on the other side. It was by far the most luscious kiss she had ever been a part of. Sweet and wet and painfully tender in its way. His tongue laced with hers in several deeply touching sweeps. Then she pulled away from it, pulled back from the temptation of getting lost in the connection he was seeking in that moment.

"The trick is making Paulson believe I am that kind of person," she said softly against his lips. "Actually, affirming it is more like it. He is already assuming I am that kind of person. Just like you have."

Have. Yes. In the past. Up until that moment, in fact. But now he realized that she had never had any intention of finding a way to kill a Morphate. Simply because the only way to prove it was absolutely unacceptable to her. As would be any of the methods she would need to use to get to that point.

"If you never had any intention of helping me do what I've asked of you, why are you here?" he asked quietly.

"You asked me to do two things. The other was to help you control the beast inside of you. I think there I can be of some help. And I admit I have other goals. I want to see the Morphate children. I want you to trust me enough to let me do what I can to help them."

"Is that why you've done this?" he demanded to know, his hand gesturing to the increasingly glowing figure on the laptop screen.

"I'm not wholly sacrificial," she said. "I need your protection from Paulson as well. I'm in his sights as much as you are. He's going to get me one day for one reason or another, and I need you to be there for me when that happens."

A strand of her hair had escaped the tight pull of her usual ponytail, perhaps because his hands were at present wrapped around her small head. He reached for it, smoothing it back into place as best as he could. It was strange, but in that moment his urges were very oppositional to his actions. He wanted nothing more than to muss her up. To pull all of her hair free, to have it between his fingers as she threw her head back in pleasure.

But despite those overwhelming urges and the insistence of his internal beast that she was the perfect mate for him, he had replayed their sexual encounter over and over enough times to recognize that she was simply not built for him. As beautiful and delicious as she had proved to be, all his hunger could ever do was tear her apart. Her pale pallor and the weariness in her features told him that more than anything.

Now if only he could keep reign over the part of him that wanted to countermand his control. The fact of the matter was, just the smell of her, just the nearness of her warmth stirred him up in ways he had never felt before.

Yes, he had had some amazing fucks with some amazing women, some of them powerful Morphates who had temporarily stepped into the role of Alpha female. But none of them had ever lasted because none of them had made him feel like this.

"Tad. That boy who thinks you're the best thing since sliced bread," Kincaid said gruffly. "He's subordinate, everyone knows I don't care for his attention to you. They see . . ." He didn't want to point out that everyone in the lab clearly knew she was his. He'd marked her hard enough, and his hovering in the lab had made it clear. He had tried to keep it low-key, knowing the trouble an outright claim on her might cause, but it had been impossible. "He'll do anything for you and for me. He's invested in the project. He'll do it and do it well."

Jenesis almost wanted to smile at him, but she muted the sunburst of pride she was feeling at that moment, though she didn't wholly understand why. But she admitted she was proud of Kin for his intelligent choice, and for trusting another, whether he realized that was what he was doing or not.

"You're right, he'll do it. And he can be trusted."

"I'll kill him for real if he fucks it up," Kincaid growled menacingly.

Jena sighed. Oh well, at least he was trying.

"Well, then, let's go kill our Tad, shall we?" she suggested, reaching to discontinue the program and shutting down the laptop. She had to brush against him as she did so, and she could feel his strong, tightly powerful body and his incredible heat against her as she did so.

She felt one of his hands close over her hip, and suddenly she felt him behind her as she bent forward, his arousal very evident as he rubbed himself up against her backside. The movement was powerful but brief, a strong act of dominance and a reflection of his true desires. But when he pushed away from her, his breath falling hard, she knew what it was taking for him to maintain control over his baser desires. She turned to look at him, her entire body hot with desires of her own that had been roused by his body contact.

He had left very abruptly the night before. There had been little explanation and she hadn't required one of him. She had just assumed they'd come to an impasse and he had thought it best to leave. But his behavior was telling a very different story. So was hers, for that matter. She should be storming furious with him for all his rude assumptions and obstinate ways, but damn him, she understood him too well. She understood his fears and his paranoia. And she felt an incredible amount of compassion and empathy. She knew what it was like to feel like you were alone and unable to put your trust in one single soul. Especially a member of the opposite sex.

She had spent seven years denying her cravings and needs as a sexual being. Her tumultuous session of sex with him had been the closest thing she'd had to a real physical connection.

She lifted her gaze to his, seeing the want and fire in his eyes.

If she could judge by the tightness of his clenching fists, it was taking everything in him to keep from throwing her up against the smart glass and giving in to his lust.

She stepped closer to him, reaching to touch his chest, her fingertips drifting over the ridges of abdominal muscles under the simple fashion of his oxford shirt.

"I won't ask an obvious question. I know you want me," she heard herself saying, her voice so sultry it was as though it were somebody else speaking. "What I want to know is why you won't act on it. You don't strike me as the sort who doesn't take what he wants. In fact, you've already proved as much."

"And nearly tore you apart in the process," he said roughly, trying to take a step back but failing in his bid to free himself of her disturbing caresses because she stepped with him, allowing her hand to catch him by his belt. She grabbed hold and used all of her strength to pull him up tight to her aching and craving body.

"There are other ways to express passion," she said. Then, before either of them could judge her actions, she had shoved them both up tight against the nearest wall and let her hands run down the front of his soft denim jeans. She could feel him, erect and hot, through the fabric. "I took you well enough last night," she said in defense of herself, although when their eyes met they both acknowledged how much he'd been forced to hold back in order to keep the episode from turning into something dangerous and very unpleasant to remember.

But as she deftly unbuttoned his pants she knew she wasn't looking to abuse her limited human vagina any further than she already had. She pulled his shirt free of his waistband, fingers working with wicked ease through his buttons until she could strip the fabric back, peeling it down the swells of his awesome shoulders, exposing smooth skin everywhere she went. She knew she wasn't imagining the increase of heat radiating off of him. Her analytical brain even appreciated that there was something about the way he smelled that just got more and more delicious by the minute. It reached the point when she felt she had to touch her mouth to him. Oddly enough it wasn't her lips that made it to him first. It was her eager, hungry tongue that licked over the large swell of his left pectoral muscle. And once the taste of him was on her tongue, she utterly forgot about the fact that the stab wound in his chest was almost completely healed, only the smallest divot in his flesh marking the spot of the occurrence.

She hadn't believed the violence she had found herself capable of in that moment. She hadn't known she could get that angry. She had wanted to hurt him and that was the only way she could think of, all the time knowing it would be a very small hurt in the grand scheme of his life.

But hurting him was by far the last thing on her mind now as she ran her tongue over the flat of his nipple. She followed the stroke up with the scrape of her teeth, and she heard and felt his fist slam into the metal frame of the wall supporting the smart glass. She smiled as she imagined what it would look like to a lab full of diligent workers if the glass were to suddenly fail. For some reason, the thought only encouraged her to be even bolder. She burrowed her hands below his waist, wrapping the fingers of both hands along the thickness of his length, her widespread fingers able to do, mostly, what her incompatible body had not been able to do last night. She surrounded his thick heat completely, stroking over him boldly from root to tip, the movement repeating again and again even as her lips drew a line from his nipple to the crest of his shoulder, though she had to lift herself to the very tips of her toes to manage it. Here she suddenly bit down on him, giving in to the sudden impulse to do so as powerfully as he had done to her, only she was missing the fangs necessary to puncture and draw up thick wells of blood like a female Morphate would.

But apparently that shortcoming made no difference to him. His hands came into her hair roughly, their strength snapping her ponytail holder. He gripped her head, holding her to the spot where she was marking him, making her stay until her less than adequate teeth broke his skin and touches of blood wetted her lips. She should have pulled back, all of her training telling her to be repulsed by exposure to blood, but there was no describing how very opposite she felt. There wasn't much blood, but it was enough to taste rust and salt, and her tongue flicked against her lips and his skin. She stood up straight and tall then, pulling her blouse back off her shoulder, stretching her hand against her shoulder until the skin broke open at the place where he had marked her last night, tempting him with a fresh show of blood. It was an incredibly painful thing to do, but it was worth it for the fierce sound that overcame him, rumbling down through his chest and over the lips he suddenly pressed against the open wound. She felt him holding back, though, felt him leashing the savage part of himself that wanted to bury his fangs in her again. But she didn't care. She didn't need those gorgeous fangs in her again . . . all she needed was . . .

One lick. One long, hot sweep of his tongue through the welling blood. She heard him swallow, and a sensation of relief and excitement ran hot and cold in contrast through her.

God, forgive me . . . I need this . . .

Feeling suddenly free, she lifted his head from her shoulder and brought his lips to hers, kissing him so deeply she tasted her own blood on the back of her tongue. She felt him flip their positions against the glass wall, felt it shudder as she hit it hard, but knew it was stern stuff and would hold up. Maybe. Still, she wasn't interested in his need to dominate. Not just then, anyway. She slipped out of his hold and the trap of his body by dropping her weight, slinking down between the press of his body, the cold of the glass, and the sharper cold of the metal wall frame. She heard his hand smack against the glass and the opposite one sank into her hair.

Kincaid was blind with need and he pushed his forehead into the cold brace of the glass wall, hoping it would somehow provide stability for him in a world gone mad. It was as though she had no fear of him at all! Didn't she know how insane this was? Didn't she know the danger she was in?

His only answer was the feel of her mouth around the head of his engorged prick. She couldn't know how hard it was for him to simply let her do that. As amazing as it felt, as much as it made him burn with beautiful need, there was no part of the beast inside of him that was happy with the way he resisted all his urges to take command, to grab hold of her and show her his dominance, show her what her true place was in the grand scheme of things.

It made the feel of her mouth and hands working on him all that much more painful and beautiful. The battle of man and masochist inside of him brought tears to his eyes, and he ejected a savage sound of pleasure and pretense. He wanted to behave normally, as normal as she might expect him to behave, as normal as he had once behaved when he had been human. But normal escaped his reach. He reacted instead with eager claws pricking into her scalp and gouging scrapes into the glass of the wall.

"You're taunting a beast you don't understand," he rasped as he felt her tongue swirling around him, shaping all the dips and contours of his engorged cock head.

"I understand him enough to give him pleasure," she said, her voice buzzing down his length in a tempestuous vibration that nearly undid everything he was trying to achieve as far as control was concerned. But at that point even his beast's attention had been fully engaged. He was tumbling into the lost sensation of giving over his pleasure to the artistic control of another. How long had it been since he had felt this sensation? Too long. The truth was, ever since his change, he had used this kind of sex as a form of subjugating his mate of the moment. It had been the only thing acceptable in those relationships.

But this was a very different relationship and a very different connection. The more he interacted with Jena, the more he understood that.

Need burned through him emotionally as well as physically. He gave himself over to both, bracing his feet hard apart as her mouth coasted eagerly all over him, as if he were her favorite candy. Her hands were both in play, wrapped tight around the rod she guided in and out of her mouth or palming the burning sac just beyond it. She was doing a thorough enough job, to be sure. The urge to come was crawling throughout his body, not just hot and low, but touching on every nerve along his back, his scalp, and even the backs of his hands.

Kincaid threw back his head and opened his mouth, but he kept the roar caught in his throat, some part of him wanting to protect her image in this, her workplace, where she needed to be respected. But that was a human foible, and the next instant the Morphate reminded him that the roar would claim her, make very certain everyone knew she was his mate. That would bring all the respect she needed.

But respect would also come with a bull's-eye. Like him, she would be in a challengeable position. Christ, she already was.

The stress of the understanding was a harsh counterpoint to his orgasm, to the amazing feel of jetting hot and hard into her mouth. He looked down at her as he did so, watching as the overflow of his come wetted her lips like an erotic lip gloss, and he knew he would taste himself on her when he pulled her up to his kiss. Suddenly he could think of nothing else; so with two strong hands around her arms, he drew her up to the touch of his mouth. He didn't lick her lips, rather just savored the soft eddy of the mixture of himself and everything swollen and passionate Jenesis had to offer of her own essence. He was breathing hard, his whole body torn and weak, his mind comprehending that this was possibly the only way they could find themselves sexually compatible.

And how very compatible they were.

But still, how much had he held in check? How much danger was there for her if he unleashed himself on her? He knew the answer to that. He knew he should back away. Create distance. He had planned on doing that when he had started his day today, but his logical mind had been thoroughly ignored.

"I want to take you on a date," he said gruffly against her lips. "Screw this lab and this building. I want to take you out on a proper date, Jen."

So much for creating distance. Well, fuck it.

She smiled, a snorty little laugh exiting her nose.

"A date? Like, going to the movies? Necking in the back of your car?"

"No, like taking you to the best damn restaurant in town, treating you like a . . ." *Alpha mate.* ". . . queen. Like the special woman you are."

He watched her left brow rise up high.

"Don't take this the wrong way, but you didn't strike me as the type to like fine dining and opera. And while I do like fine dining, I'd much rather hit the movies after. Wow. I haven't been to a movie since . . ." She broke off, her brow furrowing as she tried to think about it.

"Clearly too long," he said with a grin. "And, yeah, opera sucks. So good food and an action flick. Or are you a chick-flick girl?"

"I love action movies. And chick flicks. I love them all."

"I'll pick you up at six."

"Six," she said, the affirmation muffled by the insistent press of his mouth.

"All right, then, let's go kill us a lab tech."

He redressed himself and fairly flew out of the door, leaving her just a little dazed and trying to figure out when and why their relationship had taken a turn from what bordered on abusing each other into legitimate courting. All she could do was ask herself over and over again, *When did he stop hating me?*

And why would he stop hating me?

8

Jen checked her figure in the mirror for the fiftieth time. Lord, she hadn't been on a date in a dog's age. The truth was, she didn't have date clothes. The closest thing was this red dress she had worn to her cousin's wedding. The skirt was just long enough to cover the top of her thigh-highs, but if she crossed her legs too quickly or sat down without putting thought into it, they and her garters would possibly show to all and sundry. She had found that out at the wedding and had spent the whole day and night gluing the dress to her backside and thighs with her hands. But tonight . . . perhaps she wouldn't be doing so much of that. The memory of how strongly Kin had reacted to her lingerie stuck in her mind. It was a memory thrilling enough to give her chills of anticipation as she leaned in to match lipstick with her dress. Perhaps it was dangerous to anticipate tempting a Morphate, but perhaps that danger was what made her feel so alive. And honestly, these past two days had been like waking up out of a coma. A coma she hadn't known she was in.

Or maybe she had, but hadn't thought she deserved any better.

It was strange walking out of the building she had been limited to for so long. She honestly would have been too intimidated if Kincaid had not been right beside her, his hand at the back of her waist.

As they walked the vast streets of Philadelphia with its old historic buildings contrasting so sharply with the high-rises that had finally been allowed to surpass the top of William Penn's head on the City Hall building. But the historic places had fared far better than the newer ones when the City had fallen Dark and into the hands of the disrespectful and disreputable. It was clear, though, that on both fronts a lot of work had taken place in the effort to restore the City to its former glory.

"It is much more difficult to restore the old infrastructure of such a vast City than it is, perhaps, to start all new. It takes a lot of money, time, and man-hours. But the history in this City was left to die . . . and living in it now I find that such a shame."

"If I can ask, where did you find the money for this? And for the lab?"

"A lot of it was federally granted. At least the government was that kind. The rest was cultivated through some wise investments and investment groups who wanted a foot in the new City when it finally develops. The CEOs that are not prejudiced against us are very smart. They can see the strength of the Morphates' future. They can see we are going to become a powerful point of interest in this world." He frowned. "Provided we don't get in our own way."

She knew what he meant by that, so she didn't ask him to elaborate.

"Even humans can be very instinct driven," she said carefully. "Yet we've found a way to flourish. I have faith that Morphates can do the same."

"You have far more optimism than I do," he said grimly.

"Perhaps. But let's try something new," she said with sudden brightness. "Let's not talk about work or Morphates for the length of dinner. I accept there's no getting around the topic completely since it's so much of our lives, but let's try to talk about the other things that make us who and what we are. Or even who we were, before all of this began. We're both still there. We just haven't taken us out for air much these past seven years."

The suggestion ought to have rubbed him the wrong way. After all, what was the use of dredging up what he no longer had the luxury of being? But perhaps she was right. Perhaps part of the problem was that he had done nothing but live, breathe, and eat being changed into a Morphate. And like any complex job, it could swallow you up if you let it.

"I accept."

His graveness made her chuckle softly.

"It's not heart surgery, Kincaid. It's relaxation. Relaxaaaa-tion." She drew out the "a" as if he needed to be taught how to say the word. "I think part of the problem here is that you've forgotten how to relate to the human in you."

Kin bit back a mean retort. It made him frown darkly. He wasn't that kind of man, was he? The kind who whined about his hard knocks and blamed everyone else for the shit in his life? So perhaps he'd had some cause, but lately . . . lately he'd begun to realize he might have been wasting precious time doing so.

But then again, all he had was time. Maybe he could afford a few years of wallowing.

That idea really grated. He wasn't a wallower. He'd never been the "poor me" type. He'd kicked ass and taken names, goddammit. And he'd been doing the same thing since walking into Dark Philly. But personally . . . he'd been wallowing. Seething in this idea of vengeance.

"I . . . I used to fish."

Jena couldn't have been more surprised if he'd smacked her

on the ass. The last thing she could picture the kinetic, aggressive man beside her doing was standing around for hours fishing.

"What kind of fish?"

"Marlin," he said with a grin.

"Of course," she said, laughing brightly.

"My brother and I would do a charter once a year, down off Costa Rica or Cancun . . . sometimes Mexico. We'd combine traveling with fishing, two weeks of every year just to cut away from it all."

"Hot sun, beer, and the boys."

"Yeah, and the biggest damn fish to be found."

"And you haven't been in seven years?"

Not that Nick hadn't asked him to. Every year he pressed him to go.

"I didn't want to go. I liked remembering what it was. Not sure it'd be a challenge anymore, strong as we are."

"So go shark fishing, Kin," she said with a little exasperation. "Get heavy-gauge equipment, find some great white sharks or something and *make* it a challenge."

Kin took her arm in hand, turning her suddenly into the aggressive leanness of his body.

"Why is everything such an easy answer for you?" he demanded on a rough growl as he pressed his forehead against hers.

"It's not easy. None of this is. I never want to give you the impression I think that! But I think not trying is easy. I think it's weak. Sitting around grumbling and growling and hating burns up a lot of energy, but it gets nothing done. In the end, it's a copout. Do you think I came to Dark Philly because it was the easy way? I could have run some cushy lab in New Mexico testing new ways of killing fleas on pets. That would have been much easier."

Kin hadn't realized she'd had another offer. It hadn't occurred to him. The understanding that he could have missed out on her left him dreadfully and suddenly cold. He reached to touch her face, the crest of her cheekbone sliding under his thumb as he shaped the high contour.

For all his gruff and seemingly mean ways, it was these moments when he made her feel so suddenly treasured that left her breathless. Maybe because it was so stark a contrast, or maybe because it was happening more and more often. One thing Jenesis knew—she was beginning to understand him very clearly. It was far from feeling guilty or sorry for him. The only thing wrong with Kincaid Gregory's life right now was Kincaid Gregory. And she suspected he was coming to realize that.

Then there was a sudden snap, and Kincaid lurched around in an awkward sideways movement. Something wasn't right, and Jen barely heard the report of the shot as it finally caught up to them.

Kincaid dropped like a bag of stones, all that rough vitality leaving him sharply and suddenly as half his neck exploded from the impact of the hardcore sniper round. His grip around her arm pulled her down with him, jerked her across his falling body. It wasn't in her to be a screamer. Her brain was just too analytical. All it wanted to do was think. Think of where the trajectory of the shot had originated. Think of how to put her hands on him to stop the bleeding. Think of all the reasons why erupting into tears and hysteria would be the very worst thing she could do. Kin was trying to speak, but nothing came of his attempts except for the gurgle of blood in his throat.

But his eyes, those keen blue orbs, spoke volumes.

Watch out!

The second shot was of compressed air. She felt the dart tip pin deeply into her shoulder, its red-flagged end making her feel suddenly like a wild animal that had just been caught because she had wasted time hovering over her fallen mate. She sat down hard beside him, looking around futilely for someone else on the street.

She turned back to Kin, looked him dead in his stricken blue eyes, and said, "Don't forget the program."

Jen opened her eyes groggily, her head twitching along the back of her scalp and aching heavily. She couldn't draw her thoughts together at first as she tried to focus on the sharply white room around her.

It was so white. Blaringly, achingly white. Ceiling, floors, walls. All of it as seamless as the cleanest of clean rooms. The only thing that broke up the white was her. There wasn't so much as a stick of furniture for perspective. It made the red dress she wore seem suddenly obscene. Or perhaps just very dramatic. She heard a soft buzzing sound and it drew her attention. She looked up into the familiarity of a security camera watching her, the zipping autofocus of the lens the sound she heard. It was amazing she could hear anything at all over the ringing in her head. Whatever she had been drugged with, it had been powerful and it was clinging to her like a determined parasite, leaving her weak and numbed along her edges. She licked her lips, the feeling like tonguing a sock. She felt very alone in that vast, stark room. And she was incredibly cold. She curled inward, trying to cover herself with the sparse length of her dress. Her black thigh-high on the left was torn at the knee, the skinning and bruising of her leg as well as on the seat of her left palm telling her she'd hit hard on that side. Her palm was no longer bleeding, but the bruising on her knee was only just coming into the full glory of its color, telling her she'd been unconscious for hours, not days.

After twenty minutes of cooling her heels and shedding the last remaining effects of the narcotic she'd been given, she hoisted herself onto her feet slowly, a cautious check to see if she had any other injuries and if she could keep steady. She was missing one shoe, so she kicked off the other one and toddled barefooted over to the near camera. There were two. Two that were visible, she conceded, remembering how well Kin had hidden others in the lab and in her apartment. She saw they were equipped with tiny, powerful microphones.

"All right," she said sharply. "Let's get this show on the road. I have things to do."

Such as figuring out what, exactly, had happened to Kincaid. She was worried about him in spite of his strength and immortality. Immortality in his case could mean he could live to be tortured forever. If Paulson had trapped him somehow . . . used his catastrophic injuries as a way to capture him?

And then there was that small, whispering voice in her brain that egged on her fear that she hadn't even deserved defending, that Kin might have happily let her go. After all, wouldn't he be very willing to risk her life for his endgame?

She shook those dark, insecure thoughts off. Things had changed between her and Kincaid these past days. She couldn't explain it exactly, couldn't give it a true description, but she sensed there was a dynamic alteration. But how strange it was for her, an empiricist, to find herself putting her faith in something so ephemeral. Something she couldn't touch, something she had no physical proof of.

Jen shook her head imperceptibly. She couldn't afford to be distracted by these useless questions and emotions. They were dangerous to her right now. Right now all she needed was to focus on the moment and how she was going to help the cause of the Morphates and the human race in general.

Not to mention getting out of this alive.

God, what had she been thinking? She had purposely thrown herself to the wolves. Suddenly all of her bravery seemed to be evaporating.

Just then the locks on the door squealed, indicating they were being triggered to open. She backed away from the corner with the camera in it in order to bravely face whatever came at her through that door. She curled her hands into fists, much in the way her lover had a habit of doing when he was under duress.

It was funny how the look of Eric Paulson shocked her even though she had been fully expecting his appearance. She had met him him numerous times and, before and after learning what he was, she had seen quite a few pictures of him. The same pictures over and over again. There had been hints of a receding hairline, indications that he spent most of his time sitting in a lab. Certainly not working out or engaging in any kind of sport or athleticism.

This was not that man. This man was bigger, stronger . . . that receding hairline had disappeared and been reimagined into something lush and healthy. Youthful.

All questions about whether or not he was a Morphate slid away. There was no cosmetic surgery available that could create this kind of change. The man looked far too healthy and vibrant for the world's most hunted man who was in exile.

Which made her wonder where she was exactly.

"Ah, Dr. DeBruchl." He gave her serious and enthusiastic applause. "I knew you could do it. I had every faith in you."

"Did you have to pump me full of drugs?" she groused. "I would have come."

"Pardon my methods," he breezed on. "It's become a bit murky to me where your loyalties lie. I'd much rather be assured of things. I work better that way."

Of course he did. The man had used six different batches of humans and six different protocols to test his theories, before committing to use one of them on himself. She wondered which batch of Morphate he had deemed his best work. Canid?

Feline? Insect? Did it even matter what this psychopath thought? All that mattered was that she stayed alive while Kincaid recovered enough to track her with that program. Or . . .

"Where are my things?"

Paulson gestured to one of the men behind him and they walked into the room, handing her the small purse she'd been carrying.

"We've removed your phone for now. You understand."

She shouldered the small bag, resisting the urge to look into it.

"So I suppose you want to know how I killed the Morphate," she said wryly.

"Of course. That is of paramount importance."

"Why? Do you want to know how to kill yourself? You never struck me as the suicidal type," she said, working hard to keep the sneer of contempt out of her voice.

"Hardly. But the Morphates have been dogging my steps most rabidly. It makes continuing my work quite difficult."

"They can't kill you."

"They can now. Thanks to you. But my resources are far better than those of the Gregorys. I can advance your knowledge into handheld weaponry ten times faster than they can. Creating a significant advantage for myself and anyone who wishes to pay for the privilege. You see, continuing my work also takes money, Dr. DeBruehl. There is little of that since the government conveniently disavowed my practices."

The implication being that the government had known all along about the atrocities he'd been committing . . . until he'd been caught at it. The idea left her sick and cold inside.

"They can't be caught funding me twice. The 'we didn't know' excuse only works once. But enough of the past. Let's focus on the future. Your future."

"My future as a wealthy woman. That is what you promised, isn't it? Sounds like you don't have much to back that up with."

"Perhaps not yet. But if you work with me, Doctor, as brilliantly as you have in the past, we will rectify that together."

"I see. And I'm supposed to trust you until then?" There was no way she would act suddenly eager and believing. He'd see right through her.

"Perhaps not, but we have time. Let's get you to more comfortable quarters in the meantime."

The one thing she noticed as they escorted her through a lab twice the size of the one in Dark Philly was that all of the light, no matter the room, was entirely artificial. There were no windows. That led her to suspect they were underground. That made her a little more anxious, but not much more so than she already was.

"Why Morphates?" she asked suddenly. There had been hundreds of speculations, but Paulson was the only one who knew the truth. "Were you looking for immortality?"

"Not at all," he chuckled. "That was entirely your doing. A happy side effect of your work. Your tags not only sought out the strongest cells, they fortified them . . . made them nigh indestructible, as you've since learned. And with a tweak here and there, they even reversed the imperfections of age." His hand went to touch his hairline, but he corrected the movement. Not soon enough, though, to keep her from noticing. It made her sick to realize that all of this tragedy and pain might have come down to one man's vanity and his fear of dying. It made sense, then, that he'd want control of her. She had, from his point of view, just destroyed all his excellent work. She was, she suddenly realized, the biggest threat to him on the planet. There was nothing he feared . . . except perhaps her. He was talking a big game about developing and selling technology, but what he wanted was control of it.

Or better yet, control of the only source of it. He hadn't

really thought she could do it at all. That would mean he'd have to admit she was better than he was. Smarter than he was. After all, it had been her work he'd used to create the Morphates. Not his own. The only thing he'd added to it was the gene splicing virus. But what if that had come from another resource, too?

What if Eric Paulson was a sham? What if he was nothing more than a sick man who had the power and brilliance to use others as the means to his ends?

"I've always been curious as to how you created the Morphate mutations," she said, trying to sound the eager scientist. "I know how you delivered it. But the mutations themselves . . ."

"There's plenty of time to talk shop later, Dr. DeBruehl. Here are your apartments. Make yourself comfortable. You'll be working in the morning. Unfortunately, your previous lab has been destroyed . . . along with all of its data. So you'll be starting over. However, a mind like yours should have no trouble reproducing its own efforts."

The lab destroyed? At least it had been after hours. But the labs were beneath the human living quarters. Had anyone else been hurt? It would be very like Paulson not to care.

"So you want exclusivity to this thing, after all." And his evasion of her earlier question told her a great deal. Any scientist worth his or her salt would have been eager to talk about their methods. At least in the broadest of terms. But he knew she was too bright to be shammed, so he was going to avoid the topic altogether.

So whose work had it really been?

They might never know. That scientist might not have ever made it out of the Phoenix Project. Perhaps Paulson had not ever intended for *her* to make it out of the Phoenix Project. Only the precipitousness of his escape had spared her life.

When the door closed to her new apartment with the snick of a strong lock closing her in, she ignored the ominousness of the sound. She tried to take relief in being left alone. But she knew that Paulson would have her private areas covered by cameras just as Kincaid had done. She tested the strength of the lock needlessly. Then she made a show of checking the place out before making her way to the bathroom. She'd read too many accounts of Paulson's labs not to know the bathroom would be covered as well. But it was easy to figure the camera was behind the mirror. There weren't any other ways of hiding it that she could think of. So she dropped her purse on the floor and checked her teeth, hair, and anything else she could think of while she surreptitiously kicked the small bag into the shower well, behind the curtain. Then, unable to help herself, she began to strip down. She was naked and yanking the curtain closed within minutes, turning the water on as soon as she had retrieved her bag from the floor. She rummaged in the purse, protecting it from the water, and pulled out the pocket scientific calculator. Okay, so maybe it was ridiculous and stereotypical to think a scientist would carry a calculator even on a date, but it had worked. They hadn't thought twice about it. She popped the cover of false buttons and revealed the small screen. The GPS inside of it might not work underground, but the sophisticated locator in it still would. She turned it on and watched the screen. A red dot immediately appeared at its base. That was her. What she didn't want to see was the second dot beeping not too much farther away.

That was Kincaid.

And unless he had taken the laptop out of her office before Paulson had destroyed it and already managed to mount a rescue effort, then that meant he'd been captured as well.

Because she had coaxed him into drinking her blood, knowing full well he'd be taking in the nanobytes she'd injected herself with.

Because she had wanted a way to track him the same way she had wanted him to be able to track her.

9

It took several days for Jenesis to gain enough trust so that Paulson let her move more freely through the lab. What she couldn't plan was what she was going to do once she found Kincaid. She had discovered she had access to the lab with the key card she'd been given, but her access ended at the dormitory level of her apartment. They would have to work that out later.

It was hard for her to be patient. Even harder for her to overcome the queasy fear she found welling up inside of herself over and over again. Not to mention she hadn't been feeling well physically since the drugging she'd suffered. She had this incredible itching sensation underneath her skin. It made it impossible to focus. So far she'd been able to forestall showing Paulson a technique that didn't actually exist using excuses like getting used to the lab and not feeling well, combined with more savvy resistance like wanting assurances that he wouldn't dispose of her as soon as she showed him what she knew. He was, luckily, willing to wait until she could be lulled into a false sense of complacency or security.

Whatever. All she wanted was to find Kincaid. This whole plan had blown up in their faces. Yes, they had found Paulson, but at the worst of prices. And every day that ticked by was a day that Kincaid was trapped like a lab rat once again, under Paulson's power. And Jena knew that was the worst thing imaginable for him. She had to find him, and regardless of what happened to her, she had to free him.

Following the tracker, she turned a corner and came up against two guards protecting a hallway. She pulled her pad out of her pocket and began to jot down the most complex-looking formula she could think of and, keeping her head down, tried to brush past them.

"Excuse us, Doctor, this area is off-limits."

She stopped and glared at them, tapping her pen to her pad in irritation.

"No shit, Sherlock," she snapped at him. "You see this?" She thrust the formula under his nose. "This is what I'm going to be injecting into that Morphate you have down the hall. Only I can't do it until I run a specialized panel and do an exam. The phlebotomist will be here directly. Send her down and try not to give her a hassle."

She pushed past them, leaving them looking after her and trading shrugs. She couldn't even cheer herself in her brain. She just wanted to get to Kincaid. Everything in her was screaming the urgency of it. The need was crawling under her skin in the most uncomfortable way. A way that was making her more than a little reckless, she acknowledged.

There was only one door at the end of the hall and it was coded for a passkey. She pulled hers from her lanyard and hoped to hell it gave her access. She didn't know what she would do if it didn't. She'd been doing all of this by the seat of her pants. She was frankly amazed she'd made it so far.

The lock opened and she pushed into the room.

Kincaid turned with a snarl for the intruder, but realizing it was she, he slammed his whole essence forward against the titanium bars of the cage they had him in. Not even a bed this time. No such illusions. He was a rat in a cage. Four walls of bars, a toilet, and a sink, all centrally located in a room full of lab equipment and, usually, technicians.

Jenesis saw him and her eyes ran over him in stark, rapid appraisal. He was covered in raw, freshly healing scars, the nature of which she could easily imagine.

They had been killing him. Over and over again. Every mortal injury they could come up with. She saw evidence of it all over his body. He hadn't had enough time to fully heal, so the scars were bright and pink. Tears jumped into her eyes as she threw herself against the bars, reaching to take his face in her hands and pulling his mouth to hers.

"I'm so sorry," she wept.

But his hands felt so good, incredibly good as they caught her by the backs of her shoulders and held her up to him as well as he could with the cold gray impediment between them.

"There are cameras everywhere," he rasped as he checked her over for changes. "We don't have time."

But even as she fumbled with her key card she felt him growling softly into her mouth. She responded in kind, the sound coming out of nowhere.

The cage lock beeped open as they both pulled back in surprise and stared at each other. Kincaid swung around the door threshold, his hands never leaving her. He bent quickly to sniff beneath her left ear.

"What?" She knew something was wrong. And she was too smart not to know what was happening. But anxiety was blocking her comprehension. She broke away from him except for his hand, pulling him toward the door. "You have to go! There're two guards at the end of the hall, and my card will take you up to the top dormitory level. But . . ."

"Jena."

He stopped her, pulling her back toward him. He lifted her hand, the fingers that gripped his with painful fear, and touched his lips to them.

She shook her head, tears leaping into her eyes, her voice suddenly gone.

"What'd he do to you, babe?"

She shook her head again. "Nothing more than what I deserved," she croaked. How ironic this was, she thought. But it made sense, didn't it? Paulson found her to be the most precious of commodities. He wouldn't want anything to happen to his golden goose. And there was only one way he could guarantee that.

She realized all of the itching under her skin had stopped the minute she'd come into contact with Kin. It had changed into something else. A hunger. A wild, unbelievable hunger. A hunger so extreme that her mouth began to ache. It made her realize she'd hardly eaten a thing these past few days. It made her realize a lot of things.

"It doesn't matter," she said hastily, trying to push all that aside, trying again to pull him toward the door. "You have to go!"

"I have to go? And what about you?" he demanded.

"I don't have the strength to keep up with you. I'll stay behind as a distraction. If I go he'll just tear up the world hunting me down again. It's more important that you get free."

"And you think I'll do that? You think I'll leave you here to suffer a lifetime of Paulson's retributions? To suffer his tactics as he tries to force you to give up a technique you don't have?"

"Actually, I already suspected she didn't have it."

They both jolted around to see Paulson standing in the doorway, and Jenesis felt her entire world bottom out. Of course. Of course, she thought numbly. Paulson was too thorough for it to make any sense that she would be able to get past guards and locks so easily. But she hadn't thought of that. She'd had a single-minded focus. She'd needed to get to Kincaid. She needed him. Even as she stood there, she felt her whole body burning with that need. As he pulled her protectively against himself, she felt her body wriggling of its own accord to burrow against him. Heat burned through her as she came into snug contact with him. A heat like nothing she'd ever felt. She forgot all about Paulson. Forgot all about their chances for escape evaporating into thin air.

"I knew that she couldn't be trusted. I figured the best way of testing her loyalties and of finding out the truth was to change her. We injected her when she was first taken. My spies in your lab suspected you had a sexual connection. It stood to reason she'd be even more driven to you if I used your protocol on her. Whether she was aware of it or not, she would be impatiently driven to you. The mating drive often impedes all logic. And as brilliant as she is, I needed something quite powerful to impede her logic." Paulson turned to the two guards at his back. "Lock them both in the cage. Maybe a few days of watching her mate suffer up close will make her more tractable. You see, she may not have found out the solution I want, but I know she is fully capable of it. Just as you knew it, Gregory."

"You just decided you weren't willing to wait for her to come to it on her own?" Kincaid snapped and snarled when the guard came forward, reaching for Jenesis. He jerked her behind him, even when she instinctively rumbled a threat of her own, gnashing her teeth at the guard. She recoiled suddenly, her hand jerking up to her mouth. He knew the pain she was in immediately. It beat through him instinctively as well as with memory. Her jaw would be hurting incredibly as her teeth made room for the fangs that wanted to explode free for the first time.

But he couldn't spare her the attention and affection, the comforting he would have given to her under other circumstances. Whatever else happened, he could not let them be locked up in that cage again. As strong as a Morphate was, titanium was stronger. Kincaid lurched toward the guards, growling fiercely at them. Both guards responded in kind.

All right. Three Morphates to two, and one of his two had no idea how to be a Morphate. Still, he'd fought worse odds.

"Big mistake," Kincaid hissed through his fangs. "I'm not an Alpha for nothing. And being a Morphate doesn't make you Alpha, Paulson."

Jenesis felt Kincaid spring away from her and into the trio of men. Her theory about the savagery an Alpha male must be capable of was nothing compared to what she was seeing. Kin went for the guard on the right first, savagely ripping his head half from his shoulders. The opposite guard pulled his weapon and began shooting wildly at Kincaid, forcing Paulson, who was in the way, to hit the deck or suffer being shot. The first guard hit the floor in a bloody, twitching mess as Kincaid turned on the second man standing.

That was when she saw the first shot hit her mate's body. It was a shoulder shot, entering the front left shoulder and blowing a hefty hole out the back.

Jenesis would remember very little of what happened next. The sight of her mate being attacked triggered everything Morphate inside of her all at once. Fangs and claws exploded in a fury, as did the vicious lunge of her body. Before Kincaid could even move forward, she was on the second guard, biting his firing arm with all of her strength and ripping at it in a head-shaking motion like a dog with its favorite bone.

The torsion against the guard's shoulder ripped his arm free of its socket. The Morphate guard screamed as muscle and sinew detached. He fell to the floor, leaving his arm between her jaws as she shook blood over herself and her mate.

Paulson saw the way of things and made haste for the door. He was only interested in more backup, and the alarm button was just outside.

"Oh, I don't think so," Kincaid snapped, burying his claws

into the man's legs. Once he had hold of the doctor, he hauled
him hard toward the cage. He missed the door by a few feet, allowing Paulson to rebound in full Morphate glory.

"I'm an Alpha in my own right," he growled. "Did you
think I wouldn't make sure of that?"

Paulson ripped into Kincaid with vicious swipes of his
claws. Hauling all his weight forward instead of back, he made
for Kincaid's throat. What he got for his trouble was a blindsid-
ing headbutt from the left as Kincaid Gregory's mate made her
bid to help and protect him. Paulson raked at her even as he fell
to the ground from the power of her charge. He caught her
along the side of her face, tearing her from forehead to chin.

His most recent mistake in a lineup of many. Kincaid was on
him in a heartbeat, teeth in his throat, compressing . . . rending.

Kincaid left Paulson much the same way Paulson had left
him when he'd had him shot through the throat. He didn't care.
He didn't even feel satisfaction over exacting some form of
one-on-one revenge. The price of it had been too high. And he
turned instantly to the one who had paid that price.

Adrenaline and Morphate mutation aside, she'd never been
injured so badly before. She'd recoiled in shock. Kin went to
her quickly, his arms wrapping tightly around her.

"I know it hurts, honey," he soothed softly.

But just the same he had to force her up on her feet. The
hallway was empty beyond the open door, but for how long?
He wouldn't have them doing to her what they had been doing
to him for the past few days. He bent to press his lips to hers in
an encouraging kiss; then sweeping her blood from his lips with
his tongue, he urged her into the hall.

Epilogue

Kincaid entered his penthouse apartment, the one he had lived in before moving above the labs in an effort to keep a closer eye on everything. The building wasn't very high, characteristic of all the historic buildings in Dark Philly. But he occupied the top two floors, the rest remaining empty for when Nick, special clients, or visiting Morphates came to town. But this apartment had a beautiful stone terrace, patiently cultivated greenery bringing a bit of living landscape to the spectacular view of the City.

He found Jenesis there, as usual, her knees pulled up to her chest and a cup of tea resting in her hand as she stared off into nothing. Her face was healing, the raking wound a soft pink and nowhere near as bad as it had been two days ago. In fact, it was almost indiscernible, if not for the darkened pigmentation that came from her insistence on sitting out in the sun. But that, too, would be gone by the next day. He wished he could say the same for the shock and depression she was in.

But he wasn't going to push. He'd be the last person to

push. So he kept talking to her, as if she were present and attentive.

"Well, the lab was gutted and Paulson's gone, as expected," he said. They'd been in Mexico. It wasn't easy to rally forces to invade the lab in a speedy manner. His position as a Morphate Alpha held little sway with Mexican authorities. As far as foreign countries were concerned, Morphates were the problem of the Federated States. So he'd had to wait until the Alpha Council could rally a force to send after him. They'd had to go Black Ops because technically Morphates had yet to be given permission to travel outside of the country. Hell, they weren't even allowed to live outside of the Dark Cities.

He pushed his testiness about that aside. That wasn't where his major concern rested at the moment.

"They torched the place this time." Much in the way Paulson had destroyed the Philly lab. It had infuriated him to hear about it while being held captive, but seeing the aftermath had hurt. Especially considering there had been loss of human life in the process. Dark Philly didn't have the fire departments it needed yet. And even though the building had been fitted with the latest in fire prevention, it hadn't been enough to prevent injury and death from collapse and explosion. The Morphates had all survived, of course. Again, not his main focus.

"Can I get you something to eat?"

"I'm not hungry for food."

He'd been reaching to pluck a dead leaf from a plant in an absent need for occupation, but he froze a moment and then turned quickly to face her. She'd barely said a word to him since their escape. He'd started to wonder if he didn't have what it took to help her after all. Maybe he ought to get her professional help; something none of them had had the advantage of originally.

Then her distinction struck him. Suddenly a wash of insecurity crept over him. Just because they'd connected so quickly in the stress of Paulson's lab didn't mean she'd want anything to do with him now. Just because his Morphate self wanted no one else but her and had come to grips with that a while ago, that didn't mean she would feel the same.

"I . . ." He couldn't do it. He couldn't bring himself to offer her alternative sources of blood. The dead leaf crumbled in the clench of his fist. "You can use me for that, you know. I won't . . . I don't expect . . ."

"Don't expect or don't want? After all, I'm not human any longer. I'm the doctor who made you. And now the thing you hate most about yourself as well. I can hardly blame you."

He was across the patio and kneeling before her in an instant, her elbows in his hands as he drew her up, the cup she'd held falling to the stone and shattering, tea splashing over his pants.

"I don't hate you. I hate nothing about you."

"Do you say that because your Morphate makes you? My Morphate says the wildest things to me. I suddenly understand how you separate the two halves of yourself in your mind." Her eyes went wet as she looked down into his. "How arrogant you must have thought me, lecturing you on how to mesh your two selves, how to find your lost humanity. With this raging inside of you, how could you?"

"You're saying that now because you've not fed yet." How had she managed to go nearly five, six days without doing so? he wondered suddenly. When he'd first awakened, there was no stopping him. He'd taken the first female he'd gotten hold of. It'd been that way for almost everyone. "Are you doing this to punish yourself? Or because you know what it will mean once you've crossed that point? Feeding won't change the facts. You are Morphate now, Jenesis. You are part of this clan."

"Tailor-made. Lucky you." She reached to touch her fingertips to his lips and he could smell green tea on them. Sugar. A touch of honey.

"I'd have been much happier if you'd stayed who you were." He cursed when he saw the hurt that entered her eyes. "Shit. I mean . . . I don't want you to have to go through this. Am I going to lie to you and tell you I'm not glad that I'll be able to touch you without ripping you to pieces? No, I never wanted to hurt you. I held back every single time I touched you, trying not to hurt you. But I'd rather do anything other than watch you struggle with this. I wish I'd never been so selfish as to think it was a good idea that you put yourself at risk like you did. If I'd been thinking, I'd have considered this possibility. I'd have realized that no one should get within inches of that maniac. Certainly not someone I—"

"Certainly not someone you felt should be your mate."

He closed his eyes and sighed.

"You know what? I've been a fuckup. I see that so damn clearly now. I wish I could take back at least half the times I acted the ass to you. But please don't let that keep you from feeding. I'll . . ." God, was he able to? "I'll promise you not to touch you in any other way if that's what you want. I hope it's not what you want because I haven't been able to think straight since the day I first laid eyes on you, and that's only gotten more intense with time. I understood that before Paulson got hold of you."

"Did you? Or is that just a convenient truth?" she wondered as she examined his features closely.

"Nothing I say will ever make you believe that unless you want to, so I'm not going to argue with you about it. However, I will say . . . I have a long time to redeem myself, if you see fit to let me."

She gave him a weak smile. "That's true. I could make you pay for your obstinacy for a very long time."

"You do recall that I'm Alpha?" he growled in soft warning to her.

"You do recall that I am Alpha female?" she countered.

His heart caught tightly, wanting to soar and yet afraid to.

"You need to feed first," he tempted her softly.

And suddenly she flashed ferocious fangs in his face, a hissing growl spitting out of her an instant before she sank them into his neck.

Clothing disappeared from both their bodies, more torn away than stripped off. When she straddled him to impale herself on him, it was with very little preamble or foreplay. None was needed. The bite itself was a form of foreplay that could not be matched. And the understanding that she now could fit him perfectly inside of herself meant much less to him than the way she was smiling down at him, licking his essence from her lips and touching her fingertips to his face with a fondness that Morphate ferocity on its own would not have allowed room for.

Or so an outsider might think. The initial feeding and mating was coarse and harsh, but by his third orgasm there was none of that left, and everything tender and human took its place. She was growing tired by then, still not accustomed to her new self and still several days deficient in her nutrition. But that would come in time.

Everything would come in time.

Project Seduction

JENNA McCORMICK

Dedicated to
The Sanibel Divas:
Ladies who know how to have a good time.
Next round is on me.

1

The rumble of thunder had Jacc transferring his disgusted look from his POS rental vehicle—which had died an untimely death alongside the North Carolina mountain highway—to the heavy black clouds gathering swiftly overhead. Fracking perfect. A fat drop of water landed on his sunglasses. The twenty-second century had yielded plenty of innovation, but unfortunately, a way to control the weather wasn't part of it. Removing his vintage aviator sunglasses, he cursed the unseasonable storm along with his own pride in renting the sleek hovercar. Since the pricey two-door model didn't have tires to ground it, waiting inside it to be electrocuted during a lightning storm was a piss-poor option.

The whole visit to his home state had been a crappy plan. His father and brothers were too busy with the apple crop to talk to him for more than five minutes, and he'd lost count of how many times his mother had crossed herself while shuffling nervously around her kitchen, sending him furtive glances. To say she didn't approve of his career choice as a pleasure companion was a massive understatement. No doubt she prayed for his immortal soul every single night and twice on Sunday. After five hours—a new record—he'd had enough and hopped in the rental to head back to the airport.

"And look where that got me." Thunder clapped again, drawing nearer. He couldn't use his comm unit to call for help because it, too, would act as a lightning rod. No sense standing next to the big metal conductor. Grabbing his duffel out of the backseat, Jace started hoofing it back the way he'd come.

The skies opened, sending a deluge of water down on him. Within minutes he was drenched to the skin, shivering against the gusting wind. The black T-shirt and jeans normally so comfortable clung unpleasantly to his skin, and his boots squished with every step.

Cresting the hill, he squinted into the gloom, looking for shelter of any kind. The rain fell so hard and fast that visibility was obscured more than five meters. Trundling through his memories, he tried to recall exactly what was around here.

Nothing, unless he counted trees, rocks, and gray squirrels.

This far into the Blue Ridge Mountains, towns were fewer and farther between. Most folks probably had the good sense not to be driving around in weather like this.

The thought had just registered when he saw the headlights coming at him. Jace waved over his head in big motions, hoping to catch the driver's notice. The lights came closer and then stopped altogether. Running over to the passenger's side of the vehicle, an ancient pick-up truck, Jace reached for the handle and yanked the door open.

And stared down the barrel of an energy pistol.

Dropping his bag in the mud, he held up both hands. "I'm not armed."

"As you can see," a soft feminine voice drawled, "I am. Just so we're clear."

Jace lifted his gaze past the weapon to the woman wielding it. She was a stunner with big blue eyes and wild curly brown hair down to her waist that was tinged with the slightest traces of gray. A few freckles spread across her nose like stardust against her pale skin. Her mouth was set in a firm line, and he gulped as he realized she had what it took to pull that trigger.

"Please," he said. "Could you give me a lift? I promise I won't try anything."

Pulling up the weapon, she stowed it in the holster she wore on her hip underneath her flannel jacket. The way she handled the sidearm—with confidence, practicality, and efficiency— mesmerized him.

He wondered if that was what she'd be like in bed.

"Well, are you getting in or not?"

Oh, baby, I'd sure like to get in you. Shoving all lewd thoughts and comments aside, Jace picked up his bag and climbed into the truck.

"Where're you headed?" Sliding him a sidelong glance, she depressed the gas pedal.

"Eventually, New New York."

The corner of her mouth kicked up. " 'Fraid I'm not going quite that far."

"Really, if you could recommend a motel or an inn, any- where I can stay the night so I can call the rental company to ferry me back to the airport once the storm passes."

"You can stay at my place," she informed him.

Jace blinked. Had she just propositioned him? There was no way for her to know he was a certified pleasure companion, and he certainly hadn't volunteered the information. Maybe this was a thing with her, trolling the mountains for men to bring home. Not sure how to respond without offending her, he shifted in his seat. "Um . . . ?"

Cutting her blue-eyed gaze to him, she grinned. "Don't look so frightened; you're not in for a full-fledged cougar attack. I own an inn, the Green Oaks just outside of Boone."

"That's not what I was thinking," he fibbed. Cougar, huh?

He scrutinized her closer. A few fine lines around the corner of her mouth and around her eyes betrayed her age. Laughter lines, he guessed from the way her face creased so naturally into a smile.

"Liar," she called him on it. "I was just being a Good Samaritan."

"More like a pistol-packing mama." His gaze dropped to her sidearm.

She threw back her head and laughed. The deep, throaty chuckle drew him in. He appreciated a woman who could let go and laugh so freely. "Hey, I'm a female traveling alone. I probably wouldn't have stopped to help you if I didn't have a little reassurance that I could handle you." She lovingly stroked the hilt of her sidearm as she spoke.

Lust stabbed Jace in the groin as he watched her long, feminine fingers trace over the sleek metal. Though he doubted she'd intended the double entendre, he imagined her "handling him" with such a sweet caress.

"What's your name?" she asked, returning both hands to the steering wheel.

"Jace Donovan," he answered, still half lost in his fantasy featuring her softness on his rigid flesh.

Dark eyebrows lifted in surprise. "Of Donovan's Orchard?"

Crap, of course she would know his father. Businesses in this area all tended to run in the same social circles. "That's my family's place, but I don't live here anymore." And never would again.

"Ah, the prodigal son. Homecoming not all you thought it would be?"

Jace turned to stare out the window. "It never is."

Silence reigned until she stopped the truck. "Sorry, I'm too damn curious for my own good. I'm Evie by the way, Evie Ripley."

Maybe it was the fact that she could dismiss his sexuality so easily, or residual wounded pride from his family's rejection, but looking into Evie's kind blue eyes, Jace knew before the night was out, he would seduce her.

"Pleasure to meet you, Evie."

Evie sagged against the bedroom wall, trying to reclaim her equilibrium while Jace showered. Even sopping wet from the storm, he was incredibly sexy, with those gray-green bedroom eyes, light brown hair, and roguish chin stubble. And his mouth. Lord have mercy, those full, sensual lips made her remember exactly how long it had been since she last had sex.

Two years, three months, and six days, to be precise.

Unfortunately, he was more appropriate age-wise for her daughter. She seriously doubted he was even out of his twenties, while she had crested the hill to forty, right after ditching her good-for-nothing husband two years ago.

No, Jace with his broad shoulders, rock-hard abs, and excellent butt was off her menu. Ogling him while he was dripping wet and shivering drove home the fact that she was nothing but a skanky old cougar on the prowl for fresh meat.

At dinner, her friends Yvette, Harley Jean, and Missy had teased her about hiring a manwhore to "water her garden after her *looonng* dry spell." Somehow Evie couldn't imagine bringing a man like that into her home/business and parading him around in front of her guests. And even though Constance didn't live with her anymore, it seemed wrong to bring a hired stud into her daughter's childhood home.

So man-meat-for-hire was out of the question, and she'd promised not to jump on Jace and ride him like a wild stallion. God, the look on the poor guy's face when he thought she meant to take him home for a little naked time. Evie had to bite her lip to keep from laughing aloud. The thought of the two of them together was utterly ridiculous.

So why couldn't she stop picturing him in the nude, in her

freshly scrubbed guest shower? In her mind's eye, she saw him soaping up those incredible muscles, letting the lather slide across his skin and eventually down the drain. Did he have hair on his chest or was he smooth to the touch? And since she was wondering . . .

He was tall with big hands and feet. In her limited experience, that usually translated into an equally sizable package. Not that she was ever going to find out, because she was going to stop entertaining thoughts of a naked Jace very soon. He was her guest, and a professional businesswoman shouldn't fantasize about the clientele.

If only it wasn't so damn entertaining.

Maybe she should join a support group: Skanky Old Cougars Anonymous.

Her comm unit chirped, giving her something more pressing to do than lurking in his bedroom, waiting to offer to dry his back. With her tongue.

Sprinting across the hall, Evie answered the call. "Evelyn Ripley."

"Hi, Mama."

Evie grinned at the stunning visage of her daughter. "Hey, baby girl. How are the wedding plans coming?" The words hardly stuck in her throat at all. She couldn't possibly have a grown daughter old enough to be getting married.

But Constance Ripley—the international supermodel—was very much a full-grown woman. At fifteen she'd been discovered when Evie had taken her to Hilton Head for spring break. A modeling agent had taken one look at Constance and the young woman's life had changed practically overnight. Despite her success, Constance was still the sweet little girl who had snuggled on Evie's lap on the back porch and watched the fireflies come out.

Constance rolled her big blue eyes, the only feature she'd taken from Evie. "You know how this kind of thing goes, a zillion details and not enough hours in the day. It sure would be nice if you could help."

Evie swallowed around a lump of guilt. She should be helping her only child plan her wedding. But her hope that Constance would call the whole thing off was still alive and well, and it seemed faithless to help plan an event she desperately wanted to stop. "It's just so busy here, you know, with foliage season coming up and all."

She felt like a heel, lying to her daughter. The only guest in the place was the stray she'd picked up along the side of the road.

"But you are going to make it to my bachelorette party next week, right? And stay for the wedding?" Constance's hopeful face would be her undoing.

"Yeah, I've arranged for Harley Jean to keep an eye on the place for me."

"Good, because Maude and I have got a hell of a surprise in store. You're gonna love it, Mama."

Evie eyes teared up a little. "As long as I get to be with you, baby girl, that's what counts. But a little free wine never goes amiss."

Constance's smile seemed a shade forced.

Evie tilted the screen. "Uh-oh, I know that look. What's the matter?"

"I never could keep anything from you, could I?"

"Nope, now spill it."

"Okay. Well, don't flip out or anything, but I asked Daddy to give me away."

Shame burned Evie's face. "Aw, baby, that's nothing you need to be worried about. Of course you asked him; he's your father, and he's supposed to give you away." Even if he had never done much to keep her. It had been Evie's family's inn that had provided for them. Yon hadn't even helped her run it. His idea of helping was to inform her when something broke.

The bitter chill of the past could stay there as far as she was concerned. "Don't worry, I'll be on my best behavior, all right?"

Constance smiled, then looked over her shoulder. "David's waiting for me. We're going to a club opening tonight."

Evie studied the green flames dancing in her hearth as the eco-logs cracked and snapped, replicating real fire without the need for chopping down trees. What different lives she and her daughter led.

"Love you, baby girl."

"Love you, too, Mama. Comm-link me your flight schedule and I'll see you next week."

Evie signed off and stared at the blank screen. Only a week to go, two 'til the wedding. It didn't look as though her master plan of waiting for Constance to realize she was too young for commitment would happen before the deed was done.

"Hey, you okay?"

Evie jumped at the sound of Jace's voice. She turned to see him leaning idly against the door frame to her room, looking like sin incarnate. The sweats he wore rode low on his hips, and the white T-shirt he'd pulled on was paper thin, barely concealing his hairless chest and miles of tanned skin. How long had he been standing there? She hadn't told him she had a grown daughter who was old enough to get married, and the thought of underscoring their age difference yet again depressed her.

He held his hands up in front of him in a peacekeeping gesture. "I swear I wasn't eavesdropping, just wondering if you had anything to eat around here."

What a crappy hostess she'd been, lusting after him and wallowing in despair while he starved. She'd have to turn in her Southern Belle card. Determined to make it up to him, she breezed past him toward the kitchen. "Absolutely. Follow me."

God, he smelled divine, like clean male skin and spice combined with her homemade lemongrass body scrub. Though the upstairs suites had sonic showers, Evie liked the old-fashioned luxury of a water shower.

Why had she put Jace in the room across the hall? With the inn empty, he could have had any room in the place. Putting him on the ground floor gave him easier access to the kitchen, the dining room, the library.

And to her.

She'd promised not to attack *him*, but if Jace sleepwalked into her room and stripped off his clothes, she would welcome him with open arms.

"This is a great place," he observed, studying the architectural detail of the newel post, the exposed rafters stained a deep mahogany, the river stone fireplace that stretched the length of the lobby, and the antique chaises she'd reupholstered herself in faux leather and edged with brass tacks.

Her chest swelled with pride. "Thank you. It's been in my family for seven generations, all the way back to the 1980s."

"Long time." He grinned as he ran his hand along the smooth railing. The way he took his time as if tactically memorizing the grain of wood made her nipples tighten almost painfully. "You live alone?"

It was a perfectly natural question, but years spent trying to convince everyone from her loser ex to her best friends that she could manage the inn alone got her back up. "Yes, Green Oaks is a one-woman operation, and I do just fine, thank you very much."

He held his hands up again in that self-defense gesture. "I didn't mean anything by it."

Blowing out a sigh, Evie shook her head. "I know. Sorry, sore subject. Come on into the kitchen and—"

The words were cut off when the doorbell chimed. Jace's brow drew down as he checked the time on his comm link. "It's after eleven. You expecting anyone?"

Evie shook her head.

"Got that pistol handy?"

"I'm sure it's just a late drop-in. I bet the storm held them up." Even so, she patted her hip to make sure her piece was ready to rock and roll as she moved to the door.

The man standing on her porch was neither friend nor guest. A burglar would have been more welcome because she could have shot him, no problem. She felt more than saw Jace draw up tight to her back, but was too stunned to notice.

"Yon, what the fracking hell are you doing here?" Evie asked her ex-husband.

2

It had been a long time since Jace had sex for the sake of sex. So long, in fact, that he'd forgotten about the nervous jitters that accompanied the possibility of rejection. Typically, a woman who hired a pleasure companion wanted sex from him. Once money changed hands, Jace could take his time reassuring the timid, coaxing the shy, or getting down and dirty with the bolder types. Part of what made him so good at his job was his ability to read women and give them exactly what they wanted before they even asked. Jace was nothing if not a hard worker. Such a dedicated service provider, in fact, that he hadn't left much time for a personal life.

Hell, he was practically a virgin again.

While he showered, he'd mulled over the dilemma. He could just come out and offer his services to Evie, lay it all out there and see if she took the bait. With her as an eager participant he could work his magic, spend hours exploring the full curves of her breasts, the dip at her waist, the smoothness of her generous hips until she begged him to fuck her.

Two things stopped him. His hostess didn't seem like the

type to hire a man for pleasure. After seeing the hard work she'd invested in her deserted but well-maintained inn, he just couldn't imagine her having extra money to toss at him for a night of unbridled passion.

Plus, his pride had taken enough hits for one day. It was one thing if she rejected him, but quite another for her to reject him based solely on his occupation. Boone was not New New York City. As his family had demonstrated earlier, people here didn't think the same way as he did. At times he hardly believed he'd been hatched here with these salt-of-the-earth types.

So he'd been at a loss as to how exactly to proceed with Evie. His plan had been to talk with her some more, get to know her over a meal, and feel his way into familiar territory. A glass of wine, a few laughs, with him carefully steering the conversation away from his family. But seeing the large and obviously drunken man looming over her, all thoughts of seduction fled.

"Baby." Yon tripped over the doorstep and would have fallen directly on top of Evie if Jace hadn't yanked her out of the way. Instead, the massive giant crashed to the floor at their feet.

"Yon, no, you can't stay here." Evie toed the man with her boot.

"You're my wife," the drunk slurred.

"Ex-wife. Emphasis on the *ex.*" Evie's little love taps to the man's ribs grew in ferocity.

Yon pushed himself to his knees and smirked at her. "Yeah, but you ain't got a man since me. Constance told me you want me back."

Evie snorted. "Like I'd want a cavity."

Color ran along Yon's cheekbones, though whether it was from the insult or liquor was impossible to tell. "No other man'll have your fat ass."

Evie's mouth dropped open. Jace thought for sure she'd kick him as hard as she could, hopefully landing the blow right on the bastard's junk. But instead she just stood there, embarrassment flushing her face as she refused to meet his gaze.

Protectiveness swelled in his chest. Evie's lush curves may not be fashionable the way they were fifty years ago, but she was built like a goddess, all soft sweetness covering that iron will. He knew plenty of men who would line up to be with a woman who looked like her, with himself at the front of the pack.

Jace didn't know who Constance was, but it was clear she was misinformed. Never one to let an opportunity slip past him, Jace put an arm around Evie's shoulders. "And you heard wrong. Evie's with me now."

Both Evie and her load of an ex stared at him with the same expression of surprised disbelief. Jace planted a kiss on Evie's forehead, a gesture of intimacy he'd seen his father use on his mother earlier that day.

Evie recovered first, blinking away tears, trying to pull away. "Jace, you don't have to—"

Jace tightened his grip on her, enjoying the soft female flesh pressed deliciously up against his side. "Stake my claim? Sure seems like it. You've been keeping me a secret for too long, honey. It's time the world knew the truth."

With great effort, Yon heaved himself upright. He might've been trying to scowl at Jace, but swaying on his feet the way he was it looked more like he was fighting the urge to hurl. "What's he talkin' 'bout, Evie?"

Jace stared the drunk down. "That we're together."

"Bullshit." Yon spat the word along with some saliva. His breath reeked of Wild Turkey, and the sour unwashed smell emanating off his body didn't help. The man must have come directly off a weeklong bender to his ex's doorstep. "There's no way in hell you're fucking my wife."

"Ex-wife," Jace and Evie chorused in unison. Jace winked at her before he stepped in front of her, blocking her body from the drunk's line of sight. "Now, I'd appreciate you taking your stinking carcass elsewhere. You've interrupted us long enough for one evening."

"Get outta my way, you little peckerhead." Yon tried to shove him aside, but Jace had prepared for it. It'd been ages since he'd been in a fistfight, but some habits were so deeply ingrained they were second nature.

Jace swung, his fist connected, and Yon fell, crashing over an antique end table, splintering the thing to bits. Braced on the balls of his feet, Jace waited, but the big bastard didn't get up.

Evie pushed past him to crouch over her ex. She heaved a sigh. "He's still breathing."

"Of course he is. What, did you think I'd killed him with one blow? The guy has fifty pounds on me." And a jaw of solid granite, but Jace kept that part to himself as he shook out his stinging hand.

Evie stared down at the drunken lout. "I can't believe you did that." Her voice was low, stunned.

Oh, no, she wasn't one of those nonviolent types. If so, he'd probably killed his chances by decking the son of a bitch. The woman had pulled a *gun* on him for crissakes. Had he completely misread her? Jace decided that even if he had misinterpreted her, he wasn't about to apologize for his actions.

"He had it coming."

"For about the last twenty-two years, at least. Thank you, Jace." Blue eyes filled with gratitude and what looked a lot like hero worship fixed on him and his heart stumbled over its next beat.

Make your move! the lecherous part of his brain hissed. *Strike while she's grateful, don't give her a chance to think on it.*

Though what came out surprised even him. "You're welcome. Could I have some ice for my hand?"

Way to go, Casanova.

Evie moved quickly to his side, then took his hand in both of her small soft ones. "Let me see that."

Jace's eyelids lowered as her thumbs glided over his skin, gently probing his bruised knuckles. "It's been a while since I hit a guy."

"Do you usually hit women, then?"

He knew she was being flippant, but her question broke him from his trance. "That was an incredibly shitty thing to say."

What in the hell was *wrong* with her? If Evie could have kicked her own ass, she would have done it. Jace had stood up for her, literally knocking Yon unconscious. Then he looked at her, eyes smoldering like the fire in the hearth, radiating sex the way her fireplace expelled heat. It had been so long since a man looked at her that way, with genuine desire burning in his gaze, it had unsettled her more than the confrontation with Yon. And then she had accused him of beating women.

Even as a joke it wasn't funny. "I'm sorry, I didn't mean . . ."

Jace moved closer, so close she could feel the heat coming off him. "Not everyone is like him. Not every man is abusive."

"Yon never hit me," she quickly corrected him.

"From what I saw he was at least verbally abusive. I didn't think you were the type of woman who would just roll over and take that."

Shame ripped through her like spikes through her veins. "I'm not. That's why I divorced him."

"Then why is he here?" Jace shot back. "Why does he think it's acceptable to show up at your doorstep smelling of booze and slinging insults? You haven't set him straight."

Her hands landed on her hips. "Where the hell do you get off judging me? It's not so cut-and-dry. Yon's the father of my child; we have history. I can't just banish him from my life." No matter how much she wanted to.

"You know what I think? I think you're afraid to kick him to the curb, because if you did, you'd have nothing to keep you from moving on."

"Who are you to tell me what I feel?" Incensed, she stormed past him toward the kitchen.

"Where are you going?" Jace called after her.

She didn't bother to answer, too shaken to continue the conversation. Instead, she grabbed a clean tea towel from the drawer and scooped ice from the freezer, dumping it into the fabric. Retrieving a rubber band from her junk drawer, she secured the ends of the towel into a makeshift compress, her mind churning all the while.

Why was she so riled up at Jace? Probably because she was burning with sexual need every time she looked at him, then having Yon show up to underscore her flaws killed even the fantasy. He represented an ugly part of her life, and she couldn't help falling back into the role she'd played as his wife. God, how she hated being a doormat!

"Evie," Jace said quietly from behind her.

Thrusting the compress at him, she waited for him to take it. Brushing it aside, he cupped her face in his big hands. Searching his expression, she saw the intent there, the hunger she felt for him reflected back at her.

He gave her plenty of time to stop him, opportunity to tell him no as he lowered his mouth closer to hers. Her eyelids drifted shut moments before his lips feathered over hers in a hot and sweet caress, before settling with a deeper pressure. His mouth molded to hers, coaxing her lips to dance with his in a timeless tango of desire.

Evie opened to him and he groaned as he accepted her invitation, pulling her body flush with his. Wrapping her arms around his neck, Evie reveled in the contrast; God have mercy, he was hard *everywhere,* all smooth muscle and sinew. And the bulge pressing into her soft belly was hardest of all. She wiggled against it, delighting when he twitched inside the baggy sweats.

Tearing his mouth from hers, Jace nibbled on her earlobe. "Christ, I want you." He murmured between pulls and sucks. "You're like fire in my arms."

She felt like fire, like a living flame desperate to engulf him. If only the layers of fabric between them would incinerate, so he could give her that thick rod of flesh she was so wet and ready for.

Jace pushed her flannel shirt off her shoulders slowly, caressing every inch of skin he exposed. She gasped when he sank his teeth into the tendon running along the side of her neck. No man had ever marked her like that before. Her already tight nipples throbbed, envious of his attention above. His fingers toyed with the snap on her jeans, tugging her tank top free at the waist and skimming his hands along the soft curve of her belly.

"What you do to me," he muttered.

She wanted to feel his reaction for herself. Dipping her hand inside his sweatpants, she wrapped her fingers around the broad head of his cock. He jerked back, but she held him tightly, holding the rigid flesh in her grip. When he stilled, she continued her perusal with slow, sweet strokes, imagining each inch of his hardness pushing inside her, stretching her, filling her up.

His eyes were heavy lidded as he watched her pleasure him. Precome beaded the tip of his shaft and she swirled her thumb into it, massaging the head.

"Evie. My sweet Evie," he groaned.

The gray T-shirt he'd donned after his shower was tight and thin, and she could see every bulge his muscles made. His nipples were hard little points and she couldn't resist tugging at one through the fabric.

Jace made an inhuman sound and before she could blink, he had her shoved up against the island counter. His hands tore at her jeans almost frantically, shoving them and her underwear down together. She squeaked in protest as he lifted her up and her ass met the cold, smooth surface of the countertop.

Spreading her thighs wide, he crouched between them, examining her vag up close and personal. Slowly, holding her gaze, he dipped his head and took her sex into his mouth.

Evie couldn't look away as his tongue swiped through her folds, lapping up her juices. Jace made a sound of pure pleasure and satisfaction as he swallowed his first taste of her. Tearing his mouth away, he blew a cool stream of air against her wet flesh, causing her clit to harden to the point of pain. "Your honey is incredible. I could spend the rest of my life buried between your thighs."

Her core clenched at his words. What could she say to that? Nothing, apparently, because Jace was busy placing her heels on the countertop, spreading her even wider. He lapped at her again, swirling his tongue lightly over her clit in a teasing caress.

"I'm going to tongue-fuck you hard until you scream my name as you come all over my face."

Then putting actions to words, he stabbed his tongue deep into her pussy.

3

Jace was in heaven. Evie's sweet lube coated his tongue, and her soft cries filled his ears. She'd tunneled her fingers into his hair, holding him close as if she worried he'd stop if she didn't clutch him to her. Certainly not now that he'd had a taste of her passion. The scent of her arousal filled his every breath, and her slickness covered him from chin to nose, yet it still wasn't enough. He stiffened his tongue and thrust deep, burying his face in her snatch up to his eyebrows to catch her sweetness at its source. Her throaty gasps were the sweetest music he'd ever heard. Slowly, he traced his tongue upward, toward that hard little button of flesh, exploring every crease and fold along the way. He fully intended to send her soaring, but not yet.

Instead, he circled the bud with the tip of his tongue before plunging deeply back inside her sweet pussy. Her feminine channel clenched against his invasion and his cock jerked in his sweats, jealous of the tight fit.

If being a pleasure companion had taught him anything, it was that all women responded to different touches. Some liked soft strokes and a feather-light caress, while others craved a hard, fast tongue lashing. Some enjoyed a slow build, and still others wanted him to dive right in. Under normal circumstances, Jace would have analyzed her response to everything, figured out the best way to please her. Little details like, was one side of her clit more sensitive than the other, or did she need his teeth as well as his lips?

But his normal detachment failed him on the first lick of her savory cunt. The flesh that yielded to him so sweetly called him back for more and he was helpless to obey. With her legs propped up on the counter, her sex was completely open to him. Using his index finger and thumb, he circled her labia, enjoying the crisp hairs that tickled his fingers. Evie's pussy wasn't waxed; the hair grew dark and wild on her mound. Somehow that small detail made her more real to him. More a woman in full bloom.

The ripe petals of her vulva puffed out and he went in for an open-mouth kiss, treasuring the contact of his lips on hers. She bucked toward him, her body urging his to satisfy it.

Looking up, he saw that she'd tipped her head back even as she arched to his mouth. Her full breasts sported rock-hard nipples. Pale thighs quivered and the fingers in his hair tightened to the point of pain. She was a woman on the edge of climax and he nuzzled her softly, wanting to keep her there and burn this moment into his brain.

Her thick lashes lifted and her irises had transformed into blue fire, hotter than anything he'd ever seen. Her face was totally enraptured.

They stared at each other for an endless moment and Jace forgot everything he thought he knew about women. None had ever looked at him with such raw wonder, as if he'd given her the best gift of her life. She hadn't even come yet, so why did she look so blissed out?

Nuzzling her thigh with his stubbled cheek, he watched her closely as his tongue dragged through her sex. Her lips remained parted around ragged breaths. Her hands left his hair and her fingers glided over his face, touching him gently as though she was memorizing his features with her hands. Or trying to make herself believe he was real. Most women would have screamed at him by now for leaving them wanting, demanded that he finish what he'd started. But Evie seemed to enjoy anticipating his next move. When her fingers traced over his lips, he kissed the pads lightly, almost reverently.

Suddenly, he realized neither of them had thought about activating their health guards. No wonder he'd been so lost in her; it'd been forever since he'd tasted a woman without the snap and sizzle of his electromagnetic shield gobbling up every trace of her DNA before it could settle on him.

Illustra required pleasure companions to use their health guards at all times with clients and always during intercourse. Training a pleasure companion was time consuming and costly, and losing one to a health code violation like fluid transfer without a permit was completely unacceptable.

But Evie wasn't a client, and pleasuring her free and clear of his shield was his choice. With that thought in mind, he held her gaze as he dragged his flattened tongue over the pink swells, drinking up the dewy nectar her body yielded. Sweeping two fingers through her sodden folds, he pushed them into her vaginal opening just as he closed his lips over the throbbing bud of her clit and sucked hard.

"Jace," she cried as he trilled his tongue over the hard little nubbin. Her eyes had filled with tears, but he'd seen plenty of women cry from relief when he finally sent them over. Evie might be a little reluctant to order him about in carnal matters, but he knew for sure she'd stop him if he hurt her. And he wouldn't give her pain, only as much passion as she could handle. With that thought in mind, he hooked his fingers behind her pubic bone and found the rough bump of her G-spot inside her core.

She came apart beneath him, a fresh coat of slick lube spilling over his fingers, just as tears worked their way from the beautiful eyes still trained on him. Her lips were parted on a silent scream and he kept the intense flicks up, pushing her higher, wanting to make her soar.

On and on it went, her orgasm so sweet and hot, he nearly spilled in his sweats just experiencing it with her. When her hips shied away from his marauding mouth, he eased his fingers from her still-clenching channel and worked his tongue back down to her opening. She was so wet her juices ran down her crease and dripped from her folds. He'd made that happen. Pride swelled in his chest and he was damn sure going to savor it.

Evie gasped as he plunged his tongue in her again. She tugged on his hair and shook her head no. With a final drag, he swept up her mound, relishing every last drop of her honey.

The thought that he'd never enjoy this pleasure with her again caused a physical ache in his chest. Though his shaft throbbed for satisfaction, he found himself resting his head against her soft belly, wrapping his arms around her waist, holding her close.

If he only got one night with her, he wanted to make it last.

Evie couldn't believe she'd just been eaten out on her kitchen counter. She'd never had sex in the kitchen before, never had it anywhere but in the bedroom. The cold press of her naked butt against the quartz countertop made her shiver, even as warmth radiated from her overheated pussy. Jace hadn't been kidding when he said he wanted a snack. The way he'd pleasured her . . . Her channel clenched again in remembered bliss, the invasion of his mouth and fingers, the intensity of his gray eyes focused on her. She'd never come so hard, or so fast, in her life.

Yon had often complained she was frigid. She'd been too

busy raising her daughter and running her inn to dwell on their love life. Most days she fell into bed fully clothed. Maybe if Yon had spent half the amount of time licking her vag as Jace had just done, she would have been eager for sex more often. Like she was right now.

But Jace was holding her like she was some sort of security blanket. It seemed almost crass to ask him to fuck her now. She certainly didn't think he owed her anything, but wasn't getting his dick wet a driving compulsion for Jace the way it was with most men? Or maybe he just didn't want her. Maybe he minded the extra weight settled around her belly, hips, and thighs. He hadn't seen her ass yet in all its massive glory, and he wouldn't if she had anything to say about it.

Running her fingers through the soft locks of his hair, she cleared her throat but didn't know what to say. Asking him if he was all right seemed a little weird after he'd been up to his ears in her snatch. Ditto for saying thank you, like he'd done her a big favor. It was all a little too polite, the awkwardness underscored because this man—this stranger—had decked her ex-husband and then feasted on her like she was a banquet.

As an afterthought, it all seemed so . . . sleazy.

She wiggled a little and Jace released his death grip and looked up at her. "Should we go to your bedroom or mine?"

Her mouth dried out. Well, that answered her question about did he want to take the next logical step. Still, to assume that she would nettled her. "Who says I'm up for more?"

He blinked as though he wasn't sure he'd heard her. "You don't want me to fuck you?"

Her channel clenched again at the words. Good thing he'd withdrawn his hand or he'd know how badly she wanted exactly that.

"I do, but it'd be a little more gentlemanly if you ask me instead of assuming I'm a sure thing. Although after the work you just put in—"

"It wasn't work," he cut her off, then rose to his feet. "I wanted to do that."

Her lips twitched. "Well, I sure hope you weren't going for a merit badge or something."

Jace grinned and scooped her into his arms. Evie squeaked in protest. "Don't! I'm too heavy."

"Are not," Jace murmured, and tightened his grip on her as he carried her from the kitchen, past the great room where her ex still snored like an old-fashioned chainsaw, and down the hall to her bedroom.

Jace kicked the door closed. Instead of heading for the bed, he put her down on the faux leather chaise in front on the fire. Evie spread her legs, expecting him to drop his sweatpants and plunge inside her. Instead, he circled around behind her, catching her gaze in the mirror above the mantel. Tilting her head back, she looked at him, waiting for him to tell her what he had in mind.

"Show me how you like to masturbate."

Wow. She wasn't sure where that came from or why it made her nipples tingle to hear it. "Why? Wouldn't you rather have sex?"

"I want this first. I want to see how you touch yourself so I can plan out exactly how I'm going to take you to make our first time perfect."

He made it sound like such a science, like the study of how best to make Evie come. She swallowed, wondering how to tell him that him caring about her pleasure was more than enough. Actions spoke louder than words, so she reached for him.

Jace caught her hand and pulled it up to his face. Fire from the hearth and from his need burned her up. "Please, Evie. Give me this gift. I want to watch you."

How could she refuse? "Okay. But only if you help me. I can get myself off alone anytime."

His grin was pure mischief. "Do you use toys?"

The thought made her blush and she shook her head, letting her hair fall over her face to hide her embarrassment. "Just my fingers."

He pushed the dark strands away. "I can't believe you're the same woman who pulled a gun on me a few hours ago. I love that you're so bold in the rest of your life and so reluctantly curious about sex. You have no idea how refreshing this is for someone like me."

Before she could ask about that cryptic statement, he sucked two of her fingers between his lips. Sharp teeth scraped the sensitive pads and his tongue swirled around the digits, getting them wet with his saliva.

"Show me." He guided her hand down between her legs. His other hand dragged her tank top up, exposing her breasts before cupping the back of her head and urging her to rest against the back of the chaise.

Evie couldn't bear to look at herself in the mirror, splayed out like this, all the flaws that clothes hid put on display. Talk about a ruined orgasm. Instead, she closed her eyes as her wet fingers traced lightly over her labia. Jace's hand rested on top of hers, shadowing her movements as she teased the outer folds.

"Slow and soft at first," he murmured in her ear as her hand skipped from one side to the other. "You like to delay the pleasure, let it build."

Nodding, she moved her right hand just a fraction of an inch, sweeping it across the inside on the left. Jace's hand moved to the right, working her slowly, sweetly, and in perfect sync with her own hand.

Together, they worked in tandem, zeroing in on her more sensitive flesh. If she went up, he moved down until her entire cunt was feeling the gentle sweep of his caress. Wetness gushed from her core, her sex more sensitive than it had ever been.

Jace's middle finger circled her opening but waited for her signal. Threading her slick fingers through his, Evie pushed both of their index fingers inside herself slowly, giving her body time to adjust to the intrusion.

"Evie, my God, you are so unbelievably hot. Look at yourself, baby. Look at what we're doing to you."

Though she didn't want to see all her flaws, Jace's command could not be ignored. She opened her eyes and stared past the swells of her breasts and belly to where they both touched her. His roughly calloused hands were so different from her own. The sight of his tanned forearm against her pale belly and pink cunt was the most erotic sight she'd ever beheld.

"Yes," he hissed as her inner muscles clamped down on them. "Oh, yeah, you love this as much as I do."

She did. Pulling their hands out, she urged his into a hot circle encompassing her whole sex. The heel of his hand rubbed across her clit as his fingers cupped her folds, the middle one dipping inside her.

Jace leaned over her and pressed his lips to hers. The thumb of his left hand caressed her collarbone as his tongue traced the seam of her lips.

"Faster," she moaned, and he complied, circling her greedy flesh at an increased rate. She gasped and pressed down harder on his hand as he deepened the kiss. Her other hand went to his hair again, holding him to her as he touched and kissed her.

"Inside," she panted, and two big fingers thrust into her core hard and deep. Again and again, he fucked her with his digits before coming back up to rub her clit, increasing the speed and adding pressure.

He'd found her rhythm now, knew it as well as she did, but she kept her hand on his as he fingered her.

"Look at me, Evie. I want to see your eyes when you come." He whispered the dark command in her ear.

She stared up at him, completely lost to this man and all the delicious sensations he brought out in her. His fingers moved faster than she could track, stroking, pinching, delving inside.

She wasn't sure what sent her flying, just knew she was looking in his eyes when the powerful orgasm swept over her like a tsunami.

Boneless, she sagged back against the chaise and tried to close her legs. Jace brought his saturated fingers to his face and sucked them clean. She whimpered at his masculine groan of delight.

His next words made all the blood rush from her head as he circled the couch, tugging off his T-shirt.

"Now, my sweet Evie. Now I'm going to fuck you."

4

"Activate your health guard, Evie." Jace pushed the sweats down to his ankles and kicked them aside. Evie's gaze was fixed on his cock and her lips parted, forming a small O. For a moment, he considered asking her to go down on him, so he could see her sweet lips closing over the head, feel her wet mouth coating his shaft. He knew he wouldn't last, though, and he didn't want to give Evie time to reconsider.

Naked and painfully erect, he stood before her and pressed the small implant inside his elbow to turn on his own germ shield. The familiar hum filled his ears and he ran a hand along her arm, listening as the shield sizzled and removed any traces of her DNA from his skin.

Evie still hadn't moved. If it were possible, he would have turned her shield on himself, but the damn things were designed to respond only to the user's touch. "Come on, babe, I'm dying here."

Her eyes flew to his. "I don't have any lube."

Jace swore. That would be a problem. The shields were marvelous inventions, part of the reason he had a job, but penetration didn't work the same way with them. Anything her body produced would be eradicated instantly. A shielded man needed health guard neutral lubricant to fit his cock inside his lover, regardless of the orifice he intended to fuck.

"I think there's some in my bag." He made for the door, then stopped as he considered her expression. Evie had looked like a skittish rabbit at the first glimpse of his shaft. "You aren't having second thoughts, are you?" It would probably kill him.

"No, well, maybe. This isn't like me. I don't even know you."

Recalling the way her eyes had filled with tears earlier, he moved back toward her. "I want you, Evie, but I need you to be sure you want me too."

Her chin angled up in a defiant tilt. She rose and activated her shield, then strode toward the bed. His mouth went dry as he watched her hips sway as she climbed onto the mattress and rolled to one side. He'd never seen such perfectly proportioned curves before—sweet, soft, an overabundance of everything he thought a woman should be. He was one lucky son of a bitch.

"Jace?"

"Hmmm?" He was too busy staring at her breasts until she covered them from view.

A small smile curved up her lips. "The lube?"

"Right." He tore his gaze away from the sassy siren and made for the hall.

His bag sat on the bed, and he unzipped it and started pulling things out. He wouldn't have packed lube for the trip to visit his family, but maybe there was some left from his vacation last summer.

Jace turned the duffel upside down until everything spilled out onto the bed. Ah, there it was, vanilla scented and unopened. He worked at the seal as he strode back across the hall to Evie. She had dimmed the lights, still body shy. After the way he'd seen her ex talk to her, he knew it would take time to build up her confidence. Time Jace didn't have, unless . . .

Would she be willing to do the long-distance thing?

It was crazy to even consider it. Her life was here at the inn, his was in New New York. Even if speed-of-sound technology made the trip a breeze, Jace had no desire to return to life in these mountains. A life that was all Evie knew.

Then there was his job. He hadn't told her what he did for a living, and somehow he doubted Evie would be okay with him fucking other women on a regular basis, even if it was completely legal.

But maybe when he made management and wasn't out in the field . . .

It was crazy. She'd made a valid point earlier. They were essentially strangers. What the hell was the matter with him, building this into a relationship? Too many variables bounced around in his skull and his balls ached too badly to think everything through right now.

The seal finally gave way and he dumped the slippery liquid on his hand and cock. Stroking too lightly to stimulate himself, he coated his shaft and sac thoroughly.

In the position Evie was in, he had to stretch behind her to access her pussy. Leaning onto the bed, he reached around her and spread his hand over her sex, coating it with the slick oil. The shields dulled the sensations slightly, but still, touching her was better than not touching her, especially knowing he was about to have her.

Pulling her to the edge of the bed, he leaned over her, aligning his shaft with her entrance. If he hadn't spent so much time pleasuring her, he would have worried about the fit, but Evie's body was primed for intercourse.

Bracing his weight on one arm and a hip, Jace curled Evie's legs up until her body formed an S-shape. Her brows drew together and she pushed her back off the mattress. His free hand caught the nape of her neck and pulled her forward until her forehead rested against his and he could stare deeply into her eyes.

Because his cock was so hard, he didn't need to hold it as he entered her, slowly, letting her body anticipate his. Evie's eyes went wide and she squeezed down on him. It was the only move she could make.

The position took stamina on his part, but he knew she'd enjoy lying side by side, their bodies merging, staring into his eyes. He watched her lips part as he rocked deeper. Her gaze was filled with passion and wonder, an innocent joy that he found addicting.

Jace found something to love in every woman he pleasured, but with Evie he loved it all. Her innate passion and hesitant lusts grew stronger the further they explored. He'd startled her a few times, but she hadn't protested anything. In fact, she seemed to love everything he did to her, accepted his needs as well as her own. Her dormant lusts were waking up, and though they may frighten her, Evie refused to hide from them.

Sweat trickled down his back and on both of their foreheads, but he refused to stop. She could come this way, with the head of his cock angled to work her G-spot on every stroke. He wanted to see it, see the surprise as orgasm swept over her and made her his.

Her eyes searched his and her hot breath fell against his cheeks. When his shaft was buried to the hilt the next time, he swiveled his hips, stirring her well with his thick club. Their shields snapped and sizzled, gobbling up foreign matter, but he barely heard it over the frantic beating of his heart.

"Jace." Her eyes were heavy lidded, her expression almost drugged. "I'm so close."

"Then come for me, Evie." He sawed his cock in and out of her as fast as he could. Gripping her hair in a fist, he tugged her head back and sank his teeth into the tendon along her neck.

She screamed and her channel clenched around him, pulling

him deeper into her body. His own release was close. Jace let go of her hair and waited for her to look at him. His balls drew up tight and his spine tingled, but he fought it until she opened her eyes.

"Come now," she urged. With a shuddering groan, he did, emptying his load into her. Her shield crackled as it eradicated his seed.

On and on it went, all the while her pleasure-filled gaze encouraged him to soar. His heart pounded against his ribs, and every muscle clenched and released. "Evie," he gasped, his world tunneling until he saw only her.

She kissed him lightly and his eyes finally slid shut, savoring the hard-won bliss, so unlike his normal postcoital experiences.

Evie's arms gave out and she flopped back onto the bed. His cock slid from her body, and he deactivated his shield before curling up next to her.

"I'm too old to be a contortionist," she groused. But the satisfied smile on her lips gave her away. Jace pushed strands of hair back from her face.

"Can I stay with you tonight?" he asked. He'd never spent the night with a woman before. Even his lovers had asked for space when the afterglow had faded, and he'd quietly gone back to his cold, empty bed, satiated but somehow unsatisfied.

"Sure," Evie said blithely, unaware of just how momentous this was for him. "I should clean up first." Deactivating her health guard, she moved to get up, but Jace pushed her back down.

"Let me." He went to her private bathroom and ran water in the sink until it was warm. Cleaning his face, hands, and cock, he wet a washcloth and brought it back with a hand towel. Wiping the sweat from her face, her breasts, and belly first, he then used the wet cloth between her legs. She purred like a contented cat as he rubbed her sensitive flesh, then patted it dry.

Tossing the towel aside, he lifted the puffy blue cover and

she climbed beneath. He followed, already wondering how to get her to snuggle up against him; but as soon as his back hit the mattress, she spooned up alongside him, throwing one leg over him in a possessive gesture.

He loved it and his heart ached with want.

"Lights off," she called out, and the room dimmed to just a few smoldering embers in the fire.

"Thank you, Jace. This was one of the best nights I've had in a long time."

His throat closed up, but he managed to croak, "Anytime, Evie."

The dreaded morning after. Evie awoke with a man in her bed for the first time in two years and a feeling of deep unease. She'd never had a one-night stand before. Well, scratch that, she'd tried, but Yon was like a boomerang; no matter how many times she tossed him out her front door, he kept coming back. Until finally he wore her down, convinced her to marry him.

And look how well *that* had turned out.

Turning to her side, she took a minute to study her new bed warmer. Jace's arm was flung over his eyes, his gorgeous lips parted as he slept. His stubble seemed even more roguish in the predawn hours, and she wanted to rub herself over his face like a cat would use a corner to scratch an itch.

But what really made her heart pound was that she knew nothing about him. Sure, she knew his father by reputation, but he'd never mentioned Jace. He lived in New New York City like her daughter, and probably led a life she couldn't even imagine. Partly because he'd said nothing about it, she realized. What did he do for a living? She could picture him as a pilot or maybe a construction worker. Somehow the idea of a desk job didn't suit his rugged appearance. What was his life like? Did he work hard and play harder? Despite his intensity, she'd sensed a playfulness within him. She could easily picture him out at the clubs every night, dancing until the early-morning hours before selecting a random woman as a bed partner.

Not that she'd ever been to a night club. It was just her imagination filling in the blanks. Deep down she realized she didn't know Jace at all, other than in the biblical sense. Hell, for all she knew, he might be married.

The thought left her shivering.

Scooting out of bed, she grabbed her robe and headed for the shower. Not the one off her bathroom either, the main one out in the hall. Heaven forbid Jace decide to join her in the shower, all her concerns would evaporate with the steam.

As she lathered her hair with honeysuckle shampoo, Evie gave herself a pep talk. No regrets about last night. Jace had given her a gift of pleasure and she would accept it as such with no expectations of anything else. He'd made his disdain for country living clear, and she had no desire to repeal her single status. Marriage was for other people, younger people like Constance.

Like Jace.

Toweling herself dry, she fought the urge to take extra time with her hair or fuss with makeup. He was welcome to look at the crow's feet and laugh lines embedded on her skin, lines even the deepest after-amazing-sex-induced coma couldn't erase. Maybe he'd already hit the road.

The scent of freshly brewed hydro bean coffee put that to rest. She expected Yon to still be passed out on the great room floor, drooling on her hardwood, but both his body and his truck were gone. She doubted he'd even know where she kept the coffee since she didn't recall him ever brewing a pot.

Jace was dressed in jeans and another black T-shirt, though his feet were bare. God, that was so intimate, him parading around her kitchen barefoot, making her coffee. She swallowed, recalling what other intimacies they'd shared, both here and in her bedroom, and moved to the percolator.

"Morning." He held a coffee cup to his lips, those gray-green eyes studying her over the rim.

She shifted her gaze away and retrieved her favorite mug. "What time is your flight?" Cripes, that could have been subtler.

Jace set down his mug. "Not 'til four, but I can catch an earlier flight out of Charlotte Douglas if you want me to go."

She didn't, but neither could she ask him to stay, to spend the next several hours reliving the magic of last night. It was too pathetic.

Moving closer until he invaded her personal space, Jace tilted her chin up. "Evie, I want to see you again."

Closing her eyes against the temptation he presented, Evie shook her head. "Last night was wonderful, a memory I'll always treasure." She paused, letting her sincerity sink in.

"But you don't want to be with me again." He withdrew his hand.

Not looking him in the eye was cowardly. Lifting her lids, she stared at him and uttered the lie she needed to keep herself safe. "No."

Jace stepped back. "All right. I'll comm the rental car company." Leaning down, he brushed her cheek with his lips. "Thank you, Evie. For everything."

When the door to his room closed, she sagged against the counter. Part of her wanted to go after him, to offer the explanations her brain had been kicking around since she woke up. No matter how well their bodies had fit together, their lives couldn't be more mismatched. Age difference aside, he was clearly at home in the big city, and everything she was resided at the inn.

But that's not the real reason, her conscience nagged. *If you can't be honest with him, be honest with yourself.*

The real reason was probably pulling in to the local watering hole, looking for the hair of the dog that bit him and turned him rabid on her the night before. Just remembering the scalding humiliation of Yon's insults hardened her heart and stiffened her backbone.

Never again would she let a man tear down her carefully constructed walls. No amount of phenomenal sex was worth being exposed as a quivering bundle of raw nerves bracing for the next hit.

Evie went to her room, ignoring the scent of sex still heavily perfuming the air, and exchanged her bathrobe for clean jeans and a denim shirt. After braiding her hair, she pulled a ball cap on and headed to the pantry for her cleaning supplies. Guests or no, the rainstorm left streaks on her windows and solar panels, and she would wash them until they gleamed in the early-morning sun.

Propping the ladder against the porch, she started from the widow's walk off the honeymoon suite. She'd offered a free stay to Constance and her fiancé for their honeymoon, but her daughter had laughed the offer away.

Honeymoon at Mom's place, was that really so wrong?

A car pulled up and Jace strode down the porch steps.

"Safe trip," Evie called out to him, like he was any other guest getting back to his real life.

He turned and looked up at her, that same smoldering look that he'd given her last night when his head was buried between her thighs. That look that said, *You can't hide from me, I see everything.*

Last night she'd wanted him to see, but now, in broad daylight . . .

Evie turned back to wiping down her window and ignored the slamming of the car door, the crunch of gravel under tires. When she did finally look back, there was no trace of him at her inn or on her heart.

5

"Hey, Jace, thought you were heading out for the weekend?" Reginald Duchamp placed the weight bar he'd been lifting back into its slot. His spotter wandered off toward the cardio machines.

"Short trip." Jace nodded at the bar. "Mind spotting me a set?"

Reg slid off the bench, which cleaned itself of his sweat, immediately preparing for the next patron. "Go for it. What are you pushing these days?"

Jace lay down on the bench and positioned his hands. "About two eighty-five."

The weight bar worked better than the clunky old disks Jace had grown up using. The bar itself cost more than he made in a year, but it was designed to reduce its pull toward the center of the earth, thereby making its weight adjustable to the lifter with the input of a code. Illustra encouraged its employees to take advantage of their health maintenance facilities as part of their job and didn't skimp on amenities.

Reg stayed silent through the first few reps, and Jace worked his body hard. He'd been too restless to go back to his apartment and had headed here instead. At Illustra, time of day or day of the week was irrelevant; there were always people hustling back and forth, always other pleasure companions either gearing up for work or relaxing after. Hopefully he could spend a few hours down here feeling the burn and exhausting himself so he'd quit thinking about Evie.

"So, how's the family?" Reg's white teeth flashed against his ebony skin.

"The same." Jace grunted as his muscles twitched and he put the bar back, taking a breather.

"Hence the short trip. That sucks." Reg had gone through the initial training program at the same time as Jace and they'd been friends for years.

Jace didn't want to talk about his trip. "So what about you, Reg? Hot date last night?" Reg held up three digits as he drank from his water bottle. Jace gave a low whistle. "You are a machine."

Reg managed to do what Jace didn't, which was to have a life outside of Illustra. He had four younger sisters who lived with him, the oldest a sophomore in high school. Reg worked and dated and still made time for his family.

"What's your secret, man? How do you manage to have it all?"

Reg shrugged. "I'm not here for life the way you are. I'm whoring for my sisters, and as soon as they are out on their own, I plan to lay off this job, settle down, and have a family. Just doing what I gotta do in the meantime."

Jace nodded thoughtfully and reached for his water bottle. "You got it all figured out, then?"

Reg snorted, his face the picture of derision. "No, haven't met the right woman yet. So I figure I'll just keep trying them on until I find one that fits."

A picture of Evie popped into Jace's head. Why couldn't he

forget about her? She'd treated him like every client he'd serviced over the last nine years. He'd woken in her bed, surrounded by the scent of sex and the memory of her soft body under his. By the time he realized she'd gone to shower, cold foreboding had filled him.

But he'd still hoped. Hoped she'd want him to stay the day, stay the weekend so they could know each other better. Everything about her fascinated him, drew him in like a moth to a flame. Her brassy attitude and stubborn streak, the way she wielded a pistol. Her dedication to the inn, he'd seen her love for it in every detail. And her laugh, he could have spent a week just holding her soft body in his arms listening to that husky chuckle.

Yes, Jace had wanted more time, but Evie couldn't get rid of him fast enough. The "connecting" they'd done the night before had been all in his head. And now he needed to get the stupid idea out and move on with his life.

He'd just reclined, ready to start another set, but his comm unit trilled. Reg's went off a second later. Reaching into his pocket, Jace withdrew the small device and keyed in his code.

"I have a job for you," Miranda Bane said. "Meet me in the conference room in ten."

"Will do." Tucking his comm away, Jace stood and looked to Reg, who had the same conversation.

"Must be some job if they need both of us," Reg said. "Wealthy Widows Gone Wild?"

Jace shrugged. "Only one way to find out."

After a quick sonic shower, he sat at the conference table with Reg and two other pleasure companions. Miranda breezed into the room, her gaze flitting across them impassively.

"Gentlemen, thank you for coming. I don't have to tell you that time is money, so I'll get right to the point." Placing a small 3-D imager on the table, she depressed the button and a hologram of a sleek blond woman sprung to life. She strode to the end of the table, paused, smoldered, then strode back to the projection box, braless tits wiggling beneath a flimsy top. "I trust you know who this is?"

Reg let out a low whistle. "Whoa, don't tell me we'll be servicing Constance."

"Constance?" Jace frowned. He'd never heard her name before, but he'd seen her all over holographic billboards in Times Square.

"She's marrying David Abernathy Junior next Saturday, so, no, you won't be servicing her. She and her intended have signed a one-on-one pact. However, Maude Abernathy has arranged a special trip, a weeklong solar system cruise leading up to the main event. You've been hired, gentlemen, to entertain the single ladies in the bridal party on board the *Trist*."

Jace blinked, utterly stunned. The Abernathys owned a line of freight cruisers that dealt with interstellar trade, as well as a fleet of luxury cruise space ships. A trip for two aboard one was a costly venture, one most people would save their entire lives to afford. Buying out the ship for a wedding party and adding four pleasure companions to the mix was unfathomable. No one else would have been able to afford such decadence.

"A bachelorette party in outer space?"

Miranda's eyes were bright with avarice. "Yes, the four of you have been selected because you have the highest satisfaction ratings. In essence, you're the best of the best. And for the kind of exposure this event will bring, I want to ensure that the pre-wedding cruise goes off without a hitch."

She rattled on for a few minutes about specifics before she said, "Due to the importance of this event, I'm granting you the rest of this week off to prepare for the trip. Your standing appointments have been reassigned to other pleasure companions. Rest, workout, take care of whatever personal business you have to, but be at the space port by eleven hundred hours Friday morning for wheels up."

His mind still reeling, Jace was about to follow Reg from the conference room when Miranda called out, "Jace, a moment, please."

Jace returned to his seat and looked up at her. Miranda had once been a pleasure companion too; actually, one of his trainers. A few years ago she'd been promoted out of the field into special projects management.

"Jace, it's essential that we pull this off flawlessly. Rumors are flying about the missing board members bailing on the company and lots of bad press to contend with. We need positive PR. You're going to be my eyes and ears up there. Make sure everyone is safe and happy. You manage this and we're both looking at big, fat promotions." Her green cat eyes glimmered.

Jace's heart leapt. To be given the chance was impressive enough, but the promise of a promotion at the end of it? "Could I be a full-time trainer?" Though it wasn't the most glamorous aspect, trainers were vital to Illustra's corporate structure, and the nature of the job would give him freedom at nights, to date, the way Reg did. To find the right woman.

He refused to think about Evie.

"Honey, you make this happen, you can run the whole training department." Miranda crossed her long legs and smiled to assure him.

Jace nodded and grinned. "If you need me, I'll be down at R&D. There's a special project, and I want to see if it's ready for the field yet."

Miranda nodded and winked. "Go get 'em, tiger."

"So, what's the big surprise?" Evie asked as a hovercab whisked them away from the airport.

Constance squeezed her hand. "You'll see soon enough."

She studied her daughter from head to toe. "You look beautiful, baby girl," Evie murmured.

Constance was always a vision, but her excitement made her effervescent. Evie loved that her daughter kept an air of innocence instead of adopting the unaffected air so common among city dwellers.

Like the one Jace had when she'd first picked him up.

Stop thinking about him! she told herself firmly. But she couldn't help herself. At first she'd believed it was the inn that was superimposing him into her thoughts. The scent of him on her sheets the night after he'd left, or the damp towel he'd left on the back of the door. She couldn't even look at her favorite chaise or the kitchen counter without recalling the feel of his hands and mouth on her body, building her arousal, stoking her fire until she burned hot.

She'd refunded his credits. He hadn't taken up a room because he'd slept in hers, and after the things they'd done she didn't feel right taking his money. She'd used the excuse to get his address from the Credit Service Bureau, an address that was only three blocks from her daughter's apartment. As soon as Constance was otherwise occupied, Evie had every intention of going to his house.

From there, her plan grew hazy. What if he was married or in a committed relationship? But as the week progressed and she thought about Jace, that idea seemed more like her own irrational fears than actual possibilities. She didn't know him well, but she doubted Jace could have made love to her so openly if he was cheating on someone else.

More likely, he'd slam the door in her face. She'd been a coward and had no right to expect anything of him. But the chance that he might still want to be with her, that they could share more of the magic they had found made her a little reckless.

First things first, she needed to spend time with her daughter, to see if there was anything she could say or do to make

Constance reconsider. She had to tread carefully, though, because the last thing she wanted was to alienate her baby girl.

"Here we are," Constance sang out, practically vibrating with energy.

Evie looked around but didn't see a part of town she recognized. Instead, it looked similar to the airport, only these planes were vastly bigger in both length and girth. "Constance, what the heck's going on?"

"We're going on a space cruise!" Constance squealed, then clapped a hand over her mouth. "Oh, Momma, I know how much you've wanted to see the stars up close. Isn't this just fabulous?"

"Fantastic," Evie muttered faintly. There would be no trip to see Jace, no second chance.

Constance's face fell. "What's wrong? I thought you'd love it."

Evie cleared her throat and plastered a bright smile on her face. "I do love it. I'm just surprised is all. And how can you do this, take time off right before the wedding?" Hope bloomed that maybe Constance had decided to call it off.

"That's the best part, the entire wedding party is coming with us! We're going to be married on board tomorrow night!"

Crap. Crap, crap, crappy crap, crap. So, no Jace and the wedding was still on. Would none of the cards fall her way?

Evie followed Constance through the terminal. Their bags were pushed on an anti-grav pallet up the ramp leading to the docking tunnel. Walking through the endless snaking gateway, Evie had the unsettling sense of déjà vu, like she was being born. Or dying. Whatever waited on the other side would surely change her forever.

The tunnel finally spat them out onto a crowded deck. Unlike a regular plane, there were no rows of seats waiting for them. Instead, people milled about with glasses of champagne, talking and laughing.

Constance grinned down on her from her lofty five foot ten height. "Well, what do you think?"

"It looks like a party in full swing, not a ship about to be launched into space."

"Oh, that's my soon-to-be father-in-law's stabilizer design. The ship will be in orbit before we even know it took off. Very expensive to make, so they only use them on luxury voyages."

"Baby, there you are." David Abernathy strode forward and kissed Constance on the cheek. Evie watched him closely, this wolf in sheep's clothing. He was a handsome devil with jet-black hair slicked back like a casino pit boss out of an old Vegas-era movie and dark chocolate eyes. His angular jaw was freshly shaven, and his white teeth gleamed as his smile flashed out at her. She didn't like the proprietary glint in David's eye or the way he placed a hand around her daughter's waist, but Constance grinned at him adoringly.

"David, you remember my mother."

"Mrs. Ripley, so good of you to come." Abernathy's grin seemed genuine enough, but it didn't make Evie like him anymore.

"My daughter is about to get married. Wild horses couldn't drag me away." Evie bared her teeth in what she hoped passed for a smile.

David inclined his head. "Can I fetch you lovely ladies a drink?"

Evie didn't drink often, because she'd spent too many years dealing with the consequences of Yon's intoxication to truly enjoy herself, but Constance answered for her. "Yes, please, a glass of champagne each."

"Coming right up." David slithered off toward the bar.

"He moves like a snake," Evie muttered.

"Momma, behave," Constance implored. "This is supposed to be fun."

Crowded rooms aboard ships about to be launched into

space had never been Evie's idea of a good time, but she'd be damned if she let her introverted ignorance ruin Constance's fun. "Sorry, love, I guess I'm just a little done in."

Her daughter's face softened and she tucked a strand of hair behind Evie's ear. "You work too hard."

"Someone's gotta do it," she muttered as David returned with two champagne flutes.

"Well said." An elegantly dressed woman with ash-blond hair moved up behind David and handed him a glass.

"Mother, this is Constance's mother, Evelyn Ripley. Evelyn, may I introduce Maude Abernathy?"

Maude extended a jewel-covered hand that Evie shook automatically. The woman's hand reminded her of holding a dead trout, if someone had taken the time to bedazzle it in precious stones.

"Constance has told me so much about you. Come, let's leave the lovebirds so we can become better acquainted. I'm sure we'll be great friends."

Yeah, they were just two peas in a pod.

Evie drained her glass as Maude whisked her off on a tour of the main room. Maude seemed perfectly happy to natter on and on, and Evie swapped her empty champagne flute for a full one from a passing server.

Maude knew everyone, of course, and a sea of beautiful faces blurred together. Evie desperately wanted to escape before she made a fool out of herself and embarrassed Constance. She smiled until her face hurt and listened, laughed at the right moments, and scanned the crowd desperately for any sign of her daughter.

"Ladies and gentlemen, this is your captain speaking. I'm happy to report we have achieved orbit around the earth. We will be turning the reflectors on momentarily."

"That's it?" Evie asked Maude, who seemed to be wavering a little.

Maude nodded. "I'll bet you didn't even feel us break gravity, did you?"

The only thing Evie was feeling were the aftereffects of too much champagne on an empty stomach. She looked around for a buffet of some sort. Nothing, no food to be seen, not even nutri gel. No wonder all these people were so thin.

Maude was still going on about the stabilizers. ". . . worth their weight in platinum, I tell you. Oh, speaking of which"— she waved someone over before turning to Evie—"I hope you don't mind, but I arranged for a little company for you. You know David and Constance barely have any time together, what with her traveling, and this trip is supposed to be a sort of pre-honeymoon for them."

"So thoughtful," Evie hiccupped.

"Yes, well, in any event, I want to introduce you to one of Illustra's finest pleasure companions. He'll see to your every desire, isn't that right?"

"It'll be my pleasure," a man murmured from behind Evie.

Whirling around, she stared in absolute shock up into Jace's gray-green eyes. The champagne flute shattered where it hit the deck.

6

Jace recovered from his amazement and grabbed Evie's arm to steady her. It was clear from the high color in her cheeks and her unfocused gaze that the broken champagne flute at her feet wasn't her first of the evening.

He couldn't have her making a scene and knowing Evie, she was gearing up to give him what for. But keeping up appearances and a lid on commotion was his number one priority. Every career goal he'd set for himself was riding on this voyage, their attainment dependent on its success.

But those goals seemed very far away with his hand on Evie's warm arm, staring into her big blue eyes again. Because Maude Abernathy was standing right there, watching his every move, he brought Evie's knuckles to his lips. "Jace Donovan, Illustra pleasure companion at your service."

"Is that right?" Evie pulled her hand back. Her lips compressed in a tight line and her eyes promised fifth circle of hell type of consequences.

Just then, the lights dimmed as the captain turned on the reflectors. The once-opaque ceiling now showed a clear view of the earth from space with stars twinkling in the distance. A hush fell over the crowd at the heavenly sight so close one could almost reach up and touch it. Every head in the room tilted upward to take it all in.

Every head but his. Jace watched Evie blink in wonder at the glory of the cosmos spread out before her. Her lush lips parted as she stared for an endless moment.

His heart rate kicked up and a grin spread across his face. He'd never thought he'd see her again and now *she* was his assignment, the prickly mother of the bride Maude Abernathy had told him to keep busy for the week.

Jace smiled. The possibilities of how to do that were as endless as the vista above them.

"Allow me to show you to your room," he muttered low in Evie's ear. She shivered but didn't argue. Placing his hand at the small of her back, he guided her out of the room and down the hall to her private suite.

The reflectors lined the entire hull of the ship and Evie had been assigned a suite on the top level. Her gaze remained fixed on the ceiling as he ushered her through the door and sat her down on the chaise.

"Lie back and look your fill," he commanded, and she did. He sat on the floor next to her, watching her face as she stared up at the cosmos. If she'd been another woman, he might have started undressing her, massaging her until she was ready for a deeper touch, but he wanted to make sure Evie wasn't armed.

"I wasn't going to make a scene, you know," she said, her eyes still fixed on the view. "It's my daughter's pre-wedding event. I may have dust on my boots and hay in my hair, but I'm not as tactless as that."

"So you're not here to break up the wedding?" Maude Abernathy had told him otherwise.

Evie finally looked at him. "I think she's making a mistake."

"You daughter is a grown woman, it's hers to make."

"Like the ones I've made?" Evie looked at him pointedly.

Jace's stomach dropped. "You think sleeping with me was a mistake?"

"I think sleeping with a man I barely knew was a mistake. Pleasure companion, Jace? Why didn't you tell me?" Her lip trembled.

He reached for her hand. "I'm sorry, Evie. I would have told you, but you made it clear you didn't want to see me again."

"And for that I deserved to be kept in the dark?"

How could he make her understand? "It's just that I wanted you to see me for me, and not as some sex toy. I wanted more from you, and I've learned that most woman who know what I do for a living don't see me as relationship material."

"That's no excuse to lie to me. In fact, it's a good thing I didn't know because when I did find out, it would have been a deal breaker."

"Because of my job," he seethed.

"Because you intentionally deceived me. Because I can't trust you." Evie shook her head and withdrew her hand. "What a mess."

"It doesn't have to be." His cock was already hard, just from feeling her soft skin, inhaling her sweet scent. Moving closer, he hovered over her, letting his enhanced pheromones work their magic, helping to relax her. "We're here now, we have a second chance."

"You're on the clock," she shot back, but refused to meet his eyes. Despite her venom, he sensed the hurt lurking in the shadows.

"How can I fix this?" he asked, tucking a strand of silky dark hair behind her ear. "How do I make it right between us?"

She didn't answer right away, and his intestines knotted up as he considered that she'd say nothing he could say or do would repair the damage. Would she report him for unscrupulous conduct? Hell, was she upset enough to go on a crusade to see him fired?

Then he saw the glistening streaks of moisture tracking down her pale cheek and all of his self-centered worries were dispersed by the wave of guilt. He'd made her feel badly, he'd made her cry. "Evie . . ."

She turned away, but he moved up onto the seat next to her and pulled her into his arms, offering her comfort he had no right to give.

"Was any of it real, Jace? Did I mean anything to you?" Her voice wobbled as she fought her emotions.

Jace could barely breathe, his lungs crushed under the weight of her question. "More than you can ever know."

She pushed him back, but actually held his gaze. "Were you even attracted to me?"

God damn her ex load of a husband to the fiery depths of hell for making her believe she was somehow lacking. "Evie, you're beautiful and, yes, I'm very attracted to you." More so than he'd ever been to another woman, but he was afraid to voice it, in case she thought his eagerness to reassure her was an act.

She searched his face and he let her look, holding his breath and praying she'd see the sincerity there.

"I want you, Evie. If I had my pick of any woman on the ship, I'd still be here with you."

Her lips twitched. "Most of those women are fashion models in their twenties. I'd think they're more your speed."

Jace shook his head. "They don't have what I like. No full hips to hold on to while I'm fucking you senseless, no luscious tits to rest my head on after we're both spent. No laugh lines that tell me you know how to have fun. I want you, Evie, all of you, exactly as you are."

"What, no poetry about my cellulite?" She grinned at him

and he felt as though someone had cut the rubber band that had been compressing his lungs.

"If that's what you want. This week you're the boss of me. Whatever you want from me, I'll give you. Just tell me what it is."

Her smile faded and the band snapped back. She might yet kick him out.

"What I want from you, Jace, is the truth. Always the absolute honest to God truth. Can you give me that?"

Studying the hard set of her stubborn jaw, Jace wondered if she really knew what she was asking for. Most women needed some pretty little lies to help keep their worldview in order. They were supposed to spend a week in each other's company, in what was a stressful situation for both of them.

"Evie—"

"No, Jace, that's my rule. No more secrets, no more masks. You have to speak your mind. Be straight with me or go find someone else to spend the week with."

"I'll agree on one condition. I'm going to reimburse the Abernathys for my fees." She opened her mouth to argue, but he covered her lips with his fingertips. "Wait, hear me out."

Evie nodded.

Jace took a deep breath. "Technically, I still work for Illustra, still need to check in with the other pleasure companions on board. But everything that's going on with us will be personal, not professional. I'll agree to be entirely honest, entirely myself with you only if you are willing to give me a fair shot."

"Meaning?"

"Meaning if you enjoy yourself this week, I want you to consider dating me for real."

Evie blinked, the champagne and high-octane emotions going right to her head. That was his condition? That she would invest herself in him for longer than a week? "Um . . . ?"

Jace leaned in, brushing her lips with his. "Just keep an open mind. If this job goes smoothly, I'll be promoted out of the field. I can be exclusive if I want to be. That's important to you, isn't it?"

It was, but he was going way too fast. She'd barely accepted the fact that he was here, never mind that he was a pleasure companion, a man who had sex for a living. Sure, she'd joked about hooking up with a manwhore with her friends, but finding out that she already had, albeit an off-duty one, unsettled her. Would she have slept with Jace if she'd known he was a professional? Evie made it a habit to never lie to herself, and deep down she knew she didn't want to be a nameless number on some man's to-do list.

Yet, the deed was done and she couldn't regret it. Jace had brought her to heights of ecstasy she hadn't imagined. He hadn't been far from her thoughts for a week. The man was beyond skilled at his job. She couldn't help but wonder if he was so dedicated to all the women he serviced.

That thought left her cold. Jace had gone back to work last week. How many women had he fulfilled in the five days since he left her alone at her inn? The thought of him touching another woman the way he'd touched her made her slightly ill.

Of course, it was her fault for sending him off without a promise of anything more. She'd been too scared to take a chance on him, so she leveled their playing field to *wham, bam, thank you, ma'am.* Would he have told her how he made his living if she'd agreed to see him again?

Call her old-fashioned, but Evie liked to be exclusive when she got naked with a man. Having him as a one-night stand was one thing, but being in a committed relationship with a man who slept with other women for a living, she just wasn't that evolved. As a certified pleasure companion, Jace could never give her exclusivity. If she'd thought there'd been obstacles in their path before, it was nothing compared with the hordes of young, fit, and wealthy women who could commandeer him from her with the flick of a credit transfer.

Even if he was "promoted out of the field," there would be a countless history of other women for her to compete with, and she seriously doubted he could go from all that to just her so easily. And now he was telling her that at the end of the week he wanted to be a permanent fixture in her life. . . .

Too much, too soon.

"Stop thinking." Jace scooped her up off the chaise and deposited her on the bed. He stretched out on top of her, pinning her with his weight. His thighs bracketed hers, his groin nestled against her sex and his chest pressed into her breasts. If they'd been naked, he'd already be inside her.

"You can't just order me to do that," she muttered, but with him hovering right above her, rubbing against her with such delicious friction, the words held no conviction.

His spicy scent cocooned her, a drugging scent that made her lids heavy.

"How about a bath and a massage?" He nuzzled her ear as he whispered the words with seductive promise. "Something to help you relax."

She shouldn't even consider it. For all she knew he was just doing his job, telling her what she wanted to hear and looking for ways to keep her in the room, away from Constance. She didn't trust him, but her body didn't care as it tingled with his every caress. Her shoulders were knotted from tension, and the thoughts of his hands on her made her flash hot, then cold.

Threading his fingers through hers, Jace lowered his mouth and his weight until he covered her. He wasn't too heavy or too light, his body the Goldilocks X-rated equivalent of just right on top of hers. Lips stroked and coaxed hers open until his tongue could sweep into her mouth. Again, he instinctively knew how deep she wanted the kiss, when to pull away leaving her wanting more.

It's not instinct, it's practice—years and years of practice with countless women.

Evie stiffened and Jace rolled off of her. "It's okay," he told her. "I thought it was going too well. Let me draw you that bath."

"You don't need to wait on me." Evie wasn't used to other people doing things for her.

Cupping her cheek, he turned her face toward his until he could look into her eyes. His gray-green ones brimmed with emotion, and when he spoke his voice was filled with longing. "I *want* to do things for you."

What could she say to that?

"Just lie here and look up at the stars." With lithe grace, Jace rolled off the bed and disappeared into the bathroom.

Evie sat up. She could leave, just run right out the door, find Constance and talk some sense into her before the ceremony tomorrow. Of course, it's not like they could open the door and go home. A seven-day space cruise loomed before them. And the thought of just running out and never seeing Jace again left her feeling hollow.

Before she'd held a small, irrational part of herself back, the hopeful idealist who Yon hadn't managed to crush under the weight of his lazy carcass. The part that Jace had tended, the part that wanted to try again, to hell with the risks to her already damaged heart . . .

Flopping back on the bed, she stared at the spacescape. That part was stunted if it thought Jace the manwhore was the answer to its yearning. Let him do his worst, she'd take it like the full-grown woman she was. Why not allow herself to experience all a physical relationship had to offer before the ship docked?

Evie smiled. She may not have the flat stomach or toned thighs of some of the other passengers, but she had experience on her side. Years of imagination, fertile and ready to be utilized. Jace wouldn't know what hit him. The name of the game was catch and release, and she knew exactly what she wanted from Jace before she threw him back.

7

Jace took his time setting the stage for seduction in the massive bathroom. The tub alone was bigger than his living room at home, plenty of room for two people to get frisky. He wished he had some of those relaxation candles Illustra used to supply, but they'd been recalled a few months back, so he had to make due with plain white pillar candles to set the mood.

Anticipation built as the tub filled and he added honeysuckle-scented oil he'd picked up yesterday because it reminded him of Evie. Though he'd been prepared to handle whatever woman—or women—the Abernathys required, having Evie to himself for a week was too good to be true.

His cock pushed against his fly as he imagined all the things he could do to her in the tub. He'd already made up his mind that they wouldn't have sex tonight. She was adjusting well, better than he would have expected, and he wanted to give her more time to truly accept who and what he was. Keeping his hands to himself, though, was not an option. Evie was in store for the week of her life because Jace wanted to have it all, the promotion and the woman waiting for him. He was so close to success he could almost taste it.

Better not get ahead of himself. He had a lot of convincing to do to turn Evie around to his way of thinking. A sensual massage ending in a few full-body orgasms would definitely help his case. Then later, after he'd dried her off, he'd enjoy licking her slowly, getting her all wet all over again. . . .

Yanking his shirt up over his head, he discarded it on the floor. He'd just unfastened his pants when his comm unit chirped. Jace closed his eyes, wanting desperately to ignore it. He was randy as hell, unused to a week of celibacy, and though he'd planned to delay intercourse, he knew just touching and kissing Evie would get him off.

But he was the manwhore in charge and if something was hinky with the Illustra staff, he was the one they'd call.

"What's up?" Jace slapped a pleasant expression on his face. It turned into a genuine grin when he saw Reg dressed in what amounted to clumps of gold glitter, artfully arranged over his junk. "Dude, did you lose a bet?"

"Laugh all you want, my man, but your costume is just as bad as mine."

Jace felt his eyebrows draw together. "Costume?"

"For the bachelorette party? It starts in half an hour, where the frack are you, anyway?"

"With a client." Jace panned the comm around the room so Reg could see the careful scene of seduction he'd staged before looking back into the unit. "As you can see—"

"No can do, Jace. They need all of us for the party. It is our main event after all."

Standing around wearing nothing but glitter to be ogled and fondled was Jace's idea of hell. He was too restless to enjoy the admiration when he hadn't done anything to deserve it. And group events were *so* not his scene. Never mind that he had the unexpected gift of Evie in the bedroom waiting for the promised massage, and the last thing he wanted was to run out on her to be turned into living art.

But it was in the contract, and he did agree to supervise the other pleasure companions. "I'm on special assignment, okay, so no quickies in darkened alcoves, no live demonstrations. My services are completely booked up for the rest of the cruise." It was easier than explaining he was refunding the money for his portion of the gig. He trusted Reg, but it wouldn't be right to tell him that via unsecured comm when he still needed to make Mrs. Abernathy aware of his change of status.

Reg whistled. "Damn, someone has some serious bank. That red-haired bridesmaid is gonna be disappointed. I saw her checking you out during takeoff."

"I'm sure you'll run interference for me. See you in five." Blowing out a sigh, Jace shut off the water and started extinguishing candles.

"You're leaving?" Evie asked from the doorway. Her expressive blue eyes revealed her disappointment.

"It's a mandatory thing. If I don't, I could lose my job." He glanced at the full tub and his voice dropped an octave. "Why don't you stay here, have a bath? I'll be back as soon as I can. If I can't spend the night touching you in the bath, I can at least picture you naked in it, waiting for me."

Evie licked her full pink lips and his already rock-hard erection turned to steel. "I'm here to spend time with my daughter. If you're not around, that's where I'll be."

Then, to his utter shock, she pulled her shirt over her head. "I'll just shower and I'll see you at the party." She unfastened her bra, a sturdy white utilitarian thing that looked like armor, and the bounty of her breasts was set free.

"You're going to the bachelorette party?" Jace blinked, doubly stunned by the sight of her lush tits with tight-tipped nipples just begging to be sucked and by her statement.

"Why not? It's where everyone else will be, right? Besides, I'm starving and I assume there will be food there." Her skirt and panties slithered to the floor and she walked past him to the sonic shower stall. "The tub will keep, right?"

"Uh . . ." Jace admired her silhouette, not assimilating the question.

"Better get going," Evie called out. Then the sound waves buffeting her body clean hummed to life.

What had just happened? Shy, body-conscious Evie had blown him off and was planning to attend her daughter's bachelorette party? Try as he might, he couldn't imagine her lost in drunken revelry playing obscene sexually inspired games and feeling up the manwhores. The thought of Evie's soft hands on Reg or one of the others made him clench his fists until his knuckles turned white.

With a start, he recognized the feeling for what it was—jealousy. He didn't want to share her with the rest of the Abernathy party, except for her daughter. And he really didn't want her to see him dressed as though someone had vomited glitter over him. Jace could have easily spent the rest of the night watching her, enjoying the way she moved, exploring the bountiful landscape of her body. Unfortunately, he had a job to do.

He'd never hated it more.

Holy Caligula, Batman! Evie did her ancient cultures courses proud by occasionally using them to curse. And if there had ever been a time for cussing, her daughter's bachelorette party was it.

The event was being staged on one of the holographic ballrooms on board, and instead of being surrounded by the universe, the inner sanctum had been transformed into a hedonistic paradise. It was twilight in this make-believe world, the perfect amount of light for human eyes to see. Gold, orange, and pink painted the sky, and a crescent moon hung above like a sentry guarding the hedonistic revelry below. A sparkling red-purple waterfall ran from some unseen point above to fall dozens of meters down and end in a pool. Blankets were spread out around the pool, and the people lounging on them were in various states of undress. Evie realized she'd made another fashion blunder by donning the sparkling red cocktail dress Constance had given her for her birthday. Well, she could unhook the halter string around her neck and let her breasts spill out to fit right in, but she didn't want to frighten all the little girls with the horrors of the aging process.

Then again, if the drunken laughter was any indication, they might not even notice.

Strictly speaking, this was a female-only event, but here and there she saw a man. A few of them danced in front of the blankets, lit by firelight moving in sensual rhythm that told carnal tales. Feminine hands reached for them, slithered across taut muscular flesh with animal caresses. She saw one, dressed in golden netting over his rich chocolate skin like some sort of sea god, bow down and kiss a hand that had been working its way beneath the glittering gold around his shaft.

He glanced up, met Evie's eyes, and winked before dancing away.

Was he another pleasure companion? Or some sort of highbrow exotic dancer? There wasn't much for him to strip off, that was for sure, though Evie's mouth kicked up at the prospect of seeing if the rest of him could possibly be as impressive as what was already displayed.

Though she'd promised herself she wouldn't scan the crowd looking for Jace, her gaze landed on him almost immediately. Good Lord, he even outshone the sea god. His light brown hair looked tussled, as though a lover had just run her fingers through it. His thick, ropey muscles had been coated with some sort of oil, highlighting the definition on his abs, pecs, deltoids, biceps, glutes, and all the others she couldn't recall the names of but wanted to spend the night running her tongue over.

Red and orange flames were his only concession to modesty, the glittery fabric pulled taut over his sex and his ass. Undoubtedly the women close up could see the outline of his shaft through the sheer material.

He didn't dance, but instead moved from group to group, flashing his magnificent smile as women offered up their unfettered breasts to him. Some even spread their legs and fingered their cunts, showing him what he did to them. Jace gave each one a slow perusal and a wicked grin, but he didn't stop to dally. The women, most of whom were young and beautiful and unused to hearing the word no, grew bolder with their offerings, kissing their friends, masturbating openly, but he continued on, making himself seen but not offering his services. Other men moved toward the women he'd scorned, not nearly as magnificent as Jace but obviously much more interested.

In all of her fantasies about his real life, never could she have imagined this. Had she ever been so young, so sexually uninhibited?

No, she'd spent too much time running an inn and being all the things Constance had needed her to be. Mom and provider first, fully sexualized woman never. How depressing.

A waiter moved to her side. He smiled at her and she heard the faint whirring of gears when he raised the tray. Android servers. "Would the lady care for a drink?"

"The lady would care for a vat." She'd taken her time dressing and was clearly well behind the average guest. Draining her glass, she plopped it back on his tray and took another. His polite smile remained frozen. "Do you know where the bride to be is?"

"Up there." He gestured toward the rock where the waterfall was spilling over.

"Is she clothed?" Evie didn't know if she should seek her daughter out or avoid her so she didn't see Constance living it up. Still, Evie was on a mission and potentially catching her daughter *in flagrante delecto* with a pleasure companion—or worse, her fiancé—was worth the risk.

"As I cannot see her from this particular vantage, I do not know. Should I check for you?" the android offered cheerily.

"Thank you, no, I'll go see for myself." Evie drained her second glass and then took a third for company. She'd just lost her champagne buzz from earlier and was downing the sparkling red wine, hoping to bring it back. A little inebriation would ease the reality of Jace being a manwhore and Constance throwing her life away. "This is good, what vintage is it?"

"It's a unique vintage made just for Constance by Abernathy vineyards. Plenty more if you like from Constance Falls." The waiter gestured to where some of the other androids were filling glasses from the water—er, *wine*fall.

"Of course it is," Evie murmured. Really? He made a wine just for her, enough to produce a waterfall? No wonder Constance was head over heels, he kept her inebriated with her own vintage. The sheer decadence stunned her.

All of the beautiful people frolicked merrily. A few health guards had come up. The sea god stared at her as not one, but two women took turns licking and sucking on his exposed shaft. She'd been right; it was just as glorious as the rest of him. He crooked a finger at Evie, calling her forth, but Evie turned away.

All this was so much more than Evie could ever give her. She laughed hollowly. Never in a million years would she even think to give her daughter a life like this. Her most debauched fantasies seemed tame in comparison.

Maybe she should just stay out of it. Just because she'd had a lousy marriage didn't mean her daughter would have the same fate.

"Allow me to escort you." A hand fell on the small of her back even as Jace's warm breath stirred the hair at her nape.

Evie looked up at him, suddenly overjoyed that he was here with her. Alone, friendless, and completely out of her element and he'd ridden to her rescue. Moral support meant the world to Evie. She had only a few people in her life who'd ever offered it to her, and in less than a week Jace had become one of them. She wanted to kiss him for seeking her out when he had so many other lovely offerings to choose from.

"I'm still not sure I want to see what's going on up there. She's my daughter after all."

"I'll stay with you until you're ready," he said. The high-handedness of his statement should have bugged her, but she loved that he didn't ask, just told her this was how it's going to be. Maybe that made her weak, but in that moment she didn't trust herself to make the right call.

"So is this a typical Friday night for you?" she asked with a nod at the people along the side of the river.

"No," he said, and her heart leapt for a moment, wondering if he felt as awkward and out of sorts as she did. Then it plummeted as he continued, pointing to the sea god, clearly in the throes of release. "Usually at an event like this I'm right there next to him."

8

Now why the hell did he say that? Jace could have kicked himself for blurting out the truth. Evie was already squirrelly, clearly overwhelmed by the party and worries about her daughter. Jace was supposed to be selling her on taking a chance with him this week, and so far he was doing a piss-poor job of it.

"Do you like it? Your job, I mean." Evie turned to look up at him.

What an odd question. He shrugged, hiding the unease her soft query stirred in him. "What's not to like?"

"Answering a question with a question, very telling." Evie drained her glass and started walking, and he adjusted his stride to match hers. "Every job—regardless of the perks—has something not to like. Me, for instance. I love what I do, running my inn. It's hard work, often lonely. There was a day last winter after it snowed. Everything was soft and quiet and I just wanted to sit in front of the fire and read a trashy novel on my comm. But then the driveway wouldn't get plowed, the steps wouldn't be shoveled, the soup wouldn't be ready for lunch.

Tech helps me manage to scrape by where in the past running the place was at least a five-person job, but doing it on my own is exhausting."

"I'm sure it is," Jace murmured softly. "My job isn't so labor intensive, though."

"No, but I bet it's draining all the same. Why else would you want to be promoted out of the field?"

Her intelligence and insight caught him off guard. Evie might not be a social butterfly, but she read people the same way he did. "It's about advancement, acknowledgment for all my hard work. Respect."

She shook her head and dark hair spilled over her bare shoulders. "There's got to be more to it. I'm sure on occasion you've been assigned to someone you don't really like all that much. You have to hide your true feelings."

"I'm not allowed to have *any* feelings," Jace corrected her. Gripping her shoulders, he turned her to face the suck-off contest. Three of the android waiters stood at parade rest, their pants and vests folded neatly behind them. The silicone shafts between their legs were hollow, and the artificial sacs below had been filled with wine from the falls. Three bridesmaids knelt before them, slurping greedily like the cocks were massive straws, trying to pull the liquid up into their mouths. The woman who emptied the scrotum first won.

He gave Evie a moment to take it all in. "Look at the androids' faces. See the distant, vacant expressions? That's what I have to be when I work. A blank slate, ready to fuck or be fucked at a moment's notice, to act happy about it."

The amount of venom coating his words surprised even him and left a bitter tang on his tongue.

Evie took his hand in hers. His health guard had been up since he stepped into the room, so he couldn't feel the true texture of her hand as she twined her fingers with his. The gesture touched him deeply. Such an innocent display of affection amidst the hedonistic glory surrounding them. When was the last time he'd held hands with a woman just for the pure joy of it?

It wasn't all innocent, though. He wanted her so badly he ached from unspent lust. In a few more hours he'd be free to love her endlessly, to explore her body to his heart's content, to make her come for days with her blue eyes staring up into his with the same comfort, same deep desire he spied there now.

He'd never grow tired of looking into them, of seeing her.

"Evie," he started, then didn't know how to continue.

She licked her lips and he wanted to kiss her, to claim her in front of the entire wedding party so there could be no doubt that she was his and he was hers.

"Hey there, lover." It was the drunken redhead, the model who had arranged this event.

Jace barely stifled a wince. He'd been dodging her all night. Frantically, he scanned the crowd, looking around for Reg to foist her off, but his wingman had disappeared.

Evie released his hand and stepped back. "I'm being selfish, keeping you by my side. You should get back to work." Without waiting for him to reply, she turned toward the stone steps and strode uphill.

"Been looking for you." The redhead plastered herself to his back, one hand snaking over his hips and heading south. She must have won a suck-off competition because her hands were coated in wine and grass, and her words slurred impressively as she whispered that he was next on her menu.

Jace gripped her wrists, but that didn't keep her from pressing her artificially inflated breasts against his back. Damn, she was determined. He'd sent two other pleasure companions to see to her, but she kept coming back to him like a boomerang.

"Come on, baby. You don't want me to report that you're playing hard to get."

Her threat made him narrow his eyes. The customer may always be right, but she was the type to hold a grudge, to complain if she didn't get her way—spoiled, selfish cow. He had to diffuse this situation before it got out of hand.

"I told you, I'm already contracted for the duration of the trip."

"By whom?"

"Evie," he called out a little bit desperately.

She turned back to him.

Help. He mouthed the word, begged her with his eyes. He might have to stay here in his ridiculous getup, but if Evie announced her prior claim on his body, the redhead would have to look elsewhere to satisfy her needs.

Evie rolled her eyes but made her way back down the steps.

"By her." Jace pointed to Evie.

The redhead peeked over his shoulder and snorted in derision. "Grandma Fatass, huh? Poor baby, I doubt she'd know what to do with you."

Jace's fist clenched. He'd never thought about hitting a woman before, but he wanted to strike the heifer down for insulting his woman.

Evie didn't bat an eyelash, though, and when she spoke, her Southern accent came out extra thick. "Age before beauty, sugar booger. Scurry on back to the party before your bedtime."

"Bitch," the redhead spat.

"Really?" Evie raised an eyebrow. Jace hoped she wasn't wearing a laser pistol in her garter, because the expression on her face told him she considered annihilating the other woman. No great loss, but he didn't want to see her arrested at her daughter's bachelorette party. "That's the best you can do?"

"At least I don't have to pay men to fuck me." The bridesmaid slurred as if she hadn't been attempting to hire him to do exactly that.

"Honey, that's nothing to be proud of. Most men would

fuck anything in a skirt, fat ass or not. This one at least is smart enough to get paid for it. And my credits are just as spendable as yours. Go find someone else to play with before I spank your spoiled ass."

The other woman backed up. Jace braced himself in case she made a grab for Evie. Job or not, he wouldn't stand by with his thumb up his butt while his woman was attacked. But Red cast them each a heated glare and sashayed off to make trouble elsewhere.

"Skippy," Evie muttered and looked at him. "Better stick close. You're like a juicy T-bone tossed in the tiger's cage. We'd be morons to think that they wouldn't try and eat you."

"Thanks for rescuing me." Crooking her in with his elbow, he dropped a kiss on the top of her head. "My hero."

Jace's job was a total suckfest, at least in Evie's opinion. She had to ward off two more drunken advances before she spied Constance sitting on what appeared to be a crystal throne shaped like a giant cock and balls, sipping from a wineglass the size of a fishbowl. Thankfully her daughter wore a slinky dress, covering all of her privates.

"Hey there, baby girl," she called out, waving the hand that wasn't entwined with Jace's. Keeping in physical contact with him had her palm sweating. Or maybe the alcohol was catching up with her.

"Mama! So glad you made it!" Constance hopped up and pushed past the flock of bridal attendants who constantly surrounded her.

Evie released Jace and embraced her child. Though she'd seen her only a few hours earlier, Constance appeared even lovelier. Definitely more drunk.

"Isn't this a great party?" Constance beamed with the jubilance only the truly inebriated could manage. Her daughter's vague gaze snagged on Jace and she smiled up at him. "Hello, handsome."

Jace smiled back politely, though she saw the panic in his gaze. Oh hell, would she have to beat her own flesh and blood off him too?

In a distant part of her mind, the thought formed that if Constance hooked up with Jace, David Abernathy might call a halt to the wedding ceremony. Evie felt ill as she imagined Jace touching her daughter the way he'd touched her. Nope, not a possibility.

Threading one of her arms through his, she smiled up at him as she addressed her daughter. "Constance, meet Jace. He's with me."

Constance blinked a few times. "Really?"

Evie huffed out a breath. "You don't have to sound so darn incredulous."

"But isn't he a manwh—" Constance blushed as she realized what she almost rudely blurted out.

Ever the charmer, Jace took Evie's daughter's hand in his, glossing over the awkwardness. "Miss Ripley, best wishes on your engagement. Illustra wishes you and Mr. Abernathy worlds of joy."

Constance's blush grew deeper and she turned back to Evie. "Can I speak with you in private for a second?"

Evie noticed the bridal party, a murder of whipcord-lean crows eyeing Jace's oiled magnificence like fresh roadkill. "If I leave his side, there'll be nothing left of him but a smear on the ground."

"What you do for my ego." Raising Evie's hands to his lips, he kissed her knuckles, a curious old-world gesture that should have looked ridiculous in his flaming outfit, but he still pulled off with machismo. "Go talk with her, I'll endeavor to survive without you."

Her heart did a ridiculous little somersault at his statement. She couldn't wait to get him alone and shred that sheer fabric before dragging him into that bed with her. Standing on her tiptoes, she whispered, "Give me five minutes; then you and I are getting the hell out of here."

"Your wish is my command." Rubbing his stubbled cheek lightly against hers, he nuzzled her before letting Constance drag her off behind the cock throne.

"Oh, my God, Mama! Oh, my freaking God! You're paying a manwhore to sleep with you? Does Daddy know about this?" Constance's eyes were huge in her face.

Evie's pride had taken one hit too many tonight, and her daughter's disbelief was the final straw. "You know, this is just great. For months you've been telling me I should meet someone and when I finally do—"

"Someone, like an orthopedic surgeon or a plumber. Not a pleasure companion you pay! Honestly, Mom, aren't you too old for that kind of thing."

Evie blinked, stunned. "Too *old*? I'm forty-two! What do you think, my ovaries shriveled up like raisins and I have dust in my vag?"

Constance winced. "God, Mom. Don't be gross. It's just that you never go on dates or talked about wanting a man. I mean he's hot and everything, but why not meet someone your own age that you have stuff in common with that will take you out to dinner and not charge you?"

"He's not charging me," Evie said through clenched teeth.

Constance actually snorted. "Yeah, right, your boy toy is just so caught up in you that he's ignoring a roomful of models for you. Good one. Is this to get back at me because you don't want me to get married?"

Evie's jaw hung slack. She'd brought this child into this universe and part of her considered taking her right back out of it.

With effort, she gathered her composure. "Jace has nothing to do with the mistake you're making."

Constance's hands shot to her hips. "Getting married is *not* a mistake. You're just bitter because of what went on with you and Daddy, and now you're making a fool out of yourself with a man half your age. You look ridiculous."

Fighting tears, Evie squared her shoulders. "Maybe I do, but being with him makes me happy. I could never say the same about your father, the load I hauled around for *nineteen* years. I hope to God you never feel the way he made me feel."

Spinning on her heel, Evie stormed off. She forgot about Jace, about the fact that she was on board a space cruiser, and just rushed blindly away from Constance and the hurtful accusations her baby girl had flung in her face.

She'd been drinking, they all had, and the scene was a byproduct of too much booze and too little sense. Yet, her chest ached as though someone had put her heart through a fan and painted the wall with it. Bitter and pathetic, that's how her daughter saw her? No word of thanks for all she'd done.

Constance was just as shallow and vapid as the rest of them.

"Wait, Evie!" Footsteps thundered down the corridor behind her. Jace gripped her arm and pulled her into an alcove. He took one look at her face and pulled her into his arms. "What happened?"

Evie leaned into his warmth. "I failed. My daughter's completely narcissistic and selfish, just like her father." She sank her nails into his back, needing someone to cling to as her world lost its focus. Jace didn't protest, just held her tighter. Distantly, she took note that he'd deactivated his health guard, that he was holding her skin to skin.

"I can't stay here." Her whole body shook as a turbulent storm of emotion and defeat whirled inside her. Looking up into his gray-green eyes, she let her tears spill over. "I need to get off this ship, Jace."

9

―――――――――

"Off this ship, babe, what are you talking about?" Jace rubbed Evie's back as her shoulders shook. "Your daughter is getting married tomorrow."

Evie shook her head. "I know, and she belongs in this world, with David Abernathy. She's not mine anymore. I barely recognize her."

Jace stroked his knuckles over her cheek. "If you miss your only daughter's wedding, you will never forgive yourself."

Pushing him away, Evie strode to the nearest stairwell. "It's better if I go now. Constance won't want me there because I can't be happy for her."

He caught up to her easily, matching her stride with his own. "Why can't you?"

Evie shook her head and didn't say anything more, her shoulders squared in grim resolve.

The door hissed open to her suite, their suite since his bags had been delivered here earlier. Opening a drawer, she started heaving clothes inside her suitcase. Damn it all to hell, she couldn't leave. He had plans for her, for them. Letting her go a second time wasn't an option. "Babe, please listen to me—"

"You can come with me." She paused in her packing and glanced up at him with a hopeful light in her eyes.

Jace forgot his argument. "You'd want that? To be with me tomorrow, instead of your daughter on her wedding day?"

"I can't have everything I want. One out of two isn't so bad." She smiled at him, and his heart stumbled in his chest.

Sinking down onto the bed, he considered his options. Tell Evie that his job might depend on her staying? No, she had enough pressure and adding the extra weight of that wasn't fair. He could go with her, take her up on her offer and just enjoy the hell out of her for the rest of the week. But he'd be just as unemployed when Miranda discovered he'd absconded with the mother of the bride.

Even if she was the one who wanted to abscond with him.

"Give me twelve hours." Jace rose and strode to Evie. "Twelve hours to change your mind. If you still want to leave in the morning, I'll go with you."

She made an exasperated noise and tossed the sling-back heels she held into her open suitcase. "What difference will twelve hours make?"

"I ask you the same. I need to check in with the Illustra employees after the party wraps up. Most likely they will be booked through the rest of the cruise, but I need to check in, make sure there aren't any problems. Come on, Evie, it'll probably take that long to arrange transportation off this boat anyhow."

She stared at him for an endless moment and he held his breath, hoping.

"Fine."

Jace grinned and grabbed his duffel bag from where it had been dropped earlier. "Thank you, love. You won't regret this.

Give me five minutes to wash this shit off of me and get dressed."

Her eyebrows drew together and she cocked her head as though she hadn't heard him right. "Get dressed?"

Jace ignored the stab of hurt at her assumption that anything they did together would involve naked time. Screwing his way up the corporate ladder had seemed like an ideal way to make a living ten years ago, but when he realized just how disposable he was to a woman like Evie—smart, successful, independent— it made him want to reassess his choices.

He wanted her to look on him as a man who could fulfill all her desires, both in and out of the bedroom. She was starting to lean on him a little; she'd talked to him about the problems with her daughter, like he was her confidant. Jace loved the way she'd turned to him for comfort, and he wasn't about to undo these fragile bonds of deeper connection by bringing her right back to bed.

Time enough for that later.

"Yup, I'm taking you out."

"Should I change?" She waved a hand across the luscious red halter dress that had drawn him to her like a bee to a flower, eager for a sip of her nectar.

"No," he murmured hoarsely. "You look perfect, just like that."

Jace took the universe's fastest shower, until all the muscle-enhancing oil was cleansed from his body. Yanking on jeans and a white button-front shirt, he didn't bother to shave, just tugged on socks and shoes.

Grabbing Evie's hand, he pulled her out the door and down the corridor at a hurried pace. "Keep up, slow poke."

She smacked his shoulder playfully. "I'm wearing heels. You try running in them. What's the rush?"

Jace didn't know where the sense of urgency came from, but he let it dictate his actions. Keeping Evie busy so she didn't fume about the run-in with Constance seemed like a stellar idea to him. "I want to show you this really cool place I found when I first came on board."

"Is it closing or something?" Evie gasped.

He stopped and she crashed into his back. "You okay?"

She grinned up at him. "You're like a little kid on Christmas morning, what could possibly be so . . ." Her words died off when she saw where they were. "Is that a sonic rink?"

Jace stepped through the open glass doors. "Ever been skating?"

"Years ago, a place in Charlotte, when Constance was about twelve. I took her to a birthday party there. It was nothing like this."

The sonic rink on board the luxury liner was impressive. The reflectors above showed the galaxy beyond the ship's hull, and the black soundboard flooring gleamed. Even the padded acoustic walls were black, casting the illusion of endless space.

"I know the one you're talking about. Gray-flecked sonic floor and red acoustic mats, right?"

Evie's eyes widened, but then she smiled. "I keep forgetting you grew up in that area. You're so polished, every cell screams big city."

Jace ignored that and eyed her feet. "Eight and a half, right?"

She shook her head. "Oh, no way, Jace. Do you want to see me fall on my ass? Because that is exactly what will happen, I guarantee it."

Sweeping his thumb over her cheekbone, he caught her gaze, held it. "I won't let you fall. Trust me?"

"I . . ." Evie swallowed and then let out a breath. He could see she really didn't want to do this but was willing to give it, and him, a shot. "Size eight, wide width if they have it."

Jace swiped his credit badge for the skates and an hour of rink time. He selected black skates for himself and bright red ones to match her dress. Striding to the bench beside the rink, he engaged the sound barrier that would keep the music from bothering anyone nearby.

He laced up his skates in a hurry, then waited patiently while Evie belabored the chore. When she couldn't stall any longer, she met his gaze. "Promise not to laugh at me."

"Never. I'll only laugh with you, love." Jace proffered his hand, shifted his weight back, and pulled Evie into his arms.

The skates on her feet warbled as they got used to her jerky movements. His remained silent, one of the bonuses of the black skates. It had taken him years of practice to move soundlessly on them, aware of how every shift of his weight would impact his tune.

Wrapping his arms around Evie's waist, he held her firmly against him so she was essentially along for the ride. With his gaze focused ahead and his heart pounding with exhilaration, he pushed off.

Evie stiffened in his arms, probably shocked at the speed he used, but she didn't struggle or try to get away, a move guaranteed to send them both sprawling. Behind him the rink absorbed their wake, and low bass notes erupted in the opening chords of a rock ballad. The side mats were coming at them, so Jace turned, guiding them around in an arc along the perimeter. The soft woman in his arms relaxed against him, snuggled into his body as theirs moved together producing a harmony he'd never imagined.

And couldn't fathom living without.

Jace was a magnificent skater, and even if he hadn't been, Evie still would have enjoyed the hell out of being held so securely against his body. The music from their skates was all his doing, she aped his movements, followed his lead. But it was lovely nonetheless, with the stars twinkling overhead and the seductive melody echoing around them.

Most sonic skating rinks were chock-full of children, and

the discordant noise could be almost unbearable at times. But Jace was a master, moving them along at a swift glide, cutting across to hit the right notes to keep the tune playing. Even in the dark he instinctively knew where the edge of the rink was, where he needed to slow or speed up.

Suddenly, he turned them and Evie gasped, partly from fear because now she definitely couldn't see the walls, but mostly in amazement. Red and black lines trailed all over the floor, marking their progress. The song, slow, yet sensual, echoed off the walls, filling her ears, her mind, her soul. He knew exactly what he was doing and she could be part of it as long as she trusted him.

She did trust Jace, Evie realized with a start. He'd proven himself to be a friend, ditching his job at the bachelorette party to come after her, and then bringing her here to experience this with him, to plant joy where sorrow had flourished.

His hands moved higher on her waist until his thumbs caressed the under swells of her breasts. Guiding her arms up, he urged her to wrap them around his neck, all without slowing their song.

Nuzzling her ear, he said, "In case I forgot to tell you earlier, you look like a goddess in this dress."

"Thank you." She shivered in his embrace as his hands slid down her waist and over her hips in a loving caress. The slow touch was completely in sync with the sexy melody, and at odds with the blurring speed they traveled.

His erection pressed instantly against her ass, but his movements stayed casual, completely unhurried as he explored her at his leisure. With a sigh, she tipped her head back to look at him, yielding to his mastery of her and everything in this moment completely.

The sexy masculinity and raw hunger stole her breath.

Gray-green eyes met hers and she saw it all there: his need for her that ran so much deeper than mere physical arousal. He wanted her, desired her, not just any woman. Jace could have picked up a model as his skate and play date; she'd seen a number of them fling themselves in his path. Yet Jace was here with her, had chosen her to share this moment with.

"Evie," he rasped, and turned her in his arms. The enchanting melody wavered, then faded away as they slowed to a stop. Her back hit the mat and he pinned her arms over her head. "I need you now."

"Yes," she whispered, tilting her chin up, ready to accept him. His mouth descended and he claimed her lips in a searing kiss.

Evie forgot they were in a public place, as his tongue swept past the barrier of her teeth to mate with hers. He tasted like coffee—sharp, dark, and spicy. His hands fisted in her hair, pulling it back so she arched into him. Her hands roved over his body, working the buttons of his crisp white shirt frantically, needing closer contact with his magnificent body.

Just like with the skating, she let his mouth take the lead, trusting him to show her how best to pleasure them both. He was the professional after all.

Where a few hours ago that thought would have brought her up short, now she was grateful for his expertise. Because it didn't matter how many women had come before her, he was with her now, by choice, giving her exactly what she needed.

One of his hands worked the knot at her nape free and the top fell down to her waist, exposing her breasts to the cool air and his white-hot touch. Her nipples pebbled as he worked them over, first gliding his palms across them before rolling them between his fingers. She moaned into his mouth when he pinched them hard and her panties grew damp, her sex aching for the same thorough attention.

Pulling his mouth free of hers, Jace trailed kisses across the line of her jaw before murmuring, "Do you want me to take you here, like this?"

She imagined him hoisting her up against the wall, her skates locking around his back as he thrust deeply into her wet core over and over until they both cried out in ecstasy. As appealing as the scene was, however, she had another plan in mind, something she wanted to try. "No."

Jace moved back, clearly stunned at her answer, and the notes from his skates sounded woebegone.

Keeping her gaze locked with his, Evie sank down to her knees before him and crooked a finger, calling him back to her. "I had something else in mind," she whispered in a husky drawl, licking her lips to make sure he got the message.

A grin spread over those sensual lips and he shook his head as though shaking off sleep. "Am I dreaming?" His hands flew to his fly and he unsnapped the button there, then lowered the zipper with frantic tugs.

While he worked, Evie took her time exploring his taut stomach, the tanned skin so soft over rock-hard abs. Raking her fingernails through the happy trail of coffee-colored hairs made him hiss out a breath. With a final push, his erection sprang free. She sighed, making sure her breath fell on his stiff cock in an airy caress.

Jace's whole body responded, his hips surged forward and a discordant noise echoed through the hall. The hand on her head shook. "Evie, love, please don't tease me. It's been so long since anyone gave me this."

Why did hearing that please her so? A wicked smile stole over her as she laid her head on one trembling thigh, looked up at him, and murmured, "How long?"

His fingers tunneled through her hair, tried to pull her closer, to force his prick between her lips. Feminine power engulfed her. The amazingly gorgeous and strong man was practically begging her to suck him off. She nuzzled him but waited for his answer.

"I honestly don't remember. It's not a usual request . . . that is, no one wants to . . ." Crimson flushed his face and he closed his eyes, clearly mortified.

Evie blinked, amazed. Not only because she'd actually made a manwhore blush, but also at the sheer selfishness of the average human female. Clearly what had been going on at the bachelorette party was an anomaly, and as Evie thought back to what she'd seen there, it was more about the women showing off their mad skills for one another than pleasuring the man. Why else suck off an android with a sac full of wine? Giving a guy head might not be every woman's sensual dream, but Evie delighted in the chance to explore every inch of Jace's body with her lips. "Well, *I* want to."

Wrapping one hand around the base of his shaft to hold it steady, Evie leaned in and lapped precome from the slit, her eyes glued to his face.

His lips parted and his fingers tightened in her hair. "Oh, fuck yeah. That feels so damn good."

Tracing the thick vein with her tongue, Evie considered how she wanted to proceed. She'd already made up her mind that he was going to come in her mouth, but how quickly did she want to get him there?

"Suck me, Evie. Take me between your sweet lips," Jace half ordered, half begged.

Keeping her gaze locked on his, she did, sucking just the crown at first and then sliding wetly down the long length of his thick shaft. She didn't know if she could take all of him, but damned if she wasn't going to try and make this the best blow job of his life.

"Yes!" Jace shouted when the tip hit the back of her throat and she swallowed, using her throat muscles to work his length. Her mouth had never been so full. She rolled his balls with her free hand, massaging the twin weights, enjoying the shuddering groans along with the salty male essence, the deep masculine spice of him.

One of his fingers traced her features. "Evie, you have to stop."

To hell with that. Evie sucked harder, worked him faster, swiveling her head from side to side on every withdrawal. Her hand explored the sensitive skin behind his sack, pressing lightly on his perineum.

He made a strangled noise as she worked upward, fully intending to slip a finger inside his ass and send him over the edge. But when her hand reached the targeted area, it collided with something hard and plastic already lodged inside of him.

Talking with her mouth still full of his cock wasn't an option, so she raised one eyebrow.

"Busted," Jace whispered, his cheeks flushing crimson again.

10

_____

Jace knew Evie was waiting for an explanation as to why he was wearing a butt plug. She deserved one, after finding out the way she had. The sexy little minx had been going above and beyond to make him orgasm, and only his lauded control had kept him from spurting hot ropey jizz down her tight little throat.

"It's a self-lubing prostate massager, to keep me hard for the event. This one is specially designed to keep steady pressure to my prostate, not enough to make me come, just so I stay at the ready. A little extra stimulation, better than chemicals, which take longer to wear off."

He prayed she wouldn't want to talk about this anymore. It embarrassed him to admit he needed extra help staying hard. Closing his eyes, he waited for her response.

Evie released him with a wet-sounding pop. So, she was done with him, maybe even repulsed by what he'd admitted. Christ, he was pathetic. He should have taken the time to remove the thing after his shower but had been tempted by the idea of having his back passage filled while he came inside

Evie's slick sex. Never had he expected her to go exploring back there or having to talk his way out of the awkwardness.

Her soft, silky hair brushed against his thigh. "Don't be embarrassed."

His laugh lacked humor. "How can I not be? Most men wouldn't need help staying hard in a room full of naked and sexually charged models."

Blue eyes full of compassion locked on him. "You're not most men, Jace. After what I saw tonight, I can only imagine what you've been through. I'm surprised you'd want to have sex at all when you're off the clock."

"I don't," he murmured. "I just want to make love with you."

She smiled shyly, the flip side of his aggressive pistol-packing mountain woman who stole his breath and made his heart beat faster. When she looked like that, so innocently curious, he wanted to protect her, to wrap her in his arms and never let go. And he wanted to fuck her until neither of them could move. He was light-headed from all the blood rushing to his groin. Her lush tits spilled from her top and her hand still lingered on the toy. Her smile turned wicked as she caressed his crease and murmured, "So this feels good?"

"Yeah," he croaked. "Real good."

She nuzzled his stiff prick, still wet from the well of her mouth. "Self-lubing, huh? Such a dirty secret, Jace. I might have to punish you for keeping it from me."

Jesus, why did her saying that make his balls draw up so tight?

His mouth went dry as she gripped the flange that locked the toy in place and pulled it most of the way out, keeping just the tip inside his puckered ring. Threading his fingers through her hair, Jace fought to remain upright when she sucked him back between her sweet lips at the same time she pushed the toy home.

A strangled groan escaped as she both sucked and fucked him, the toy gliding across sensitive nerve endings before bumping against that magic spot. Steady pressure was one thing, but having this big-breasted goddess working the plug while she rhythmically swallowed his cock wasn't something he could ever get used to.

Another pull from her sweet mouth as the toy retreated. His eyes rolled up in the back of his head. "Evie, Christ, I'm about to blow."

She made a soft humming sound of satisfaction and the plug was forced back in, more quickly this time.

Every cell in his body shuddered. Jace had experienced pleasure before, but never with this blinding intensity that made him want to go everywhere at once. His job, his training, every time he'd had sex were all pale imitations of the vivid euphoria Evie delivered with every stroke of her tongue, every push of the toy.

Blue eyes locked on his and he could almost hear the command he saw there. She wanted his orgasm, demanded it. Jace shuddered as he could almost hear her honeyed voice whispering in his mind, *Come for me.*

With a hoarse shout he did, emptying down her throat. The intensity of his orgasm was almost violent, but it seemed to go on and on, prolonged by the satisfaction he saw in her face and the swelling of another organ altogether.

His heart.

He loved her. Not just because she'd given him pleasure beyond description. She accepted him, all of him, eagerly, wantonly. She may detest his job, but she didn't hold that against him, or use it as a wedge between them. Hell, she didn't even ask him to abandon it for her. Finding out he was a pleasure companion hadn't changed the way she treated him because, although it had come as a shock to her, Evie saw him as more than a manwhore, more than the sum total of his job. In a million years she could never know how much that meant to him.

Totally spent, his knees buckled and he slumped back against the wall, pulling her with him, needing to hold her close, to breathe her in. Jace always thought he was the type to run from soft, fuzzy feelings. But the instant he recognized his devotion to the magnificent woman in his arms for what it was, he embraced it the same way he did her.

Now if only he could get Evie to do the same.

As they returned to the room, Evie had never been more turned on in her life. The power she'd wielded over Jace, the way he'd trembled as she touched him and the pleading in his eyes. A girl could easily become addicted to that.

Jace held her hand as they maneuvered the corridors. Such a sweet gesture, but somehow a little provocative too. The warmth from his skin and the roughness of his palms reminded her that she hadn't come yet.

As if she could forget.

She wanted him to toss her down on the bed the instant they were in the room. To tear her clothes from her body and impale her with some part of his. She needed to be fucked good and hard, to the point it almost made her crazy.

Instead, he bypassed the bed, hauling her instead into the bathroom. Removing the temperature cover from the bath he'd run earlier, he stripped off her clothes efficiently. Doffing his own, he led her down into the water of the deep pool until they sat on the bench with her between his legs.

"Close your eyes," he murmured softly.

"Jace, I need to come." Fire scorched her cheeks at having to put it so crudely, but she was past the point of pussyfooting around.

Pressing a kiss to her temple, he murmured, "Trust me."

With a sigh, she let her lids drift shut. Jace pressed his wet front to her back and swept her hair over her shoulders. Digging his thumbs into the stiff muscles of her shoulders, he worked the tension loose.

Evie groaned, her head lolling forward as he kneaded her shoulders and upper arms. She'd just relaxed into his touch when he said matter-of-factly, "I'm going to quit my job."

Her eyes flew open and she glanced at him over her shoulder. "Why?"

"I don't want to do it anymore. All the skill in the world doesn't make a difference if the will isn't there."

"When did you decide this?" she asked, both hopeful and afraid she had something to do with his decision.

"I've wanted out of the field for a while, been working toward it. That's why this gig was so important, it was supposed to be my golden ticket. Pride has kept me going for a while now, pride that I've managed to do something most people can't. I like my reputation, the fact that I was selected because I'm the best at what I do. Even if I don't want to do it anymore."

"What are you going to do now? Is there like a pension plan for pleasure companions?" Evie winced at how moronic the question sounded, but Jace grinned.

"Not exactly. I've been smart with my money and have plenty of options. Maybe I'll build my own sonic rink so I can run it."

She could imagine him doing that. Jace was made to lead a life of ease, of pleasure and fun and all the things she wasn't. "In New New York? Hope you saved up a pretty penny."

"I was actually thinking I'd open one in Boone, not that I couldn't in New New York if I wanted to. One of my regular clients was a stock trader. I'm flush with cash. I'll show you a bank statement if you want."

Evie frowned, irritated that they were having a financial dis-

cussion when what she really wanted was a baker's dozen orgasms, give or take a few. "Why would you want to show me
your bank statements?"

Jace picked up a comb and ran it through her hair, working
the tangles free painlessly. "Because I'm hoping to convince
you to marry me."

Evie froze. Every molecule in her body just stopped what it
had been doing, paralyzed.

Jace sighed, put the comb down, and hauled her back against
him. "Too soon, right? Okay, how about you just use me for
sex for a while? I'll rent a room in your inn and you can tie me
to the bed whenever the urge strikes you, get exactly what you
want from me."

Her body shook, overloaded. "Jace."

He kissed the back of her neck, thumb sweeping across her
collarbone. "I'm prepared for you, you know. I walked away
from you once because I thought that was what you wanted.
It's a mistake I don't intend to repeat. Now I have a new strat-
egy, want me to tell you?"

Evie didn't, but he kept on talking, his hands sliding beneath
the waterline to play with her breasts.

"I'm going to be there with you all the time. Helping you
whether you ask me for it or not, cornering you at every opportunity. We'll work hard all day, you running your inn, me
overseeing the building of my sonic rink. And at night we'll sit
on the front porch, you watching the sun go down with my
head in your lap, pushing your skirt up and pulling your
panties aside so I can go down on *you.*"

"What if I'm wearing pants?" she croaked. Of all the dumbass
things to say, but then what could she say to his crazy declara-
tion? He was moving back to the mountains, was essentially
moving into her inn, wanted to build an attraction that would
boost the local economy, including her own business. And he
was doing it for her.

Jace shook his head. "Won't matter. See, I'm determined to have you and only you. I don't care if it takes me fifty years of cajoling, if we're both old and gray, you will marry me."

She shook her head because his madness was catching, the picture he painted so damn alluring that she was starting to yearn. "You'll get tired of me, will want more than I can give you."

His hands cupped her breasts as he nuzzled her neck. "How could you think that? I'm not Yon, Evie. I know a good thing when I've got it and I don't intend to let you go."

In a sudden move, Jace pulled her to her feet and bent her over the side of the tub until her breasts pressed onto the cold tile. A hand roved over her back, a softly sweet caress. "I didn't expect this to be easy, and I'm prepared for a long siege. Let me show you what I bring to the table."

Wedging himself between her legs, he buried his face in her cunt. Evie gasped as his tongue found the wet entrance to her body and dove in deep. His roughly stubbled chin prickled her inner thighs and his jaw worked over her slit. A wet digit stroked the seam between her ass cheeks, swirling over her tightly puckered hole.

Evie wriggled, but he had her trapped beneath him, at his mercy. Her body melted for him from the inside out, liquid lust dripping from her core, and when he latched on to her clit and sucked, she stopped fighting, stopped resisting him and just went with it.

"That's my girl," Jace murmured, thumb circling over that forbidden opening. "Relax and accept it, trust me to take you where you need to go."

Spreading her legs wider, she did. His confessions were too much, she couldn't think about the future of their relationship right now. Letting go, she focused only on the wet slide of his tongue through her folds, the press of his thumb against the sensitive nerves that came alive under his tender ministrations.

As he flicked his tongue relentlessly against her clit, she barely noticed the increased pressure on her sphincter until his thumb breached her and wriggled inside. Sensations overloaded her and she cried out as a sharp climax made her body clench.

"Shield, baby." Jace withdrew from her and she just managed to activate her health guard when he surged inside her, riding her hard through the decreasing wake of her orgasm.

Gripping her hips, Jace circled an arm around her, pulling her flush against him. The slick slide of his body from the lubed-up water sent her soaring even higher. Stirring his thick cock in her dripping channel, he murmured nonsensical words of encouragement, of praise.

Of love.

"What am I going to do with you?" she asked, mostly of herself.

He held her tighter, their shields snapping and sizzling as his body worked hers. "Keep me. Love me. Let me love you. Just let go, Evie."

He made it sound so easy, his body rutting on hers so carnally, as though sex alone could forge an unbreakable union.

She wanted to, wanted to love him, to let go, but she knew better.

Didn't she?

And then that wicked thumb was back, applying pressure to her rosebud until it opened for him. Just a few slick strokes over those sensitive nerves sent her careening again. Her body clamped down on Jace at both openings and he shouted his own release, her shield eradicating every trace of him from her body.

If only it could do the same on her heart.

11

Jace awoke with a stupid grin on his lips because Evie was curled up next to him, soft and warm. He'd worn her out last night, between their play in the tub, on the chaise, and again, finally, in the bed. And his cock stood up eagerly, anticipating more.

His comm unit dinged and Jace was tempted to ignore it. What was the worst that could happen, they fire him a few hours before he quit? But Reg was his friend and if he needed help with something in taking over, Jace would lend a hand.

But it wasn't Reg or even Miranda calling to check in. "Mom?"

"Jace, honey, how are you?"

"Fine?" Talking to his mother while he was naked in bed with Evie weirded him out. "What's up?"

"It's your father. He's had a heart attack."

Jace couldn't even blink, the news was so startling. "When?"

"Last night. They're taking him in for surgery in a little while."

A cool hand touched his back and he turned his head to see

the concern in Evie's eyes. His mind was reeling. "I'm on a space cruise, though I can probably hitch a ride to the Mars outpost and take a shuttle back to Earth."

"I'm not sure that's such a good idea." His mother's hands weren't visible on the screen, but he would have bet every last dollar he had that she was wringing them. "He didn't even want me to tell you, sweetheart."

Jace grunted as though he'd been slugged in the guts. Evie made a pained sound and shifted closer. His mother's spine straightened as though she just realized he wasn't alone. "Well, you're so busy and all."

Hell, she probably assumed Evie was a client. Shame burned through him that his own mother would think so little of him, that his job was more important than his father's life. "Mom, it's not what you think."

But his mother kept going. "I'll have the doctor cc your comm with any updates. I just thought you should know." The line went dead.

"Jace"—Evie reached for him, wrapping her arms around him—"it'll be okay."

He held her close, just breathing her in. "I have to go."

She stroked his hair. "Of course you do. I'll go with you."

"No." He pulled back and almost winced at the hurt he saw on her face. "You have to stay for the wedding."

Her mouth opened and he covered her lips with his, stealing a kiss, probably the last one he'd get for a while. He'd expected her to fight, but she melded right into him, opening her mouth, clinging to his body so sweetly.

He was the one who broke the kiss and moved away from her, then climbed out of bed. "You'll regret it if you don't make things right with your daughter before she gets married."

His mind was whirling. He'd comm the bridge first to find out what the fastest way back to Earth was. En route he'd contact Reg and let him know what happened, along with Miranda to officially resign. Yanking on clean clothes, he was haphazardly stuffing items into his bag when he noticed that Evie hadn't moved.

He hated to leave her looking like that, so out of sorts. "Hey, what's wrong?"

She shook her head, hair falling over her face. "Nothing, just go." The words were sharp, meant to cut.

"Baby, I don't want to leave you, you know that, right?"

Her chin came up, that defiant angle he knew so well. "Of course not. You have to go, your dad is sick."

Something was going on with her, but he didn't know what. "Evie, leaving you is hard enough, but I don't want to leave when you're obviously upset."

"I'll see you, Jace." Throwing the covers aside, she strode for the bathroom. "Safe trip." The door slid shut behind her and the red glow from the comm panel told him she'd shut him out in every sense of the word.

What had he done wrong? Indecision warred within him. His dad didn't want him there and Evie seemed to need him. Maybe he should just stay, wait for an update.

But that was the easy way out. He'd meant every word he'd told Evie last night, he was set to make her the center of his universe whether she wanted him to or not. Leaving her at such an early stage pained him, but he knew soon enough he'd be back with her.

Picking up his duffel, he leaned against the doorway. "I love you, Evie. I'll comm you as soon as I get planet-side."

There was no answer. He hadn't expected one, no matter how badly he wanted it.

Evie stood outside Constance's door trying to think of a good reason not to go in. She wanted to wish her daughter well on her big day, knew it was the right thing to do. But going to a reception with a bunch of catty bitches who called her Grandma

Fatass and watching Constance morph into a snotty brat made her guts roil.

Or maybe that was because Jace hadn't wanted her to go with him.

So much for his conviction. Not even six hours and he couldn't escape her fast enough. Next thing she knew he'd become a raging alcoholic like Yon, mocking her and demeaning her and ripping her heart to shreds for sport.

"Shame on me for letting my guard down," she whispered. Letting Jace in had been the most intensely erotic experience of her life. But like all good things, it had to end, displaced by the cold void of reality. Sighing, she'd just made up her mind to find her own way home when she heard the muffled sob.

"Constance?" She called over the door. "Are you all right?"

The door spit in half and retreated into the wall. "Mama?" Constance sniffled.

Her daughter was a vision in her sleek white satin gown and sparkling tiara. If not for her blotchy, tearstained face, she would have looked like a fairytale princess.

Her child may have behaved badly, but she was still her baby girl. Evie pulled her into a hug and asked, "Hey, now, what's with the waterworks?"

Constance blubbered uncontrollably. "Oh, Mama, I'm so sorry I was such a bitch to you last night. When I think about the awful things I said . . ." Her words became unintelligible as great, heaving gasps for air took precedence.

Evie stroked her smooth hair. She hated seeing her daughter in such pain, and shame burned through her as she realized it was partly her fault. "Hush now, it's all right. You had every right to chew me out. I came here hoping to change your mind, and that was wrong of me."

"I know you were just looking out for me," Constance said. "Like you always do."

They hugged it out for several minutes before Evie's tears dried up. Searching for tissues, she set to fixing her daughter's makeup. "I guess it's too much to hope that my neuroses wouldn't warp me. I'm sorry, baby girl. Honestly, I've got nothing against marriage. I just want you to be sure."

Dabbing the corner of her eyes, Constance smiled. "Oh, I'm sure."

Evie ran a brush through her daughter's long hair. It reminded her of the way Jace had combed hers out the night before. Swallowing past the lump there, she tried to exorcise Jace's ghost from her mind.

Constance caught her hand. "What's wrong, Mama?"

"Oh, no, I'm not burdening you with my man troubles on your day."

Constance's chin lifted and her shoulders went back in a maneuver straight out of Evie's playbook. "I want you to, so it's not a burden."

While she helped fix her daughter's hair and makeup, Evie told her about Jace, glossing over the more explicit parts.

Constance was frowning by the end of it. "So you're mad that he went to go see his father who might be dying?"

Evie huffed out a breath. "No, I'm not that self-centered. I'm mad because he didn't want me to go with him."

Constance looked at her as though she'd sprouted a horn. "Yes, he did. He just wanted you to be happy more. Don't you get it? Jace knew that you wouldn't truly be happy as long as we were fighting, and that you'd always regret it if you didn't see me get married."

Evie sank down on the bed. It was true, all of it. How had she missed that? "I'm such an idiot."

Constance patted her hand sympathetically. "You didn't want to see it. You weren't ready to accept it because you're so afraid of what happened with Daddy."

"When did you get so smart?"

Constance made a squeaking sound and dove for her comm. "What shuttle was he leaving on?"

"I don't know. Why?"

Constance was busy, furiously typing away. "Because there might be a way you can have it all."

"What the fracking hell is the holdup?" Jace asked the shuttle pilot. He had a long trip ahead of him and the longer it took them to get off the *Trist,* the more irritable he became. He'd almost gone back to find Evie twice, to shake some sense into her.

"Message from the captain, we're waiting on a few VIP guests."

Way to make him feel like a useless lump of crap. Closing his eyes, Jace leaned back against the bulkhead and tried not to think about all the ways this day had sucked.

The sound of running feet up the access ramp made him huff out a relieved breath. "It's about—"

He cut himself off when he saw David Abernathy, Constance, the captain, and Evie all squeeze on board the shuttle. "What the hell?"

"Launch whenever you are ready," the captain instructed the pilot. Opening an actual book, what looked to be a bible, he cleared his throat. "All rise."

"Evie? What's going on?"

"Ssshh."

Tugging Jace to his feet, Evie turned to face the captain as he recited, "Love is patient, love is kind—"

This was nuts. "They're getting married on the shuttle?"

"Sorry, Captain. Love might be patient, but the man I love isn't."

The captain gave him a grin. "No rush."

"Jace, I'm sorry I was so difficult earlier. It's just that I was upset about you not wanting me with you."

That's what she'd believed? "I did want you with me."

"I had to have someone very smart explain it to me."

"And I owed Mama for being such a pill last night, so David and I decided we'd come with you as far as the Mars station and get married here, so she can be with both of us when we both need her."

"You did this for me?" His mind, strained from worry, was just catching up. Turning to Evie, he tilted her chin to face him, not daring to breath. "You said the man you love."

Her smile nearly blinded him. "That would be you, handsome. Forgive me?"

"Always," he rasped before claiming her lips and kissing her the way he always intended to. With all his heart.

The captain cleared his throat again. "So, should we make it a double wedding?"

"I'm game if you are," she whispered.

Jace had always been ambitious, and keeping the goddess in his arms for the rest of his days was no exception. He swore to whatever power had decided to bless him that he would do whatever it took to make her happy. "I'm totally game."

The captain cleared his throat. "Love is patient, love is kind. It does not envy, it does not boast, it is not proud. It does not dishonor others, it is not self-seeking, it is not easily angered, it keeps no record of wrongs. Love does not delight in evil but rejoices with the truth. It always protects, always trusts, always hopes, always perseveres."

"I love you," Evie whispered and became his wife.

It wasn't until sometime later that Jace read the message from his mother, though he already believed it.

Everything is going to be all right.

A Pirate's Pleasure

CASSIE RYAN

To my wonderful agent, Paige Wheeler, for all that you do

Acknowledgments

To Kayla Janz, author of *Sapphire Blue,* for brainstorming and support. To Brit Blaise, author of the Cave Creek Cowboy series, for critiques, love, and support during the writing of this story.

1

Dani McGovern lay on the bunk in her cabin, staring out into the blackness of space as her body hummed with pent-up arousal. Her breasts were heavy with need; her pussy aching and empty. Even the soft friction of her clothes against her skin was a small torture to the heightened awareness of every inch of her body.

"We're at fourteen minutes now and counting."

"If you just shut up and stop giving me countdown updates, maybe I could get there!"

Dani needed to take her pleasure probe in for adjustments. The damned thing had started mimicking her snarky voice. Why the hell had she picked the talking model?

What had she been thinking?

Lately there had been way too much work and too little play. Something needed to give soon or she was sure she'd explode—literally. That's what had prompted her to take a few hours for herself away from the control room and her responsibilities. She was hoping that a little *pressure release* would return some of her concentration—not to mention her sanity.

She edged the tip of the pleasure probe inside her slit, hoping to fill the emptiness that ached as a very real reminder that it had been too long since her pussy had been filled with a nice, thick cock.

"Partial penetration detected. Would you like to engage the heat setting?"

Dani cursed, then remembered that the pleasure probe often exhibited unpredictable results when all she did was curse at it. Straightforward answers were best if she didn't want it to suddenly turn ice cold or slimy with space lube. "I want you to shut up and vibrate. Adopt normal body temperature for a human and just shut the fuck up!"

"Fuck mode engaging."

Dani groaned as the penis-shaped tip of the pleasure probe extended and retracted in rapid succession. Since she didn't have the probe fully inserted, it didn't even hit her cervix, which might have pushed her over the edge, and she was afraid she'd end up pinching something tender if she tried full insertion now with the wildly moving tip.

The ship rotated quickly to port, and Dani stared out the viewport wondering what was happening up in the control room.

"Discontinue fuck mode," she barked at the snarky pleasure probe. Its antics slowed, but it continued to vibrate softly as the newest galaxy medical-grade silicone heated to normal human body temperature.

If only it were attached to a real man who could kiss and caress her . . . and get her off without giving her five-minute progress reports.

The sight of a small ship through her view screen made her pause. What was such a tiny ship doing way out here? They were a few light-years from the twin Gavin planets and were watching everything on long-range sensors. She considered contacting the control room but was confident that Dahlia, her first officer, was fully capable of running things. And besides, she hadn't yet accomplished what she'd come to her quarters for.

She returned her attention to the task at hand and figured as soon as she came she could contact Dahlia. The woman would contact *her* if anything serious happened.

"Pleasure probe, program four." Program four was the highest vibration setting the unit had, and Dani rarely used such drastic measures, which only further convinced her she'd been working too hard and needed to de-stress.

"Dani, as a safety warning, too much high-powered stimulation against the human clitoris can cause loss of sensitivity and even nerve damage with long-term use."

"Oh, for God's sake. Just turn on program four and shut up."

"Engaging program four," the snarky voice informed her.

The sudden increase in vibrations against her sensitive clit was like a touch to a live wire against her most sensitive parts, but she refused to change the program just to spite the snarky pleasure probe, so she breathed deep and relaxed into the sensations until her body absorbed them and the steady, high-powered vibrations turned into sweet, warm arousal spilling through her veins like a nice tall shot of Gavin whiskey.

She welcomed the sensations she knew were a precursor to the explosive orgasm she both needed and craved. She eased the pleasure probe deeper inside her slit while still maintaining its contact with her clit and began to grind against it, undulating her hips and sending sharp, sudden spikes of arousal spearing through her entire body.

She was breathing heavy, but the orgasm she craved hovered just out of her reach. With a frustrated sigh, she raised her other hand and lightly pinched her nipple. When she realized the light tweak wasn't enough to match the heights of the rest of her arousal, she pinched harder and twisted just enough to send a lance of molten lava from the tight bud of her nipple straight to her clit. She didn't bother to hide the gasp that escaped from her lips. In order to reach her goal, she needed something more, but what?

She allowed her thoughts to wander and lost herself to her fertile imagination. In her mind's eye, a virile and sexy man stood next to her bunk, his pants tented with one of the most generous erections she'd ever seen.

She kept her eyes closed, even as she gasped, enjoying the self-made vision. She licked her lips as her body reacted to the manufactured anticipation of his touch.

The extra stimulation and the very detailed vision helped, but only edged her closer to climax, not all the way there. What was she going to have to do to get there? Hook up her pleasure probe to the hyperdrive unit?

"Main power cell depleted . . ." the mechanical voice trailed off and slurred down to a deeper tone of voice as it stretched the last word into several long syllables.

Dani huffed out a breath as her newfound arousal drained away like water in a cracked cup. She considered throwing the pleasure probe across the room, but at the last minute remembered just how many credits she'd shelled out on the thing on their last R&R stop.

"Damn it. I'll never get to come at this rate."

The sudden explosion and resulting fireball outside her viewport shattered her anger and chased all thoughts of sex and arousal from her mind. As a slight edge of fear burned though her, she sat up so quickly her head swam for a moment before she breathed deep to regain her equilibrium.

"Boss," her first officer's voice came through over the room's small intercom. "A small arms ship just tried to sneak past us toward the Gavin planets. There were only four life signs on board, one human and three unidentified."

Relief slid through Dani. She didn't like killing, and although even a few lives lost bothered her, it could've been so much worse.

"They refused to stop, so I sent a warning shot to their cargo hold. I guess their cargo must've been flammable since I'm sure you saw the explosion."

"No explosion detected," her snarky pleasure probe piped up in its slurred voice thanks to the depleted main power cell. "Orgasm still elusive."

Dahlia's snicker was clearly heard over the intercom, and Dani resisted the urge to curse again.

"End program."

"Still having arguments with your pleasure probe, boss?" The amusement in Dahlia's voice was obvious.

Dani forcefully returned her thoughts to the situation at hand. "Anything else, D?"

They were used to having ships self-destruct rather than be boarded and captured, but it was relatively rare for them to make one explode with just a simple warning shot to a nonvital area. She shrugged. This would just add to their notoriety, already overblown thanks to her predecessor, but did make it easier to force ships to surrender in some instances. Fear was a powerful motivator.

"Yes," her first officer's voice broke back into her thoughts. "I've picked up a large ship headed toward the twin Gavin planets. Shall we move to intercept?"

Dani sighed. "Take us into the system, but keep us out of sight and sensor range. We don't want to spook our prey before we know what they're up to. I'll be up there in five minutes."

Dani put her clothing to rights and made sure her hair didn't show any disarray from her time rubbing against the pillow while she'd ground against the pleasure probe. She also took the time to wash her hands and snap the damned pleasure probe into its charging base before she cast one last longing look toward her bunk, stepped outside her cabin, and turned toward the lifts. "Duty calls, Dani," she chided herself, and headed toward the control room.

Five minutes later, she was sitting in her captain's chair, her feet propped on the ship's console in front of her as she scanned the situation forming outside the large view screen. A Galaxy class space cruiser was headed toward Gavin 2, the second planet in this tiny solar system just outside of Earth's, and would most likely set up a standard orbit to deliver supplies to continue the bloody war that had waged for four generations between the twin planets.

"Oh, no, you don't," she admonished, even though only her first officer was in the control room to hear her.

"What do you think, boss? Weapons or supplies?"

Dani pursed her lips as she turned to study her first officer. They had stopped so many ships trying to give aid to Gavin 2 that they'd gotten pretty good at guessing the cargo long before they captured and boarded the ships.

Distaste was still thick on her tongue from the last ship they'd stopped the previous week. It had been filled with children bought and paid for from neighboring solar systems to be raised and trained to be laborers and the lower class on Gavin 2. Heaven forbid the wealthy residents of Gavin 2 use their own citizens to help run the planet. She couldn't even refer to it as *their* planet since they'd stolen it from the current residents of Gavin 1. Most likely that's why Dahlia had told her how many life signs had been on the ship that had just blown up, so she didn't worry they'd inadvertently blown up a ship full of children. But hopefully Gavin 2 had learned its lesson on that—although she doubted it.

As someone who had grown up on Gavin 1, seeing the war firsthand, Dani's stomach had turned at the lengths the Gavin 2 populace had gone to in buying children from off-world to act as their common laborers. After all, four generations before, they were the ones who had deported all the lower- and middle-class citizens off of Earth to the twin Gavin planets in the first place. They were the super wealthy on Earth at the time, and after decades of suppressing the lower classes, the mistreated populace had risen up against them. In response, the wealthy upper classes had paid off-world assassins and enforcers to move the unwanted classes of Earth. She supposed she should be thankful they hadn't simply all been killed, or she wouldn't be here today, nor would most of the people she'd ever known or loved.

A large sigh from Dahlia reminded her she still hadn't answered the question. "Sorry, D. Just woolgathering. Although I'd bet on weapons."

"No," Dahlia admonished, "you're dwelling on ancient history again. You're doing all you can to right the wrongs in this war, so let the rest go or it's going to eat you alive. And I agree. Definitely weapons."

Dani huffed out a breath, which fluttered the long chunk of hair that had slipped down across her right eye while she'd been silently stewing. She should've pulled her long hair back into a pony tail before leaving her quarters, but her mind had been on other things.

"I know you're right, D, but I just can't help thinking that the Gavin 2 residents brought this on themselves. And now since only the propaganda is taught in their schools, their populace will never even know the truth about it."

"You know history is written by the winners, boss. And even though they haven't technically won the war yet, they have the resources to buy the opinions of half of the galaxy, so only people like you who saw the plight of Gavin 1 firsthand will be willing to intercede for them since they don't have the credits Gavin 2 does."

The Galaxy class space ship chose that moment to take up a far-lying orbit around Gavin 2.

232 / Cassie Ryan

"It's time, D. Let's do it."

Dani punched the ship-wide intercom button. "All right, everyone. We have a Galaxy class space ship setting up orbit around Gavin 2. It looks like a standard cargo ship converted from a pleasure liner, so I doubt they have much, if any, weaponry. Time to go to work and earn your credits. Report to your stations and prepare for boarding."

Klaxons sounded all over the ship in time with yellow and white flashing lights. Red lights would make it harder for the crew to see the action taking place out in the blackness of space, so when she'd taken over the ship, she'd promptly changed the lights to yellow and white, and had updated the Klaxon to something still attention getting, but slightly less annoying.

Anticipation curled through her veins as it did every time they were about to capture a ship. Part of it was the excitement of never knowing quite what they would find, and part was the knowledge that she was doing a tiny bit to help end the ongoing war between the Gavin planets.

"D, take us in."

They were several light-years out watching the scene unfold under maximum magnification. All the better to sneak up on unsuspecting ships without letting their prey slip through their fingers, and without letting the small armada on Gavin 2 interfere—although a few good torpedoes would take out the entire armada. Gavin 2 had bought fighters from other worlds, but their loyalty lasted only as long as their paychecks held out, and while the residents of Gavin 2 were extremely rich by the Galaxy's standards, they were also known as spendthrifts who didn't like to part with more credits than they needed to for each situation.

Dahlia's fingers flew over the control panel as if she were a concert pianist. And in many ways, the comparison was apt. Not only was Dahlia the best ship mechanic in the sector, other than herself, but the woman was a genius at flying ships and just about anything else that could break a planet's orbit. Dani had been lucky to recognize Dahlia's talents when she'd captured the ship the woman was being transported on to bring skilled labor onto Gavin 2. That had been five years ago, and Dani had never regretted her decision to both let Dahlia live and offer her a long-term job. They'd become fast friends . . . and more. After all, space travel was a lonely business, and Dani couldn't afford to get too friendly with the male personnel on her ship and risk losing their respect. It was difficult enough being a female captain without undermining her own authority by advertising that she was putting out to one of the crew—or worse, several.

She mentally scolded herself for getting caught up in her sex life and not concentrating on the unfolding situation in front of them. She needed several amazing orgasms and soon, or she'd end up getting her entire ship captured and her crew killed.

It took only a glance down at the long-range sensor readings to bring a scowl to Dare MacFadyen's face. "Carl, do you see what I see?"

Carl cleared his throat. "Unfortunately, I do."

Dare hit some buttons on the console in front of him and brought the view of the incoming ship up to maximum magnification.

He let fly his favorite round of curses and swallowed hard against the bile that tried to inch its way up the back of his throat. "It appears we're about to have an encounter with the infamous Red Death."

"Fucking evil bastard." Carl had a way with words.

But Carl had nailed it—Red Death had struck hundreds of ships throughout the surrounding quadrants. The bastard had been attacking ships for two decades, and was known to be extremely ruthless and very efficient in not only stalking his prey, but also in confiscating cargo, dismantling ships, and selling them off for scrap or whatever else would bring the highest price.

"Carl, I don't think I'd be too happy losing my own flagship on its maiden voyage. What do you think our chances are?"

"They've already exploded one ship this morning, so maybe they'll be lenient with a second. Who knows."

The vision of the tiny ship exploding just ten minutes ago flashed across Dare's mind and tightened his shoulder muscles. "This is a really bad time to only have a few seasoned crewmen on board out of our twenty. But I hadn't counted on running into Red Death. It's been rumored he's been marauding in the Relion sector lately."

Carl nodded. "I'd heard that, too, so you're not the only one surprised. I wonder what fascination two tiny war-torn planets have for Red Death unless he's found a way to make a profit off the situation."

Dare's blood chilled at the mention of making a profit. He'd recently tried expanding the business by taking on side delivery projects, so when Gavin 2 had offered a king's ransom for a hold full of munitions, he hadn't questioned it. He'd jumped at the chance to put his own stamp on the company he'd just inherited from his grandfather, Devil MacFadyen. He knew there was a war raging between the two planets, but he was here purely as a delivery agent—he wasn't about to get involved in their politics.

"Red Death is a complication we just don't need right now, Carl."

"You can say that again. We only have a few more hours in the delivery window to get these munitions to Gavin 2 or they won't pay us one credit for the lot."

"Don't remind me. If that happens, it will be the first large mistake I've made at the helm of the company, and I won't be very happy about that either."

Dare hit the ship-wide intercom button. "All hands, we are

about to encounter Red Death. In the event we are boarded, your priority is to guard the cargo until you hear otherwise from me or Carl. Those munitions are worth your weight in credits if we can survive this encounter and get them delivered to Gavin 2 within the delivery window. Just remember, Gavin 2 is notorious for not paying for partial orders. We need every last pound of those munitions to collect, so do what you have to do to protect our next payday and we'll get through this in one piece."

He knew that lame pep talk would only work for some of the crew, and the more desperate and greedy at that, but the rest would probably be the ones to run and fall in battle first anyway, so what did he have to lose by trying to remind them why they were here and what the potential rewards were?

As the other ship closed in, Carl executed some expert flying moves that Dare would've bet five minutes ago couldn't be done with such a large ship. But then, that's why his grandfather had recruited Carl to be the main pilot for the company several years ago. Carl was one of the *old-timers,* and Dare knew if his grandfather had trusted the man, his own life was in good hands with Carl as well.

However, Red Death's smaller ship easily matched their maneuvers and even stayed ahead of them, cutting off any escape route and catching them between the planet and their smaller and more maneuverable ship.

The communication console beeped urgently, alerting Dare to an incoming message.

Interesting and unexpected.

He'd heard Red Death shot and boarded first and only talked later—at least to those few who were left alive on the newly captured ship. But since there were no other ships in range to send them a communication, it had to be from the small pirate ship.

Dare glanced at Carl and shrugged. "What do we have to

lose by talking a bit? Just keep trying to maneuver us out of here if they give us any opening."

Dare took a deep breath and punched the open channel button on his com panel. "Unidentified ship, this is Captain Mac-Fadyen. We have business on Gavin 2. Will you clear a path?" Lame, but then, how did one address an infamous pirate ship?

Some static that almost sounded like soft laughter came across the channel. "You and I both know you're no match for our firepower, so unless you want that nice, pretty ship blown out from under you, drop your shields and prepare to be boarded." The obviously artificial computer's voice made Dare frown. He would've preferred an actual human voice so he could get some clue as to their character.

Dare took his finger off the com button so only Carl could hear him. "That's it? They aren't going to disable us first?"

Carl shook his head. "I keep forgetting you've never spent much time captaining before. Hell, your grandfather and I were being attacked by renegade space pirates when you were still a dirty thought in your daddy's mind." He chuckled and gestured with his chin toward the pirate ship. "They want the ship intact so they can dismantle it or sell it. You and I both know if they send one good hit to the hold, we're nothing but a fireball thanks to all those munitions Gavin 2 wanted. We have a better shot at staying alive if we surrender. I've heard that over the past five years Red Death is much less likely to kill the crews if he doesn't need to, and he's even recruited a few captured crewmen to work on his ship. Let's see what we can finagle, shall we?"

Dare waved a hand at the com panel, silently turning the conversation with the pirate ship over to Carl, who obviously knew more about this type of situation than Dare did. Dare had spent time in the business offices with his grandfather, but other than learning to fly, operate the ships, and run the company, he'd never actually done a lot of the piloting and traveling. Now he regretted not spending that time and learning all he could from Devil. The older man had taught Dare quite a bit, but obviously there had been a lot more to learn. Regret warred with sadness inside Dare's chest, and he took a deep breath to hopefully hide both of those emotions from the too-perceptive Carl.

Carl pressed the com button and leaned toward Dare so he could speak more closely to the com mic. "Unidentified ship, we are carrying ordered supplies for Gavin 2. If you agree to expedite our delivery, I'm sure we could come up with a suitable split of the profits that would benefit us both." Carl took his finger off the com button as he shrugged. "Can't hurt to try. We'll see what they come back with, but I'm thinking we're going to have to let them board unless you're up for setting the self-destruct and going up in a ball of flame all for the principle of not being captured."

Dare shook his head. "No way. If they want me dead, they're going to have to pull the trigger up close and personal. I refuse to make it easy on them."

Carl winked at Dare. "That's the spirit. Let's make the old man proud! Lots of people thought he was insane when he appointed you to head the company after he was gone, but I have faith you can do it." Carl slapped Dare on the back and grinned over at him. "You've always been the spitting image of Devil, regardless of what your deadbeat father thinks."

Dare smiled over at the older man, oddly touched by his show of support. His grandfather's opinion had always meant a lot to him, so knowing that Carl thought Devil would be proud warmed him, even in this dangerous situation.

The computer voice broke into Dare's musings. "If Gavin 2 ordered those supplies, then I'm sure they're a lot more explosive than food rations or building supplies, so let's cut the clutter and be honest, gentlemen. I'm betting we could take you out with one well-placed shot to your hold. So shall we end the day explosively, or are we going to play nice and give as many people as possible a good day?"

Dare nodded at Carl. "Do it."

Carl pressed the com button and winked over at Dare. "Unidentified ship. We would prefer not to be picking up pieces of our vessel for the next century, so we would be happy to invite a small boarding party on board."

Dare heard what sounded like a snort in the voice of the computer and wondered if that was a good or bad sign.

After several minutes where Carl continued to try to edge away from the pirate ship and the smaller ship kept them blocked in, Dare began to think they would get no answer.

"Your offer is accepted. Send your command crew to the port air lock to greet our boarding party."

Carl cursed, but stood from his chair. "Come on, Dare. Time to earn that captain's title."

Dare nodded. He as the boss should be the one to face the first danger rather than his crew. He just hadn't thought he'd be given the choice in this instance. He slapped Carl on the back and nodded as he hit the ship-wide intercom button. "Attention all hands. We will be welcoming a boarding party in a few minutes. Please wait for me and Carl to greet them. Be ready, but don't make any aggressive moves unless needed to defend yourselves. Captain out."

Dare sent up a silent prayer for strength and wisdom from his grandfather and headed toward the air lock.

The walk to the air lock seemed to take forever, and Dare just hoped his lack of experience didn't make his crew pay the ultimate price. He could stomach dying for his own mistakes, but not making others suffer for them.

When they reached the air lock, Dare stepped in front of Carl, pressing the older man behind him before he looked through the air-lock window to make sure the other ship was securely attached against their hull. The green screen across the outside of the window showed him it was, so he pulled the lever to equalize the pressure between the two ships and when the hissing sound of equalizing air stopped, he pulled open the door and stuck his hands in the air surrender style.

A group of at least ten men with laser weapons stood looking at Dare with their weapons unerringly trained on him and the few crewmen behind him.

Dare cleared his throat before speaking. "Please take me to your captain so we can finish discussing our terms." Dare nearly smiled at the audacity of his words. If situations were reversed, he'd consider that speech damned ballsy by their captured prey.

One of the men stepped forward with a large smirk splitting his beefy face. "The captain has requested you and your first officer be taken to the ready room to be interrogated at the earliest convenience. Please follow me."

Dare motioned Carl forward and then for the rest of the crew to stay put until they received further instructions.

"What about my crew?" he stopped to ask before going any farther.

The beefy man nodded. "A good captain ye are to be asking. You'd be surprised how many captains aren't concerned about the crew, only saving their own backsides. They'll be safe and sound as long as they give us no reason to leave them in another condition."

Dare nodded and stepped forward to follow Mr. Beefy.

The path through the ship and up two levels toward the ready room was winding and long, but it gave Dare a chance to evaluate the ship. It wasn't fancy or comfortable like his, but then this was no pleasure liner booked by rich vacationers to see the galaxy. Every inch of the ship was utilitarian and devoted to sensors, weaponry, or some other vital function, which would make sense for a pirate ship, but still surprised Dare. He supposed he expected more posh accommodations from an obviously rich space pirate who had been marauding for so long. But the stark show of function over form and flash chilled Dare's blood as he mulled over what that could mean in other areas. He was ready to give his own life if needed, but he fervently hoped to spare Carl's and his crew's.

"Here we go, gentlemen." Mr. Beefy stopped just in front of them and motioned to a doorway on their left. "There are a few of our associates inside who will ready you to await the captain's and first officer's pleasure."

Dare frowned back at Carl, not sure what the speech meant, but at the sight of Carl's stoic expression, Dare mentally shrugged and walked through the doors into the ready room. Four very large crewmen stood eyeing Dare and Carl with threatening expressions. Not that Dare blamed them. If he were in their situation, he wouldn't trust the newcomers either.

"Sit, gentlemen," the largest man said as he motioned to the metal chairs spaced around the wide metal table. "We've housekeeping to take care of before you can see the captain and first officer. If you cooperate, this will take no time at all."

"What do you need from us? You already have our ship." Carl's voice was matter-of-fact and held only curiosity and not anger or any sign of fear.

Dare hoped he could be as stoic the next time he was in this situation, because he damned well intended to survive this one long enough to become the *old-timer* to a child of his own who would take over MacFadyen shipping from him when the time came.

Carl sat, and Dare followed his lead.

Only then did the large man reach in front of him and hold up an injector tool. It was like a twenty-first-century shot but didn't actually break the skin. It pushed whatever was to be delivered between the molecules of the skin and left little or no sign behind depending on the size of the molecules in the substance being delivered. Dare had only ever experienced slight redness from their use, but he frowned as his mind catalogued just what Red Death's crew wanted to inject them with.

Carl cleared his throat. "Truth serum or shock collars?"

Dare started at the term "shock collars." He'd heard that the human body could be implanted with a microchip near the base of the neck, and when an external control button was pushed could be forced to experience different levels of discomfort from a slight bump to a sensitive area all the way up to excruciating pain. He'd also heard about Gavin 2 using them on the populace of Gavin 1 that they'd captured, but he'd discounted the tale as embellished war stories. After all, why torture someone in this day and age when you could just inject them with either truth serum or compulsion serum where you could ask them to jump out of an air lock and they would happily do it?

The large guard cleared his throat before answering. "Red doesn't need or use truth serum. So definitely shock collars, but trust me when I say they won't be used unnecessarily. If you cooperate and remain civil, then there will be no need for their use. It's just a precautionary measure before we put our command team in here with two unknowns."

Carl nodded and tipped his head to the side, a silent invitation for his injection.

"Wait. I'm the captain," Dare broke in. "You can do mine first. Give Carl a few more minutes of peace."

Carl practically beamed over at Dare, and the approval in that one look warmed Dare down to his toes.

Since his own father had always been quite clear that he'd wanted a daughter and not Dare, who reminded him of his surly father-in-law, Dare had grown up seeking male approval from his grandfather, and more recently from Carl, who had been a boyhood friend of Devil's. Dare chided himself that as a man of thirty-eight he should no longer seek approval from anyone, but he heard his grandfather's amused laughter in the back of his mind and forced his thoughts back to the task at hand. He tilted his neck to the side and laid his hands in his lap so as to look more nonthreatening as the burly crewman approached.

The cold metal of the injector pressed against the tender skin of his neck, but before he could brace, purely out of reaction and habit, a hiss sounded in his ear and the device was pulled away. Whatever microchip they'd implanted him with was now in place. He rolled his neck experimentally but didn't feel anything out of place or different.

A hiss from beside him made him turn his head in time to see Carl's chip implanted.

Dare watched Carl for a minute to make sure all was well. When the older man leaned back in his chair and winked over at Dare, Dare relaxed.

"Good." The beefy guard slipped the injector device into one of the holsters on his uniform and motioned for the others to follow him. "The captain and first officer will be with you momentarily. You seem like nice lads. Behave yourselves, treat them with respect, and we won't have to provide any demonstrations of the equipment. Like I said, Red doesn't like using pain unnecessarily."

The guards filed out and Dare was left looking across the table at the stainless-steel wall lockers and the small view screen that showed the blackness of space just outside the hull of the ship.

"You did well, boy," Carl nodded. "Keep cool and we'll be able to get out of this one with all of our skins. I know you've got old Devil's temper, but just keep it under wraps. I'm not sure how Red Death interrogates, but it's probably a normal tactic to piss off men to throw them off their game. Your deadbeat father would never be able to keep his calm, but I know you will for the sake of the crew and the ship."

Dare knew that Devil had tried to dissuade his only daughter from marrying the young, dashing ship's pilot who ended up being Dare's father, but his mother wouldn't listen and Devil loved her enough in the end to relent and reluctantly give his permission on the condition that she keep her last name and that any children from the union also be MacFadyens. Dare shook his head. What would he have done in that situation? He knew he wanted children someday, but a daughter or a son, either would be fine by him. Women could be just as effective piloting ships and running a business as men, sometimes more so. So who was he to follow in his father's footsteps and make his offspring feel unwanted for the rest of their existences?

The doorknob rattled, and Dare turned at the same time Carl did to see who would enter the small room.

2

Dani turned the corner dashing toward her ready room and slammed into a wall of pure muscle. As the *wall* tried to steady her, they both tumbled into a tangle of arms and legs.

Jared, one of her oldest and most loyal crewmen, might have taken this in stride if not for the fact that her hand landed on his family jewels, and damned if it didn't want to linger.

What the fuck was wrong with her? When had she become all about being so horny she couldn't think straight?

"Ahem, Red?" Jared pointedly stared at her hand that still rested quite comfortably on his tender parts.

Dani jerked back and banged her head on the floor.

It served her right. She needed to get her head back in the game.

As she scrambled to her feet, she caught Dahlia rolling her violet eyes as the corners of her mouth twitched upward.

Speaking of Dahlia, where had she come from? Maybe she'd been hanging out with Jared? Dani pursed her lips as she let the possibilities percolate through her mind.

Good for D. Maybe at least one of them was getting some regular cock.

"Status on the prisoners?" Dani barked in her best "nothing just happened" voice.

Jared cleared his throat in a very self-conscious gesture and then took a deep breath before continuing. "They both have the chips, boss. I think you two will be fine, but you hit the alarm if you need anything at all." Jared held out his hand, showing her two silver control panels the size of an old Earth half dollar. Dahlia stepped between them and took one of the control panels and handed the other to Dani, cementing Dani's suspicions about Dahlia and Jared.

Pulling her mind back to work, Dani smiled at Jared. Devil MacFadyen had taught her enough hand-to-hand combat skills that she was confident she and Dahlia could handle the two prisoners no matter what, but she appreciated Jared's gesture and smiled up at him. "Thank you, Jared. You always take good care of us." She looked meaningfully over at Dahlia and tried not to grin to let him know she was on to them.

Jared blushed and his expression turned sheepish. "Oh, Red. You're much better than our last captain. You treat us well, you've made us all rich, and you're not unduly vicious with the captives. Not to mention you actually have red hair, unlike the previous Red Death." He laughed. "You're a good woman, and we're all behind you a thousand percent."

"Me too, boss," Dahlia chimed in with a grin.

"Thanks, guys. Let's get this going, shall we?" She headed toward the ready room and tossed a smile over her shoulder to Jared, with Dahlia close on her heels. When the door opened, Dani nearly gasped as both men stood. One of the men was an even better version of her earlier fantasy man. His dark hair was a bit too long on top so it edged over onto his forehead, making her want to push it back. His intelligent blue eyes burned through her, giving her the impression that he saw and catalogued everything, not to mention he liked what he saw. A study in virility, he was muscular without going too far. His face was ruggedly handsome with a cleft in his chin and a dimple in his right cheek that she ached to reach out and touch. The tent in the front of his pants impressed her much more than her dream man's.

A sudden rush of moisture between her thighs gave her body's agreement as to his attractiveness, and she bit her tongue to keep her reaction in check. Now was the time to think with her head, not with her aching pussy.

The second man was older, but looked hearty and spunky . . . and oddly reminded her of Devil MacFadyen. She wondered briefly if he was Captain MacFadyen, or if the tall, dark hunk next to him held that title.

Only one way to find out. She stepped forward with her hand extended. "Gentlemen, welcome."

The tall hunk took her hand and shook—a firm, dry grip. No he-man tactics or sweaty palms for this one.

"I'm Dare MacFadyen, ma'am, and this is my first officer, Carl."

One mystery down. The sexy man before her had to be Devil MacFadyen's grandson since she knew Devil only had one daughter and no sons. Now that she studied him again, he did have Devil's stubborn chin and blue, blue eyes.

Her nipples were tight and sensitive, it was as if they were pointing at what they wanted—straight at Dare MacFadyen. And while she couldn't argue with their logic, now was not the best time to voice or act on that preference.

Carl shook hands with Dani as well, and then remembering they were in the middle of introductions, Dani motioned to Dahlia. "This is my first officer, Dahlia."

Dahlia shook hands with both men; then the sexy hunk cleared his throat. "When can we expect to meet Red Death?"

Dani couldn't help the grin that curved her lips, and she smiled wider at the small laugh that sounded from Dahlia beside her. She was used to men not expecting Red Death to be female. But many of them took that as a sign of weakness and didn't realize their colossal mistake until it was too late and they were writhing in pain on the deck. She hoped that wouldn't be the case here.

"I'm Red Death, Mr. MacFadyen. And, no, there's no Mr. Red Death waiting in the wings. I'm the one you're looking for. But please call me Dani."

She watched as confusion and then acceptance played over both men's features.

The men stepped back near their seats as if to look more nonthreatening. Carl raised his gaze to meet hers. "If you don't mind, ma'am, you look very familiar. Have we met before?"

"I'm not sure. But you remind me of Devil MacFadyen, even though I'm assuming Captain MacFadyen here is his direct descendant."

Carl grinned. "You were one of his *projects*, weren't you?"

Dani laughed as out of her peripheral vision she caught the dark confusion on Dare MacFadyen's handsome face.

Carl turned his gaze toward Dare. "Your grandfather would find underprivileged people or those down on their luck and he'd help them however he could. He did it so often that I dubbed them his projects. I'm sure he helped hundreds of people over his long lifetime, and Dani here was apparently one of them."

Dani nodded, thinking back through all the valuable lessons she learned from Devil MacFadyen. "Let's sit, shall we?" She gestured for Dahlia and they all sat around the sterile metal table.

"I grew up on Gavin 1. Devil caught me trying to steal bread one day and took it upon himself to teach me to fend for myself. Not by stealing, but by fixing ships. He also taught me to defend myself, to barter with the shopkeepers for what I needed to survive, and to think for myself."

A small sound from Dare had her glancing his way. The look of awe and reverence on his face showed Dani that even though he'd most likely already thought a lot of his grandfather, she and Carl had just raised the man in Dare's esteem a bit further.

Carl gave her an appraising nod and then shook his head as if he were having his own internal argument. "Well, now, I'm glad old Devil was there to help you when it was needed. But what are you doing marauding the skies and boarding one of his ships? That's not the best way to repay him for his kindness."

Dani sat back feeling like she'd been struck. But Carl did have a point, and she felt compelled to give both men an explanation.

"After Devil left to return to his life, I stayed on Gavin 1 and watched the pain and suffering of the populace—especially the children. So when the original Red Death put in at Gavin 1 for repairs, not only did I repair his ship, but I charmed my way on board and promptly engineered a mutiny. That was five years ago, and ever since I've been trying to end the war between the Gavin planets the only way I know how—by blocking the weapons to either planet and trying to right the wrongs done here."

Dahlia sniffed. "Now wait just a minute," she aimed at Carl. "I'm sorry if you don't feel Devil would approve, but I think in an odd way he would. Dani has used the skills he taught her to make a difference, and the new regime of Red Death doesn't kill indiscriminately or torture. Yes, our men are now rich from the bounty off of the ships that would help bring more death to this system." She glanced at Dare MacFadyen, who suddenly looked sheepish. "But whereas you and your ship were transporting a hold full of munitions, I'm sure for a very large profit,

Dani here is trying to end a bloody war that has lasted for four generations. Which one of you do you think Devil would approve of more, Mr. MacFadyen?"

Silence fell inside the little room, and it took a long while before Dare MacFadyen broke it. "I don't think Carl meant anything by his remarks. It's just very odd to find a benevolent space pirate, especially since the name Red Death is synonymous around the galaxy with death, destruction, and profit."

Dani studied Dare as her body continued to react to his close presence. The electricity in the air was so thick she was sure Carl and Dahlia could physically see it. She knew she felt it and was pretty sure from the way Dare held her gaze and continued to shift in his chair, most likely to find a more comfortable position for his rather large erection, that he was experiencing something similar.

Her smugness lasted until she looked down to where he'd directed his gaze. The girls were noteworthy, but not her best feature.

Crap! Her uniform had come undone during her tussle with Jared.

Dare sucked in a large breath and tried to wrestle his traitorous body under control. He'd been thrown for a loop to find out that Red Death was not only a woman but had known and been helped by his grandfather. Now that he'd heard her story, he could see that Devil would be proud she was using the skills he had taught her to do some good, even if it was in the guise of a vicious pirate with a sweet set of tatas.

"So what happens now?" he couldn't help but ask as she wrapped her arms around her chest to hide what she'd shown when she propped her arm on the table.

Dani smiled and the entire room seemed to light, or maybe it was just Dare's libido. It had been a long time since he'd had a woman, and this one was definitely intriguing and attractive. And who knew? Maybe he could work out some better circumstances for him and his men. After all, women had been using sex as a bargaining tool for centuries, so what was wrong with a man using it for once?

"My men are offloading the munitions as we speak, and I'm assuming you've already missed your delivery window to Gavin 2. So we discuss like civilized human beings what's next. Any preferences, gentlemen, other than returning your munitions?"

The cultured words rolled from her lips and made Dare think of nibbling those lips like the finest chocolate until she sighed beneath him. Perhaps bargaining with Dani using sex wouldn't be such a bad thing. He'd taken one for the team under much less enjoyable circumstances.

Heat burned up his neck and into his face as she caught him staring, and he forcibly dropped his gaze.

Carl made a small noise in the back of his throat and Dare turned toward him, happily turning the conversation over to someone who had more blood in his brain than his cock right now. Dare knew it had been a while since he'd had a woman, but for some reason this particular woman sent his libido into overdrive. He'd tried to reason with his body, to remind it that this woman had hijacked his ship, kidnapped him and his crew, and made them miss out on a small fortune, but his erection only tightened.

"I assume since we've come this far that you've decided not to kill us." Carl smiled and raised his brows, which made his comment sound almost wistful.

Dahlia laughed. "That would be awfully rude at this point, don't you think? Speaking of rude, Carl, was that you doing the flying over there? I'll admit, some of those moves you were executing made me curse in very unladylike ways." She grinned to remove any sting from the "rude" comment. "Any way you could give me some flying tips while you're here?"

The corners of Carl's lips slowly curved as if the smile was reluctant, but he couldn't help himself. Dare knew what he was going through. These two women were charming, even though they were supposed to be ruthless pirates and they'd caused him and his crew a whole lot of trouble. Time to use his manly wiles to turn the situation in their favor. He caught Dani's gaze and held it before letting his lips curve into an inviting smile.

"Well, Miss Dahlia. Don't discount your skills. That was some damned good flying." Carl broke into Dare's thoughts. "I've been piloting for thirty years and you gave me a good run for my money. Why don't you and I retire to your control room and we can discuss flying tactics and possibly some next steps while we leave these two alone? I'm afraid if we stay here much longer, we'll be caught in the aftermath of the fiery explosion that's sparking between these two."

Carl sent Dare a meaningful look and Dare got the distinct impression that Carl was all for plan "taking one for the team."

Dahlia laughed as more heat burned into Dare's neck and face. So the old man was on the same wavelength? At least it didn't seem like Carl would disapprove. One glance toward Dani showed him a blush burning brightly on her cheeks. She hadn't exactly been subtle about her attraction to Dare, so being called out on it probably would cause some embarrassment.

Dahlia stood signaling an end to this portion of the conversation and Carl followed suit.

Within seconds Dare and Dani sat alone staring at each other across the expanse of the metal table. Dare wasn't sure which one of them would break the ice, but he had to clench his hands into fists to keep from reaching out for her and pulling her against him—probably a great way to find out firsthand how the shock collar worked. But he wasn't sure how to smoothly break the ice in this instance. It wouldn't be a hardship to seduce and bed her, but getting his ass kicked in the process didn't seem like a good part of the plan.

"So, Dare . . ." Dani trailed off and then wanted to bang her head against the table. *Very smooth, Dani.* Not!

Dare grinned back at her, making her think he was just as affected as she. Not to mention the way he'd been staring at her as if she were a tall drink of water and he was a man dying of thirst.

"Dani, I know this is highly unusual, but I tend to be very straight talking." He took a deep breath and held her gaze with a sensual smile curving his lips. "I know I'm your captive and we still haven't determined what you're going to do with all of us and my ship, but you're the most attractive woman I've ever seen. And it's not just that you're physically attractive, or that you learned all your skills from my grandfather, but also that you took a very bad situation and turned it into an altruistic one. Not that I appreciate being robbed of quite a bit of credits that we would've received from Gavin 2, but I do understand why you did it, and even think my grandfather would be proud of the way you've taken the twists and turns in your life and made them into something good." He shook his head. "Don't get me wrong. I have no intention of getting involved in the politics here in the Gavin system, I was just delivering ordered goods, but I can see your side. Anyway, as I was saying, I just can't stop staring at you like some teenage idiot. I would apologize, but I'm not the least bit sorry."

A smile blossomed across Dani's face that instantly brightened the entire room and made Dare's heart skip a beat. If he had that smile to wake up to every morning for the rest of his life, he'd be a happy man.

Where the hell had that thought come from?

Sure, he expected to settle down someday. But someday was a long way off. He was still a young man, and there was plenty of time for domestics later on.

She really was an enchanting woman. He wished he could be practicing this seduction, inept as it was, under better circumstances. But then again, how would it look for the owner and operator of MacFadyen Shipping to suddenly take up with an infamous pirate. It wouldn't matter if she was the second Red Death or not, his business would most likely take a hit, and that he couldn't allow. The news of his flagship being captured and him not making his delivery would already require quite a bit of reputation repair. After all, the Universe's wealthy hired MacFadyen ships for safe pleasure cruises around the galaxy—with safe being the keyword. Although Dare suddenly wondered if there would be a market for excitement cruises where millionaires got the experience of being hijacked by a gorgeous and more friendly version of Red Death. He smirked at the thought.

Dani stood quickly, her chair scraping against the floor with a loud screech.

Dare braced, not sure what would happen next, but then Dani leaned across the table, grabbed the front of his shirt in her fist, and held him still for a fiery kiss.

Her lips were warm and insistent against his, and his gasp of surprise allowed her entry. She didn't waste time slipping her tongue inside his mouth. Dare slowly stood so as not to spook her and edged around the table so he could hold her in his arms. She melted against him, and his body silently sent up thanks for every luscious, warm curve that pressed against him.

He speared his fingers into her hair and she made an *mmm* sound against his mouth as she reached around and grabbed his ass in both hands.

His erection throbbed where it pressed against the soft skin of her stomach, and he wanted nothing more than to pull her down to the floor and plunge inside her until she clenched around him and cried out in ecstasy.

The door burst open and Dare started as Dani pulled back—all the sensations of having her close and warm against him suddenly ripped away.

Dare held his arms out at his sides in his best "I'm harmless" stance and glanced toward the intruder, who turned out to be Mr. Beefy who had led Dare and Carl to this room earlier. Mr. Beefy's face was dark and stormy—not a good omen for Dare's continued health and existence. He hoped Dani wasn't Mr. Beefy's woman. He couldn't stomach the thought of the red-headed goddess in front of him with the stocky, harsh-looking man looming in the doorway.

"Jared." Dani's voice sounded calm and cool even though her chest still rose and fell in a choppy rhythm showing Dare she was still fighting off the same arousal that still pumped through his veins.

"Dani? Is everything all right? I saw Dahlia and the other prisoner in the mess hall and figured I'd come back to check on you."

Dani raised one brow and turned a chiding look toward Jared. "While I appreciate your concern, I have everything well in hand here. You can return to your station and I'll ring for you if I need anything at all."

Jared's expression turned sheepish, and Dare thought he also detected a bit of hurt. Maybe Jared did have something of a crush on his boss, but then who could blame the man. Dare had been here less than two hours and his body was on overdrive with this woman. What would it be like to work with her day in and day out and not be able to touch her, hold her, or possess her?

"Yes, boss. I apologize. I should've known you could handle

yourself in any situation. It's just we—the crew and I—are pretty protective of you. You're the best boss we've ever had, and we're not keen to lose you."

Dani smiled, and the hurt drained off Jared's face as if it had never been there. "I know, Jared. And you men are the best crew I've ever worked with. But as you know from our fight nights, I can handle myself in pretty much any situation, and even without the shock collar, Mr. MacFadyen would be no match for me if he chose to do something I didn't want or like."

Surprise slapped at Dare. She'd said she'd been trained to fight by his grandfather, but then so had he, and he was bigger and stronger. He wondered if she was really that good or if that last statement had been purely for Jared's benefit.

Jared cast Dare a last warning look and left, closing the door firmly behind him.

"Fight nights?" Dare couldn't help but ask.

Dani nodded. "Yes, I started them when I took over to gain the crew's respect and to make it clear that if they saw me as an easy mark somewhere along the line, they were mistaken. There are bets placed and I fight anyone who volunteers. First one to say 'Uncle' loses. To date, I've never said 'Uncle.'"

Dare whistled long and low, impressed and intrigued. "If Devil taught you to fight, then I'm not surprised. He taught me as well. Just out of pure curiosity, I'd love to see which one of us would win."

Dani ginned. "Maybe later, Dare. Right now I can think of a whole host of other things I'd rather do with you."

A knock on the door had Dare turning to see what would happen now.

"Come in," called Dani, and the door swung open to reveal Jared again.

"I apologize, boss, but Dahlia has news for you. She said she'd meet you in the control room. Would you like me to take this prisoner to your quarters to await your return?" Jared's voice was carefully neutral, but Dare was surprised he'd even made the offer after the earlier scene.

Dani looked back and forth between the two men and nodded. "Yes, thank you, Jared." She looked at Dare and grinned. "I'll go see what news Dahlia has and then I'll return to my quarters."

3

Dare had no business wanting to fuck the woman who meant sure death to his future. Yet here he was.

As much as he could deny it, the attraction was more than he'd like to admit. If he couldn't handle this, what business did he have taking over his grandfather's legacy?

He scanned the furnishings inside her personal cabin while Dani was being briefed by her first officer. One minute he was in the captain's ready room talking to Dani about which one of them would win in a fight, and now he was facing a much bigger battle.

Jared had brought him here, warned him not to disturb anything, and tethered him by his ankle to the metal bunk with a chain. That had been about an hour ago, and he wondered if Dani was going to return or if he'd misunderstood her intent to join him in the first place. After all, how often were invitations to personal chambers extended from infamous space pirates—female or not? Dare had no idea, but from his little time with Dani he didn't think it was often.

He had to admit, this was better than he'd expected. After Jared had walked in on them kissing, Dare thought he'd be dead or writhing in pain for the rest of his existence for daring to touch their boss—even if *she* had touched him first.

And oh, what a touch it was. His body still reacted to her as if she were held close, her soft curves melding against him.

Things like this happened in old Earth novels and movies, but never happened in real life, right?

Or maybe it was purely that they were two captains who hadn't found anyone lately to share intimacy with, and when sparks flew between them unexpectedly, neither could deny the realities? Either way, his rock-hard cock reminded him that he was right where he wanted to be for the moment; well, not exactly, but much closer than he had been.

Besides, he still had a goal to reach. He needed to get Dani firmly on his side so he could get himself, his ship, and his crew out of this situation in the best and quickest possible order. He just had to sort out how to make that happen.

"Hello, human male."

Dare startled at the mechanical voice coming from across the room. He turned his head and saw a rather large purple pleasure probe sitting in a charging station on Dani's dresser. He chuckled and wondered if Dani realized she'd left it out.

Unable to contain his curiosity, he stepped closer to the probe and touched the Power button.

Instead of powering down, it flew off the pedestal and hovered just beyond his reach.

"I'm sure you're not here to use my services. Are you here looking for a pretty pussy? Dani's is pretty and soft and hasn't experienced the explosion of orgasm in at least two month's time. That's when she purchased me. Although she did try locking me in one of her drawers for nearly a month, so I can't vouch for her activities during my exile.

"I hated it in that dark place, even lying on all her soft lacy panties. I like the open air much better. It doesn't dry out my lovely synthetic exterior."

Dare frowned at the pleasure probe as it flitted about the room. He'd never heard of a talking model, especially not one with such a sarcastic sense of humor or such sentience—not that he'd had a lot of experience with pleasure probes.

He'd seen them in marketplaces, of course, but not having need of one himself, and preferring to use his own equipment when the opportunity presented, this was the first one he'd seen up close and personal, so to speak.

"I doubt Dani would want you telling everyone her business, pleasure probe." He nearly smacked himself on the forehead as he realized he was having a conversation with a sex toy. Not exactly a distinguished pastime for a ship's captain, not to mention someone who considered themselves a very masculine man.

"You can call me Pussy-do."

"Pussy-do? Really? I don't think so."

"Male human, you're the only one besides Dani I've had a conversation with, and since I assume you're here to see if you can succeed where I have failed her, we are in somewhat of the same capacity."

The prod to his pride annoyed him. Dare didn't like being lumped in the same capacity with a pleasure probe, but he refused to argue his point with the talking rod of silicone . . . or whatever. Especially since the damn probe had a point.

After all, wasn't he here to use his body and Dani's arousal against her to get himself out of the situation he'd gotten himself and his crew into?

"I want to see your equipment." Pussy-do dive-bombed Dare's head. He batted at it, moving back until his legs hit the bed. The damned contraption had herded him. No way in hell was he going to show his cock to a toy.

"Pussy-do off."

Dani's terse words behind him startled Dare, and he turned to find her with red flaming into her cheeks, staring at him with mortification clear in her expression.

The probe fell from the air onto the bed near his leg. "Good thing it was hovering over the bed or it'd be in pieces."

"I'm so sorry, I forgot all about that damned thing. I have to take it in for adjustments. It's begun to pick up my snarky speech habits."

Dare couldn't help but laugh, especially since the damn thing had him cornered before Dani had arrived. "No problem. I'm sorry if it embarrassed you."

She shrugged, which did great things to her generous cleavage.

"My fault entirely. I shouldn't have left you for so long, but Dahlia and I had business to take care of." She smiled, but it didn't quite reach her eyes, which made him wonder just what business they'd had to discuss.

"I'll make you a deal. You don't tell anyone what my obnoxious probe said, and I won't tell anyone—especially your crew—that you just held an entire conversation with a large, flying, purple pleasure probe in the captain's private quarters."

Heat flowed into Dare's cheeks as he thought about the ribbing he would take if his crew ever found out about this. "Deal." He laughed and picked up the probe. "Why don't you just toss it in a drawer? I know it said it wasn't happy there, but at least that would shut it up."

She appeared horrified to see it in his hands, but she didn't reach for it. He ran his free hand over the length and tried not to show how uncomfortable it made him. "It's hard to imagine this little thing making so much trouble."

"L-little? Ahem. So it told you about that." She blinked hard before looking away from the probe and down to the juncture of Dare's legs.

Dare drew a slow, deep breath as he fought not to laugh.

Was she wondering if the probe was indeed little compared to him?

"I think you traumatized it . . . er her."

Don't smile, he told himself.

She sighed. "It becomes positively impossible when I try to stuff it into a drawer. It yells and thumps around and screams like a banshee until all its power cells are depleted, and that, of course, is when I want to use it. I've learned it's just easier to leave it on the power station and ignore it. I just need to take it in for adjustments soon before I'm tempted to carry it through the ship just to toss it out an air lock for some peace and quiet. I dropped too many credits on it not to figure out a way to co-exist with it peacefully."

Dare restrained himself. He'd tormented her enough. A prolonged pause ensued as he studied her clothes. If he was in her quarters, how had she managed a change of clothing? Maybe she'd borrowed it from Dahlia?

She now wore some type of gauzy top and pants that allowed Dare to see her turgid nipples and her dark areolas through the cloth, not to mention the dark red thatch of curls at the juncture of her thighs that proved she was a true redhead.

A jolt of pure anticipation caused him to drop the probe on the bed.

Dare's mouth went bone dry, and he swallowed hard to try to break the mesmerizing spell her body seemed to suddenly have over him. He wondered if she'd known the effect this outfit would have on him, or if it was purely accidental. Regardless, his body liked it a lot, and his brain didn't mind it either.

"Anyway," Dani began. "How about I take that ankle restraint off and we can pick up where we left off when Jared originally interrupted us? Unless you have any objections, of course. I know this is an odd gender reversal, but I don't force my attentions on my captives. In fact, I've never . . ." Dani trailed off, and Dare took the opportunity to close the gap between them and pull her flush against him again. He searched her gaze for signs she didn't want him. Her eyes, a startling color of green, reassured him. She definitely wanted him.

She was warm and soft and melted against him just as she had in the ready room. He slid his fingers into the lush red hair at her nape and when her tongue flicked against his lips, he pressed his mouth to hers.

She opened for him immediately and allowed him to taste her sweet feminine heat. He fought not to make too much of the way sensations pinged along his nerve endings from the kiss. Something about her was so different . . . and yet too familiar. Thankfully she distracted him by running her hands over his chest, his abs, around to his ass and then back again. When her hand reached his aching erection, he groaned into her mouth and slid his hands down from her hair to begin to slowly explore her wondrous curves. He'd seen her beautiful breasts up close and personal in the ready room—accidentally, if he'd read the situation correctly—but they fit in his hands perfectly and he couldn't wait to taste them.

But this was a woman to be savored, not one to be plundered quickly and forgotten. He was quite sure he wouldn't forget Dani McGovern, aka Red Death, for quite a few years to come.

"I should still get that ankle restraint off, unless you want to see if we can continue this with you still chained," she said against his mouth, then pulled back with a smirk. His arms felt empty without her.

"I think removing my chain is a good idea. I promise not to do anything that would piss off Jared . . . unless . . ."

Dani raised one brow. "Unless what?"

Dare mentally stumbled and wondered if he'd fallen into one of those woman traps of things you're never supposed to say. But it was too late to back out now, so he manned up and answered her. "Unless you're his woman?"

Dani frowned and pierced Dare with a steady gaze. "First, no man owns me, Mr. MacFadyen. And second, I don't make it a habit to sleep with my crew. He's just protective . . . all of them are. I've been good to them since I took over, and they return the favor. Besides, I think Jared and Dahlia are seeing each other. I've been seeing some signs just today that convince me I'm right. So there's no competition standing in your way. Unless you're just not interested." She squared her shoulders and kept his gaze.

Dare's respect for her edged up another notch. He appreciated the straightforward approach in both women and men. Although he wasn't interested in men the way he was interested in the sexy woman who stood before him. Dare was definitely heterosexual, and his cock agreed.

Dare pointedly glanced down at his very full erection and then slid his gaze back up to Dani's. "As you can see, I'm quite interested . . . Dani. I just wanted to make sure I wasn't stepping into any territorial disputes. After all, this is uncharted territory for me." Those words worried him. They were far too close to the truth. This was about getting free with his crew and cargo intact, nothing more.

She laughed. "For me, too, Mr. MacFadyen, I assure you."

Dare frowned. "This is so not going to work if you keep calling me Mr. MacFadyen. Please, my name is Dare. I think we should already be on a first-name basis, don't you?"

Dani nodded as if acceding to his point.

"Dare," she said, as if trying out how saying his name would feel on her tongue, which sent thoughts of what else she could feel with her tongue skittering through his already blood-starved brain.

When Dani knelt in front of him, his erection twitched; then Dare realized she was just removing his ankle tether like they'd spoken about a few times now before they'd gotten distracted by other things.

A distinct clicking noise signaled the lock disengaging; then the chain holding his ankle loosened and fell away.

"Sorry about that," she said from her still-crouched position. "I suppose Jared felt you could get into less trouble this way." She tossed a pointed look toward the pleasure probe still lying where he'd dropped it. "Or not."

Dare stifled a laugh. "Don't forget, we have a solemn oath to not speak of what went on with that pleasure probe in this cabin today."

A huge grin curved her lips and she nodded. "Don't worry, Dare. I never break a promise. Now, where were we?" She slowly stood, her breasts brushing his erection as she rose, the top of her head coming up even with his chin. Their gazes locked and held with fierce hunger on both their parts. If she dared deny it, he'd call her on it.

He took one step back and then lowered his face to hers so he could capture her lush mouth and fall back into the kiss that they'd started earlier.

Dani sighed against his lips and this time let him lead. All constraints of duty were pushed aside, and he threw himself into the task of seducing this amazing woman . . . for his own pleasure.

He ran one hand down her shoulder and brushed it along the side of one full breast, reaching out with his index finger to graze the rock-hard nipple.

He was rewarded with a moan and Dani leaning harder against him.

She placed both her palms on his shoulders as if for balance, and Dare took that as an invitation to continue. He reached around to the back of the gauzy top and found the hook and zipper combination at the neck that kept the top closed and up. He made quick work of the hook and zipper, then pulled back just far enough to whisk the shirt over Dani's head and toss it aside.

The vision of Dani's translucent bra, a filmy piece of material that teased and tantalized, made a deep groan fill Dare's chest. "You are lovely."

Filmy material didn't match the mood overtaking him. His need became a roaring fiend.

He wanted, craved skin-to-skin contact. His pulse raced and his breath quickened. With one quick flick of his fingers, he opened the clasp to her bra and let it fall between them.

"Now we're getting somewhere. I think it's time for the human male to show his equipment too."

Damn! How had he forgotten about the damned probe? Dare turned a quick scowl on Pussy-do and realized one of the arm straps of the bra had neatly lassoed the probe and now hung on the thick purple tube.

He was about to toss it against the wall when Dani grabbed his face in both hands and turned him back to face her. She pulled him close and recaptured his lips. Her breath was coming in choppy pants, and Dare couldn't resist tracing one blunt finger around the waistband of her pants and dipping it inside to tease the tops of her curls just under her lacy panties.

Dani pulled the tail of Dare's shirt from his pants and tugged impatiently until he pulled it off and tossed it on top of the probe . . . or at least he assumed he did since no more snarky comments interrupted them.

Her dainty hands running over his chest and her dexterous fingers tracing through his chest hair sent lances of molten lava throughout his body and tightened his balls almost painfully.

When Dani placed a trail of open-mouthed kisses along his jaw and then down his neck and torso, he nearly exploded, and had to take several deep breaths to keep from embarrassing himself as he imagined that insistent set of lips sliding up and down his cock.

"Mmm, salty," she murmured as she continued to kiss and started unbuckling his belt and unzipping his zipper.

Dare adjusted his stance and speared his fingers into the silky mass of her hair once again, purely to be able to touch her while she tantalized and drove him crazy.

Dani reached in to free his aching erection and then swiftly pulled down his pants and underwear at the same time, leaving them pooled around his ankles. His cock stood out proudly, pointing toward Dani as if it were a homing beacon and she was the destination he sought.

"I wish my programmers would have been as generous with my design as yours, human male. Are you artificially enhanced?"

Dare's eyes widened in surprise as he took a direct hit to the male ego. He couldn't help but turn toward the pleasure probe and retort, "No, probe. I am most certainly not artificially enhanced. And you can bet that once Dani and I are finished today, she won't have a need for you for quite a while. I'll make damn sure of that."

"We'll see, human male. Sometimes silicone is stronger than flesh."

"Like you've done such a good job in the past few months," he couldn't help but retort.

Dani stiffened, and he realized too late that his comment would only embarrass her.

"Touché, human male. Time will tell."

"Do you two mind?" Dani demanded. With the tips of her fingers she touched the crown of his erection, tracing an invisible line around it before caressing his slit. "We're in the middle of something here. If you two would like to trade bedtime stories later, I'll try to leave you time."

Dare reached out, picked up his shirt, and unceremoniously wrapped it several times around the probe before dropping it to the floor where he could pin it under his foot. He wasn't sure how the thing *saw*, but maybe that would curtail some of its mischief.

It immediately began to complain, but the muffled sound didn't deter him. Rather than being drawn back into more banter with the inanimate object, he turned his full attention to Dani, who was still on her knees in front of him with one hand on his cock.

"I apologize. I've never encountered a pleasure probe before—especially a talking one."

"And you let it prick your male pride, pun intended."

It wasn't a question, but Dare nodded self-consciously anyway. "I suppose I did."

"Well, you have nothing to worry about on that score." She gently squeezed his cock and lightly cupped his balls with the other hand before slipping her lips over the head of his cock, and in one swift move took him deep.

Tingles of arousal burned inside his balls and deep inside his pelvis. He used all his willpower not to spill down the back of Dani's throat like some teenage boy receiving his first blow job.

As if she sensed his predicament, she stopped sucking to place little butterfly kisses around his cock head. It gave him time to compose himself until her head dipped lower and she teased the tag of skin just behind the crown. First she worried it with her tongue before nipping with a gentle touch.

It took a strong man to allow a woman to use her teeth.

He sank his fingers into her soft hair, telling her with his massaging touch that he liked what she was doing to him. The slow, sweet, downward slide of the flat of her tongue changed his mind. He didn't like it . . . he loved it, and the moan escaping his lips echoed in the small space. She licked him until he found it difficult not to grab her head and fuck her mouth.

This was her party, and he didn't want to meddle with perfection.

After she made her exploration a couple of times, a drop of precome dotted his crown. When she noticed, she made an audible hiss as she sucked in air. She stopped and glanced up at him with a mischievous gleam dancing in her green eyes.

Yes.

He grew harder.

With a flick of her tongue she captured the drop just as it grew large enough to dribble. Her smile of contentment warmed his heart and made him feel all-powerful . . . virile.

In the next moment, she lost her smile and took on a look of seriousness. Engulfing his cock with her mouth, she worked him in and out, each time going a little deeper. When the strong muscles at the back of her throat clutched him tight, it was all he could do not to thrust.

He turned his concentration to making his breathing deep and even, anything to distract him from the exquisite sensations traveling up and down his cock. He had to take control of this encounter before he totally embarrassed himself. "I want to be inside you when I come."

4

Dani took Dare's cock deep inside her mouth until he bumped the back of her throat; then she lightly cupped his balls between her fingers. His balls were firm, yet soft, with a light dusting of hair around the base where they attached to his body and edged up against his thick cock.

He was quite an impressive specimen—no wonder the pleasure probe had seemed threatened by him.

Dani glanced up past his stiff cock and firm, tight abs to see the bronzed expanse of his chest dusted by crisp dark hairs. She remembered the sensation of running her fingers through those hairs a few minutes ago and her core throbbed, reminding her she was tired of all this foreplay. She wanted him inside her, and she wanted him now.

Dare must've been on the same wavelength because he placed a gentle hand on the top of her head and then stepped back, pulling his cock out of her mouth with an audible *pop*.

"Not that I don't love your mouth around my cock, but if I don't touch you soon, I'm going to come. I want to be buried deep inside you when that happens." He knelt and picked her up as if she weighed no more than the pleasure probe—which she definitely did. "I hope you don't mind, but I'm going to speed things along a little."

"I'm good to follow your lead." And she meant it. Dani didn't mind speeding things up at all; in fact, she nearly sighed with relief. Every part of her body ached to orgasm, and it was long past due.

Dare laid her gently on her bunk and then made quick work of her boots, pants, and panties. He slid into the bunk and curled against her—a comforting warm weight that she'd waited far too long to enjoy. The seduction of skin on skin made her arousal soar. She showed her appreciation with a satisfied moan.

His large hand cupped her breast and his calloused fingers sent sensations skyrocketing through her. But then he guided one aching nipple to his lips. When that insistent heat closed over her, she thought she would die from the pleasure it sent ricocheting through her.

Her labia throbbed and her clit ached, begging for its own attention.

Be patient, damn it all! she thought to her traitorous body. *I'm busy enjoying here!*

Dare swirled his tongue over her nipple one last time before switching his concentration to the other breast.

While Dani appreciated the well-balanced attention, she nearly wept with gratitude when he slid his hand down over her stomach and delved his fingers into her already moist curls to find the aching nub that had been begging for attention just a moment ago.

As soon as that wonderfully calloused finger touched the soft, sensitive skin, lava lanced through her and she arched against his hand.

"I can see I'm not the only one impatient to have me inside you."

Dare's deep voice vibrated through her, and she could only find the energy in her foggy brain to grunt in agreement as she continued to grind against his hand.

"Please. Soon," she finally huffed out in between ragged breaths.

Dare chuckled and shifted them so she lay on her back and he lay between her thighs. "But first, I have to see if you taste as sweet as I've been imagining."

A groan ripped from Dani's throat and she clenched her fists in her bedding to keep from grabbing the man and impaling herself on his thick cock right then. It's not as if he were unwilling, but it was nice to have a strong man set the pace for once. Most of the men in her past had been content to let her lead, and she'd always craved a strong, virile man to set the pace and leave her to feel like the pampered woman in the equation.

Dani might be a strong woman, but she could definitely admit that in this capacity, she didn't mind being a follower. She wouldn't even mind being someone like Dare MacFadyen's woman.

She frowned at the thought. She wasn't quite ready to give up her single days, but she did admit she craved the touch and company of a man. A man who was hers in every respect, not just the friendship she had with her crew and with Dahlia. Dahlia might share her bed on occasion, but the dynamic was different between two women than it was between a man and a woman.

Dare's tongue made contact with her clit and Dani nearly had to peel herself off the ceiling as the myriad of sensations ripped through her and left her gasping for both breath and reality.

He swirled his tongue over her again and she widened her thighs to give him better access. But when he plunged his tongue inside her, she cried out, fisting her hands in his hair and silently begging for more as she ground her hips against his mouth.

Dare's talented tongue continued to pleasure her, raising her arousal to a fevered pitch for a few more long minutes before he lifted himself and slid inside her with one long, slow stroke.

She groaned long and low as he filled and stretched her. It had been so long, and Dare was so well equipped that it took her body a minute to adjust and remember she could easily accommodate this welcome invasion, and there was more and better to come.

Dare began to move, burying himself to the hilt so the hard tip of his cock bumped against her sensitive cervix and then slid nearly all the way out before delving back inside again.

Dani arched her hips, moving with him and enjoying the closeness and arousal that she hadn't experienced in so long.

When Dare leaned down to capture her lips in a slow, sweet caress, she sighed and smiled against his mouth. She tasted her own sweet, tangy essence on his tongue and groaned with the memory of how he'd *acquired* that taste. With each thrust, the crispy hairs on his chest brushed against her aching nipples, sending a wonderful warm wash of arousal through her. When he fully impaled himself, his hard stomach bumped her aching clit, pushing her higher and closer to her impending goal.

The walls of her sex tightened around him and he groaned into her mouth in response.

"Are you ready to come, Dani? I'm more than ready to feel you pulse around me."

His sensual words tightened her further and she mumbled an affirmative response against his lips before recapturing her wits. "Please, Dare. Make me come, and then I want to feel you spill inside me."

Her words had the immediate effect of making Dare speed up his thrusts and plunge even deeper inside her. Then he surprised her by rolling them both over while still keeping her firmly impaled until she straddled him and he lay on his back in the bunk.

"Ride me, Dani. Pleasure yourself, and let me watch."

Dani groaned at the new, even deeper penetration and wasted no time in experimentally moving to see what felt best. When she found a motion that seemed to please them both, she relaxed into it and leaned her hands on his chest for balance as she moved, rubbing his hard cock inside her just the way she craved.

She was glad she still had two months to go on her yearly birth control cycle and that her STD vaccination was up to date. Not that she thought Dare would be carrying anything, but it was always better to be safe than sorry, especially with some of the more nasty STDs that had broken out during the twenty-second century.

Unaware of her thoughts, Dare reached up to cup her breasts and tease her nipples as she moved, which only complemented the growing sensations curling inside her and waiting for release.

She gasped as he bucked up inside her, and the walls of her sex gripped him impossibly tight. Steady, tingling sensations began deep inside her pelvis, churning and twisting as they rushed out to the rest of her body, picking up speed and intensity until her entire body exploded with orgasm.

Then something happened.

Instead of a climax, she'd entered into a state of bliss unlike anything she'd ever experienced. Now she prayed he wouldn't think she'd come. "Don't stop. Please don't stop." She looked into his gaze and could see he was there—on the edge. "A little more." The pleasure was so intense blackness encroached upon her vision. "Hold on."

Each thrust took her higher. White lightning flashed inside

her brain as she came with a force that snapped her back. Her toes curled with the overwhelming sensations, and her fingers clenched tight against Dare's chest as she cried out his name.

The aftershocks of her explosive orgasm came one after another, each giving her satisfaction worthy of individual thanks. She continued to move, wondering what would happen next.

Dare grabbed her hips and thrust up inside her twice, until with a gasp and a bellow he spilled inside her. The sound of his satisfaction gave her a final burst, so sweet it made her boneless. She collapsed on him with mewling little squeaks.

"Who are you? I sure as hell hope you weren't sent by my enemies, because I surrender."

His warm seed tickled her ass where the cool air contrasted. She buried her face against the side of his neck as she fought to breathe.

What was that? How could she make it happen again? This wasn't just a long overdue orgasm, it was a taste of heaven. It couldn't get any better than this . . . could it?

Unsure of her sudden emotions, she craved the comfort and closeness of a man, and Dare didn't seem to mind fulfilling that wish. In fact, a few minutes later, he rolled them both on their sides, slipping out of her and tucking her against him spoon style, his arm draped over her stomach, holding her close.

"Dani, are you all right?" he asked in his gravelly, deep voice.

"Mmm-hmm," was all she seemed to manage before she asked him the same question.

He chuckled and the vibrations spilled through her body from their close contact, bringing warmth along with them.

"I'm more than all right. I just wanted to make sure I hadn't hurt you. I have had a few women in my past comment that I can be a bit much to accommodate."

His words were said matter-of-factly and not as any kind of boast, which raised him even further in her esteem. Dare Mac-

Fadyen seemed like a good man all the way around, and if he weren't her captive, and if she hadn't just found out some new information on him from Dahlia, she would be in serious danger of falling hard for this man. As it was, she admitted she might be in danger anyway, but it was too late to do anything about it at this point.

After a few more minutes of silence, she realized she'd never answered him. "Sorry, I was wallowing in the aftershocks of amazing sex."

Dare laughed. "I can't argue with you there. My body is still buzzing, and I'm enjoying just lying here next to you and sharing some time. It's been a long time since I've had both the opportunity to do this and someone who was willing. Believe it or not, most women I meet are completely done with me once they orgasm, and I guess I'm that rare breed of man who loves the touching and intimacy that can come after sex as well as the act itself."

Dani filed his words away to study later. "To answer your original question, I'm more than okay. You didn't hurt me a bit. And if that was pain, I'd like a lot more of it and soon." She stopped suddenly as she realized what she'd said and how vulnerable and needy that would make her sound. She must've stiffened, because Dare stroked a gentle hand down her side and nuzzled her nape.

"We're in agreement again. We'd better be careful or we might become friends here."

His words implied the "or something more," and Dani wisely chose to withhold comment since she already knew she was in dangerous territory.

She took a deep breath and delved into the conversation that she'd been avoiding since she came back to her quarters but knew she needed to have.

"Dare, there's something you and I need to talk about."

"Yes, I agree. I'd like to talk about the release of my men, my ship, and Carl and me if you're ready. I know this may not be the best timing, but since you brought it up."

Dani sighed, not looking forward to telling him what she'd learned. "That's not exactly what I meant, but we can definitely discuss that too. I was serious that we don't intend to kill you or even hold you beyond what's necessary. However, there has been a development."

Dare pushed up onto one elbow and looked down to meet Dani's gaze. "What type of development?"

"Gavin 2 has put a price on your head. Yours and Carl's."

"A price?" His brow knit and confusion flowed across his handsome face. "What for? Not delivering their munitions? They can just not pay us for that. Putting a price on us wasn't necessary."

"I'm afraid it's worse than that. They say you're in league with Red Death."

She couldn't help but smile self-consciously at her mention of herself in the third person. "Since your ship is still fully intact and tethered to ours, and there have been no gory stories of crew thrown out air locks or killed outright, they think you're working with us to block their supplies, and since they've tried to take me and my crew out in the past and failed, they figure you and Carl might be easier targets for the mercenaries they hire for this type of job. Even if we let you all go at this point, you'd all be hunted down and exterminated."

"Fuck."

Dani couldn't argue with his sentiment. Both she and Carl had said pretty much the same thing when Dahlia had brought them the news. She'd meant to keep the munitions out of the hands of the Gavin 2 residents, not make the descendant of Devil MacFadyen public enemy number one—behind her and her crew, of course. But hopefully the plan she, Carl, and Dahlia had come up with would give Dare and his crew a fighting chance. At the very least, it was better than sitting and doing nothing until some lucky assassin got through their defenses.

"I know this isn't your problem, but my crew and I need to get out of here. We're sitting ducks, and I refuse to let anyone take me out that easily."

"Dahlia, Carl, and I do have a plan if you're ready to listen."

5

Dare stood on the surface of Gavin 1 hugging a pole, hand-cuffs digging into his wrists with each breath. His pride was about to take another big hit, but if the coming fight could help him and his crew prove to Gavin 2 that they weren't in league with Red Death, he'd do it.

He glanced to his side where Carl also hugged a pole and was handcuffed tightly to keep him from escaping.

The idea was that he would fight Dani . . . and let her win. And Carl would fight Dahlia with similar results. Just the first step in a plan to try to show that they weren't in league with each other. Apparently Dare's pride was well-known and by being beaten by a woman, in a very public setting, it would help to show that he was truly a captive. Especially since Red Death's fighting prowess was also well-known.

He was pretty sure he could make this a convincing fight even if he had to throw it, but he hoped he didn't hurt Dani. And truth be told, since she'd learned to fight from his grand-father, there was a very real chance that she could do some serious damage to him as well.

When she'd outlined this portion of the plan, he'd been more concerned about Carl fighting Dahlia. Carl wasn't a young man, but that would make it easier for him to lose. And Dahlia knew she needed to make it look convincing without hurting his first officer seriously.

Honestly, this was the worst part of the plan for Dare, so he'd rather they get on with it and get it over with. No matter how often he explained to his male pride that this was just for show, and this was *definitely* taking one for the team, his ego smarted and sent him accusing twinges for agreeing to such a crazy plan.

A chorus of shouts rang out from the large crowd that made Dare think the entire population of Gavin 1 had come out to watch. Dahlia came to uncuff Carl and lead him to the far sand-pit. From what Dare could tell, there were approximately twenty large sandpits, each roughly the size of an old Earth basketball court, scattered across the landscape. Each one sloped down into a flat base and as far as he could tell held all kinds of gaming events, including fights. He could see tall buildings off in the distance, but the main landscaping here was the sandpits.

Dare couldn't see the action in the far sandpit from his current position, but with the large crowd gathered, he was sure he'd hear a play-by-play, or at least some portion of it.

A few long minutes later, the fight began, if the shouts were any indication, and Dare gritted his teeth hoping Carl could hold his own. Carl was a seasoned fighter, but Dahlia was much younger and much quicker, and to make it a convincing fight there would definitely have to be some blows exchanged.

About ten minutes later, a general groan came from the crowd and Dare took that to mean the fight was over. When Carl and Dahlia emerged from the sandpit looking no worse for wear except a slight limp for Carl, Dare breathed a sigh of relief.

Now for the hard part.

Dani appeared in front of him and unlocked the cuffs.

"Are you ready for this, Dare?"

He sighed. "As ready as I'll ever be. Is everything else going as expected?"

While they were down here dealing with appearances, both crews were up in space moving all the weapons and armament from Dani's ship to Dare's. Dare's ship could easily hold both crews, and since he would be the one under fire if bounty hunters came after him, they'd decided to be ready. More appearances, but then perception was everything, wasn't it?

Dani led Dare down into the sandpit and when they both stood about a foot apart, she raised her hands to let the crowd know the fight was about to begin. A shout rang out from the crowd and then a loud murmur as bets were exchanged.

Dare almost felt bad for those who would mistakenly bet on him. Dani had quite a reputation, so maybe she would garner most of the favor, but again, that dented Dare's pride. He would let Dani win, but he'd give a damn good show on his way to the loser's circle.

Without warning, Dani executed a perfect jump kick, and Dare reacted just in time to take only part of the blow on his cheek and let his head snap back in a realistic approximation of the aftermath of such a blow.

While her leg was still in the air and she was off balance, Dare swept her right foot out from under her and heard a small chuckle from her as she landed square on her ass.

At least the soft sand would break her fall. He definitely didn't want to hurt her just to save his pride.

Dani was on her feet within seconds and throwing a right hook straight into his solar plexus.

He tucked slightly to absorb the blow and tried to give the correct "aftermath" of such a hit.

In response, he threw an uppercut and Dani's head snapped

back and then lolled forward, a fine performance of perfectly absorbing the blow. Then she twirled away as if his punch had knocked her off balance.

The crowd yelled and Dare couldn't tell if it was in approval or disappointment.

His momentary distraction with the crowd nearly caused him a painful injury when he noticed, almost too late, that Dani's foot was headed straight for his crotch. He turned slightly so his upper thigh absorbed the blow, but then he doubled over, his hands clutching his family jewels protectively as he crumpled to the ground. He was glad they'd worked out the choreography in advance or he might not have caught that blow in time to avoid a very painful hit.

If he could've thrown up on command he would have, but that was a bit too much to do even for theatrics.

Dani advanced on him in his *vulnerable* state and he grabbed her ankles, pulling her down to the ground before she could kick him or stomp on him.

He figured not protecting himself in such a situation would be too unbelievable, and besides, he wanted Dani to know he still had a few tricks up his sleeve.

He pulled her forward and covered her body with his own heavier one.

The crowd went wild, catcalling and shaking their fists in the air—again, Dare couldn't tell if it was in support or not.

"Good job," Dani hissed in his ear before she maneuvered her elbow into his side and rolled them both over so he was now on the bottom.

Once she straddled him, she wrapped her hands around his neck and squeezed.

Dare tried to remain calm and relax, even when he felt the blood pool in his face and his airflow became severely restricted.

He threaded his arms between hers and with a grunt and a heave broke her grip and rolled her over once more.

"Okay, let's finish it," Dani whispered just loud enough for him to hear. "None of my fights last this long. Roll with me and make sure your thighs are apart so we don't damage anything we'd like to use later."

Dare rolled them both over again until Dani straddled him, but as she came to rest, she placed her knee hard between his open thighs, just missing his tender bits and digging her knee into the soft sand.

Dare took the imaginary hit as would be expected and flung his arms wide to lay on the sand, in effect giving up and watching as Dani scrambled off of him and held her arms in the air victory style.

Dare wasn't sure if the fight had been convincing enough or not, but it was time for them to flee Gavin 1 and start stage two of their plan.

Before he could pull himself to his feet and make a shaky retreat off the playing field, a huge explosion rocked the world and he glanced up into the sky to see the resulting fireball.

Confusion flashed through him since this had definitely not been part of the plan, at least as far as he had understood from the briefing. The only two ships he knew of in orbit above them were his and Dani's, so one of them had obviously just blown up. He selfishly hoped it was Dani's and not his.

The crowd erupted into chaos and stampeded in all different directions, the noise level growing deafening in the process and showing they hadn't expected such a display either.

Dare turned to Dani as she led the way out of the pit. "Was that part of the plan you forgot to tell me?" He glanced up into the sky meaningfully.

When she shook her head, Dare's blood chilled in his veins. Had one of the bounty hunters decided to take out his ship while he and Carl were down here fighting? Only one way to find out.

They met Dahlia and Carl at the top of the hill by the posts, and the four of them filed through the surging crowd toward the shuttle craft they'd flown down to the planet earlier in the day.

A tall man in shiny chrome armor stepped out from behind their craft and sent two laser shots toward Dare and Carl.

Dani swept both men's feet out from under them, narrowly saving them from being shot. Dare landed with a thump that knocked his breath from his lungs and left him momentarily dazed.

Two more sizzling shots rang out and Dare turned to see Dahlia with a laser gun in each hand.

The man crumpled and fell, and the four wasted no time in boarding the shuttle and starting the preflight sequence to escape the planet.

"Well," Carl began, "we've survived our first bounty hunter. I wonder how many more we'll have to escape before they get us? The odds definitely are not in our favor."

Dare left Carl and Dahlia to fly the ship and took a seat next to Dani. "Thanks. We would be dead on the ground right now if you hadn't stepped in."

"It was just a reflex action, but you're welcome. How about you thank me in person later when we can find some alone time?"

Dare's cock surged to life as he thought about exactly what that thanks would entail. "You're on. And maybe we can trade some more fighting moves in an interesting manner when we're alone."

Dani smiled, her green eyes sparkling with mischief. "Too bad Carl can't thank Dahlia in the same way, but I think he's a bit too old for her. Maybe we'll reward her with some time off with Jared. The plush beds on board your ship will be a nice change from the hard bunks on my ship. That is, if your ship was the one that survived." Her face clouded. "However, from the size of the fireball, I doubt it was yours. So it looks like I may be in the market for a new ship sometime soon. Know of anywhere I can find one cheap?"

"I thought you were a rich space pirate. Why do you need one cheap?"

"I never spend more than I need to. How else do you expect me to stay rich?"

Dare laughed but couldn't argue with her logic. "We'll see how the rest of the plan goes and if we're all still alive at the end of it, I'm sure I can help you locate a ship, if you're still going to be pirating, that is."

Dani's cheeks turned red and Dare knew he'd hit a nerve.

"I have been thinking about retiring for a while now. Jared and Dahlia are more than capable of running the operation; but to be honest, I have no idea what I would do with myself."

"I'll be damned." Carl's voice brought Dare's attention to the front view screen where he could clearly see both his ship and Dani's, perfectly sound except for a few new scorch marks on the hull of each ship.

Dare blew out a long breath as relief flowed through him. Even though he would've physically survived the destruction of his ship, he would've felt he'd let his grandfather down in a large fashion to lose it in such a way.

"Let's dock with the ship and find out what happened," Dare said.

Neither Carl nor Dahlia answered, but their hands continued to fly over the controls, and the view on the screen showed Dare's ship growing larger, which meant closer.

"MacFadyen ship, we request docking." Carl's voice was

calm and flat as if none of the earlier events of the day had happened at all.

"You're clear to land," Jared's voice answered back.

Dani laughed. "I guess my crew has already taken over your ship since the men you left in charge aren't answering."

Dare laughed and then frowned. "That wasn't part of the plan either, right?"

Dani grinned up at him as she shook her head. "No, I'm sure they just worked out a shift rotation and not a capture. Don't worry, Captain, your ship is safe and secure. But like you said earlier, perception is everything."

A few minutes later, they were docked with his ship and someone from inside was equalizing the air pressure and then opening the air lock.

Dare stood and motioned for Dahlia and Dani to file out first. Carl followed close behind, and Dare brought up the rear. When he stepped inside the ship, Justin, the man he'd left in charge, nodded. "Dare, we had a small tussle, but everything is all right."

"What happened?"

"A ship fired on us, but we had already completed moving all the weapons over here, so we held our own and then hit a vulnerable spot. We think it was a bounty hunter but can't be sure since they are now nothing but space debris."

"To be honest, from the planet we thought it was Red Death's ship, but I'm glad it wasn't either of our ships. So why is Jared at the controls when I left you in charge?"

"We've been working around the clock, boss, and since he's an expert with their weapons systems, he's training our crew in teams to be proficient with them as well."

Dare nodded. He approved of the decision and was glad he'd left Justin in charge since everything had turned out well.

"Good job. Go get some rest. Carl and I are back and ready to take charge."

Dani and Dahlia craned their necks as Carl led the way through the posh hallways and upstairs to the control room. But Dani was the first to break the silence. "Wow. I've never been on a pleasure liner before. I can see why people pay top dollar to take a vacation on your ship, Dare."

Dare grinned as pride flowed through him. "We also offer excellent customer service and are thinking about expanding our offerings."

"Really?" She raised her brows in question.

"We had thought perhaps people might pay extra for a pleasure cruise where the ship was boarded by Red Death. Of course, not to take captives or rob them, but purely for the adrenaline experience. And that might give you something to do in your . . . retirement."

Dani's expression turned thoughtful. "I'll talk it over with my crew and let you know. I'm assuming there will be compensation involved?"

"Perhaps a cut of the fee for the trip?"

Dani nodded and Dahlia laughed beside her. "It would cut down on danger for the crew, so they just might go for it."

Dare caught Carl's gaze. "I'm a little worried about losing customers by going into business with Red Death, but the adrenaline of the experience might attract more business than it scares away."

Carl grinned. "I think you're right, boy. Don't underestimate the willingness of the rich to live vicariously. I think it would be a large draw. Now, if we can just get the bounty hunters off our tails, we could think about putting it into practice."

When Carl reached the control room he motioned for the women to precede him and then for Dare before he stepped inside.

Dare immediately straightened and resumed command.

"Jared, I hear you're training my crew on the weapons systems. I appreciate it."

Jared shrugged. "If we're going to keep this ship safe, then everyone on all shifts needs to be proficient at covering our asses."

Dare couldn't argue with that.

"Justin updated me on the blown-up ship as well, so we're ready to contact Gavin 2."

Dani sighed and glanced out the view screen where her ship hung motionless and empty. "Let's get it over with so we can move on. But even though it's not as fancy as yours, I must admit I'll miss my ship."

Dare wasn't sure what to answer, so he remained silent and took the seat next to Jared at the control panel. "All right, everyone. Quiet on the set. I'm opening a com channel to Gavin 2." He tapped the appropriate controls and when static came on the line, he took a deep breath before he spoke. "Gavin 2, this is Dare MacFadyen requesting a conversation with the president of the council."

More static sounded on the line for a few minutes until finally a man's voice cut off the static. "Go ahead, Mr. Mac-Fadyen. President Everly is on the line."

"Mr. President, my crew has won our freedom from Red Death and we now control their ship. We are offering to sell the ship if you're interested."

"And what would we want with a pirate ship?" came the snide reply.

"Since Red Death has plagued you for nearly two decades, I thought you'd like the ship as a showpiece that Red Death will no longer be marauding your part of the galaxy." Dare wasn't quite sure that was true since Dani felt so strongly about the war, but if he wanted Gavin 2 to buy the ship, he had to convince them of the incentive to do so.

"Let me consult with the council. I'll contact you again in ten minutes."

Dani met Dare's gaze and held it. "A little presumptuous, aren't you? I haven't accepted your offer yet, and who else is going to keep weapons from going to both sides of the war? Otherwise, this war is going to last another four generations."

"I think Dare was trying to convince them rather than cornering you into a certain action." Carl glanced back and forth between Dare and Dani until finally Dani nodded.

"You're right, I'm sorry. I just don't think I can leave the Gavin planets on their own long term. I know the plan involves a little time away, but I'll have to think long and hard about my convictions and what I want my future to hold."

"Fair enough, Dani. But to get past this part of the plan, we need them to buy the ship and accept the idea that we won our freedom."

"What are you going to tell them you did with us?"

Dare grinned. "We released you on Gavin 1, of course. Especially since you grew up there and have friends there, that won't be too far-fetched of an idea for them to take in."

Dahlia nodded. "I could see the residents of Gavin 1 protecting you and even the crew after everything you've done for them over the last five years and even before you took over as Red Death."

"MacFadyen ship," the snide voice came over the intercom again.

Dare hit the com button. "We're here."

"The council has agreed that we will purchase the ship for five hundred thousand space credits. Is this acceptable?"

Dare took a long moment to answer, even though their offer was much better than he expected. "Agreed. If you send a small shuttle-craft convoy, we'll turn over the ship before we break orbit."

"Just one more thing: what happened to Red Death and her crew?"

"We released them on Gavin 1."

There was a long pause before the president said, "Acknowledged." The disappointment was clear in his voice. "Stand by to receive our shuttle craft."

Dare hit the com channel to close the connection and then glanced over at Jared. "As soon as we turn the ship over, lay in a course for MacFadyen headquarters . . . unless you're ready to turn the controls back over to Dahlia and Carl."

Jared grinned like a child with a new toy. "If you don't mind, I'd love to fly her, at least for a while. The journey will take approximately sixteen hours, and I've never had a chance to fly anything like this before."

"I'll keep you company," Dahlia offered, reminding Dare of what Dani had said about Jared and Dahlia.

Carl cleared his throat. "I'll relieve you in four hours. I need a good meal and a hot shower after letting Dahlia kick my ass down on the planet."

6

_____

Jared's expression turned sheepish and Dani frowned down at him. "What aren't you telling me, Jared? There's guilt written all over your face." She let the corners of her mouth curve to take any sting out of the comment. Jared had always taken good care of her, so whatever it was couldn't be that bad.

"Well . . . boss, there was one other thing that happened while you were gone that you might not be too happy about. And we're all very sorry."

Dani's blood chilled as dozens of possibilities for disaster flashed through her mind. "All? Jared, just tell me and get it over with. You're worrying me, and besides, it's obviously bothering you, so there's no use putting it off any longer." She glanced over her shoulder at Dare, who gave her an encouraging smile. She appreciated his strong presence of support behind her and warning bells clanged inside her brain.

When had she come to rely on his presence? Did she dare trust him? Things were happening too fast between them and even though it scared her, she wasn't sure she wanted them to slow down. It had been too long since she'd allowed herself to care about a man—even a tiny bit.

Jared cleared his throat, bringing her attention back to him. "Well, since you weren't here when we were moving everything to this ship from ours, I packed your quarters and brought everything over here. You were kind enough to share your quarters with Mr. MacFadyen last night, so I figured he wouldn't mind sharing *his* quarters here with you. At least until you both work out other arrangements. So that's where you'll find all your things."

Confusion speared through Dani. When was he going to get to the worrying part? She had a bad feeling about this and was just waiting for the other shoe to drop. "Go on," she prompted.

"Anyway . . . to get right to the point, I shot your pleasure probe."

"Damn," Dare muttered from behind her. "I wanted to shoot that damned thing."

Mortification flowed through Dani and heat flowed into her neck and face. She remembered him saying *all*. Did the whole crew on both ships now know she had a pleasure probe? And probably much more than that thanks to the mouthy device.

"Anyway, it kept asking to see my cock and kept telling me that mine couldn't possibly be as well designed as Mr. Mac-Fadyen's. So finally I got fed up with the thing, ended up chasing it around half of the ship while it taunted the rest of the crew, and then I shot it. It's a smoking pile of debris and I left it on the other ship in the trash bin."

"That's it?" Dani tried to play off her embarrassment but was sure both Jared and Dare knew her reaction all too well from her instinctive blush. Damn curse of being a true redhead, she couldn't hide her blushes.

"You can take the cost out of my next paycheck. I just feel

horrible for letting it taunt me into killing it, and letting it flit around the ship destroying your privacy. But it's done now."

"I'm not too worried about it," she lied. "I was about to toss it out the air lock myself. I will never again buy the talking model."

Dare laughed. "Jared, if I would've had a laser pistol last night, it would've already been a smoking pile of debris before you found it."

Dare's amused words from behind her nearly made her smile. She still remembered their pact not to talk about Pussy-do outside of her cabin, but she guessed the silicone was out of the bag, so to speak.

Dani turned to face Dare. "I don't know about you, but I'm tired, and like Carl, I could use a hot shower and a hot meal, and not necessarily in that order. Care to show me around? I'm sure one of your crewmen can handle the turnover of the ship. Especially since my crew and I aren't supposed to be aboard anymore."

Dare grinned with mischief in his gaze. "I'd consider it an honor. Jared, can you make sure the transfer of the ship goes smoothly? From a distance, of course. We don't want to give away our game."

"Absolutely. Leave it to me."

Dare gestured toward the door. "Turn right and follow the corridor around until we get to the lifts."

Dani followed his instructions and tried to keep from gawking like a tourist. Every inch of the ship was elegant and screamed of class and sophistication. Nothing like her poor Spartan ship. Dare took her up in the lift to a large dining room where they ate steak, vegetables, fresh baked rolls, and the most sinful chocolate cream pie she'd ever tasted—not that she'd had it more than twice in her life previously.

"If you eat like this regularly, you must have to work out

constantly; otherwise, you'd be close to four hundred pounds by now."

Dare ran his hand over what she knew was a muscled stomach and winked. "The crew and I have regularly scheduled workouts, even during voyages with customers. And sometimes the patrons like to watch or join us. It's quite a draw actually."

Dani's insides clenched with far too much eagerness at Dare's implication. She could totally see a bunch of pampered rich women wanting to watch Dare and some of his crew sweat and flex. She wouldn't mind watching a few sessions herself, although after that meal she would need to participate—unless she could talk Dare into more calisthenics like last night. She was sure they burned off at least two entire chocolate cream pies. And if they kept that up, Dani would be in the best shape of her life, even with the overindulgent food on Dare's ship.

"Are you ready for that shower now?" Dare asked when she pushed her plate away and drained the rest of her drink.

"Most definitely." She tried not to think about just how many *calisthenics* they could do in the shower, depending on the size of his shower stall.

"My cabin is two floors up on the port side. Shall we?"

Dani followed Dare back to the lifts and then to his cabin when they reached the correct floor. He led her to a hardwood door that displayed a plaque that had CAPTAIN emblazoned on it. He placed his palm on the security keypad and waited while it scanned his finger and palm prints to prove his identity.

The lock clicked open and Dare opened the door, pushing it wide and gesturing her inside.

This time Dani did gawk. Dare's personal quarters were like nothing she'd ever seen. The entire room was done in rich maroon and hunter green with hardwood accents to match the hardwood floor. There were silver handles on the drawers and doorknobs that led to rooms she figured were the restroom, the closet, and a few she couldn't even guess at.

"Do you like it?"

"Like it? This is amazing. You actually live here when you're in space?"

Dare chuckled. "It's good to be the captain. Although the crew and passenger quarters aren't bad either. I'll have to show you so you can see the difference."

Impatience snapped through Dani. "Tour later, shower now. And then I believe you mentioned something about thanking me properly for saving your life?"

Dare's smile turned to high wattage, and moisture dampened Dani's thighs in anticipation of what was to come. Apparently there would be more *calisthenics* like last night, so she didn't need to worry about the rich lunch she'd just eaten.

"This way, Dani." Dare made a wide gesture toward one of the doors and then turned the knob and pushed it open.

More than likely grinning like a fool, she managed to contain a gasp. The bathroom was just as elegant as the bedroom, with wide marble counters, double ceramic sinks, and all silver hardware. The mirror took up nearly the entire wall, and when she stepped farther into the room she could see the glass-fronted shower was big enough to hold six full-grown men. There were spouts on all four sides up and down the wall at various intervals, and the far wall held a long cushioned bench that brought to mind all kinds of interesting ideas that tightened Dani's nipples and made her sex clench. There was even a small viewport so the occupants could see out into the blackness of space dotted with twinkling silver stars and planets. She could see how rich couples would find this romantic and tantalizing. Hell, *she* found it romantic and tantalizing, and she was jut a guest here, not to mention Dare wasn't hers.

Her toiletries were already in the shower and arranged on

the counter next to Dare's, and Dani suddenly felt like she was on a luxury vacation rather than on a ship fleeing bounty hunters.

She whisked her shirt off over her head and tossed it on the toilet lid before turning to Dare. "I hope you're not going to mind me being straightforward, but a shower sounds amazing right now and I'm not in the mood to wait."

In answer, Dare stripped off his own shirt and then started on his shoes, pants, and underwear.

Dani caught up stripping off the rest of her clothes, slid the large glass door open, and stepped into the cavernous shower, gesturing for Dare to join her. A few bruises already peppered his torso from their fake fight earlier and she wondered if she'd sustained any but didn't want to waste time to ask. Dare's generous cock already jutted out from his body, and she took a moment to playfully run her fingernails down the shaft.

Dare groaned and lightly tweaked one of Dani's nipples before pulling her close for a searing kiss. He explored her mouth thoroughly with teeth and tongue and lips, nipping at her lightly as he kneaded her lower back and ass, and pulled her flush against him so his full cock pressed against her stomach and made her sex clench in protest of still remaining empty.

Dani sucked in a breath as she realized what she'd started and where. She'd never had sex in a shower before, but chances were she was about to, and nothing but pure excitement and arousal speared through her at the thought.

Dare turned the twin spouts and warm water suddenly jetted from all sides, soaking Dani's skin in wondrous pulsing waves. She groaned and Dare laughed.

"Not all the cabins are equipped with this shower, however. I had this specially installed. After all, like I said, it's good to be the captain."

"It's much better being captain on this ship than on mine. I was lucky if my shower even worked half the time. That along with the toilet were always breaking down, forcing me to borrow Dani's or Jared's, which were also always broken."

"That's another great thing about this ship. I have crewmen dedicated solely to maintenance and keeping everything running smoothly. After all, the rich and powerful expect fully working showers and toilets when they vacation with us."

Dani stepped back just far enough to reach between them, wrap her fingers around Dare's cock, and gently cup the heavy sack that hung just underneath.

Dare responded by running his fingers through the springy curls at the juncture of her thighs and finding her sensitive clit.

Dani made an *mmm* sound in the back of her throat and tipped her pelvis against Dare's seeking fingers.

He skimmed his lips over her neck and around to her shoulder, turning her and placing his hand behind her knee. He lifted her leg and placed her foot up onto the padded seat, then leaned her forward and placed her hands against the tile wall.

Dani caught her breath as the large, swollen head of his erection pressed against her aching slit. Water cascaded over her ass and against the sides of her breasts as Dare slowly pressed inside her, his large hands on her hips keeping her anchored and still.

As he slowly filled her, heat spilled through every inch of her body, teasing to life nerve endings that hadn't been used in far too long. She'd thought last night had been amazing, but when Dare's stomach finally pressed against her ass and he was firmly seated inside her, she knew today would make last night seem pale by comparison.

Dare reached around to find her clit and she shook her head. "I want you to pound inside me and make me come that way. My clit can wait for its turn."

Dare made a sound deep inside his throat that was part arousal and part primal male possession. Dani was both thrilled and scared by the possessive sound, but only tipped her ass higher so she could take him deeper.

Dare apparently took her at her word because he slid nearly all the way out and then thrust back inside her until the swollen head of his erection bumped against her cervix, sending waves of heat and arousal through her pelvis and on a straight path to her clit and both nipples, which all swelled in anticipation of a very large orgasm.

"More, Dare. Please."

His grip tightened on her hips and he began pounding inside her as she'd asked, the sound of flesh slapping against flesh loud inside the echoing chamber.

The wave of sensations built within her, churning and twirling tighter with each thrust. Dare's fingers dug into her hips harder as he pounded inside her, and she gloried in the sensations of both his rough grip and his pistoning cock hitting her cervix.

She gasped as the wave reached her chest, making her pant to take in enough air. "Almost," she gasped and nearly shouted when Dare adjusted his grip on her ass and lifted her until her other foot was above the tile floor of the shower. The angle of his penetration deepened and ecstasy spilled through her as he continued to pump in and out. Four hard thrusts later and the wave engulfed her, causing her world to explode in silver sparkling diamonds behind her eyelids. She was dimly aware of shouting Dare's name even through the continuing thrusts. A few more hard thrusts later and Dare came, his emission sending more warmth through her body. Even through the ringing in her ears she heard Dare shout her name before she collapsed bonelessly on the padded seat, not caring that the water continued to pound down on her.

Dare gently pushed her hair back away from her face and then surprised her by taking the soap between his large hands and tenderly washing her from foot to face. When he reached

298 / Cassie Ryan

her hair, he gently sat her up on the seat and then pulled down her shampoo from the upper shelf and soaped up her hair, lightly massaging her scalp until she nearly purred under his attentions.

Dare towered over her as she lifted her head. She gazed at him through errant strands of hair as her heartbeat began to slow.

After brushing back her hair, he bent down to kiss her, just a brush of his lips, but so tender. A smile curved his lips as he took the soap and lifted her foot to the platform he made with his knee. Starting with her little toe, he soaped her foot. The slow massage of each digit turned her inside out and upside down.

By the time he finished both feet and legs, and made it to her now overly sensitive sex, her breathing came fast again. He had her lathered up in every way possible. However, he didn't stop there.

The effort he put forth to clean her breast was admirable. Such a nice man . . . or evil depending on point of view. She couldn't decide if he was being tender or calculating. A quick glance at his unaffected cock told her. The man was caring for her.

She'd never had a man be this tender and attentive, especially after sex. Once they came they were usually done with her, or wanted *her* to minister to them. It caught her off balance and forced her to examine him closer.

When he gently tipped her head to the side and rinsed the soap from her hair, she sighed and realized she felt pampered and cherished for the first time in her life.

She expected the warning bells to clang inside her brain again, but then she realized it was too late. While she wasn't quite in love, she was definitely smitten, and the rest was a slippery slope. Not that she minded landing *atop* him.

Dare brushed a gentle kiss across her forehead before pulling back and soaping himself and washing his hair.

He was glorious to watch, his muscular arms flexing with each movement and his tight, muscled thighs doing an erotic dance that she just couldn't tear her gaze from. The defined ridges of his abs were like stair steps down to the magical part of him. The sight that enchanted her was his cock, deflated now, but still large and inviting. She resisted the urge to reach out and stroke him, not quite ready for another round of heaven before she got some much needed sleep. She trusted that he was more than capable of fulfilling the silent promise of good things to come he'd made while washing her. It would be a difficult transition to be in the habit of trusting someone, but if anyone deserved a chance to try to earn her trust, Dare just showed himself worthy.

7

Sunlight filtered in to spill across Dani's face. She groaned and cringed away, enjoying the warm, comforting weight against her back that had been there all night.

Sunlight? Warm, comforting weight?

Confusion filtered through her brain and she forced open her eyes to find a beautiful sunrise showing through the large viewport in Dare's quarters that she hadn't noticed until he'd opened the maroon curtains last night. That was just before they fell into a deep sleep on the most comfortable bed she'd ever laid on. And as reluctant as she was to move, the sunlight was bright and insistent and had broken her out of her warm cocoon.

She reached back behind her and came in contact with a very warm, muscular chest.

Dare.

Memories of last night flitted through her mind, bringing with them her body's instinctive reaction. She was afraid she was becoming very much addicted to the attentions of Dare MacFadyen. She shoved that thought aside to worry about later. There were still several stages of their joint plan to complete before she would have to worry about what leaving him behind would mean.

Dani sat up, blinking and trying to let her eyes adjust to the yellowish warm light.

"Sorry," Dare mumbled, his voice low and gravelly. "I forgot about the sunrise and sunset program when I opened the drapes last night." He rolled over, reached for the large hardwood headboard, and pressed a few controls until the light faded to a tolerable level and the curtains slowly slid closed.

Blessed darkness, or at least murkiness, returned to the room and Dani resisted the urge to burrow back down into the covers and see if she could recapture the warm, comforting safety of a few minutes before. After all, she probably already looked too needy and dependent after letting Dare take so much care of her in the shower last night. She needed to remember that she was an independent woman, and that she definitely liked it that way.

"Why do you have a sunrise and sunset program in your quarters?"

"It's actually in all the rooms. The guests love it since several of their planets only have close moons and the suns are too far away to be visible from their homes."

She laughed, a low chuckle that took only minimal energy.

Dare pulled her back close against him, his morning erection cradled against her ass crack. "I haven't slept so well in ages. I should keep you captive here in my quarters and tempt you in my bed as often as possible."

Dani instinctively curled back into the covers and the warmth she had been craving a few minutes ago. She looked back at Dare over her shoulder and nearly laughed at the surprised expression on his face. Apparently he was just as surprised by his revealing words as she was. But on the bright side, she wasn't the only one who seemed smitten. She could think of nothing worse than having this attraction be one sided. Well, not attraction exactly. She knew there were emotions involved, but she was still afraid to examine them too closely. There had only been one man to ever earn her trust, and that had been Devil MacFadyen. And while his grandson was like him in so many ways, she wasn't quite ready to fully trust Dare Mac-Fadyen. Sex—even amazing sex—was one thing, but trust was an entirely different notion, and one she didn't give lightly.

A soft knock on the door startled Dani, and Dare's large hand stroked a path down her arm, soothing her. "It's all right. Probably just Carl to give me some sort of update. Stay here and I'll find out what's going on."

Dare climbed over her, lightly rolling out of bed and grabbing a robe from the end of the bed before pulling the bed curtains closed to give Dani her privacy.

The soft sound of him padding to the door made Dani smile. For such a large man, he was very graceful and light on his feet. She wondered suddenly if he danced, and if he did how it would feel to dance with him and be in his arms in a slinky black dress where she actually felt feminine and petite.

Where the hell had that thought come from?

Probably part of the whole *smitten* package. It would definitely take some getting used to, these unguarded thoughts that popped up without warning. Thoughts she would've bet several days ago that she would never have for this man who was her captive.

"There's been a development, and Dani needs to hear it too." Carl's voice was pitched low but carried clearly to Dani anyway. She could hear the concern and worry in those words, and her blood chilled.

What now?

A few seconds later, the door closed and the curtains around the bed swished open. "Duty calls. There's apparently some news both of us need to hear. Are you all right to get up?"

Dani forced a smile. "While I'd much rather stay here lounging in bed curled against you, I think you're right. We need to go find out what's going on."

Dani reluctantly pushed up out of bed and went to find her clothes. They were all neatly arranged in Dare's closet and in his chest of drawers. She cut the thought short that the arrangement seemed rather comfortable and homey. Thinking about dancing with him was one thing, thinking about always having their clothes side by side was another thing entirely.

By the time Dani found her clothes and pulled them on, Dare was already dressed and ready.

Dani took the time to use the restroom, brush out her hair, and brush her teeth. Ah, vanity, she chided herself, but that didn't stop her from performing the tasks.

Dare led the way out of his quarters, pulling the door shut with an ominous click behind him as the security system engaged.

In the lift, they found several crew members from each of their ships and Dani smiled in greeting. However, the return expressions seemed to all be off somehow.

Maybe she was just still tired from the rather vigorous activities of the previous evening.

She'd have to ask Dare when they were alone if he had noticed it too.

When the lift opened, everyone filed out and Dani immediately heard loud laughter and voices from down the hall.

The crew who had preceded them out of the lift had disappeared headed toward the noise.

Dare lay a warm hand on Dani's shoulder. "I don't like the looks of this. The dining room is the other way, but let's check this out."

"So it wasn't just me who noticed the odd way they were all looking at us?"

"No, definitely not. Something's up, and I'm going to find

out what it is before we head to the dining room to hear this new news." Dare shook his head and kneaded Dani's shoulder before dropping his hand. "You know, I could use a few days of boring once all this is done. No news, no developments, no mysteries." He laughed. "Maybe you and I could invoke the captain's privilege and just lock ourselves in my room for a long weekend once all this is done."

Dani bit her tongue to keep from answering, but managed a small smile and nod.

The laughter and catcalling ratcheted up a few notches, and Dare's lips tightened into a hard line. "This had better not be what I suspect it might be. Come on."

Dani followed him down the hall to a large recreation room, and he slowly opened the door and peeked inside.

One entire wall was made up of a view screen, but instead of the blackness of space, there was—Dani blinked a few times to make sure she wasn't seeing things.

No, still there.

Dahlia and Jared were very naked and definitely having sex of the caliber that she and Dare had enjoyed last night.

The sounds of flesh slapping against flesh and gasps and soft sighs snapped Dani into full reality, and heat seared into her face. It wasn't as if she'd never seen people have sex before, but not two of her closest friends and confidants. From the elegant background in the room, Dani assumed the action was happening right here on Dare's ship, but how . . . and why?

Dare stepped farther into the room and a sudden hush fell as the crew from both ships noticed him and Dani.

"What the hell is the meaning of this?" Dare's bellow caused several of the crew to shrink away or to scurry to the far side of the room since Dare and Dani were blocking the only exit.

When only silence greeted Dare's question, he flipped on the overhead lights and pierced Justin with a hard glare.

Dani almost felt sorry for the man—almost. But then a chilling thought formed. If they were watching Dahlia and Jared right now, did that mean that they had all watched her and Dare last night? Vivid memories of some of the more steamy scenes they'd shared replayed inside her mind and she cringed. If that was the case, no wonder the crewmen had looked at her strangely this morning.

"Justin?" Dare's voice rang out again.

Justin slowly stood, obviously reluctant to face his boss.

"Boss, one of the men accidentally hacked into the security system while he was installing the weapons systems onto the ship, and, well . . . things got out of hand last night when we accidentally realized the channel was still open."

"Last night?" Dare's loud voice made it clear he wasn't pleased with this explanation, and Dani's stomach fell as her worst fears were confirmed.

"Yes, boss. Although if it's any comfort at all, both crews thought last night's *entertainment* was much hotter than this morning's."

Dare's fists clenched, his muscles tightened, and the crews only cringed away farther as Dare's expression turned more murderous. "No, it is *not* a comfort, Justin. But dealing with you and the hackers later will be *very* enjoyable."

Justin's face paled and he only nodded. Finally, mercifully, Jared bellowed on-screen and then slumped on top of Dahlia.

With the action obviously finished, someone turned off whatever was projecting the image and the screen went dark.

"No one leaves the ship, understood? I'll deal with this later."

Dare rested his hand on Dani's lower back and guided her out into the hallway and down the hall toward the dining room.

*   *   *

Ten minutes later, Dare sat next to Dani in the dining room with cups of coffee in front of them. Carl was already there and seemed to be several cups of caffeine in already.

When Dahlia and Jared walked into the room, it was everything Dare could do not to make eye contact and give away what he knew. There would be time enough later to fill them in and right now he needed to hear what had happened to necessitate Carl pulling him and Dani out of bed so early this morning.

"News or breakfast first?" Dahlia stifled a yawn.

Dani smiled over at Dare and he knew she was struggling with not meeting Dahlia's and Jared's gazes also. "Definitely news."

Carl, Dahlia, and Jared seemed clearly agitated, so Dare thought whatever it was needed to be said as soon as possible. And while he assumed Carl was astute enough to know about what had gone on in the recreation room, Dare didn't think that's what had the older man agitated.

Dahlia blew out a long breath and then fixed Dani with a concerned gaze.

Dani's brow furrowed and Dare resisted the urge to reach out and smooth the furrows away. After seeing Dani so relaxed and happy last night, he hated to have anything destroy that. And due to the implied seriousness of the news, he resisted replaying last night inside his mind, or wishing they could go back upstairs and start all over again.

"Dani," Dahlia began. "Gavin 2 got hold of a nuclear black hole device . . ."

Dani sucked in a breath that hissed through her teeth.

Dare took her hand in his under the table. He had heard those devices were a hundred times more destructive than the nuclear warheads from Earth back during the twenty-first century. He could only imagine the kind of damage that could be done to poor Gavin 1.

"What happened? Tell me, Dahlia." Dani's face had blanched and her fingers tightened around Dare's.

"Something went wrong and it detonated. But no one is sure which planet it detonated on. There were only limited messages from the planets giving that information and then nothing as the radiation began to interfere with communications."

Dani's blood ran cold as the ramifications of the news filtered though her mind. No matter which planet the device had detonated on, it would mean millions of lives lost. What could possibly be worth that high of a cost? And what had Gavin 2 been thinking? Obviously only about winning the war.

Dani's thoughts turned to all the places on Gavin 1 she knew so well from growing up there and all the people who had been part of her troubled childhood before Devil MacFadyen had found her. Faces swam in her memory, and her heart clenched at the thought of them all dead.

"Dani," Dare began, "I know how important Gavin 1 is to you. We can take the ship back and find out what's going on since we can't get communications through. But you need to eat something first. This entire morning has been full of shocks and you need your strength."

The implied *after last night* hung in the air between them. She couldn't argue with his assessment, although she didn't feel like eating.

"I'm not sure I could eat without throwing it up right now."

"You need to try. Let's see what's on board for breakfast and then we can make plans for how to handle everything."

Dare motioned the waiter over and then ordered a full array of breakfast items for the table.

Five minutes later, the table was full of all manner of delicacies, but Dani's stomach bucked at the thought of even nibbling on any of them. Dare was right, there had been too many shocks this morning and she needed time to process them.

Several times while everyone else ate Dare squeezed her

hand and sent a concerned look her way. Something warmed inside her chest each time he did it, and she finally convinced herself to try some hot tea and a plain butter croissant. The bread seemed to help settle her stomach and she didn't push her luck any further.

Jared pushed his plate away. "If we're going to go back to the twin Gavin planets, we need to get started. Dare, Dani, is there something wrong? You mentioned several shocks this morning and I only know of one. You wouldn't be holding out on us, would you?" He and Dahlia exchanged a look before pinning Dare and Dani with identical expressions of expectation.

Carl cleared his throat and it sounded like a cross between that and an aborted chuckle. "I'll break this news so we can make plans and move on. Dare, Dani, you two finish eating."

Carl filled them in in a concise and fact-based fashion as Dahlia's cheeks turned bright red and Jared's gaze turned nearly as murderous as Dare's had earlier.

"Boss." Jared caught Dani's gaze across the table and held it. "We don't need anything but a skeleton crew to go back, even if we encounter bounty hunters. Although depending on which planet had the . . . incident . . . that may not be an issue anymore."

Dani hadn't thought that far ahead, but Jared was right on both counts. "You're right. Handpick the skeleton crew, offload the rest, and we can deal with this entire situation when we return. Just make it clear that no more of these invasions of privacy will be tolerated."

"I can guarantee you that message will be clearly communicated. Although we might have to hire more crew when we return." Jared turned his attention to Dahlia and squeezed her hand while shooting her a reassuring gaze.

Dani's heart clenched. Apparently she wasn't the only one on board who was *smitten.*

Dare turned to Carl. "Why don't you get us refueled and ready for departure, and we'll all meet in the control room in an hour? Oh, and, Jared, you can let the crew take the two shuttle crafts. We shouldn't need them on this trip and they're going to need them to get everyone down to the MacFadyen headquarters."

"Thanks, Dare."

"It's going to be another interesting day," Carl said matter-of-factly.

The understatement hung in the air and no one bothered to break the silence.

8

An hour later, Dare sat in the control room with Dani beside him. Dahlia, Jared, and Carl sat around the room in front of the different consoles. "It's going to be another long sixteen hours. We should probably take shifts."

Dani shifted in her chair. "Dare, do you want to take first watch with me and we can wake the next shift in six hours?"

"I'll take the next shift," Carl jumped in. "Just call me on the com and I'll be up here in ten minutes with a few pots of coffee to get me through."

"I guess that makes us third shift, Dahlia." Jared's voice clearly communicated he didn't mind, and would enjoy spending the first and second shifts with Dahlia while they waited.

The three filed out with well wishes for an event-free shift.

Dare turned his attention back to Dani. Her long red hair was pulled back into a pony tail, and even though she wore no makeup her pale skin was lovely. She wore a simple T-shirt and jeans, but her ample curves still made his mouth water.

Dare!

Get your mind back on business. If Dani's not already too

sore, you'll have second and third shift to trace those amazing curves.

Dare started the preflight sequence and Dani seamlessly took over the controls where he left off, so within ten minutes they were on their way to the twin Gavin planets under full power.

"Dani," he began.

She turned to him, her brows risen in question.

"I know you grew up on Gavin 1, but I don't know much about your childhood other than the few references you've made to the fact that it wasn't the happiest. Would it be too personal if I asked you about it?"

Dani laughed and shook her head. "After everything we've shared over the past few days, I think we're past worrying about personal boundaries, don't you? Besides..." She shrugged. "I'm sure there are things about you I'd like to know as well. So we can trade stories." She leaned back in her chair as if gathering her thoughts. "As you can imagine, growing up on a war-torn planet wasn't the best childhood. My parents sold me off to a budding shipping company when I was twelve."

She cast an amused glance toward Dare and his blood ran cold. His grandfather would never buy children, no matter what anyone would try to convince him.

"I can see I've offended you, Dare, but it's true. However, old Devil never had the heart for human trafficking, and he found most of us new homes or trained us with enough skills to make lives for ourselves. In my own case, Devil taught me not only hand-to-hand combat, but also how to pilot, fix just about anything mechanical, speak a few languages, and how to read people." She paused. "I was saddened to hear of his death."

Relief and a renewed sense of loss slid through Dare as he thought about his grandfather. At least he hadn't been a human trafficker. Dare would've been shocked if he had been, but leave it to his grandfather to turn something so repugnant into a humanitarian gesture. Devil had always used his credits for good, and Dare had been proud of that.

Dare turned to find Dani watching him and realized he'd fallen silent. "So that's how you ended up on Gavin 1?"

She nodded. "Devil found me a family there who needed someone to work, and I made money for us as a ship mechanic and pilot until about five years ago. My foster parents were old and passed away within a few months of each other, and I found myself without direction. So I charmed my way onto a pirate ship that had taken up orbit around Gavin 1 looking for supplies and fuel. They gave me a place to stay and by the end of the week, the old Red Death had decided he was ready to re-tire, the crew had decided that they'd be loyal to me, and I promised to make them rich beyond their wildest dreams. The second ship we captured after that had Dahlia aboard, and the rest is history. I've taught my crew to be very careful about their pronoun usage, but even with that, the news that I was a woman filtered out. Although most people chose not to believe it, thinking that Red Death was just trying to throw them off his scent. But here we are."

Dare smiled over at her even though he couldn't understand how this woman had turned out so amazing having had such a hard childhood. "I don't know what to say. My childhood was a cakewalk compared to yours. I almost feel bad for having things so good."

"Don't. I would've traded places with you in a second if I could. Especially if it meant I could be related to Devil. He was a great man and even though he treated me like his own grand-daughter, I always knew it wasn't true and always felt the lack deep inside my heart."

Their six-hour shift sped by with them chatting about their childhoods, Dare's family, and his time with and memories of his grandfather.

In six hours, they called Carl on the com, and true to his

word he arrived ten minutes later balancing two pots of coffee and a cup. "I talked the cook into sending me up some food in about an hour, so I'll be fine. You two go get some sleep, you'll need to be fully rested to deal with whatever we find on the Gavin planets."

Dare glanced over at Dani, noting the dark circles under her eyes, and silently vowed not to paw at her when they reached his quarters. She needed sleep and that wouldn't hurt him any either. The prospect of curling up next to Dani was inviting and even without the sex sounded like a heavenly way to spend six hours.

Five minutes later, they were inside his quarters. Dani had already stripped off her clothes and lay naked on her side on the bed. "Can I ask a favor, Dare?"

"Of course. What do you need?"

"I've very much enjoyed our sex together, but I think I'm much too tired for another round right now. However, I've been fantasizing all day about having that wonderful thick cock back inside my mouth. Do you think I could do that and we could restrain ourselves for just sleep after that?"

Dare's fly suddenly tented as his cock gave an instant answer. The thought of her full lips wrapped around him definitely wasn't a hardship, and although he would crave being deep inside her again, he thought he could restrain himself for just a little longer if the payoff in the end was getting to fall asleep next to her.

Dani chuckled as she stared at his fly. "I'll take that as a yes."

When Dare didn't argue, she arched one brow. "So strip," she chided as her lips curved up at the edges. "I can't wait to taste you."

The erotic words made him even harder and tightened his balls up against his body. He took deep breaths as he slowly began to strip. He didn't want to come as soon as she touched him. After all, he'd shown her in their past few sessions that he had some stamina; he didn't want to ruin that in five seconds flat . . . or two.

When he stripped off his underwear and dropped them onto the growing pile with the rest of his clothes, his cock stood out from his body, pointing directly at Dani as if beckoning her forward to keep her promise.

Instead, he stepped toward the bed and Dani scrambled to the floor, dropping to her knees on his pile of clothes and wrapping her hand around his aching cock.

His member jerked when she touched him and as soon as she cupped his balls, a heavy bead of precome formed in his slit.

Dani made a deep *mmm* sound in the back of her throat and then lowered her head to capture the heavy drop on her tongue as she traced his slit.

Dare fisted his hands at his side to keep from reaching for her. He didn't think he could contain himself if he even allowed himself the indulgence of removing the band that captured all that thick red hair and spearing his fingers into the mass. He knew it would be too tempting for him to take things to the next step from there.

Unaware of his struggle, or just trusting him to keep their bargain, Dani traced a path with her tongue up the long vein on the underside of his cock, starting with his balls and ending with the sensitized tip. He thought she would slip him inside her mouth then, but apparently she wasn't done teasing him. She traced a path around the head with her tongue and nipped him gently, which sent pure lava racing through his veins and pooling deep inside his pelvis. He adjusted his stance since he found himself suddenly unsteady on his feet, and glanced down to watch her lick and tease him.

He couldn't remember a more erotic sight than Dani kneeling naked in front of him with his cock in her beautiful mouth. His cock jumped in response.

"I'm sorry. Too much teasing?" she said in a tone that told

him she wasn't the least bit sorry and, in fact, was enjoying herself quite a bit.

"I don't think that's possible," he lied only slightly. "Although I am exercising superhuman control to not pick you up, throw you on the bed, and thrust inside you."

She laughed as she took the head of his cock inside the tight O of her lips and the vibrations tickled down his hard member. "I appreciate your restraint, Dare. This is my show and I'm loving my feminine power right now. I've never had such a beautiful man at my mercy and I'm reveling in it."

"Beautiful?" Dare couldn't help but ask.

"Yes, beautiful. You're a handsome man, I'll admit; but when I get to see the whole bare package, you're absolutely beautiful. Michelangelo would've loved to sculpt you—even with that blush and frown you're wearing now."

Dare hadn't noticed his cheeks heating or his frown until she'd mentioned it, but now that she had, he noticed that wasn't the only part of his body that was heated. "Thank you. I appreciate the sentiment, but I think you're far more beautiful than I am, and watching you suck my cock is the most erotic thing I've ever seen."

She hummed as she took him deep, and once again the vibrations teased him and caused his balls to tighten against his body. "My pleasure . . . really." She opened her throat and took him even deeper, and he had to fight not to thrust.

She reached up to cup his balls and gently knead them between her fingers as she began a slow, steady rhythm of sliding him out of her mouth until her lips ringed the head and then taking him back in until he bumped the back of her throat, sending deep tingling sensations roaring through his pelvis and threatening to make him come.

When she pushed his stance wider and tipped her head forward so she could take one of his balls inside her mouth, Dare thought he would die from pure ecstasy. She swirled her tongue over the orb, and the deep tingling inside his pelvis reached a fever pitch. He sucked in large lungfuls of air to keep his climax at bay and sighed as he chased it back just far enough so he knew he wouldn't embarrass himself.

"Dani," he warned. "I can't last much longer."

"Then I'll have to give equal attention to the other one some other time."

Dare swallowed hard and his balls tightened hard against his body in response.

Mercifully, Dani slipped his shaft back inside her mouth and began a steady, quick rhythm of sucking him fully inside and then sliding him back out again.

A few seconds later, the tingling in his pelvis exploded and he spilled down the back of her throat, chiding himself that he hadn't given her warning.

But Dani swallowed and then laughed around his cock while she reached around and grabbed his ass. "Thank you, Dare. I've been wanting that all day. And now I'm ready for some sleep." She slowly stood, her full breasts brushing against his bare skin on the way up. She grabbed his hand as mischief danced in her gaze. "Join me?"

Dare was more than willing and climbed onto the bed, beckoning her forward. As soon as she curled under the covers next to him, he pulled her back against him spoon style and draped his hand over her slightly rounded stomach.

Warmth and contentment engulfed him and he realized how deeply his feelings had grown for Dani. Regardless if he lost some business or not, he would convince her to partner with him and share his life and his bed.

He waited for the familiar fear of commitment to flood over him, but when it never came he sighed and settled in for a long, content slumber.

9

"Dare, Dani," Jared's voice came over the com unit in Dare's headboard, jarring Dani awake. "We're about twenty minutes out from the Gavin planets and we thought you might want to be in the control room for this."

"We'll be there soon. Dare out."

Dare's voice from behind her sounded low and gravelly with an edge of sleep still in it. "Good morning," he said as he stroked a warm hand over her hip.

Dani rolled onto her other side so she could face him. "Good morning." She was probably grinning like a loon and she didn't care. "I'd suggest we grab a quick shower, but then we'd never make it upstairs."

Dare reached around and grabbed her ass in an affectionate squeeze. "You go first and that will save us both from temptation."

Dani couldn't help the swift tug of disappointment that swirled through her, but Dare's suggestion was a good one. She rolled out of bed and headed toward the shower. Maybe it would finish waking her up out of the delicious slumber that still clung to her.

Twenty minutes later, they were both walking through the door to the control room, dressed but sleepy, or at least Dani knew she still was. But it probably had more to do with cuddling with Dare than actual sleep.

"The planets should be visible in about five minutes," Jared supplied. "Still no communications traffic from either planet, but the radiation levels are rising as we get closer. Nothing in the dangerous range, but that is probably what's interfering with their communications."

The seconds ticked by slowly as Dani kept her gaze glued to the front view screen. Finally, Gavin 1 came into view and grew in size until they'd reached a close enough position to take orbit around the planet.

Dare shifted in his chair. "Jared, how are the radiation levels?"

"Higher than normal, but still not dangerous, at least not on this side of the planet. Long-range sensors are showing higher levels on the other side. That may be where the detonation occurred . . ." Jared must've realized he just implied the detonation had happened on Gavin 1 and she promptly fell silent.

"Let's get down there and find out the scoop." Dare sat back, letting Jared, Dahlia, and Carl man the controls. After all, the three of them were the experts. Even though he was proficient, he knew his skills couldn't match any of theirs. He had other skills that could, but he wasn't ashamed to admit he wasn't an expert at everything.

Ten minutes later, they landed near the sandpits on a large, flat stretch of ground. They didn't have any shuttle crafts to take down, so it had been necessary to take the whole ship down. Luckily they'd found a good spot that was uninhabited.

Radiation levels remained constant and they all filed to the air lock. Dare opened the door and lowered the ladder since there was no need to equalize the air pressure now that they were no longer in space.

A small crowd had gathered near the sandpits, and as soon as they stepped down onto Gavin 1, the crowd rushed toward them shouting greetings and questions.

A small, elderly woman beelined for Dani, and Dani opened her arms to give the woman an affectionate hug.

"Katya, are you all right? What happened down here?"

The older woman beamed up at Dani and then spared a glance for the rest of them. "You remember me, Dani."

"How could I ever forget you? You were so kind to me."

Dani turned to Dare. "Dare, this is Katya. Devil was very close to her while he was here and she took me in before Devil found my foster parents."

Dare glanced back at Carl, and at Carl's confirming nod he turned to study the woman more closely. Dani knew this was a lot to digest, but there had been no easy way to tell him that his grandfather had had an ongoing affair with this woman.

"Dani, you all come to my house and I'll tell you what I know. It may not be much, but it's as much as everyone else here knows. We were as surprised as I'm sure you were. And we haven't been able to send or receive communications since it happened."

When they were all gathered in Katya's small house and she had provided everyone with cups of water, which was probably all she had, the old woman sighed and took her own chair.

"All we know is that Gavin 2 got hold of a nuclear black hole detonation device. I'm sure they were planning on firing it on us, but something went wrong. No one is sure if it was a saboteur or if it just malfunctioned. Anyway, it was in the middle of their capital city when it went off. Most of the residents are dead. We received a small burst of messages after we saw the fireball, but since then it's been total silence."

Dani nodded, relief flowing through her that it wasn't her

home planet of Gavin 1, but sadness followed quickly that there was such a loss of life. Katya didn't know much more than they'd heard previously, and really the only new piece of information was that the detonation had happened on Gavin 2. But she was glad they'd made the trip and found out. Her heart warmed as she realized that Dare hadn't even questioned her need to come here, he'd just mobilized his crew and brought her. He was truly a worthy man—worthy to be Devil's grandson and worthy of her trust.

"I need to go out and talk to some people and see the city. If you all will wait here, I'll be back in a few hours."

Everyone nodded and told her to be careful. Dani took the gentle well wishes in stride, but she knew the residents of Gavin 1 would never hurt her. She'd been something of a Robin Hood for the past five years, bringing them supplies and taking people off-world when needed. The only things she wouldn't provide them with was weapons, but they never seemed to blame her or be angry with her for that omission.

She spent the day finding old friends and talking to those she'd never met before. The stricken faces of the children broke her heart, and she remembered all too well being one of them before Devil had found her.

Most of the populace seemed like they had lost all hope, regardless of the fact that they'd won the war and that the bloodshed was over for good.

She found out that several ships of Gavin 2 residents had been off-world at the time and had asked Gavin 1 for asylum. The Grand Council had denied them entry and they'd dispersed to find other places to live. They still had their credits deposited in the Galactic bank, so it wouldn't be hard for them to find new places to live, but Dani wished Gavin 1 had welcomed them and started the healing process that Gavin 1 would need long term to survive.

When she was exhausted and hungry, she slowly made her way back to Katya's house, her heart and her mind longing to see Dare and feel his comforting hand in hers.

When she stepped through the door she found only Katya sitting in the main room and a trickle of unease slid through her.

"Katya? Where are they?" Her voice came out more demanding than she'd intended and she immediately felt bad for snapping at the older woman.

"They're gone, child."

"Gone where?" Dani hadn't bothered to scan the horizon for the ship as she'd returned, never thinking that they would leave her here. She was surprised she hadn't heard the ship break orbit, but it could've been while she'd been out by the waterfalls. While the water was calming and soothing, it was also very loud.

"I don't know, child. They took the ship and left."

"Did they say when they would be back?"

When Katya shook her head, tears burned at the backs of Dani's eyes and she blinked to keep them from falling. Betrayal and sadness cut deep. Not only had Dare left her, but also Jared and Dahlia.

This was why she never trusted, because she always got hurt in the end.

When Katya hugged her and rubbed circles over her back like Dare had done many times, her emotions finally broke down the wall she'd kept them behind and large, fat tears streamed down her face as sobs wracked her.

How could she have been so wrong? Not only about Dare, but Jared and Dahlia, whom she'd known and trusted with her life for the past five years.

Her legs gave out from under her and she managed to sit on the threadbare couch before she toppled both her and Katya to the ground. The tears kept falling and she wasn't able to stop them until she felt hollowed out and exhausted.

When she blinked open her eyes and realized that she'd cried herself to sleep, her eyes felt like someone had installed sandpaper on the backs of her eyelids. Her face was swollen and sore, and her chest still ached, as well as her heart.

She slowly sat up, her stomach growling, and she realized she hadn't eaten for over a day. Thoughts of when they had all had breakfast and found out about the detonated device in the first place tried to intrude and she shoved them aside. She couldn't function if she continued to let herself wallow in her emotions. She needed to function. It was time to go back to being totally independent and figure out what she was going to do next.

It was obvious that for at least now she was stuck on Gavin 1, but she knew other ships would eventually come and she could talk her way on board and away from here. After all, she was an excellent ship's mechanic and could fly nearly anything—both very marketable skills. If she had to, she could also play up her time as Red Death.

Dani spent the next four days fixing small appliances for the residents and helping do things like patch roofs, forage for food in the forest, and fish in the lake by the waterfalls.

She was walking back to Katya's with a string full of fish when she heard a large ship break orbit and begin the descent to land.

She tried to keep from looking up and battled back the stab of hope that speared through her. They had left her without explanation. She refused to forgive or give them the chance to hurt her again, no matter what excuses they had.

When she reached Katya's, the woman was more exited about the string of fish than the obvious ship that was landing beyond the sandpits.

Dani offered to clean the fish, but Katya would have none of it, pushing past Dani to clean the fish in her small front yard and rinse them with water from the old-fashioned water pump.

When Dani heard Jared's voice and Dahlia's light laughter, she hugged herself and sat back on the threadbare couch where she'd had her emotional meltdown days ago.

The voices came closer, prodding her until she finally stood and went to the door to peer out.

Dare trailed them both and although he tried to catch her gaze, Dani purposefully looked away, keeping the hurt close so she wouldn't soften toward him.

"Dani," Dahlia called as she entered Katya's small yard.

Dani turned around to face the house, unwilling to lose the tight rein on her emotions in front of them.

Jared said her name, too, but she refused to turn around.

When Dare said her name, she couldn't stand it anymore. She turned and ran directly for him. When she was close enough, she planted her right foot and pushed off into a jump kick. Her boot connected with his jaw . . . hard. His head snapped back, toppling him back onto the ground. He landed with an *oof,* then looked up at her with obvious confusion and hurt flowing over his features.

"Bastard," she accused. "Don't look at me like that. You left me without a word and now you come back trying to act like you're the one who is hurt. And you two." She whirled, fixing Jared and Dahlia with a lethal glare. "I would've never thought you'd betray me like that."

Before either of them could speak, Dare broke in, "Dani, we told Katya where we were going. It did take us a little longer than we expected, but we didn't leave without a word. We couldn't find you that day to say good-bye."

Dani turned to look at Katya and when she read the truth on the woman's face, another knife of betrayal slid deep. "Katya? Why?"

The old woman looked sheepish but raised her chin in a defiant gesture. "To protect you, child. That was the same way Devil broke my heart. He said he would be back for me and he never came. The MacFadyens can't be trusted, and I didn't want you to go through the same thing I had."

Dani resisted pointing out that she'd been put through the pain regardless of Katya's efforts. Instead, she turned away from Katya and faced Jared and Dahlia. "I'm sorry. I didn't know. I thought . . ."

Dahlia rushed forward and captured Dani in a bear hug. "It's all right. We know what you thought. We would never leave you like that, Dani, but I'm so sorry you thought we did."

Dani's heart melted just a little and she stepped toward Jared, who gave her a similar hug to Dahlia's. "I'm sorry, boss."

She nodded and blinked back the tears that threatened to fall.

Then she took a deep breath and decided to face head-on the situation she'd dreaded since she'd heard the truth.

Dare still lay on the ground and she went to him, kneeling to trace the growing bruise on his jaw where her boot had connected.

"You really do have a killer jump kick. I'm glad I didn't get the full effect the other day in the sandpit. It would've rattled my brains."

Dani couldn't help the small chuckle that escaped even as a fat tear began to roll down her face.

Dare sat up and this time caught her gaze. "Dani, I'm so sorry. I can't imagine what it felt like to find us all gone like that. Let me make you a promise that I thought I'd never make to any woman in my life. I'll never leave you like that. If I do have to leave for some reason, I'll talk to you first and be up front. I'm not a secretive man and I would never hurt you on purpose."

Dani leaned over and brushed her lips over Dare's, the only

apology she could manage unless she wanted a flood of tears instead of just a few.

A small crowd had gathered and they rushed Katya's yard calling to all of them in excited voices.

"Just where did you go, Dare?"

She'd never seen Dare look self-conscious before and she frowned as confusion swirled through her.

"We went to find food, medicine, and supplies. Most ships will avoid the system for a while afraid of the radiation from the device, so we figured while we were here we'd drop off some supplies to hopefully hold them over until we can send more ships or find some others who will deliver them for us."

Dani's heart melted the rest of the way and a surge of emotion swamped her, but this time it was warm and comforting instead of painful and scary.

Could it be true? Did she love this generous, tender man?

She thought it might be true and she'd have to sort out the implications later, and figure out if Dare loved her too. A lot would ride on whether he felt the same way or not. She'd always prided herself on being independent, but somehow she knew if she were with Dare she wouldn't be giving that up, and neither would he. A few more tears fell, but she brushed them back and smiled at Dare. "Well, then what are we doing sitting here? Shouldn't we be helping offload?

Dare laughed and swatted her ass as she stood. "Let's get to it."

Jared and Dahlia led the way, but the four of them spent the next several hours offloading and then distributing the supplies. The Grand Council took the medicine and some of the supplies to distribute to the outlying areas, but the rest was divided up among the residents who were close by. Dani knew they would share with those in need, that was the way on Gavin 1, and she was proud that Dare had thought about doing this.

Six months later

Dare led Dani out onto the dance floor and the guests on his latest voyage made room for them. Her black slinky dress felt smooth and silky under his hands, and he had to fight not to drag her back to their quarters and peel her out of it.

It had been a busy day for them both and there was still work to do.

Their day had started early by being "attacked" and boarded by Red Death and her skeleton crew. From there Dani had joined the patrons for breakfast. She'd charmed them through the rest of the day, even participating in the crew's exercise regimen and regaling the patrons with stories from her marauding days.

Dare had managed to steal her away for lunch back to their quarters where he'd made love to her until they'd both fallen into an exhausted sleep until it was time to clean up for dinner.

Now they were both attending the nightly dance in the large cleared-out rec room. The first dance was traditionally theirs; then they would separate, Dani charming the older men who frequented these voyages and Dare charming the women. Although he'd noticed that he did a lot more fighting off roaming hands than she did. Perhaps because the men were afraid of the wrath of Red Death? He smiled at the memory of their fight in the sandpits. Those men were right to be concerned.

Movement to their right caught Dare's attention and he turned in time to see something flitting in the air just outside his reach. In the darkened room it was hard to make out just what it was, but then something swooshed down, capturing it and pinning it to the floor.

"Careful, human male. I was just repaired!" The familiar mechanical voice made Dare groan. Not Pussy-do!

Jared closed the distance between them and Dare could see

he was holding the end of the net that had captured the obnoxious piece of silicone.

"I thought you shot that thing!"

"I did. One of the crew took pity on it, brought it over to your ship when we moved, and repaired it. Unfortunately, it still has its memory banks intact and has already taunted half the crew and a few of the patrons."

"Dare, show us that rather impressive cock! It's bigger than me, and I know Dani has to have been quite happy with it these last six months. Come on! Bring it out and show us. I'm sure all these people will want to see."

A titter rose from the patrons and a few women called out for him to show them.

Embarrassed and ready to have Dani alone, he led her off the dance floor calling for Jared to shoot the offending pleasure probe again.

The denials and begging for its life followed them out of the rec room and down the hall to the lifts.

Dani smirked up at him as they stepped onto the lift. "I'm glad I don't need a pleasure probe anymore. But Pussy-do was right, I've been quite happy with your wonderful cock for the past six months."

"Care to extend our agreement? I know we agreed on an eight-month trial for this arrangement, but I'd like to talk about extending it indefinitely."

Dani's heart clenched and a rush of warmth spilled through her. "What did you have in mind, Dare MacFadyen?"

He grinned and fished a small box out of the pocket of his jacket. "I propose that you make an honest man out of me and that I finally tame Red Death once and for all. What do you say? Are you up for the biggest challenge of our lives?"

When he snapped open the box to display a delicate platinum ring with one of the largest gems she'd ever seen gracing the top, Dani sucked in a breath.

Where did he get that? Only on Earth did they still make such things as engagement rings. When did he make the trip, and why hadn't she noticed he was gone?

"Remember when Jared and Dahlia went on their honeymoon a few months ago? Dahlia picked this out and brought it back for me."

Tears threatened at the backs of Dani's eyes and she blinked them back. What an old-fashioned romantic gesture. She loved every minute of it, and she loved this man.

"I love you, Dani McGovern, and I'm pretty sure you love me too. So what do you say?"

In answer, Dani threw her arms around Dare's neck, stood on her tiptoes, and kissed him, exploring his mouth with teeth and lips and tongue like she had when they'd first met.

A groan rose between them and she wasn't sure which one of them had made it.

"Let's get back to our quarters before I take you right here in the lift."

Dani laughed. "Who knows, it might be a good draw for your patrons."

Dare swatted her ass as the lift doors opened.

"I'll do a lot for my patrons, but I draw the line at letting them watch."